PRAISE FOR *JUDE*

"Julian Gough gives a new shine to an antique m̶
Quixotic picaresque, as he relates the antic ad̶
Tipperary orphan. It's clever, it's nuts, and t̶ t̶s of
comic greatnes̶
Kevin Barry (author of *City of mes* Books of
the Ye

"Clever and laugh-out-loud hilarious" *Mail on Sunday*

"This is funny. It is also, possibly, quite serious. Certainly, it endears"
Irish Times

"Sheer comic brilliance… The ultimate Irish joke"
The Times

"Gough's novel is like the picaresque bastard love-child of
Flann O'Brien and Matt Groening, and yet is all Julian Gough.
Possibly the finest comic novel to come out of Ireland since *At
Swim Two Birds*, it recounts the story of Jude, an orphan, as
he wanders through Ireland in a quest to find his true love and
uncover the secret behind his parentage… Gough makes it look
easy, with an instinctive sense of timing, and a razor sharp and
subversive intellect"
Sunday Tribune Books of the Year, 2007.

"Twenty-first century Irish satire has well and truly arrived
thanks to 'Toasted Heretic' frontman, Julian Gough"
Metro, Fiction of the Week

"*Jude* makes most other contemporary Irish novels look like a
pile of puke" Olaf Tyaransen, *Evening Herald*

JUDE IN LONDON

JUDE IN LONDON

JULIAN GOUGH

First published in Great Britain in 2011 by Old Street Publishing Ltd
Trebinshun House, Brecon, LD3 7PX
www.oldstreetpublishing.co.uk

This paperback edition published 2012

ISBN 978-1-908699-19-0

10 9 8 7 6 5 4 3 2 1

All of the people – the known and unknown, the living and the dead – in
this book are fictional, or used in a fictional context in a fictional world
which comments on, but is not, our own.

Except Jude. Jude is real.

A CIP catalogue record for this title is available from the British Library.

The seven interior illustrations are by Gareth McNamee Allen.
© Gareth McNamee Allen 2011.

Typeset by Old Street Publishing Ltd.

Printed and bound in Great Britain.

For Anne Marie Fives

Also by Julian Gough

Juno & Juliet
Jude in Ireland (formerly known as *Jude: Level 1*)
Free Sex Chocolate: Poems & Songs

To come:

Jude in America

Welcome.

You don't need to have read Jude in Ireland *to enjoy* Jude in London. *Like many before him, Jude starts a new life in exile. But, should you be curious, here is a brief account of his earlier adventures.*

Jude is raised in an orphanage in Tipperary. On his 18th birthday, a letter arrives which may contain the secret of his origins, but it is confiscated. Jude is sent to the official opening of the sacred boghole in which Ireland's legendary liberator, Éamon de Valera, had his vision of Irish maidens dancing barefoot at the crossroads. Jude urinates, in error, into Dev's Hole, and onto Dev's descendant – the Minister for Beef, Culture, and the Islands. An angry mob pursues Jude, and burns down the orphanage. Jude saves a corner of the letter from the flames before escaping across the fields. An enigmatic stranger, Pat Sheeran, rescues him, and takes him to the Sodom of the West, Galway City. Pat also gives Jude a prototype of his invention – the Salmon of Knowledge – which can distil, from all the information in the world, a single drop of wisdom. Jude discovers it was Pat Sheeran who delivered the mysterious letter. Pat has not recognized Jude. But Jude is afraid to reveal who he is, and ask Pat's help, because Jude, by urinating on the Minister, has destroyed Pat's chances of selling the Salmon of Knowledge to the Irish government. Pat abandons Jude in Galway, where Jude falls in love with the first woman he sees, Angela. He makes his home in a church. Angela sets him a quest: she would look more favourably on his love if he looked like Leonardo DiCaprio, and made a million. Then she vanishes. Jude seeks his million from billionaire industrialist

Barney O'Reilly Fitzpatrick McGee, who gives Jude a job (while Barney's daughter Babette gives Jude a smile). But Jude blows up the factory and himself. He persuades the doctors to reconstruct his damaged face in the image of Leonardo DiCaprio. However, the doctors' experimental skin grafts, using penile tissue, leave him with an uncontrollably erectile nose. He leaves hospital, to discover that property developer Jimmy "'Bungle" O'Bliss has demolished his home. Jude pursues Jimmy O'Bliss to the private island of Ireland's former leader, Charlie Haughey. Jude does battle with both, and sends Charlie Haughey floating into exile on an iceberg. Jude returns to the factory, liberates the workers, makes love to Babette, defeats Barney O'Reilly Fitzpatrick McGee, and sets up a socialist paradise in an abandoned gated luxury estate. Jimmy O'Bliss meanwhile seduces and corrupts Angela. When Jude discovers Jimmy has committed Angela to a Dublin lunatic asylum, Jude reluctantly leaves his Galway paradise to free her. Before he walks to Dublin, Babette gives him a ring with unusual powers. In the inferno of Dublin, he liberates Angela from the lunatic asylum, defeats her lover Jimmy O'Bliss in battle, and follows her into exile on the largest car ferry in the world, the Ulysses. It hits Charlie Haughey's iceberg, and sinks. Jude awakes on the iceberg, makes his peace with Charlie Haughey, and decides to swim towards England, and Angela...

CONTENTS

Jude Saves the Universe 1

The Snowy Walk 91

Goats and Monkeys 111

Alice in Ordnung 169

Gents Anal Cruise.. 261

King of the Artists 289

The Journey in Oil.. 333

ABOUT THE AUTHOR 354

Jude Saves the Universe

I began at the beginning,
like an old ballocks,
can you imagine that?
~ Samuel Beckett, *Molloy*

I left the iceberg behind me and swam towards England. Yes, somewhere in that dark and uncivilized land I would find her. Angela! The thought warmed my naked limbs, and drove me faster through the water.

On my head the black bag that contained all my worldly possessions began to feel heavy, and to force me under. I adjusted my stroke to one that held my head higher. Then, as I breasted a wave crest, I saw something in the water ahead of me.

Huge.

Very pale in the dim light before dawn.

As I sank into a trough it disappeared, and reappeared as I rose again. Another iceberg? No, there was something not right about it... I blinked the water out of my eyes and looked harder.

The bloated corpse of a white whale?

Its shape was too regular, its lines too straight...

Was it large and far, or small and near?

I heard a scream.

I flicked my gaze along the smooth waves, pausing for an instant at each piece of debris, looking for a human face. I saw nobody.

Another scream.

I looked up, to see a dozen, two dozen seagulls, flying inland.

What were they fleeing? I twisted my neck, to look back over my shoulder.

Dark grey clouds. Black. A storm.

My right calf spasmed in the cold water. The muscles relaxed, then cramped again.

Unable to kick, I gasped with pain, inhaled a little seawater, coughed it up and out. The weight of all I possessed again pushed my head under the water. Gagging, spluttering, I reached up into my black bag, and pulled out the first thing I touched, to lighten it. The jacket of my stained and tattered suit fell to the water.

Not enough.

I pulled out the trousers.

The waistcoat.

The suit floated, grew saturated, and sank, heavy and slow, into the depths of the Irish Sea.

I reached up into my dark bag, again, and touched the cool, curved, metal sides of Pat Sheeran's gift to me.

The Salmon of Knowledge.

No. That, I would keep.

I dug deeper. A small tube. The stub of her lipstick. All I had of her now. No. I dropped it back in the bag.

I pulled in a hard breath, as the cramp began to pass.

But the shore was very far away.

Too far.

I swam, as fast as I was able, towards the white... Whatever it was.

Oh, I did not wish to die in the gap between Ireland and England.

I let a roar out of me, in a language that was considerably older than English, or Irish.

In instant response, high on the mysterious white object, Angela climbed to her feet. Naked but for scraps of lingerie, her golden hair blazing in the dawn light, she and the sun rose together above England.

I was blinded by the nuclear light. When I had blinked the dancing suns out of my eyes, she was gone, vanished in the dazzle. Gone, the curve of her hip. The V of her thong.

Had Angela then drifted with me on the same currents from Ireland? So close, all along? I swam harder, towards the long shadow of her white island.

As my chilled body made its way through the water, the unnaturally warm low winter sun baked my forehead.

Thus I began to suffer simultaneously from both heatstroke and hypothermia. I had not experienced that particular duo of discomforts since the hot, thundery summer of my eleventh year, in the Orphanage, in Tipperary. The Orphanage! My happy home, before catastrophe and exile! The memory, enhanced into vividness by the heatstroke, came rushing back, obliterating my view of the sea, the waves, the white object…

I was eleven. Breakfast was about to be served. A rumour swept the length of the Dining Hall: Brother Quirke, in his rush to be off to the races at Limerick Junction, had left the Banned Books Section of the Orphanage Library unlocked.

By the time the food arrived, I'd summonsed my courage. Quietly, I left my fellows and my prunes.

I exited the Hall, unheeded.

Now, the Orphanage's Universal Christian Library itself, full of improving fiction by God-fearing authors, containing indeed the literary fruit of two thousand years of Christian culture, was always unlocked, and I had read each of its books a dozen times. But today I walked past the open biscuit tin containing all seven slim volumes, pressing on instead to the Banned Books section.

The rumour was correct. Though the padlock was looped through the chain, it had not been clicked shut: and so I gently loosed the chain, pulled back the bolt, swung open the mighty double doors, and stepped into the vast, dim, echoing space.

The immense room was divided into the three major categories, in order of Bannedness.

I walked past Obscenity.

I walked past Godlessness.

I headed straight for English Literature, picked up *Beowulf*, and began to read.

Brother Quirke's return from the race meeting was delayed somewhat, after he was struck by lightning in the Paddock. And so, by the time he had returned from Limerick Junction, I had made my way as far as the Seventeenth Century, and my head was full. Another summer thunderstorm was brewing, and outside the soft ions gathered trembling on the tips of every leaf and branch and blade of grass.

Inside, in the dense, cool air of the Banned Books Section, deep in Thomas Shelton's original English translation of Miguel De Cervantes' *Don Quixote de la Mancha*, I feared for my life.

Or rather, I feared for the life of Don Quixote. But the two had become profoundly confused: I was both observing and being him. I had, too, mentally translated Shelton's translation of Cervantes' place-names into names more familiar to me; and so my Don Quixote was not of la Mancha but of the featureless lowlands of Offaly, and loved a Dulcinea not of Toboso but of Ballylusky. Thus I walked my own fields as Quixote.

I winced as he was struck, and my legs twitched as he ran.

My hand moved to protect my teeth as he was struck again.

Thus it was that Brother Quirke entered the Banned Books Section entirely unobserved. He walked the long aisles of Obscenity and Godlessness, looking for intruders; I read on, oblivious.

A steady rattle of hail against the windows disguised his approach.

Yet as he raised his iron-tipped stick above me, the brief storm ended; the sun came out; the shadow of his stick was flung across my page. I ripped my eyes free of Shelton's translation of Cervantes' account of Quixote's life, just as a stick was descending on Quixote, to see the stick descending on me.

My mind and body being already fully engaged in battle, the transition was effortless, and I used the heavy book as my shield to fend off the buffet.

"Zounds!" I said. "Sirrah! Would you besmirch the honour of your name with a Sneeking Attack? Face me, in combat fair and courteous!"

Something was terribly wrong. I put my free hand to my mouth. "Why, my voice sounds quite English!" I said, astonished. My native Tipperary tones had vanished, and with them certain words, certain ways of building a sentence so it would stay up.

I reached for my sword, and realised I did not have one.

I tried to say "Shite and onions," but it came out as "Soup and fish."

Brother Quirke, unused to such insubordination, took a step back and scowled. His scorched electric hair stood frightful and erect as he raised high again his smouldering stick.

"Well, this is a most pretty pickle I find myself in, I must say!" I said. Shocked, I said: "I say! Must I say, 'I must say'?"

I appeared to have suffered some form of Mental Catastrophe, and lost all my sweet and beloved Irishness. When I reached for words, all I could find were those I had just read, a great pile of language going back to the Anglo-Saxon, built up and unprocessed in my head.

Trapped, under attack, without a sword or a language of my own to defend me, I turned to Sancho Panza to request his aid.

He was not there.

How lonely a feeling, to lose so good a friend so thoroughly that he never was at all. The closing of a book is a massacre.

I ran.

Wishing to have my friend back again, I opened the book, and as I ran I read. And back he came, smiling, frowning, living, and all was well.

Brother Quirke pursued me, roaring, through the Orphanage, across a number of nearby fields, and back around through the vegetable garden to the Orphanage again.

The trick of being pursued across rough ground while lost in a good book is to tilt it down slightly, and use the upper peripheral vision to ensure the route ahead is clear.

In this manner we passed a happy hour.

At length it began to rain, then hail again. I did not wish the book to get wet or damaged, and so, still reading, I took shelter in the South Tower. The only way was up: I took the stairs two at a time.

As we passed, some of the Orphans shouted words of encouragement.

"Leather the head off him, Brother!"

Their noble Tipperary speech reminded me of my Mental Catastrophe. I ventured an experiment with my deformity: I spoke a Catholic thought, and it came out Church of England. I tried another: I praised a fine All-Ireland semi-final performance by the Tipperary Under-21 hurlers against Kilkenny, and from my mouth came alien speech of an FA Cup semi-final replay at Villa Park.

Sweet Mother of Jesus, I thought, astonished.

"Queen of Heaven!" I said.

Christ on a bicycle, I thought.

"Good Lord!"

Holy fuck.

"Blessed Union!"

I gave up the attempt to accurately express myself, and returned to my book.

I reached the top of the South Tower, and made my way up and out through a skylight, onto the tower's sloping pyramidal roof, as Brother Quirke came round the end of the stairs.

Scrambling down the wet slates to the roof's edge, I lay down, unobserved, in the deep stone channel of the rain gutter, holding the book above the water as I read. My head, above the water, baked in the high summer sun. My body, below the water, chilled in the icy runoff as the melting hailstones flowed down the roof as slush into the gutter.

And so, when he finally found me, the hot blood in my head raced, full of images and language; but my languid limbs lay cool and still, numb and asleep in the chill water. As his red face loomed above me, I realised I would be able to answer his blows only with language.

The air around us was electric.

"I don't know what's got into you today, Jude," said Brother Quirke. He shook his head. "Your refusal to cooperate is a most ferocious breach of etiquette."

"By Our Lord's Wounds," I said sadly, "it is."

The justice of the coming beating was indisputable, yet I felt a reluctance to cooperate. It would interfere with my reading of my book. Art made its call to me, and Life made its call to me, and I must decide. I felt the very air crackle with the potential of this moment, to create me or destroy me.

To whom would I discharge my duty? Brother Quirke, or Don Quixote?

For some reason an old physics lesson of Brother Brophy's

came back to me now. Ah, Brother Brophy's fine advice is always useful in a crisis.

Art, or Life?

"Assume the position," said Brother Quirke.

I sighed. And decided.

"Brother Quirke," I said, "I am currently unable to move my frozen limbs. You would get a better run at me from the top of the roof."

"True," said Brother Quirke. "It is hard to get momentum into such a low stroke from a standing start."

He walked back up the wet slate roof, to the peak. I sighed a second time at what was about to happen.

"Remember to take a good high swing," I urged.

Brother Quirke swung the iron tip of his copper-clad stick high into the electric air.

Every ion on the Orphanage, and indeed the surrounding fields, rushed up to this new highest point, and Brother Quirke's hair leapt momentarily erect as the electrical potential of half of Tipperary expressed itself through him.

For the second time that day, he was struck by lightning.

Blazing, he rolled past me and over the edge of the tower roof and, still blazing, down into the vegetable garden.

I sighed with satisfaction for a third time. Physics had always been hard chewing for me, and it was most gratifying to find a practical use for it.

I returned to my book.

My eyes adjusted to the cross-fading light, as the moon rose and the sun set, and I brought the living book closer to my eyes so that it replaced the world entirely.

When I had finished reading it, and closed it, and the hot tears had finally dried on my cold cheek, I looked up from the gutter and found that I was looking at the stars.

Oh happy memories!

As my head, above the water, baked, my body, below the water, chilled, it all came rushing back. And I thought, Mighty Stuff! And I said, "How wonderful!"

And I entered the shadow of the iceberg, or whatever it was.

I touched its sheer sides. Brilliant white.

A curiously regular shape. More like an ice cube than an iceberg. No, not a cube either, I realised, as it rotated slightly, caught by a cross-current as it came nearer the shore.

It was neither cold nor hot. Neither hard nor yielding. It was definitely there, but it was barely there at all.

I trembled. Where was she? Had I, like a man in a desert glimpsing a shimmer of sweet water, only seen what I most desperately wished to see?

"Angela!" I cried, and back came the high cry of a gull.

There was no other reply. I swam around the enigma. Smooth. Featureless. No steps, no ladder.

Even my eye could find no purchase on it.

A fresh spasm of cramp. I inhaled water.

This blank thing stood between me and life. And love.

I spat the water at it. Punched it. My fist bounced, but left a dent. Sinking, gasping, I poked it, with a single finger. The finger crackled half an inch into it. Yes…

I drove the rigid fingers of my strong right hand into it, hard. They crunched in as far as the second knuckle.

Lifting myself halfway out of the water, I drove the rigid fingers of my other hand through the surface, pulled myself higher.

Crunched another hole, got my toes into the first handhold, and I was up and over the lip...

As I lay there, face down, gasping, shaking the cramp out of my leg, I saw words stamped into the blank white surface, too close to focus. I raised my head and read "Styrofoam Packaging", accompanied by some mysterious symbols.

I rose to my feet and stood, unsteady, on the flat top. No sign of Angela. It had been a hallucination, then. I sighed.

The rising wind whipped the heat from my wet naked body and I shivered. My manhood had shrunken till it was as small and tight-wrinkled as a barnacle. My erectile nose, too, had tightened to a hard nubbin.

I looked back, across the Irish Sea. The dark shadow of the black clouds snuffed out the sparkling light from one wave crest after another, as the storm blew towards me.

In the far, far distance, I saw Charles J. Haughey, the last Tribal Leader of Old Ireland, floating on his vast white ice mountain into the past. Melting, melting.

I strained my eyes, but the land of my youth was gone. Ireland lay beyond the horizon now.

The last white horse turned grey, and the storm's shadow fell on me. I turned to survey my little artificial island. My only refuge from the coming storm.

The iceberg was made of immense white styrofoam blocks, all held snug with plastic ties. These blocks surrounded and supported a single tremendous object, set down about a foot inside its thick walls of styrofoam. The styrofoam roof which had guarded the top of the object was long since lost, in shipwreck or gale. All that protected the upper surface now was a cloth of fine black wool, ripped and unravelled on the side nearest me. I pulled it back.

The object was a vast, black, concert grand piano.

I knelt, and lifted up the keyboard's curved wooden cover, longer than a man, to reveal the keys. The number of octaves seemed excessive. I knew of no music which required so many. Reaching down, I struck a black key.

From inside the piano, in a voice like nectar flowing down the throats of a thousand hummingbirds, came a muffled "Owch".

The enormous lid of the great piano began slowly to rise, and Angela emerged from its dark interior into the fading light. Her golden hair blew about her in the gathering storm. In her right hand she held a large number of the thongs, knickers, and string-like things that she had acquired for her new life in London. In her left hand, she held a selection of bras, bra-like objects, and cloth scraps of uncertain function. She herself was naked. I myself was naked.

Nothing stood between us but a grand piano.

She stepped up, onto the far end of the keyboard. An immense chord boomed from the piano, blending with the booming chords of the sea, the wind, my heart. She walked towards me, along the keyboard, and at each step drove music to the sky. Heel-to-toe, each footfall a little run of ever-lighter notes, ever higher, soaring with my heart, until she arrived, smiling, naked, stopping in a flight of notes almost too high and delicate for human ears.

Would you believe it? I thought.

"Would you Adam 'n' Eve it?" I said, astonished, my brain still damaged into random forms of Englishness.

Oh, Angela.

My head was spinning.

No, it was the great world that spun. The wind, stronger now, was bringing us towards the shore, and a small stray current had caught us.

Angela and I rotated towards the future on our vast white styrofoam block.

She dropped her thongs in a little heap and reached out to me.

I reached out to her.

She took my hand and pulled me gently towards her.

Were my sufferings over?

Was this the end of my lifelong quest for True Love?

With her beautiful, naked foot, Angela tapped my right ankle behind my left and tripped me, sideways, into the piano.

The wires rang and sang as I fell on them, and I felt the great throb as they yielded, then resisted my fall. I noted that several wires were missing.

I felt her heel pressing into the small of my back, sliding me over the gap in the wires.

I fell through it, and lay winded on the deep-set sound-board, looking up at the sky through a prison of wires.

At first I had trouble making out what I was seeing. The huge interior of the piano was almost entirely filled with unravelled threads from the piano's black woollen cover. They hung tangled in the wires and hammers.

I had been briefly incarcerated like this – though obviously in a much smaller piano – in the Orphanage, years before. The memory made me nervous.

With a crash, the vast black lid descended. And now, in the middle of my life's quest, I grew lost in the dark wood. Angela did not yet think me worthy of her love.

My eyes adjusted. A little light spilled through a crack.

I wriggled towards it. The lid had been held from closing by the little heap of thongs. I reached up through the gap in the wires and touched their bright materials, backlit by daylight, vivid in the dark. I looped my little finger through the string of a thong of gold and tugged it gently. It slipped free of its sibling thongs.

In the distance, a dozen hammers lunged up and struck a dozen tight wires, and a high cry, almost unbearable, almost too loud to hear, filled the tight chamber, and a blast of brighter light came through the narrow crack.

Angela had stepped back on the keys at the far end of the piano.

The dozen hammers dropped. Another dozen rose, and struck.

The hammers and the sound approached me, deepening to thunder, mingled with true thunder as the storm broke outside. The soundboard vibrated against my naked skin, like a gentle beating. I should not fear the hammers. They could not reach me. Soft hammers of dense felt. They could not hurt me. But I feared the hammers.

There was a pause.

Now she was no longer walking on the keyboard, but playing it. Or was it her playing? The music was strange and wild. Sunstruck and frozen, trapped in a dark space, I wondered was it music at all, or noise? It contained patterns, repetitions, areas of chaos and beauty. Above all this, Angela sang words that were neither Irish nor English.

And then the hammers came for me, in their rising thunder. The energy of the beaten air was almost overwhelming. By turns it caved and vexed my lungs with its power.

I rolled back as far as I could along the pulsing soundboard, under the wires, and was wrapped in a hundred, then a thousand threads, around my torso.

The hammers were almost upon me. I threw myself back the length of the piano.

All my threads pulled tight about me, and a dissident, right-angled thread, running in and out of all of mine, was pulled down through the lot of them like a comb through hair.

The hammers came for me again, descending now the scale.

I threw myself back the way I had come. The thong I held snagged for an instant, on what I could not see, and jerked me to a startled halt; I pulled free, and kept rolling, leaving the thong behind. Angela's thong! Her colours, my talisman! I reached back and pulled it free, leaving a golden thread dangling.

The hammers pursued me. One snatched at the trailing thread, stretching it taut. Another slammed the thread and, with a high clean note, plucked it from my hand. Threads slid through each other and pulled tight. The unseen player hammered out a charged, charming, strange-flavoured music that spun up and down the keyboard, paused, then repeated.

And now the invisible pianist, by the correct choice of small, perfect movements, used the great machine of the piano to reorder the chaotic air into a sublime order. Air and water transmitted a code which led the fish in the darkness beneath us to swerve; halted the rabbits in the distant dunes; and caused the birds a mile above to shriek their appreciation and fear of the suddenly meaningful air.

The pattern of the music was rich, dense and repetitive. With each pass, as I threw myself through the threads that hung from the hammers, I grew more enmeshed. For the threads, in their passing and repassing, were weaving themselves back into their old relationship. And I, caught in their dance, imposed my naked shape upon their dark material, as it wove itself about me in a pattern rich, dense, and repetitive.

As the web wove tighter about my torso, I tried to push the threads away, but then the web wove itself about my outstretched arms too, until I was jacketed in the finest black wool, precisely suited to my contours.

I began then to worry that the invisible weaver would not halt, would continue to glove my hands and mask my face, as mummies with the mummy cloth are bound.

Mother of mercy, I thought to myself.

"Mummy! Mummy!" I cried, in anguished English.

And I was afraid then, and exerted all my strength, and broke the threads that bound me.

I crushed myself into a corner, warmer now in my perfect jacket, with its delicate pinstripe from the golden thread of Angela's thong. But my legs still stuck out, into the area of music and danger. And soon – after a quiet passage drifting the length of the keyboard which merely reorganised the broken threads, catching them again on the hammers – there was a lunging, attacking piece of music which shook the ribs in my chest. The taut threads rippled in octaves, embracing one leg, then the other, as I tried to swing them free. Then the left hand and the right hand of the unseen player clad my legs in fine cloth, coming together at my crotch with a bravura display of staccato and legato that made me gasp, crescendoing magnificently as it hugged my hips, finally running out of thread at the stirring climax.

Well, you would get used to anything. Now that I had a most marvellous jacket and trousers, I felt the lack of a waistcoat. Something bright, I thought, to shine against the darkness of the suit. I slid back under the gap in the wires and, with trembling hands, freed several of Angela's thongs from the grip of the piano lid and unwound their silk threads. Cautiously, I threaded the mighty machine.

I waited a moment and, sure enough, the unseen player soon started up a sprightly little tune, with elegant variations on each return, which sent a herringbone pattern through the coloured silks.

My waistcoat was soon finished, woven into an unorthodox yet pleasing relationship to jacket and trousers.

The music stopped. The silence was almost unbearable.

Now what? I thought.

Oh yes! My True Love.

Clad in pinstriped woollen suit and silk waistcoat, my brain crippled into Englishness, I felt ready for the ordeal ahead. Which was good, for it was about to begin.

I heard, far off, a splash. Could Angela have fallen? Jumped?

With an almighty scrunch, the high-floating plastic iceberg struck England's shore, caught on an English rock, and tipped over on its side. The lid of the piano swung open, and crashed down onto the pebbles of the beach, forming a ramp.

I stared through the wires of my prison. The light was stunning, too much.

After a while my eyes adjusted, and I squirmed out from the warm dark through the gap in the wires, and looked up into a pale blue sky.

The storm had passed.

I walked down the ramp and onto England's shore.

I had never before walked upon land that was not almost excessive in its Irishness. My bare feet touched the beach, each with a crunch. I looked down at the alien shore with great interest. So this was England! Or perhaps Wales.

I picked up a stone, and examined it for signs of Englishness, without result. No doubt a magnifying glass, or microscope, was required. I dropped the stone.

More than the weight of the stone seemed to leave me. I felt lighter. Light-headed, light-hearted.

I looked around me at the long curve of stony, sandy beach. At the dunes beyond.

Pulled in an enormous breath. Held it, savoured it. Sharp, salt air. I drove it out, pulled in another. Ah, the rich rot of the shore.

It seemed to me that to be a young man in a foreign land, journeying on a Quest to win his True Love, was a splendid thing, and I let out a yell of joy that rattled stones along the beach.

But where was she? I looked around me, at the piano and the sea. I scanned wave after wave. Further and further out. Nothing.

Debris.

Broken things.

No life.

Dread, in me.

But then, close to shore, her head, then shoulders rose up out of a trough. Her strong legs bore her up the steep approach; bore up out of the creamy, foaming water her breasts, torso, bellybutton, then the great curves of her hips. I was dazzled and dizzied by the sight of her tiny golden hairs, their captured water-drops glinting in the sun.

As she drew close to me, I drew everything I felt into its simplest sentence and said, "I love you."

"Fuck *off*, for fuck's sake," she said, and she ran.

Her strong legs carried her up the beach in a long diagonal and into the dunes.

I nodded approvingly. It was a tactic I was familiar with, from the shop-lifted copies of women's magazines the Lads read in the Orphanage, the better to understand Female Psychology.

She was Playing Hard to Get, in order to make me value her, appreciate her, and love her all the more.

The tactic was working. I began to run after her.

The stones were hard on the soles of my feet, softened by so long in saltwater. Angela began to widen the gap between us.

I saw two shoes further along the foreshore. I broke off my chase and ran down and got them.

Excellent English black leather shoes, of the highest quality.

Though on closer inspection no longer black, as the dye had been dissolved by the water and altered by the sun so that they were now a strong dark blue.

And no longer leather, for being scraped up and down the beach every few seconds by the tireless sea, for several weeks, had sanded them to a soft suede finish.

I hesitated. Blue suede shoes, with a black wool suit? I would do aesthetic violence to all I passed. But can we afford such scruples, in the pursuit of our true love? I pulled them on.

We pursued our flirtation for some time among the dunes.

Angela had set a brisk pace: the sheep and rabbits had to step lively to get out of our way.

The long day wore on.

At length my new shoes began to chafe my feet.

I resolved to manufacture miraculous socks for myself, in the manner of Saint Christopher as he fled persecution.

I stopped to gather handfuls of black wool from the brambles on the landward side of the dunes. I stuffed the rough wool into the big shoes, then wriggled each foot into its warm nest.

Off again, through the dunes, running hard in search of lost time.

The pounding rhythm of my feet massaged the fibres of the wool, back and forth, back and forth.

Soon the warmth and moistness of my feet opened the tiny scales covering each fibre of the wool, and the fibres aligned themselves into a new and more stable order, their scales meshing like the teeth of tiny gears. After a couple of miles of strenuous running, I had manufactured a fine sturdy pair of black felt socks.

Or perhaps, I pondered as I ran, pedifacture would be the more accurate term.

The judicious application of energy to a disordered system had created order. Though, of course, the overall entropy of the universe had gone up, as it always does, the entropy within the zones of my shoes had been greatly lowered.

Ah, pleasant it is, to pump order into a disordered system on a warm winter's day.

However, it occurred to me that, should I ever need to wash my socks, I would have no spares. And so I stowed my new socks in my little bag, and stuffed my shoes with black wool, and made a spare pair of socks.

All went well for a while. I made better time in my comfortable socks, and was rewarded with frequent glimpses of Angela's buttocks. Her brief stay in the Merciful Hour Lunatic Asylum on Dublin's North Side had put meat on her, and I was impressed by her speed and stamina.

As we covered a dozen, or perhaps two dozen, miles of beach and dune, I absently plucked the fur of some class of local rabbit from the passing brambles, and at length I had an excess of it. I mused on this as I ran. There was always the option of the third pair of socks.

But no, with two pairs of socks you know where you are. One pair on, and one pair drying. What would a man do with three pairs of socks? It would lead to confusion and decadence.

I ran past a rock the size and shape of my head. Ah! Here was my way out of this crisis of overproduction.

Running briskly on the spot, I felted at a fierce rate. Then I quickly stretched and shaped the fresh felt around the rock. Removed it. Hmm... Perfect!

I adjusted my new bowler hat as I ran. Yes, now I would be able to hold my own among the heathen English.

But where was my True Love?

Far ahead, I glimpsed the curve of a familiar, a beloved, buttock, high on a dune's crest against the pale blue sky. Like a crescent moon.

Then it was gone.

Angela was heading inland.

I reached the crest of the dune. No sign of her…

There! Angela's thong! Or, more accurately, one of her many thongs. I picked up the squiggle of tangerine, and clutched it to my heart. I looked about me.

Her naked footprints on the sand.

I followed them inland through the labyrinth of dunes.

They stopped at the edge of a stream that cut through the sands, exposing a rocky bed. The footprints did not reappear on the far side. An old trick for evading one's True Love, often practised in Tipperary. In which direction had she waded? Upstream? Downstream?

Ah. Dark splashes of water on smooth, pale rocks by a quiet pool.

Upstream.

I ran on…

I followed the stream towards its source.

Sand became grass.

Dunes became low hills.

I emerged into a valley of great beauty. Old oak groves grew in its shelter. The stream chuckled to itself. The air was warm and fragrant.

Across the stream, a red deer appeared, and bent to sip, unaware of my presence.

I stopped my breath. A pregnant doe.

The trees sighed as time passed, and water ran over stones. I could hear her drink.

Finally she swung her casual head, water dripping in a curve, to face my exhalation. She froze a moment to stare at me, then unfroze, and spun, and away with her through the dappled light of the oak forest. A breeze shuffled light and leaves so that the forest imitated the pattern of her skin in every dancing direction, and the deer in mid leap disappeared.

Somehow the warm valley seemed exempt from winter, and all the trees within it were in fruit. I walked on, upstream, and plucked wild plums from a tree as I passed, and ate them.

Further on, I paused in a glade, to listen to the music of the bees. Endlessly the same, yet never repeating.

At length I emerged from the trees into open grassland, punctuated with thorn bushes and young hazel groves, at the far end of the valley. Here, a group of men were improving the situation with shovels.

The native inhabitants of England! Or perhaps Wales.

I adjusted my bowler hat, and strode up to the workers, in my pinstriped wool suit, pleased that I would blend in so easily.

They were labouring in the vicinity of a fine pair of freestanding gates with long, sharp, interlocking steel teeth. The gates blocked a rough road. Beside the gates was a small hut or guardhouse. Beyond that, a few portable cabins, and scattered bushes.

How're ye, lads, I thought to myself, but I said, "Good day, gentlemen" – and in even fruitier tones than usual, for I still had a plum in my mouth. One by one, they put down their shovels.

"Eh?" said the first of the fellows, in a strong Lorrha accent.

"Who the feck is this fecker?" said the second, in an aristocratic Ardcrony brogue.

"Jaysus, it's Bertie fecking Wooster, what?" said the third, in the noble tones of Terryglass.

"Little Lord For Fuck's Sake," said the fourth, in the unmistakable accents of Knockalton Upper.

Dear God in Heaven, I thought. These were Lads of the Orphanage – but aged and tanned like leather by hard work and Sun Holidays. They had been the elite among the Orphans, those who had known the true name of their Father. Saints, and scholars! After they left the Orphanage, we had heard nothing but tales of their glory. The Men who Rode the Celtic Tiger. The first Lads in our nation's history who hadn't had to feck off to England to work on the sites…

Yet here they were.

And they did not now recognise their own, behind my new face, my plummy voice.

The companions of my youth took a step towards me, in a line, and raised their fists as one.

Are ye dancing the Siege of Ennis, I thought to say, to lighten the tone. But it came out as, "Ah, the old Arsenal defence…"

They scowled and took another step.

Shite, I thought. I'd better introduce myself straight away, before the notion that I'm of the English ruling classes takes root, and perhaps prejudices them against me.

I concentrated hard on distilling the pure drop of my Irishness. I structured my sentence in the glorious grammatical forms of the original language of all these islands. I would be authentically Irish.

I'd be Jude. And what name would you be after having yourself? I thought.

"The name is Jude. May I enquire as to your identity, sirs?" I said.

The more Irish I tried to be, the more English I sounded.

Holy shite.

"God's dung!"

"What?" said the Lads.

"My speech," I explained, "has been corrupted by English novelists."

They nodded their understanding. "The same thing happened to my sister," muttered one. "The bastard."

They did not recognise me, yet their sympathy reassured.

Perhaps, I thought, given that my past actions had led to the burning of our beloved Orphanage, it was best if the motherless men who ran Ireland did not recognise me.

Yes, I would speak to these companions of my youth as a fellow Irishman, and yet also as a stranger. We would build a new friendship on new ground. Ah, there was a liberty in wearing a new face, speaking a new tongue, in a new land.

I gave up entirely on stressing my Irishness, and lapsed into a more neutral tone that was less banjaxed by my affliction. "But why do you – noble Irish souls – labour here in heathen England, when Mother Ireland needs her sons to build the New Jerusalem, and mixed retail?"

"Jesus fuck," said a Lad I recognised as Finian, of far-off Clonard. "Where've you been, on an iceberg?"

I confessed that I had.

"The Celtic Tiger died long ago," he said. "In agony, after getting its goolies caught in the credit crunch. To spend, we now must earn."

All shuddered.

I nodded. "So, you were tradesmen in the construction industry."

"Jaysus no," said Finian of Clonard. "That was all Poles, Lithuanians and Turks... But property now, well, of course we dabbled in property, as a hobby, on the side, who didn't..."

Ruadhain of Lorrha nodded. "I financed fifty flats in Fulham."

"I bought Bond Street," said Brendan of Birr.

"I briefly owned Birmingham..." said Columba of Terryglass.

"We all worked in the Irish Financial Services Centre," said Finian. "Derivatives, chiefly. Ruadhain there invented the credit default swap."

Ruadhain gave a modest nod.

I gazed beyond the Lads as Finian talked on, hoping for a glimpse of Angela. Which way had she gone? And what was that thing in the distance? I edged a little sideways to see past some bushes obscuring the view. A great white curved building, at the very end of the valley. A dome. No windows at all. A single, tiny door.

It looked like the moon, half buried in the earth. What the feck is it? I thought.

"Would you care to enlighten me as to the nature of that structure?" I asked the Lads.

But Finian was still talking. "I myself assembled goat-backed securities for the UN, with a nominal value bigger than world GDP. But such jobs are in temporarily short supply everywhere. We wangled the gig here because we knew the foreman, Dick Fuld. And also the man who makes the sandwiches – Fred Goodwin. And Seán FitzPatrick, of course. He's in charge of the chemical toilets. Old friends all of them. It's only our first day here, so they have us building a wall."

"It's an insult!" burst out Ruadhain of Lorrha. "We, who structured products of infinite complexity!"

They all stared at the small stretch of crooked, hump-backed wall they had built.

Finian sighed.

The wall fell over, breaking back into its component blocks.

"I have always had difficulty with physical objects," confessed Brendan of Birr. "Now, if that was a derivative of a wall – or better yet, a derivative of a derivative of a wall – sure, we'd be laughing."

I trembled with the need to be off. Yet these were the companions of my golden youth. Oh to be able to go back and fix the broken past. But you can only fix what's in front of you.

Do you need a hand, lads? I thought.

"May I offer my assistance, gentlemen?" I said.

"Ah, not a bother."

"It should be nothing, for mighty men of money such as ourselves."

"Celtic warriors of Capital."

"High Kings of High Finance."

"Lords of Leverage."

They stared at the hole in the ground, the scattered blocks.

"Well," I said, after a long pause, "Someone's done the hard work anyway, and laid a foundation."

"Yes…" Brendan of Birr poked a block cautiously with his toe.

Nearby, the steel gates roared open automatically, then slammed closed again, though there appeared to be nobody there.

Ah, the different paths our lives had taken. I owned nothing but whatever I could carry in a small bag, and the immaculate suit on my back. What had we still in common, now that they were successful Irish businessmen and financiers, owning, no doubt, immense wealth in property? Evidently they had forgotten even the block-laying classes of Brother O'Driscoll. There was no past for me to go back to. It was time to move on.

I glimpsed, behind them, in the bushes, a flash of lurid colour. Angela? I leapt over the toppled blocks, and headed after it.

Finian grabbed my arm, and hauled me back.

"Hold hard there, Lord Snooty." I detected a certain toughening of his tone. "No one's allowed through the perimeter."

"What perimeter?" I said.

They all looked at each other. Then they took the legs from under me with a deft hurling move, and sat on my chest while they began to consult in the Irish language. An old Orphanage habit, when in the hearing of Foreigners. It gave me a queer feeling, to be on the outside of it.

I understood their speech effortlessly, though wincing at the barbarous grammar of Brendan of Birr.

Were their bonuses at risk if they didn't build this wall?

Should they tell me the secret of the white building at the head of the valley, in return for my help?

What secret, I wondered, but could gather no hint…

Finally Finian crouched beside me. "Look," he said. "What happens in that building is Confidential. But if you help us with this wall, we'll pretend we never saw you."

Sound man, I thought.

"Stout fellow," I said. We shook hands.

The Lads unseated themselves from my chest, and helped me up.

"So," I said, "you just need to lay a block, like this…"

Brother O'Driscoll's block-laying classes had seldom been far from my mind. The dreams were particularly vivid. I rubbed the scars behind my ears, then mixed a little cement, going easy on the sand, and laid a block, hoping it would jog their memories.

"OK, off you go," I said.

"Right!"

"Right."

"Right…"

They stared at the block.

I would have to use some other method.

"Well, drawing on your years of experience at the heart of the biggest construction boom in world history, what do you do next?" I asked, glancing past them at the bushes. No sign of her now. Feck.

"Right! OK!" said Finian. "Somebody's given us a…" – he looked at the block – "… a unit. We'll call it our capital base… Now – as the Pharaohs discovered while building the pyramids – the secret is leverage… I know, I'll ring Brendan."

He rang Brendan of Birr on his little phone.

Brendan, three yards away, answered. "Brendan," said Finian, "I've an asset I want to leverage. Will you give me ten on it? Sound." He hung up. "Now I've ten blocks."

"You have?" I said, blinking.

Finian nodded. "Oh, Brendan's word is his bond."

The others winced.

"I lost both my yachts investing in his bonds," muttered one. "Insured with fecking Lehman Brothers indeed."

"Sorry…" said Finian. "I should have said, as good as money in the bank."

They all groaned. "He never fecking told me his bank was registered in Iceland," muttered Columba of Terryglass.

Finian coughed. "Ah… yes…. I meant, as safe as Houses."

The muttering was louder, and general, and there was weeping.

"Anyway," said Finian hastily, "now all I need to do is just invest my ten blocks." He rang a number on his little phone. "Ruadhain, I've ten blocks I want to invest."

"Ten blocks, eh? Well, there's great demand for blocks. I'll put your blocks into more blocks," replied Ruadhain. He grinned. "Ah, it's all coming back to me. The good old days."

"Brilliant," said Finian. "Oh, and if you could assemble them into a product…"

Behind Finian, a rabbit hopped over the single grey concrete block of the Perimeter.

It seemed this method of block-laying had little in common with the – perhaps old-fashioned – methods of Brother O'Driscoll. Still, these were the men who had created the greatest property boom in world history and built Modern Ireland. They must know what they were doing.

Ruadhain rang Brendan, and the Golden Circle was complete. "Brendan? I've ten blocks I want to leverage up."

"As the man said when he was asked to paint the shed brown, consider it dun," said Brendan.

Ruadhain hung up, and rang Finian. "You've a hundred blocks, assembled into a product."

"Mighty." Finian hung up, dropped the phone into his inside pocket and slapped his hands together. "A hundred blocks! Assembled! Well, that's the wall built."

I looked at the single block.

"You're right, you're right!" said Finian. "We're not safe yet. Now I need to put in place a Hedge, to protect it."

He rang Brendan again. "Short or long?" asked Brendan.

They put in place a short Hedge.

"Hurray!" shouted the Lads.

"Bonuses all round," said Finian.

Fred Goodwin arrived with the sandwiches.

I hadn't known I was hungry till Fred handed me a sandwich. As I lifted it to my lips, I grew dizzy with desire.

My teeth slid through the layers of bread, butter and meat, to meet. The curved bite of sandwich sat on my tongue for a minute while I marvelled at it, its starches slowly turning to sugars in the deepening pool of my saliva, so that the bread turned gradually sweet in my mouth. Oh, the familiar chemical miracle! Overwhelmed, I closed my eyes and chewed it.

Dear God! It was a Tipperary sandwich!

13

The amylase and lipase of my saliva opened up the layered chemicals of my ham sandwich like a book. My eager tongue and teeth devoured a fond, familiar tale of Fethard pigs smoked over Oola oak. And – by the rich taste of it – butter churned from the cream of the milk of the cows of Ballydine, left to graze all summer in the lush grass of the Rainy Meadow, only moved on the hottest days to Tadgh's Pond field and its harder water... Oh, the long, languorous protein chains! And the bread... By the bite and tang of the crust, made with wheat from the Golden Vale. Ah, the familiar surprise of those minerals, that iron! Grain grown in the south-facing fields just past Knockavilla, up on the shoulder of Cooper's Hill, yes, the fields just below the last rough fifty acres of untended hilltop where a cunning fox could always throw the chasing pack into milling chaos by urinating in the four corners of the last green field, then off away with him silently into the exile of the scrub – and if you weren't quick to get back to your snares after hearing the screech, you'd find only the rabbit's head left in the noose.

Tears came to my eyes.

I swallowed.

The Lads, too, ate their sandwiches in thoughtful reverie. All about me, familiar faces were transformed. The hard lines softened as they relaxed, and youth returned. I observed dear Senan of Iniscathay, or Scattery Island as the poor English map-makers, afflicted by their speech impediments, had been obliged to call it. He ate, as ever, in a kind of religious ecstasy. He dunked the crust of his ham sandwich in his milky tea and, taking a bite, overwhelmed by memories of a lost love, cried,

"Madeleine! Ya wagon, ya!" He closed his eyes, in remembrance of things past.

Behind the chewing, swallowing, weeping Lads, the pregnant doe emerged from the oak woods, pushed through the short Hedge which was rooted in nothing and already dying, and walked up to the single grey concrete block, firm in its setting cement, off to one side of the steel gates. She nuzzled the block with her nose a moment, and snorted. Her pregnant belly almost brushed the block as she stepped over it. A ripple of breeze rattled the leaves of a thousand oak trees behind me, making a noise like the sigh of the sea, as she faded into the swaying bushes.

We finished our sandwiches. Finian stood up, and slapped the crumbs off his hands. "Ah, it's a great relief to have that Wall built," he said. The Lads murmured assent through the last bite of crust. Ruadhain nodded, got a crumb up his nose, and tried to sneeze it free. "Time for a nap, I think," said Finian.

I stood too. "I should be off," I said. "However, I can see but one block, and I laid that myself with my own hands."

The Lads stared at the single block. Finian poked it with his toe. "But it always worked before," he said.

I sighed, and quickly built the wall in the old manner, by cementing blocks together. "There you go," I said. "Well, I'll be off." I stepped forward. And was stopped, by the high wall I'd just built.

Fuck, I thought.

"Bugger," I said, pointing. "I need to go there."

"You must pass between these symplegades," Ruadhain snuffled, and blew his nose.

"Pardon?" I said.

"These simple gates," he said.

The huge steel gates, their interlocking steel teeth meshed in a vertical grin, flew suddenly apart, hauled back along their deep, steel tracks by invisible motors, or demons.

I took a cautious step towards them.

And another…

The jaws roared shut. Their teeth met with a clang that set the tall bars, twice the height of me, vibrating.

I looked down to see the slamming gates had neatly shaved the suede from the toe-tip of my left shoe.

"Why do they not let me through?" I said, vexed. "I'm on a quest, and my Heart is Pure."

"Ah, I'll send over the Guardian of the Threshold, so," said Ruadhain of Lorrha, and headed off to the portable cabins.

14

Ruadhain of Lorrha returned from the cabins a few minutes later, chatting to a wildhaired man.

As they came close, I gave a start that almost knocked my hat off.

It was Pat Sheeran. The man whose business I had inadvertently destroyed, back in Tipperary.

The man I had nearly killed, by mistake, in a Dublin pub.

The man who… I tilted the brim of my bowler to cover as much of my face as possible.

"Hmmm," said Pat Sheeran. He poked at one of the Gates. "It seems to have developed a mind of its own."

"Could you open them, my good man?" I said, the plummy voice aiding my disguise.

"Ah no," said Pat Sheeran. "Neither I nor anybody else can open them. I'm only here to install a Salmon of Knowledge, to manage the gates." He poked the other Gate. "Hmmmm… Are you familiar with my invention?"

Shite. I swung my black bag, containing my Salmon of Knowledge, behind my back. What if the Salmon – Pat's gift to me on my far-off 18th birthday – were to detect my fright, speak Wisdom, and betray me…?

"Please," I said. "Enlighten me."

"A Salmon of Knowledge," said Pat, "is an electronic device which searches the vast, surging, global ocean of Information for the single, suspended speck of Wisdom that, at that moment, you most need."

"I trust business is thriving," I said.

Pat shrugged. "Well, I nearly sold it to the Irish Government.

But some Bastard urinated on the Minister before our meeting…"
He picked up a spanner.

I gulped. "There are plenty of other governments, thank the Lord," I said.

Pat shook his head. "Governments turned out not to crave Wisdom as much as we had hoped. And when they did get Wisdom, they were upset. So we changed our business plan, to concentrate on less emotional areas: economics, global financial data."

"And how did that go?" I asked.

"It went great," he said. "We got so many orders, from every bank in the world, that production was overwhelmed, and we had to stagger our deliveries. Wonderful times…" He looked off up into the clear blue sky. "I remember Bear Stearns got delivery in March that first year. Fannie Mae and Freddie Mac in early September, Lehman Brothers a week later…. We'd sped up production by then, so AIG got delivery the day after Lehman Brothers. Then Washington Mutual, Wachovia, Fortis, Citibank, Royal Bank of Scotland, Anglo Irish Bank… We had to charter a container ship to satisfy the demand from all the banks in Iceland…"

"And did the arrival of Wisdom and the delivery of Truth revolutionise their businesses?"

"It certainly did," said Pat Sheeran.

Dick Fuld and Fred Goodwin walked past, carrying more ham sandwiches. They avoided Pat's eye. On the soft breeze came the sound of whistling from the chemical toilets, as Seán FitzPatrick applied his skills to his new area of responsibilities. The whistling stopped abruptly, and there was a startled cry, and a splash.

Pat Sheeran looked down. The blue sky was reflected dimly in a muddy puddle in the rough road. He spat into it, raised his head, and smiled.

"Still," he said, "they have turned out to be great for controlling gates." He ran his knuckles across the steel bars so that they sang. "As each, unique, visitor arrives, they are Judged by a complex code as subtle and terrible as God. And they pass through… Or they do not. And the judgement is Just; and it is Final. It makes," he paused to clear his throat, 'All the Sense in the World™'."

I committed the sin of despair, in the shadow of my hat: how was I going to get through these infallible and omniscient gates?

"But," said Pat Sheeran, frowning, "for some reason, this Salmon seems to be letting through the Evil, and barring the Righteous."

I cheered up. There was hope for me, so. I raised my face to the sun, and my hat fell off. I caught it.

He stared at my face, and raised his spanner. "You remind me of…"

"Leonardo DiCaprio," I said hastily, ramming my head into my hat. "Everybody says so."

The gate roared open again as he took a step back to look at me.

Beyond the gate, I glimpsed motion.

Far off, at the head of the valley, a door in the vast white dome slid open.

A strange perfume drifted to me on the mild air.

I squinted into the distance. Yes… Angela darted from behind a bush, and ran for the door, holding a supple branch like a spear. She jammed the closing door open with the branch, and disappeared inside the white building.

The pregnant doe, ambling along in Angela's wake, sniffing the air, leapt the branch with a casual ease that surprised, given her huge belly, and vanished too into the darkness.

I strained forward, squinted, and discerned a dim stir or struggle in the distant doorway. The branch, jamming open the door, curved up still further, under pressure.

Then a small man, hairy even at that distance, sped under the branch and out the door on a yellow bicycle, into the bright sunshine. He cycled towards us at some considerable speed. Two taller men pursued him on foot, shouting.

"Stop!" yelled a man in brilliant white, waving the branch that had held open the door.

"You little bastard!" yelled a man in deepest black, brandishing a broom.

Pat Sheeran, distracted by the mysteries of the Gates, poked away at the Salmon, oblivious.

"Strange…" he murmured. "I've lowered the definition of virtue so the Salmon should let in nearly anyone, but still no go."

I passed my hand through the invisible beams, in the direction of the gates.

They Judged me, and slammed shut.

My hand retreated back through the beams, in reflex.

The gates slid open.

"You have it in upside down," I said. "It's closing when signalled to open, and opening when signalled to close. Look."

I plucked out the Salmon, reversed it, and slotted it back in.

"Now they'll open automatically at the approach of the virtuous," I said.

"Shite, I'd better tighten up the definition of virtue, so…" Pat Sheeran scrambled back into the Guardhouse, and began adjusting the controls.

The hairy man approached the gate. The two pursuing men accelerated, and diverted him off the road onto the grass. They chased the hairy cyclist round a clump of bushes, and disappeared from view.

The Salmon of the Gates spoke abruptly:

> "Although my belief in the world returned to me, I have never since entirely freed myself of the impression that this life is a segment of existence which is enacted in a three dimensional boxlike universe especially set up for it."
>
> **Carl Jung, *Memories, Dreams, Reflections,* 1963**

Hmmm. The Salmon of the Gates had evidently not enjoyed the reversing of its sensors.

The bicycle reappeared from behind the bushes, and headed straight for us now at great speed. The two men followed.

I glanced into my black bag, to see was my own Salmon all right. It murmured in the darkness:

> "How do I know that I am not being deceived by an infinitely powerful evil demon who wants me to believe in the existence of an external world – and in my own body?"
>
> **René Descartes, French thinker, 1641**

How, indeed? I shivered as the wind died. The whispering leaves fell silent.

I looked around me for the Lads. Yes, they had all gone to sleep, after their lunch, in the shade of the oak trees. My opportunity...

The small hairy cyclist approached the gates, ringing his bell with a hairy thumb.

The Salmon examined his Virtue, Honour, and Credit History, made a Judgement, and opened the gates.

The hairy man cycled out of the high security zone.

I stepped through the gates, into the Zone.

In the guardhouse, Pat Sheeran pulled on a chain from which hung an enormous round red sign reading "Do Not Pull". The gates slammed shut behind me, in a blaze of sparks.

Pat Sheeran leaned out the window of the guardhouse, to observe the damage. "Shite," he said thoughtfully.

15

The hairy man headed off downhill, down the valley, on his little bicycle. The man in black arrived at my side.

"Bah!" he said, and banged his broom off the gate.

The man in the white suit limped up to us. "Stop him!" he gasped. He leaned on his branch and breathed heavily.

"Why?" I asked.

"Because the fate of the universe depends on it."

Oh arse, I thought.

"Top hole!" I said.

I frowned, and performed the exercises taught us in the Orphanage by Brother Lovett, who had spent some time in the Missions in China.

One did not merely lash a rock in the general direction of the enemy. Oh, no. First, I visualised an ideal rock striking that which was impeding my spiritual progress; only then did I lift an actual rock into the gusset of Angela's tangerine thong, and swing it like a slingshot, faster and faster. My muscles performed the release without conscious command: the rock lofted straight up into the blue sky. I looked up after it, into the dazzle of the noon sun. A storm of dancing black dots flashed white and black as I blinked, trying to see the descending stone.

The stone emerged from the cloud of unknowing, and struck me firmly on the crown of the head – the very seat of the Self – crushing my bowler hat.

When I came round, I sighed, brushed the wreckage of my hat from my bruised head, and stood up. This was always the risk with such exercises. Indeed, back at the Orphanage, the Self had proved to be the chief obstacle to my spiritual progress so often that I had been forced to give up both conkers and archery. "Shite," I said, and realised that the blow had cured me of my Englishness.

"Ah! You're Irish!" said the man in white, in tones of great Englishness, having recovered his wind. I sighed. Once again, I did not fit in. Bugger.

"Fuck... So I am," I said. Still, it was, on another level, a relief to finally meet an Englishman. There seemed little point going Abroad if you didn't meet Foreigners. I picked up another rock, and put it in the gusset of Angela's thong. The tiny cyclist was accelerating away down the valley. It would take some shot to stop him now.

"Bastard!" said the man in white.

I wondered how he could tell just by looking.

He grabbed my upper arm. "You lucky, lucky bastards were never Colonised: You never had your minds Raped and your native culture Destroyed by a murderous invader who despised your rich, deep, ancient culture as primitive and vile. But England, poor sweet gentle Celtic England, fell to the Roman legions. They forced on our broken nobles Latin and Greek, and thrust those vile, foreign tongues so far down our throats that we choke on them yet in our best schools."

I was having the very devil of a time aiming at the escaping cyclist, with this fellow hanging off my arm. Also, there was a word I wished to get in edgeways, but it was hard to find a gap.

"Only in the past few decades," he said, "have we begun – begun! – to cease cringing before our old colonial masters. For centuries, we wrote... Nothing. Scared little farts of books, each starting with its epigraph in Latin or Greek, an apologetic clearing of the throat before," he spat, "the Classics."

He paused to draw a breath.

"Shakespeare," I said, relieved that I had got my word in edgeways.

Far off down the hill, the cyclist tinkled his little bell.

The man in brilliant white moaned, and wept, and squeezed my arm the tighter. I noticed that there was something odd about his face… "Yes! Yes! The golden exception, proving the iron rule! Only one great English writer in all that time, and he achieved all the glory that the world can bestow not *despite* but *because* he had little Latin and less Greek. The only free man in England."

"Ah now, England has produced a rake of great literature since then," I objected.

"Name them!" he cried.

I searched my mind. "*Peter Rabbit*," I said. "*Alice in Wonderland. Winnie the Pooh… The Jungle Book.*"

"A retreat to childhood!" he cried. "Afraid to take on the Classics! No, who are the great English names to match James Joyce and Flann O'Brien? The nimble, the free Protestant English geniuses of the written word? Beckett. Wilde. Shaw. Yeats. Swift. Sterne. Only in Ireland were we ever free to speak! Away from the land of our shame!"

I nodded, and gave an unobtrusive wiggle, but he gripped me all the tighter.

"The suffering English, trapped between Hadrian's Wall and the Roman Ports!" he cried to Heaven. "Still ruled from the colonial capital, Londinium! You cannot understand it, because you are free, authentic, unselfconscious. Yes, Sterne and Wilde and Swift our tongues in Ireland!" He released my arm, to gesture freely at the sky. "Sterne! And Swift! And Wilde!"

I took advantage of the liberation, and swung the thong.

His fist froze halfway to heaven. "Oh Lord…"

I relaxed, timed my release, adjusted for the light breeze; the drop of the valley; the acceleration away of the target…

I had given up on the pursuit of perfection, and, in renouncing it, achieved it.

The rock's curve was a line of beauty.

The arc of its fall intersected with the vector of the target's acceleration…

Yet the bike continued downhill. Could I have missed?

The rider began to tilt slowly sideways; the bicycle toppled, crashed, and lay still.

No.

16

"Oh dear," said the man in white. "Oh dear."

A figure wild of hair and wild of eye joined us. Pat Sheeran, waving his spanner.

"Open!" Pat shouted at the Salmon of the Gates.

And the gates opened.

We walked back down the valley to the small, still figure, lying face down in the grass.

He really was remarkably hairy, even for an Englishman.

The back wheel of his bicycle clickety-clickety-clicked to a halt.

"My God, you've killed their monkey," said Pat Sheeran.

The still figure groaned, and turned over, and blinked. One eye stared straight up at us. The other stared off sideways. Both were bloodshot.

"Oh, crumbs…" said the man in white. "We've only got half an hour to resuscitate him. Someone put on the coffee."

I watched carefully, as the man in black ran back to the dome. He was stopped in the doorway by a Security Guard. The Guard interrogated him briefly and examined his credentials before letting him in.

Hmmm. How was I to gain entry, with the place now in such a state of high alert?

The man in white grasped the concussed monkey under the armpits and, with a grunt, threw the groaning figure over his shoulder. With difficulty, he bent down to pick up the bicycle.

"Let me give you a hand," I said, and hefted the bicycle up onto my shoulder.

"Sorry, yes, sorry, thank you. Sorry," he said. There was definitely something unusual about the man's face, though what it was I could not rightly say.

The bicycle was surprisingly light. We passed back through the gates. The rough road wound through bushes, and approached the dome.

"It must often be nice to be English, all the same," I said, to cheer the man up.

He groaned. I tried to think of a nice thing about being English. An image came to me.

"Sipping, um... Darjeeling," I said. "Whatever that is.... In your pyjamas..."

"A beverage of the Bengali Himalayas!" he cried. "In garments of the Hindustani highlands! No, the entire English breakfast ritual is wretched with inauthenticity."

"Well, at least you've your own Church," I said. "That's all the important rituals taken care of."

"The Church of England? Whose Holy Land is in the Middle East?" A tear appeared in the corner of his eye.

"The English Royal Family," I offered. Safe ground, surely.

"*Entirely* comprised of Germans and Greeks."

Nonplussed, I circled back to the literature. "But, ah, England's publishers are justly reknowned for, for..." I was having trouble with this one.

"For books," he said firmly, "written by chancers from Ireland."

"Oh, England's great literary prizes aren't always won by the Irish," I said. "They're sometimes won by..." I searched my memory. Hmm...

"By inhabitants of the subcontinent!" He sobbed, briefly. "In the land of Robin Hood, our books are all by Cowboys and Indians."

I had not cheered him up as much as I'd hoped. Indeed, he seemed somewhat traumatized by our conversation.

We were waved inside by the Security Guard. I kept my head down, as I carried the bicycle past the Guard, and through the doorway. The words of the man in white had stirred me deeply, almost as though I myself had some kind of buried childhood trauma associated with England's prize-winning literature. A memory came rushing back to me: Ethel the Orphanage Cook walking away from me; the taste of coconut; the sight of a shelf, bending under the strain of...

No. Luckily I did not have a buried childhood trauma, and the feeling passed. "I'm sorry..." I said in sympathy.

"Oh, gosh, no need to apologise," said the man in the white suit, blushing. "Forget I said anything. Sort of slipped out. Sorry."

He looked away, biting his lip, and lowered the concussed monkey gently to the smooth white concrete floor. "It's just... you must understand, I had a deprived childhood. A post-colonial education of the narrowest kind. We learnt nothing – nothing! – of the rich culture of these, our own islands. And so the limitations of my provincial schooling have left me without a single verse of the meanest vision poem of Eoghan Rua Ó Súilleabháin, not a line of the accentual poetry of Ó Rathaille, not a word of the simplest *Filíocht na nDaoine*, or so much as a *remscéla* from the *Táin Bó Cúailnge*. Why, I left Eton not knowing a *fada* from a *sébhú*!" He wept.

I patted him gently on the back. "Ah, you're grand. Sure, don't you have the *Beano*," I said, to console him. "And the *Dandy*."

He wept harder.

I looked around the vast, open space for Angela.

It was like being inside half a giant eggshell. The curved white walls seamlessly became curved white ceiling, the space under it criss-crossed with rafters and lights.

Across the white concrete floor, low white partitions made a maze of cubicles, each containing a Man and a Machine. Some men studied glowing squares of light. Some typed, and tapped, and sighed, and typed again. Laboratory benches loaded with equipment stuck out like jetties from the walls. I could see no women at all. Other men walked fast, almost ran through the maze. I sensed that this chaos of activity was aimed toward a single, urgent goal.

Set into the far end of the great white egg of a building was a single thick black circle.

Not quite a circle.

No trace of Angela. No trace of the deer, either. Where the feck could they be hiding, in this vast illuminated labyrinth? Bright horizontal tubes of light hung from the rafters high above. The only shadows were directly above the rafters.

In the cubicle nearest us, a man wearing a rainbow-patterned shirt studied a row of glowing lights, a dozen of them green, the last one red.

"Did you see," I said, "the most beautiful…" He waved me away without even looking up. "…Woman…" The red light turned green.

I trailed off.

"Temperature achieved…" he murmured. "So we should have…" There was a rising, wavering, whistling sound from the far end of the room. "Yes…"

A distant figure ran towards us, everyone stepping smartly out of his way. The man in black! He held… something gleaming, silver… from it came… was that smoke, no… I strained to see…

"Coffee!" he cried. "It's hot! Coming through!"

"Well," said the man in white, shaking my hand. "Thank you for your help…?"

"Jude," I said. That black disc at the far end of the room seemed to be some kind of door… or door*way*… Was that a flicker of movement, in its darkness?

"Good to meet you. I'm Dan," said the Man in White. "Well… er… You can make your own way out… ? I had better… sorry…"

The aroma of the coffee arrived, followed by the Man in Black and the coffee itself. The monkey shivered, and abruptly opened its eyes.

I edged closer to the round black door.

Dan followed me. "Ahem…" he said. "The way out is…"

I had to purchase more time, to find Angela. "So," I said, "what do you all do in here?"

Dan sighed. "Well…" He looked around him. "Are you familiar with the Scientific method?"

"I've heard of it," I said cautiously.

"And its recent crisis?" said Dan the man in white.

"Ah, I've been away…"

The monkey stared straight at me with its bloodshot right eye; with its bloodshot left eye it stared straight up at the rafters.

"Science has achieved many great things," said Dan.

The monkey began to acquire a substantial erection.

I looked up, to where it so urgently pointed.

There. At last. Just visible, emerging from the shadow of the rafter on which she hid. Angela's immaculate posterior.

It glowed, pale as the moon in the dusk sky. Her long blonde hair beyond it in shadow; the sun in darkness.

Well, it was an honourable tradition. Hadn't King Sweeney himself, naked, taken to the trees in his madness, and crossed Ireland without touching the ground, conversing in song with the little birds?

I would not betray her, if she wished to hide. But how would I reach her?

She returned to the rafter's shadow, in modest retreat from my gaze, or the monkey's. She was gone.

Oh, how I longed to sink my face into her…

"But!" said Dan.

"Yes," I said, startled. "Though you express it more crudely than I would myself."

"Ours is the first generation in three hundred years," said Dan, "in which Physics has made no progress… We have played twenty questions with the universe for three centuries. We brutally interrogated it, at the tiniest and the largest scale. And always the Universe came up with some answer, to satisfy us. But the object it described is not in the room. The game has broken down. The set of answers we call General Relativity and the set of answers we call Quantum Mechanics are not compatible. We've spent decades trying to join them up. Mostly with String. But they do not describe the same universe. Now, of course, our theories could be wrong…"

The man in black interrupted. "But what if the Universe is wrong? Has contradicted itself? Has screwed up? Why does it always have to be our fault?" He stepped up, onto a swivelling chair. "Must we live under these physical laws, which we did not choose? Laws which condemn us – every man, woman and child – to random and arbitrary death!" The other scientists gathered round him and cheered. He shouted "No! We must throw off the yoke of the oppressor!" and swung his arm wide, in a revolutionary gesture.

The swivelling chair, brutally enforcing Newton's Third Law, rotated beneath the man in black, in an equal and opposite reaction. He fell to the ground, and twisted his ankle.

"Gah!" he said. "Oogh!"

"The Universe conspires against our leader!" cried the rainbow-shirted scientist.

"Gravity sucks!" cried an immensely tall man in a squeaky voice.

"Repeal the Second Law of Thermodynamics!" boomed a dwarf.

There was an excited babble.

"Enough changing our theories to suit reality!"

"Let's change reality to suit our theories!"

"Hurrah!" they cried, "HURRAH!"

"A big step, that," I said. "More of a leap..."

"Pah!" said the man in black, getting, with difficulty, to his feet. "It is the natural and logical next step. The Chemist merely studied matter, until he understood its laws: then he created forms of matter never seen before. Californium. Promethium. Bose-Einstein Condensates... The Biologist merely studied the creatures of the earth, until he understood their reality and laws. Now he rewrites their genetic codes, in poems of flesh. In this very valley, my colleagues have built trees that fruit in winter. Pigs that wish to be eaten. Bees that sing Bach."

"Would that not be considered by some to be against Nature?" I said.

"Exactly!" cried the man in black. "Who could possibly be *for* Nature? That totalitarian torturer?"

I recalled my childhood in the lush Tipperary fields. "But there are days when many are happy," I said, "and nature is kind."

"Hah! No doubt Stalin smiled at babies, and Hitler loved his dogs," said the Man in Black. "Nature? Kind? Nature breaks us, degrades us, murders our children. The lovers of nature have merely internalised their oppression. Collaborators!" He looked around. Dan was squatting a little way off, coaxing the monkey to sip from the mug. The man in black nodded towards Dan. "The old man thinks we wish merely to improve a little on a benign system. No! We wish to kill a tyrant." His voice lowered in volume, but rose in passion. "Our new universe is far more radical than he knows. There is no point throwing off the laws and forms of the oppressor, only to replace them with identical laws and forms. Why, that would be as absurd as labouring to throw off the most powerful empire in the world, only to replace her parliamentary system, court system, prison system, and civil service with an identical parliamentary system, court system, prison system, and civil service."

"Indeed!" I said, with fervour. I had always felt it to be one of the glories of Ireland's revolutionary history that, on achieving our freedom from the British Empire, our nation's founders had fearlessly made profound and radical changes, replacing the Crown with a Harp on the cap-badge of every prison officer, and painting the Post Boxes green. "But it's a big job, that, radically improving the universe. When were you planning to do it?"

"Well, we'd been planning to take our time and get it right. A few years of modelling, a few years testing... But, in our eagerness to discover its secrets, we interrogated the universe a little too energetically over at the Large Hadron Collider, and, er..." The man in black grew silent. He sighed, and pulled from a drawer a crumpled one-piece suit made from some stretchy silver material.

"What did you do?" I said, alarmed.

"We, ah," he blushed. "Broke the universe."

"We didn't mean to!" squeaked the tall man. "It cracked under questioning."

"Theory clearly stated…" boomed the dwarf.

"Well, perhaps we shouldn't have run those two experiments simultaneously," said Dan, rejoining us. "The universe contradicted itself, at the most Fundamental Level, and its internal contradictions are due to tear it apart in…" He looked up at the clock on the wall, over the black circle. "Whoops! Less than half an hour… We'd better get a move on!"

17

As they continued to talk, I nodded as though I was interested in the fate of the universe, while looking around me surreptitiously. Angela must have used some kind of rope or cable to get up onto that rafter. It had to be somewhere.

"So you see," said the man in black, helping Dan pull the monkey into the crumpled silver one-piece suit, "we had to design our new universe rather faster than we'd have liked." He slapped the lolling monkey's face, right to left, then backhand. The monkey groaned, and dropped the mug. "Hmmm. More coffee…"

"Still, given the time constraints," said Dan, "we're pretty happy."

"By cunningly and intricately folding certain aspects of matter into other dimensions," whispered the man in black in my ear, "we have abolished Death."

"We got in Jonathan Ive," said Dan, "the great English designer of the original iPod, which transformed listening; the revolutionary iPad, which transformed watching; the chocolate-flavoured iPud, which transformed eating; the iPid, which transformed going to the toilet; the iPed, which transformed having sex with children, and the Salmon of Knowledge, which… er, well… yes…"

"Anyway," said the man in black, "Jonathan Ive has totally rethought the usability and ergonomics of the universe. Lighter, brighter. Better use of space."

"Jonathan has fixed our interface with the universe," said Dan. "In the old one, you might have noticed people kept getting cut, stabbed, mutilated, heads sliced off… It was ridiculous, from a Health and Safety point of view. So his new universe has no sharp edges."

"Fair play to you," I said politely. "But how exactly is the trick to be done?"

"We have designed the Most Fundamental Particle..." said Dan, "... super-symmetrical in every dimension..."

"Which, if we can bring it into Being, and carefully unbalance its Symmetry," said the Man in Black, "will quite naturally collapse into complexity, unfold into structure..."

"And create a new universe, to our design."

"An entire new universe?" I said.

"Yes," said Dan.

"But it takes a lot of energy to make a lot of mass," I said.

"Ah... yes. It does, doesn't it? Well, anyway..." he said.

But, secure in the knowledge vested in me by Brother Brophy, the Orphanage physics teacher, I persevered. "I mean, you'd need an astonishing, an immense amount of energy... Where will you get this energy from, to build the new universe?"

"Ah, well..." Dan cleared his throat. "The old universe. This one." He slapped the partition of a cubicle almost entirely filled with stacks of paper. The partition wobbled, and knocked the stacks of paper in a sliding white avalanche. The inhabitant of the cubicle, a pale, nervous-looking fellow, thinking perhaps that the experiment had started early, threw himself under his desk.

"Sorry about that," said Dan.

"And how much of our old universe will it consume?" I said.

"Well... All of it..."

"But..." A drawback had struck me. "Everyone now living will die." I looked at the clock. "In eighteen minutes."

"Yes, progress always comes at a cost," sighed Dan. "Believe me, nobody has suffered more than us. The stress of finding funding. And the paperwork!" He pointed under the desk. The pale young man crouching there blinked up at us. "Just ask Mortimer." Mortimer crawled further back under the desk. "Oh, you haven't seen paperwork till you've written the Environmental Impact Assessment for the total destruction of the universe..."

Mortimer, far under the desk, wept helplessly.

"Thank God for the US Federal Reserve," muttered the man in black, a few yards away at a lab bench. He looked at the clock, and turned up the heat under the fresh pot of coffee. Glanced back at the clock. Turned the heat up a bit more. "Their funding at least came with no questions, no forms, and no strings attached."

"Why," I said, glancing surreptitiously under Mortimer's desk for any hidden ropes or cables, "would the US Federal Reserve help fund the total destruction of the universe?"

"Well," said the man in black, "they had some toxic assets they were trying to dispose of… And they'd tried everything else."

The coffee started to come through, and he busied himself with it.

Wait. *There.* Behind the monkey: A long ladder, leaning at a tipsy angle against the wall. Angela must have used it to climb into the rafters, then kicked it away.

"All it needs now is an Observer," said Dan.

"Ah, yes," I said, while I edged towards the ladder. "The Observer can force light to behave as either a wave, or a particle…" I reached out, Unobserved, behind me. My fingers touched, tip, tip, tip, the cool metal rungs of the tall ladder. If I could swing it back out, and across to the rafter; race up its rungs and embrace my beloved… My imagination failed at this point. But something would occur to me.

The Man in Black was staring at me. "Obviously you need an *Observer*," I continued, playing for time, "in order to force a decision on the Most Fundamental Particle. To unbalance the perfect balance."

"No," said Dan, looking up from a steel jug in which he frothed warm milk.

"Bollocks" said the Man in Black, pouring fresh coffee into the mug. "We've understood the behaviour of light, with none of this 'Ooh, the Observer influences the Observed' mystical bullshit, since Feynman, Dyson, Tomonaga and Schwinger developed quantum electrodynamics."

"No," said Dan, handing the monkey a cappuccino, "we only need an Observer because someone has to see the old universe actually recycled, and sign off on it, or we don't get the last tranche of our grant."

"The only sense in which the Observer influences the Observed," said the man in black, "is that he'll cock it up and break everything if he touches it."

"So," said Dan, "we trained an Observer, from birth, to be Objective, Logical, and Dispassionate."

They looked at the monkey. He seemed almost recovered and was sipping his cappuccino with a wounded expression.

While their attention was on the monkey, I braced the base of the ladder against my foot, and hauled on the highest rung I could reach. The top of the ladder came away from the wall and out, in a high arc above me. I stepped smartly sideways to let it past so that it could come to rest against the rafters.

But as the ladder toppled, one of its two rubber feet slipped in the spilled coffee from the monkey's original mug, and juddered a vital few inches back toward the wall. This, unfortunately, rotated the whole immense falling ladder just enough so that it fell short of the rafter by about a foot.

It therefore kept falling, ever faster.

The recovered monkey, in the ladder's plunging shadow, shrieked, dropped his cappuccino, and ran. He ran along directly beneath it, almost the whole length of it, flickering through the falling shadows of the rungs, frame by frame. The crash of the long metal ladder landing was muted by the soft monkey, whose shriek came to an abrupt end as the final frame pinned him to the floor.

There was a long silence. We all drifted closer to the unmoving fur bundle. Somebody lifted the ladder clear of the body.

"Our innocent mind!" said Dan.

The silence throughout the great space grew terrible.

"Can you not get another monkey?" I said.

"There is no other such. That beast was trained from birth to be innocent of all preconceptions. Brought up to see things as they Truly Are…"

"A great pity you didn't think of training a spare," I said.

"We had twelve monkeys. The other eleven, ah, em…"

"Killed themselves," said the man in black.

We looked down at the doubly concussed monkey. He stirred, opened his eyes. One bloodshot eye stared up at my bright silk waistcoat. The other stared down at my blue suede shoes. The monkey groaned. He did not seem impressed by the sight of things as they Truly Are.

He passed out.

"And now we have no innocent observer, and the Universe is fucked," said the man in black.

I felt bad then, for my actions had led to the likely destruction of the Universe. I really should stop and help… But… Pursue Angela, or save the universe?

I thought of the universe, and everyone in it.

I thought of the pale moon of Angela's rear, the golden sun of her hair, the apples of her breasts against my chest. I imagined my warm body merged and blurred into her warm body so that I no longer knew my state or position, and she no longer knew hers.

On reflection, fuck the universe. I lifted the ladder, and began to head off with it.

But… I paused, one foot in mid-air. Should the universe cease to exist, she too would cease to exist!

Now, that would be a blow.

I put down my foot, and pondered anew.

The monkey groaned, reached for the pot containing the coffee dregs, and missed.

My dilemma reminded me of that faced by the young Setanta, who slew with a rock the guard-hound of Culainn. Yes, I would do what noble Setanta had done.

I turned back.

18

The scientists were clustered together, talking in low, anxious tones. I cleared my throat behind them. They jumped, and turned.

"I have done you wrong, and injured your animal," I said. "Allow me to replace your innocent beast."

"With what?" said Dan, looking around him.

"Well, I am poor but honest," I said. "With myself."

Dan clapped his hands. "Yes! Brilliant! No one could be as innocent as an Irishman! Why, you are almost as good as a monkey!"

All nodded their agreement.

"Great. So, can I save the universe now, then?" I said. "Only I'm keen to be off."

"You'll have to wait a few minutes," said Dan. He looked up at the clock over the round door. "Eleven, to be exact."

I sighed.

"Well, we'd better get on with it and train him," said the man in black.

I began to recover from my disappointment. True, helping them would delay my blessed union with Angela, but on balance it seemed well worth it. Surely few things were more likely to impress a woman than saving the Universe.

The scientist in the black leather jacket decanted the stunned monkey from the silver suit, and began to test the seals and joints and air supply.

He caught my look. "Don't worry, she'll stretch," he said.

Dan cleared his throat, in the manner of Brother Brophy preparing to explain the Nature of Reality to the slower lads in the back row. "Right…" he said. "Pay careful attention. Your life, and the fate of the universe, depends on this. The Most Fundamental Particle, being heavy with the potential seed energy of an entire universe, is immensely massive."

His accompanying hand gestures reminded me irresistibly of Angela's rear, and I grew light-headed.

Dan continued, "It behaves rather like a Black Hole."

I had a Vision... of Angela's... Still more blood rushed to my extremities, and I passed out, briefly. When I came round, he was still talking.

"... so Light has the devil of a time crawling out of it. That means that you cannot truly Observe it from a distance. You must get very close – technically, cross its event horizon – in order to Observe."

"And it is vital that you cross the event horizon at a speed as near as possible to fifteen miles per hour," said the man in black. "Vital! A bicycle complete with speedometer will be provided for the purpose."

"But..." I said, worried now – for in Brother Brophy's Honours Physics class we had once created a small black hole in error, and I was all too familiar with their properties – "Will I not be torn to pieces and utterly annihilated in a shocking blaze of energy as I approach the event horizon?" I could still hear the Doppler-shifted screams of poor Collie Moran.

"No," said the man in black, and whispered in my ear. "Remember, we have abolished Death, in the New Jerusalem. You will safely cross the non-event horizon..."

"Pardon?" said Dan, frowning.

"Oh, nothing," said the Man in Black. "Instructions... Right, we'll have to get this off you." He began to tug ineffectually at my clothing. "Nice suit... Jermyn Street? Where's the...? Why is the...?" He pulled harder at my jacket.

At my waistcoat.

At my trousers.

"I see three... Yet they seem to be... One..." He marvelled at the mystery.

An immense tug on each part of the whole, by three scientists at once, merely succeeded in breaking a single thread. It gave off a high, clean note like a seagull's scream as its tension was released.

They gave up on removing my clothes, and hauled me as I was into the silver suit. It was indeed considerably stretched, for Angela was still on my mind.

"Most importantly," said Dan, "you must truly Observe."

"And what would that involve?" I asked.

"You must see the Universe as it is," he replied.

"But aren't I doing that now?" I said, puzzled.

"To use the beautiful language of your people (for I briefly attended Trinity College, Dublin, and thus my idiolect is redolent of Dublin's linguistic riches): in a pig's hole you are observing," said Dan. "What colour is this apple?"

"Red," I said.

"Wrong," said Dan. "The world has no colour."

"It does not?"

"No. What mortals call light… what scientists once called electromagnetic waves… which are in fact particles… the energy that truly is, beyond those words, unknowable… is detected by the chemical orbs you call your eyes. They signal to what you call your mind, which is a structure of carbon-based molecules. But in fact you See nothing, you just wildly exaggerate an unreliable internal chemical reaction into a dream of a solid external universe."

"Beware the human brain," said the man in black, "it is Unscientific. It is Hardwired to go beyond the data."

I thought about this.

"Fair point," I said.

I concentrated hard on not being made a fool of by space, time, and the illusions of matter. It was a good minute before I felt I'd got there.

The red went from the apple.

The appleness went from the apple.

The thingness went from the thing I had formerly seen as an apple. The isness went from what remained.

I no longer saw. I Observed.

Then I did the same with my hearing. Then my sense of touch. All my external senses.

All my internal impulses.

There was soon no separation between me and the universe. I was merely a fragment of the whole, Observing myself, itself. Then I lost the illusion I was a fragment. I was part of the whole. "I" was not. All was.

"God, this is mighty craic altogether," I said, and took a bite of the apple, revelling briefly in the illusion that I existed and that it was delicious.

"Ready?" said the man in black.

Reddy? I gave the apple a suspicious look... Oh. "Ready," I replied, and dropped the apple.

"Into the airlock then." He gestured towards the small black door.

"The airlock?" I said. "Ah... Where exactly will I be, while I'm doing all this Observing?"

"Well..." said Dan, his white suit dazzling against the black of the airlock door, "we accelerate the Particle along a tube in total vacuum, at close to absolute zero. You'll be, ah, inside the tube, approaching the Particle from the other end."

"Inside the tube?"

"That's right. Now if you don't mind..."

"Hang on a minute," I said. "It cannot be very healthy and safe to be struck at inconceivable speed by so massive a particle." Had Setanta had these doubts, I wondered sadly, after volunteering to replace the hound of Culainn?

"You are correct," said Dan. "Normally, we'd accelerate you toward each other at close to the speed of light using a magnetic cannon."

"However," said the Man in Black, "Our new universe has been designated an urban play space containing children. So the Most Fundamental Particle cannot exceed fifteen miles per hour."

"Therefore," said Dan, "you'll be perfectly safe approaching by bicycle."

Hmm. Even if I made a total bags of my approach, a fifteen-mile-per-hour collision shouldn't cripple me entirely.

A final thought occurred. "How long is the tunnel?"

"Infinite," said Dan.

My heart sank. "Ah, now," I said. "I'm not that good a cyclist…"

"Well, naturally I exaggerate for effect. The tunnel is a circle; and thus has no end; and is infinite. Alpha, and omega."

"But particularly omega," muttered the Man in Black.

I did not like the sound of that.

"Don't worry," Dan added hastily, "our calculations show that you will encounter the Most Fundamental Particle early in your first circuit."

I closed my eyes, the better to make up my mind without distraction. If they were wrong in any aspect of their theory, my body would be ripped limb from limb, then cell from cell, then molecule from molecule, then crushed to a super-dense plasma, then… But they were Scientists who had received Funding, and therefore they must know what they were doing.

I opened my eyes.

"I'll save the universe, so," I said. "Only I can't stick around afterwards, if you were thinking of having a few drinks or whatever."

"Great." Dan looked at the clock above the black door. "Let's go. And remember, at this delicate, early stage in the evolution of the universe, every step you take…"

"Every move you make…" said the man in black.

"… will ripple and echo throughout the ever-expanding future, forever changing everything. So just sit quietly on your bicycle, pedalling at precisely fifteen miles per hour, and Observe. Rationally. Logically. Objectively."

"Right so."

He shut my helmet.

The temporary pattern of energy which sustained the illusion that it was me hesitated. Should I bring my bag? I had grown used to having it with me. But did I really need anything in it? As I peered through the thick, dark glass of the helmet into the bag, the Salmon gave me a parting word of advice.

"What-is-not," it said, "… is not."

Parmenides, the father of science. Greek thinker, early 5th century BCE

"What-is-not… is not," I repeated.

If what-is-not is not, then there is no what-is-not for stuff to come from.

So nothing can come into being. And nothing can go out again. All that is, is. And always was. And always will be.

And there is no past, for it is not. And there is no future, for it is not.

All is one, unchanging.

Holy shite. I decided to take my bag.

"Go," said Dan through the dark glass of the helmet, and I beheld him, as though through a glass, darkly.

I crouched, and stepped into the tiny, dark airlock.

I touched the walls. Squinted around the shadowy space. Hard to see. It seemed to resemble the interior drum of a Washing Machine, but large enough to stand up in.

They passed me my small yellow bicycle, and softly closed the round black door. The only light now came from a few pale, glowing dials, showing air pressure, and temperature, and time.

I groped around and found a hook to hang my bag on. There was nowhere to sit. I stood and waited for the end of the universe to begin.

The giant pumps began to suck the warm air from the airlock. The baggy joints of my silver suit twitched and stiffened as the suit's air expanded out into the dropping pressure of the small space and my ears popped. My backpack drove more air into my suit, to equalise the pressure. The new air was cold and clean. I swallowed hard. My ears popped again, and cleared.

19

I relaxed in the dark.

The big, slow pumps of the airlock, like a mother's lungs and heart.

The rapid, intimate hiss and suck of the valves in my suit, as thick air was drawn through it by my little pump, as busy as a child's heart in embryo. For a warm moment, in the chill of the cold recirculating air, I did not feel so all alone.

The sound of the big pumps faded, like a mother dying, as the air thinned. My suit inflated a little more, and its wrinkles vanished.

I received an almighty blow in the back, and whirled around.

I glimpsed the blur of someone else in the dark of the airlock.

I sensed a beautiful, muscular, curved, female presence.

Angela! Had she hidden here? But she had no suit, and the air was vanishing.

A face loomed out of the gloom, struck the face of my helmet, rebounded. We faced each other. Such beautiful eyes, such eyelashes… It was the pregnant doe, hiding in the dark cave of the airlock, panicking in the thinning air.

"What's happening?" said a thin voice in my ear, and I jumped.

An electronic voice. Some class of radio device, within the suit. The Man in Black.

"There is a pregnant deer in the airlock," I said.

"A what?"

A babble of voices, arguing. Then the Man in Black again: *"You'll have to kill it!"*

"What with?"

"Anything!"

"Why?"

"It is not part of the Design!"

"Well…" I said, "It is not part of *your* design…"

I stared into the beautiful eyes. She had stopped trying to escape, and was breathing as fast as she could, sucking in as much air as possible, flooding her blood with oxygen for the ordeal ahead.

The pumps removed the last air from the airlock. I took a firm hold of my bicycle.

The far door opened with no noise at all, and I left her behind me and stepped into the coldest place in the universe.

I was the only heat here. My little body, burning its chemical fuel.

I mounted my little bicycle, took a deep breath, and cycled towards the birth of the universe.

20

I hammered down the pedals. The bicycle gave satisfying resistance to my push.

The curved walls flew by, a smooth pale blur, interrupted only by the hooped bulge of the buried magnets.

I tried to switch off my Consciousness, but that just slowed down the bicycle. No, better get there first.

I stood on the pedals, and rose from the saddle to drive them faster. Faster.

I made good time, my pumping knees almost brushing my chin.

There: in the far distance, floating towards me around the curve of the enormous ring. The Most Fundamental Particle.

Here goes…

I abandoned all my habits of thought, all my preconceptions, all my self, and saw it as it truly was.

Big.

Round.

White.

It looked inconceivably… Grotesque? Unprecedented? Bizarre? Unbelievable? No, it had floated free of words. Oh, mighty stuff altogether. I could hear the scientists through the helmet's radio. Cheering. The pop of champagne corks.

The Most Fundamental Particle, so big, round, and white, was already beginning to split symmetrically in two. The new Universe was about to scratch the itch of itself.

I was just in time.

I congratulated myself on the purity of my vision, on my refusal to impose a meaning on it.

That was a mistake.

To congratulate myself, I had to notice myself. The pure impersonality of my vision was tainted: my self woke up, and had a look at what had previously been selflessly observed.

It looked just like a smooth, curved…

Exactly like her…

Yes.

And the cheeks beginning to part.

21

Something flickered at the edge of my vision. I turned, to see.

The doe's rippling, dotted flanks, designed to disguise her in a sun-dappled glade, stood out vividly against the white concrete walls. Her large belly swayed as she, running hard, came slowly, stride by stride, alongside my madly speeding bicycle.

I glanced down at my speedometer for a second. Dear God! Almost fifteen miles per hour!

In vacuum, at near absolute zero, she was beginning to die. But the life in her was so hot, and the vacuum so good at insulating her from heat loss, that she still ran, though her blood was beginning to boil in her lungs. Specks of bloodied froth leapt from her lips.

The liquid on the surface of her eyes had frosted over in the almost unimaginable cold, and so she ran without seeing. The vacuum was absolute, so she ran without hearing. And her nerve ends were beginning to freeze and die, so she ran without feeling, or tasting, or smelling. All communication between the universe and her was ceasing. Did she even know that she ran?

Yet she ran.

As she drew level with me, she stumbled. Tears filled her frost-blind eyes, and froze immediately. I reached across, and brushed the thick white lens of ice from the surface of each eye with my clumsy glove. As the two milky discs spun free, she recovered her footing, and turned her head. I Observed her.

And she Observed me.

Her perfect eyes, her long lashes… I felt the lurch of blood to my erectile tissues, and my legs grew weak and the pedals slowed. I looked away from those clear eyes, back up the tunnel.

I blinked, tried to concentrate. I must see everything Innocent and Pure, or I would fuck up the Universe.

Ahead of me, the pale cheeks parted, to reveal a Black Hole.

After an immense interior struggle that set the bicycle wobbling, I managed not to Interpret it. I merely observed an absence, an absence of... An absence of presence. There you go.

Nearly there.

I felt both positive and negative about all this.

The black hole began to shimmer. It quivered like heat-haze. Or jelly. Or a slapped bottom... I repressed. The. Thought.

And suddenly, generated perhaps by the massive energies between the cheeks, no, halves, a ray of golden light emerged from the black hole.

The ray, which should have been invisible in vacuum with no dust to scatter it, shattered itself on the atoms of breath and blood that had been gasped by the dying deer all around the ring.

Glowing like the sun, it shot over our heads in a beam of Mercy for the Living, and off down the tunnel, bent round the curve by the mighty magnets.

Relativistic effects, enforced by EU regulations, ensured that it appeared to me to be travelling at only fifteen miles per hour, but what it lacked in speed it made up for in beauty. Even my untutored eye could see that this new stuff was quite clearly a superior form of light.

I felt a squeak rise through the seat of my pants.

I felt another, transmitted through the frame of my bicycle, as I passed the next magnet. Squeak. And the next. Squeak... What was it? I ceased Observing and glanced down for an instant, risking the destruction of the universe, in order to examine my bicycle.

The screw that held on the front wheel was working its way loose. We passed the next magnet, and I felt two squeaks, in very rapid succession. Inside my helmet, I heard the clink and fizz of champagne being poured, and someone saying something in an urgent voice.

Two squeaks?

I looked behind me. The screw holding on the back wheel was emerging from its hole.

"*Oh dear*," said Dan inside my helmet. "*We hadn't thought of that…*"

As I passed the next magnet, the two screws worked entirely loose and shot off sideways like rifle bullets, to slam into the wall and stick to it head first and quivering.

The wheels of my bicycle fell off.

While still in mid-air, I began to run as fast as I could. The deer ran hard alongside me. My running feet hit the ground. I nearly toppled… rebalanced… kept running. The suit's tight joints were optimised for cycling, so my ankles almost immediately ached with strain. And running at fifteen miles per hour took a lot more energy than cycling. I began to breathe heavily.

I looked from the doe – a deer, a female deer – to the ray – a drop of golden sun.

Me – a name I call myself – had far – a long, long way – to run.

"So!" I said…

Having switched off my Consciousness, it was rather difficult to know what to do next. I made a note to follow "So!" with some kind of a thought, as soon as I could think.

It was quite nice, not carrying the burden of consciousness.

"La! La la la lalalaaaaa…" I sang as I ran.

Side by side we strode, towards the black hole, and the beam of gold.

I ran towards the darkness.

She ran towards the light.

The Black Hole itself began to glow, and evaporate.

Something more than light was emerging from it now. Something of great strangeness, and charm.

Here comes everything.

Almost upon it…

Dear God, it's too high in the tunnel! I'm going to pass under it!

Cool perspiration beaded my forehead, and I smelt the sudden chemistry of fear in my tight suit.

Could I jump? I experimented, as I ran. The ankle joints did not have enough bend in them for a full jump, and I hardly left the ground.

I got a thump in the shoulder that almost knocked me off balance. The doe was moving into the centre of the tunnel, lining herself up, tensing to leap.

I swung an arm around her neck, a leg over her back, and hauled myself aboard as she kicked free of the earth, and we rose and entered the light.

As I crossed the non-event horizon, I felt myself massaged gently by the changes in gravity as they moved along my body. The tension melted from my muscles. I slipped free of the doe, and did not fall. She and I hung suspended in a place beyond, or before, space and time.

No pain no fear no death.

No sharp edges.

I vowed to sit there quietly and Observe. And to be rational, logical, and objective as I did so.

No alarms and no surprises.

The doe kicked me in the face, shattering the dark glass visor of my helmet.

Feck, I thought, as the air gushed out of my shattered helmet, and the newborn universe was showered with broken glass.

A faint voice, almost overwhelmed by crackling, said in my ear through the thinning, outrushing air, *"Jude, do you read?"*

It seemed an odd question at such a moment.

"When I have the time," I gasped.

Double feck, I thought, as the remaining broken glass fell down inside my suit. No air. I felt a wrestling in my cells. They were from the old universe, in which life spent every second of its existence fighting its way up the ever-collapsing cliff of entropy. On the crust of a cooling speck of dust drifting in an infinite ocean of hostility to life. My cells had fought, and fought, and fought to maintain their complexity in an ever simpler universe, and now they were tired, and had no fuel, and they wished to die. But this new-born place, where death was impossible, wished to stop them dying.

As I reached to undo my shattered helmet, I felt a hot stab from a trapped shard pressed into my side by the gesture. Moving more cautiously, I took off the helmet, then carefully undid the zips and clamps and fasteners of the silver suit and climbed out, before I did myself a serious injury.

I was alive. I was very alive. I was alive in a place that would not let me die.

I looked at the doe. This safe, mild universe was going to have its work cut out saving her. Every cell of her body was busy either giving birth or dying. And they'd all had a good head-start on mine.

22

As the doe died, she gave birth.

And as she gave birth, she died.

I could not stand back and do nothing. I held her, so she would not feel alone. And she thrashed life and death into the pattern of the forming universe.

Death? Shite, they won't like that, I thought. And just look at the state of my suit: nicked by glass splinters, threads dangled from trouser, waistcoat and jacket. The doe swung a flailing leg and caught all three threads in the cleft of her hoof.

And as she thrashed and rolled in the mild void, she unravelled my jacket.

My trousers.

My waistcoat.

She, too, had been nicked by the shards of glass. Thrashing, rolling, she wrapped my threads about her, and staunched her wounds.

The three threads unwove, back and forth, back and forth, in the same patterns as they had been woven. And as the three threads were plucked free of their garments, they sang, each to each.

Vibrating in the warm, mild, amniotic soup of the unborn universe, each thread gave back the music that had made it. And their musics meshed to make new harmonies never heard before.

The dying animal played the recording of my suit.

The vibrations of the plucked threads, as they wrapped around her, transmitted their music deep into her flesh, and she was soothed. And as the vibrations passed off, out and away through the clear, unformed, universal substance, forming it, changing it, rippling order into it, I understood that music properly for the first time.

There had been no piano player. The world, the universe, had played the music of itself. The storm had played the keys. Wind, rain, hail and lightning.

Subtle, in among the notes of the music of the universe, were the rhythms of the ocean. The sea. The waves that had rocked me gently in the piano, I heard clearly now in all their detail. The galaxies, rotating, had tugged on the orbit of the sun, which spun the waltzing earth and moon, whose dance made waves, which broke against the styrofoam of my strange island with a vibration that gently adjusted the tensions and the pattern of the thread. Each part was merely the whole, in code.

Everything sang of every other thing.

It took an entire unfolded universe to make the storm. And the storm brought debris, ice, branches torn from trees, birds, hail; fish leapt from the deep to pound keys made of bone in rhythms never heard before, but…

Now I realised.

Always known.

There, during the making of my waistcoat, a rain of frogs, lifted from some Irish pond by a funnel of twisting air.

I could hear them all pour out of my disintegrating universal suit, a recording which could only be played once. And at the end I heard, in a last little run of notes, as the final feet of thin thread unwrapped and plucked free of me, Angela's footsteps along the keyboard, but retreating from me this time, back, away.

Gone.

Off, away into the ever-expanding void went the waves of sound and memory. A rainstorm in sunlight on the Irish Sea, the sun rising, and Angela singing to me.

In my arms, the doe gave birth, and died.

And I Observed, as the old universe was annihilated to make way for the new.

And I was annihilated.

And in that moment, I was father to a trillion sons – and a moment later grandfather to a trillion trillion suns – and with a rush of infinite intricacy, complexity, and absolute inevitability the familiar universe came into being, growing, spreading, filling out the primal void to the limit of the limit, through the billions of years of expanding time until we reached the moment of my annihilation, and I came back into being, observing my observation so that it could happen, *had* happened.

The new universe came into being, and replaced the old universe with an exact replica of itself.

"Well, that's a relief," I said as I both vanished and appeared. Built and abolished, neverpresent and eternal, I stood there and did not.

Was.

Wasn't.

Was, again.

In a universe the shape of Angela's...

The astonishing ray, its job done, faded and died with a final flicker of light that lit the wet, dappled sides of the newborn fawn, the dead deer shrouded in black wool, the broken glass, my blue suede shoes.

I stood in a universe that, now that I looked at it – doe, ray, me – was filled with unbearable yearning, sharp edges, and death.

Oh dear.

I feared I had perhaps Influenced, rather than merely Observed.

I stood weeping on the tunnel's concrete floor, beside the corpse of the doe. Tight to her belly, her fawn nuzzled a dead nipple through the thread that wrapped her mummy, and began to suck.

I sniffed the breeze. Breeze? And I realised the surprising thing lay one layer of logic back.

Air? Yes, it was thin but it was air.

I shivered in the grotesque and shocking cold of the super-cooled tunnel, naked but for my blue suede shoes and a pair of miraculous felt socks.

Well, it could be worse.

I had destroyed the universe, but I had, to be fair to me, also created the universe.

I sighed. It had been a long day. My teeth began to chatter and my muscles shivered. It would be a great shame to freeze to death now, after doing all the hard work.

I'd better get out of here. Fast.

There was an uncertain clatter behind me.

I looked over my shoulder, to see the tiny newborn fawn release the dead nipple, stand unsteadily, and totter after me on legs like drinking straws. Born ready to flee death.

I scooped her tiny life up to my chest.

I turned, and walked back along the ring, in the direction of the airlock, into a thickening breeze.

Warm, moist air blew towards me, down the super-cooled tunnel.

As the water vapour in the new air condensed in the shocking cold, puffs of cloud appeared.

I stopped for a moment, to examine the wreckage of my bicycle. Unusable.

The fawn gave a sleepy suck on my nipple, but found it unrewarding. She fell asleep in my arms.

I walked on.

A thick, white, soft frost now rose in long crystals from every surface, an inch long, two inches. The soft crackle of a trillion crystals forming was, when you added them all up, remarkably loud.

The temperature differential between tunnel and air was of an extreme not found in nature. The air rushing towards me, cooling rapidly at the walls, began to tumble, and rolled along the pipe in furious doughnut rings of cloud. They raged for a minute and died, as the ragged frost stole their moisture and heat.

I walked shivering and roasting through five-second snowstorms, through humid warm fronts a few yards wide, and I was spun around and knocked over once into a soft bed of frost by a hurricane no taller than myself.

And now the weather settled for a little longer, and I enjoyed a sixty-second summer. The fawn woke, complained woozily, gave a hopeful suck on my other nipple, and fell back asleep.

By the end of that long summer, I felt restored, and ready to face the rigours of a full minute of winter.

But the winters grew milder, as the thick ice coating the tunnel began to melt. Soon a chill lake formed on the floor of the tunnel, and I had to walk high up the cold curved sides.

I walked on, through the tiny weather of the flickering seasons. And after many a summer, I returned to the place I had come from.

At the airlock, all the doors were open.

25

The pressure had not yet equalised, and a river of air roared through the airlock. I leaned into the wind and pushed inside. My bag still hung on its hook, swinging wildly in the dark. I threw its strap over my bare shoulder with my free hand. I could feel the small heart of the tiny, orphaned fawn stutter against my chest, as she dreamt her first dream.

The open outer door was a circle of light.

I hesitated.

The Salmon spoke.

> "They know that a system is nothing more than the subordination of all aspects of the universe to any one such aspect."
>
> **Jorge Luis Borges, from "Tlön, Uqbar, Orbis Tertius"**

I nodded.

"I am afraid to go through the door," I said. Or I think I said. I could not hear myself in the wind.

The Salmon spoke.

> "Fairytales are closed systems, that is what makes them so terrifying."
>
> **Cees Nooteboom, a novelist of the Netherlands; from *In the Dutch Mountains***

I stepped through the door, and reentered the vast control room.

White sheets of paper swirled and circled above like gulls in the churning air.

26

The scientists were clustered round their instruments, talking loudly over the roar of air, and waving their arms.

The man in black punched his left fist into his right palm.

"Shankaracharya?" exclaimed Dan, studying a sheet of paper. "Wankaracharya, more like."

As I walked closer, Dan looked up and saw me. His white suit glowed. I looked closer, and closer again, at his face, which had always puzzled me. Now I saw it was not black, as I had supposed, but rather a dark blue.

"Dan," I said, "where exactly in England are you from?"

"Oh," he said, "the last surviving, authentic, English town. Cricket on the green, warm beer… more a village, really."

"Its name?" I pressed.

"You would not have heard of it. Ah…" He closed his eyes in reminiscence. "Tucked into the folds of the rolling hills near Calcutta…" He opened them again. "I cannot get used to this new name, Kolkata."

"The Dan is short for…?"

"Sorry…" His dark-blue face blushed. "Dhanvantari. I'm, ah, the Fifth Avatar of Vishnu… And, um, Doctor of the Gods. But everybody calls me Dan."

I nodded as though I understood.

"Well," said Dan, "will you join us for a celebratory drink? There's finger food, too."

I stared, cross-eyed with tiredness, at the two cups and two plates held out by his four arms.

I forced myself to focus, and their numbers halved.

Dan shrugged. "Our first attempt at proactive physics may not have turned out quite as we had hoped…"

"He has totally banjaxed the universe," muttered the man in black, studying another piece of paper. "It appears to have been Observed by both Animal and Man, both Logically and Sensually. Its truths exist on all kinds of different levels, none of them given a higher priority than the other. Everything is other, and yet all is one, in a most irritating way. It is not Scientific."

"Well anyway," said Dan, "you must be starving, have some Amrita – it's a rejuvenating nectar." He passed me a glittering cup of thick liquid. The fawn stirred in my other arm.

I sipped. My mouth burned and I gasped.

"And you must try these quite delicious medical herbs," said Dhanvantari.

I crunched a bunch of greenery. My mouth froze and I roared.

"And… ah! You must wash it all down with this." He handed me a cup containing a steaming brown liquid, and a plate bearing white rectangles covered with a thick, translucent red jelly in which seeds hung suspended.

"Wad id id?" I said through traumatised lips.

"Tea – a drink with jam and bread."

That brought me back to… D'oh!

I had forgotten Angela. My Quest. The meaning of my existence. I knocked back all the tiny sandwiches, washing down each one with a sip of scalding tea. I had to find her.

"Would you like a drop of milk?" said Dhanvantari. "I've an ocean of milk."

"No, thanks… The fawn, though…"

I handed Dan the trembling fawn, and he fed her an ocean of milk.

I threw my head back, and gazed up into the rafters. All I requested of the new universe was that my true love be unchanged from the old version.

There! What was that? I altered my position, and no longer knew my own state. Something moved, high above. A curve, in the darkness. Angela! I thought, and "Angela!" I cried. And the curve shifted, and moved into the light.

An enormous hairy arse. The creature turned.

"That is not Angela," I said.

His… It was smeared with her lipstick. I did not want to think about that.

"The blessed monkey won't come down," said Dan.

There was an awkward pause.

"Thanks," said Dan. "For saving the Universe. However imperfectly."

"No problem," I said. The tea was delicious. I felt rejuvenated. Well, I felt something. "Can I go now?" I took a final bite of jam and bread.

"You certainly can," said the man in black, studying some Data on sheets of paper. He looked up. His white face floated before me, glowing above the soft folds of the black skin of his jacket. "You have completely ruined the Universe." He shook the data in my face. The top page slipped free; he caught it as it fell. It gave him a nasty paper-cut. "Look!" he said, sucking on his wound. "A wasteland of death, and sharp edges."

"I'm sorry," I said.

He spat red blood on the white concrete floor. "But was it not, briefly, perfect, the new universe? The one we Designed? Before you screwed it up, and left it the same as it ever was? I yearn to know that Heaven."

I thought back to the warm nothing of the unformed and perfect universe, before the doe and I brought it death and life.

"Describe," he said, thrusting his face into mine, "in infinite detail" – I smelt on his breath the faint tang of warm iron – "every aspect of its lost perfection."

Other scientists gathered round us, murmuring.

I would do my best.

"Heaven," I said, "Is a place… where nothing… ever really happens."

The Man in Black closed his eyes, sighed, and removed his face from mine.

"Sorry," I said. "I did my best." My eyes prickled: saving the universe wasn't all it was cracked up to be. "Can't you just do it again," I said, "if you don't like it?"

The scientists shook their heads. "The Ring is broken."

"I am very tired," I said. "Can I not now rest?"

They shook their heads: no.

"But I have saved the universe," I said. "Can I not now rest?"

They shook their heads again. No.

"Have I not fulfilled my quest?" I said. "I am very tired. Can I not now rest?"

"That was not your quest," said Dhanvantari, placing his four arms on my exhausted shoulders. "That was our quest. Yours is still ahead of you."

I nodded. Yes, I had to be off. I could not sleep. I still had my quest.

"Goodbye, then," I said.

They did not shake their heads.

I opened the door to the outside. Snow covered the world.

"But... is this not the door into summer?" I said.

They shook their heads: no.

"Where is the fruit?" I murmured. "Ripe out of its season... Summer was held in this valley."

No more. The wall, the hedge... They were gone... What remained?

The oak trees.

The stream.

Standing in the doorway, leaning out into the cold breeze, I searched the snow for Angela's footprints. "There was a woman... Did you see her...?"

"The beast used the ladder. He found her in the rafters and..." They hesitated.

I bit my numb lip. "Go on," I said.

"They... and he... then she..."

I closed my hot eyes for a while.

"Afterwards," they said, "she left, before the snow. For London."

On my way out of the valley, I met the Lads from the Orphanage. They were commemorating a triumph – or disaster – in the traditional manner of our people.

Finian of Clonard broke off from admiring his reflection in a pool of his own vomit to address me.

I stood with my black bag slung over my naked shoulder, shivering in my miraculous socks and blue suede shoes. I must have looked less English without the bowler hat and pinstripe suit, for he addressed me now in the old tongue.

"Níl míniú ar an saol atá iniú ann", he said. "I Sasana go háirithe. Tamall ó shoin d'imigh muc ar seachrán uainn agus nuair d'fhill sé bhí culaith fhiúntach éadaigh uime. D'imigh tusa uainn lán-ghléasta, agus táir tagaithe arais anois, tú có lomnocht is bhí tú an chéad lá! Seachas na stocaí, agus na bróga gorma svaeid."

The words did not arrive in my mind as fluid music, but as shards of broken language. With pain and difficulty, I assembled them into a pot of message. *There's no understanding the world that's there today at all, and especially in England. A pig rambled off on us a little while ago and when he returned, he had a worthwhile suit of clothes on him. You went off from us fully dressed and you're back again as stark naked as the day you were born! Apart from the socks, and the blue suede shoes.*

It was true I had little to show for my adventure. First I had been replaced by a monkey; now I was outshone by a pig? I felt my shame fully. I reached for an answer, and found no words of my own. Rummaging in the shards of the broken old order, I eventually found a fragment which would answer my case. "D'fhéachas isteach in áit nár shaighneáil an ghrian ariamh," I said.

Finian recognised the quotation, though it was from a different island to our own. It was Tomás Ó Criomhthainn, as he stared in awed delight up the skirts of the girls, in a high wind on the Great Blasket. *I looked into a place where the sun never shone before.*

Finian of Clonard, the last saint and scholar of the lost Celtic universe, nodded his understanding and acceptance. "You lucky fecker," he said.

I was absolved. I moved on, a little lighter in spirit; not much.

Crossing a clearing, I noticed dark marks in the fresh snow. They seemed almost meaningful. I stopped, and bent to examine them. Fuzzy round the edges, half-buried in the snow, each no bigger than the top joint of my thumb.

A scatter of dead bees in the glade.

One stirred, and rolled over.

My heart leapt. Oh, to hear their music now!

From a small hole in its belly emerged the head of the larva of a parasitic wasp.

It Observed me, the snow, the universe; and it went back inside.

The bee moved no more.

I stood, and returned to my course.

The snow fell heavier, and night would soon fall. Oh, for some help with the ordeals which lay ahead.

The ordeals which lay behind.

The Salmon of Knowledge spoke.

"The greatest sorcerer (writes Novalis memorably) would be the one who bewitched himself to the point of taking his own phantasmagorias for autonomous apparitions. Would not this be true of us?"

Jorge Luis Borges, "Avatars of the Tortoise"

"Perhaps," I said. "Perhaps."

My feet crunched the crystal snow. In the distance, I could hear a roar that was not the sea.

The Salmon of Knowledge spoke again.

> "I believe that it is. We (the undivided divinity that operates within us) have dreamed the world. We have dreamed it strong, mysterious, visible, ubiquitous in space and secure in time, but we have allowed tenuous, eternal interstices of injustice in its structure so we may know it is false."
>
> **Jorge Luis Borges, "Avatars of the Tortoise"**

"No doubt you mean to console me in my desolation," I said. "However, your wisdom is leaving me even less happy than before. I have fucked up the universe, shattering the fond dreams of many who had laboured long to improve it; and I have lost the trail of my True Love, who in my absence has been Ravaged by a Monkey. It would take some fecking wisdom to console me under such circumstances."

There was a pause. At length, the Salmon of Knowledge spoke once more.

> "When at last I had disabused my mind of the enormous imposture of a design, an object, and an end, a purpose or a system, I began to see dimly how much more grandeur, beauty and hope there is in a divine chaos – not chaos in the sense of disorder or confusion but simply the absence of regular order – than there is in a universe made by pattern. This

draught-board universe my mind had laid out: this machine-made world and piece of mechanism; what a petty, despicable, micro-cosmos I had substituted for reality."

Richard Jefferies, English thinker and writer, "Absence of Design in Nature – The Prodigality of Nature and the Niggardliness of Man," from *The Old House at Coate: And Other Hitherto Unpublished Essays*, 1948

"You console me," I said. "Yes, you console me now."

The Salmon said nothing.

I wept for the orphaned fawn. I wept for the lost dream of order. I hoped that my chaos would prove divine.

I walked on, into the thickening snowfall, through the deepening snow.

No two flakes alike.

The Snowy Walk

The purpose of a rabbit snare is to catch rabbits. When the rabbits are caught, the snare is forgotten. The purpose of words is to convey ideas. When the ideas are grasped, the words are forgotten. Where can I find a man who has forgotten words? He is the one I would like to talk to.
~ Chuang Tzu (Fourth century BC)

Repetition is a form of change.
~ Brian Eno & Peter Schmidt,
  Oblique Strategies (1975)

28

I approached the roar that was not the sea.

At length I came to a tremendous road, running south-east. I clambered down the embankment, and began to walk toward London along the rough stony path at the road's edge.

As I walked, the snow grew heavier. The flakes falling through the crisp, cold air were firm, and settled on my shoulders and hair without melting. The slush thrown up by the passing trucks, however, threatened to soak and chill my naked flesh. A Tipperary childhood, though it makes you hardy, does not make you infinitely hardy. I stopped, and harvested some of the many plastic bags that gaily adorned the bushes of the embankment. From these fine, waterproof bags I fashioned a crude suit. To allow me to perspire, I incorporated flap-covered slits, made with my little knife. Next to my heart, I made a special pocket for the stub of Angela's lipstick, and the scrap of paper the tube contained. The corner of the letter I received on my 18th birthday. My only clue to the Secret of my Origins.

An eternal river flowed forward forever at my right hand as I walked on; vehicles of all sizes, all colours; some tiny, low, and fast, some huge, swaying, slow and sloshing; some with lights flashing; and occasionally my favourites: immense vehicles carrying many other smaller vehicles on their backs.

At the far side of that river was a thin, never-ending island of grass and bushes.

Beyond that island flowed forever a second mighty river of vehicles, in the opposite direction.

That first day's walking, the vein and the artery of the nation's body pulsed in a long, slow rhythm beside me, the great pulse into the city after dawn, the great pulse out of the city as night fell. And at night, the red river of light flowing into the city, the white forever leaving.

Above it all, the high orange lights illuminating the vast road, the vehicles, the swirling orange snow.

In the full of the night, the snow grew heavier and began to drift deeply at the foot of the high embankment to my left, pushing me out into the slowest lane of traffic.

I was encouraged to keep going for another hour by the friendly horns of the truck drivers, who willed me on with long blasts, but at length I grew too tired to continue.

I harvested another crop of plastic bags from the embankment bushes, and added more layers to my costume until I was as snug and warm as any man in England. Wading uphill, through the deep snow of a deeply drifted drainage gully cut into the embankment, I found the deepest spot and dug a simple snow-hole.

The dense snow above and around me muffled the river's roar. I looked up, along the snow tunnel, at a little patch of sky. I settled my plastic-clad hip into a dip in my snow-bed. Wisps of steam drifted through the slits and from under the flaps of my suit as my perspiration escaped me, into the cold air.

At the tunnel mouth, as the orange clouds cleared, a single star appeared. The star stood steady in the sky as the last snowflakes danced about it, then died away. At last it stood, alone.

Imperceptibly, as the world turned, the small star, too, drifted away from me.

Love… love is a puzzler.

The soft, distant swoosh of trucks through slush lulled me at last to sleep.

The next day, I was awoken by the low morning sun shining on my shelter. A light drift of fresh snow had closed the entrance to my snow hole with a thin crust, so that I opened my eyes in a space as weightless, translucent and featureless as the centre of a pearl.

I stretched and yawned. Perspiration had saturated me in the night but, trapped against me by the plastic bags, it had warmed agreeably. Comfortable and snug, I stank pleasantly of myself.

I stood, and broke out through the powdery crust. The sunlight, bouncing off the surrounding snow, dazzled me. Squinting, I walked hip-deep down the gully, with a great crackling of plastic and crunching of fresh snow, toward the roaring rivers of cars. I melted handfuls of the fresh powder in my mouth and drank the clear, pure water. Then I searched through the debris under the snow at the mouth of the gully until I found a large plastic cider bottle, of the traditional amber hue.

I cut a broad, curved strip from the bottle with my small knife, then made a notch in the middle for my nose, then two more notches at either end for my ears. After a couple of fine adjustments, I had serviceable protection from the glare of the snow. The curved plastic clung snugly to the sides of my head, and left little weight resting on my nose. This was good, for my nose had shrunk in the cold until it was so diminutive it would have had difficulty supporting my eye-protector unaided. After urinating through a flap in my plastic suit, I rubbed my nose vigorously to make it bigger, and continued my journey.

It was long, hard walking of a kind I hadn't had to do since my teenage days in Tipperary. It brought back pleasant memories of rounding up sheep on the low hills around the Orphanage, and of herding the sheep along the road into Town, to the Market or the Abattoir. Indeed, my happy memories extended back to a time when the grandparents of those sheep were lambs, and I was but a boy.

When I was a young Orphan of nine or ten summers, nothing pleased me and the other young Orphans more than to chase and tackle lambs, rolling them over in the long wet grass as they kicked and bucked and bleated, before letting them go, so as to chase them again, till all were exhausted and the Orphans lay down with the Lambs. After that we would usually bite off the testicles of the males, for which we were paid five pence per gonad by the farmer – and there was an ice cream from Father Madrigal for the lad with the greatest haul of Balls at the end of the day. Later, we would play hurling with them until finally it grew dark, and we lost the last testicle in the long grass. Oh, surely there is no childhood as happy as the Tipperary childhood!

Those particular lambs, of course, would not have been the grandparents of the sheep we herded later.

These and other memories filled my heart, and I sang as I walked.

Occasionally, colossal signs warned of tributary streams of vehicles soon to join the great river. Such tributaries were often the very devil to cross, and I decided at length to make my way over to the more pleasant and continuous woodland path that ran between the twin rivers of cars. I set off across the river.

In Tipperary, all who knew you would beep their horn and wave as they passed you on the little roads. In England, I was delighted to discover that even total strangers did the same, one after the other – hundreds of them. Indeed, the friendliness of the drivers was almost embarrassing. I tried to wave back individually at everyone who waved at me, which slowed my progress across the torrent of machines considerably.

One or two drivers were so distracted, waving at me with one hand and beating out a merry tune on their horn with the other, that their vehicles mounted the grassy central path, jumped the low strip of metal that ran like a spine along the middle of it, and passed into the oncoming river of traffic. These cars were then borne away whence they had come, backwards, and so quickly that I had no time to return their waves.

Despite these diversions, I finally made the central path. The snow-carpeted grass was pleasant beneath my feet, and I began to make good time toward London. The occasional tarmacèd breaks in the grassy track were easily crossed, for they seemed rarely used. I tried to ignore my growing hunger, and walked on.

31

Towards dusk, I began to gather up some of the freshly slaughtered rabbits which lay, mixed in among the corpses of crows, rats, foxes, hedgehogs, badgers and cats, all along the river's edge. Most of the freshly killed rabbits had been immediately crushed, recrushed and eventually flattened by subsequent vehicles. However, some had been thrown clear onto the grass by glancing impacts. The best, with their guts unburst and their flesh unbruised, were those rabbits who had merely broken their rear legs, and dragged themselves off the road into the grass to die.

I had so forgotten the lessons of my youth that I lifted my first rabbit by the ears. How the other Orphans would have laughed, could they have seen me! Gravity, of course, caused it to piss copiously down my leg from its death-loosened sphincter. Thankful for my plastic suit, I quickly reversed the rabbit.

Bending one rear leg back at the joint, to raise the tendon out from the bone, I made a slit behind the raised tendon with my little knife. Tucking the paw of the other leg in behind the tendon, to make a loop of the legs, I was able to carry the rabbit easily on my bent little finger, in the usual manner. I did not wish to place the rabbits in my black bag, due to the fleas, and blood, and excrement. Besides, the narrow strap of my bag, even with the little I was carrying, tended to cut a groove in my shoulder and numb the arms after a while.

Soon I had four good-sized rabbits dangling from my fingers. Night was falling, and the temperature with it. Where should I set up camp? The central path was delightful, but exposed. I needed dry wood for a fire, and trees for shelter…

I had noticed, when passing the mouths of the tributaries, that they seemed to harbour within them huge circular islands, around which cars swirled clockwise. The largest islands were often wooded. I decided to set up camp at the next one I saw.

Fording the broad river and making my way up the tributary to the island was peculiarly difficult. The planners of the Approach to London, though they had done a lovely job with the path, seemed neither to have laid pedestrian crossings, nor to have installed bridges to the islands.

Several of the drivers seemed under-prepared for the sight of a pedestrian walking out in front of them. But a couple of friendly waves were all it took to sort out these little misunderstandings.

In the heart of the small grove at the centre of the island, I found dry sticks, an old metal hubcap embossed with the letters VW, and several types of edible fungus. Selecting two rabbits with intact skins and good thick fur, I gutted them, skinned them, and laid the skins aside.

I started a fire with flints and dry moss and the steel of my knife. Then I trimmed a narrow strip from one of the skins, and threw it into the hot hubcap. When I'd rendered a little fat from it, and the metal was oiled and sizzling, I cut the best meat from the legs and backs of the two rabbits, and tossed it in, along with the mushrooms.

As my meal cooked, and darkness fell, I carefully built a shelter of branches,

Great open lorries circled the island, mechanically scattering rock salt into the river of slush, to stop it freezing again in the long night. I watched from the central grove, as I ate my rabbits.

When I'd finished eating, I made wet clay from earth and snow. I gutted the last two rabbits, and stuffed each with a different variety of wild mushroom. Carefully I covered them in thick casings of mud, buried them in the hot ashes to one side of the fire, and packed earth on top of them. That was breakfast sorted.

Now to do the washing up. I licked the fat off the hubcap, then made my way to the edge of the island and searched the shore for rock salt. The drowsy waves of the tributary's late-night traffic swept past me, around the curve of the island, down into the great river, and away to London. Carefully, I collected my salt, and filled my pockets with the discarded plastic cutlery that was abundant on the island's foreshore.

I returned to my little spark of heat, clutching a double handful of whiteness: the hard white cubic crystals of the rock salt mingled with feathery, brittle crystals of snow. I poured the soft fistfuls onto warm, flat stones at the fire's edge. Soon the snowflakes collapsed and melted away into a dark puddle on the flat rock, then drifted off as steam, leaving small piles of dry salt.

I unfolded, one across each knee, the skins of the two rabbits I'd eaten earlier. With the plastic cutlery (for my own little knife was too sharp) I scraped them clean of the last fat, which blazed and spat in the fire, giving good light. I thoroughly massaged the dried salt into the skins, to dry and tan them. As the fire died, I wove a frame from hazel wands, and pegged out the skins to stretch and cure.

Before I slept, I took the lipstick from the pocket by my heart and removed the top. I slipped free the brittle yellow triangle of paper – all I had saved from the burning Orphanage. I read it again by the glow of the dying fire in the heart of the glade: the mysterious clue to my origins: Gents… Anal… Cruise…

As I read, I wafted the open lipstick beneath my nose, its feminine perfume dizzying me so that the letters blurred before my eyes. As I inhaled, a female figure shimmered at the edge of vision, at the far side of the fire. Beyond the warm, trembling air, the dark became a woman.

Carefully, I put it all away.

At length I fell asleep, the lipstick moving with my heart.

In the morning, I used the hubcap to dig up my two baked rabbits. I cracked open the dried mud. It came away with the fur and skin. I feasted. They were moist and delicious. The flavour of the mushrooms had penetrated the flesh.

I set off. The skins and frame were easily carried on my back, and I made my way down to the landscaped path. As I walked, the skins cured in the sun and wind. Once they were dry and supple, I would take them from the frame. A few more days. Then I would sew them, with bone needles, and with sinew and tendon as my strong thread.

Within a few days, I had a jacket of rabbit fur, lined with rabbit fur.

By the end of a week, I had a whole suit. For variety, I added hard-wearing badger trim at hem and cuff. My amber goggles I decided to line, for comfort, at the nose-notch and ear-notches with white rabbit fur. First, using a wire heated in the fire, I melted sewing holes in the plastic. The wire slid through with a hiss, leaving a raised rim of molten plastic around each hole to cool and set into a reinforcing eyelet. Then I sewed on the shaped strips of skin using the bone needle and the delicate but strong front-leg tendons. The warmth of the soft fur, and its gentle caress, caused my nose to maintain a decent size on even the coldest morning. The goggles sat better, and I was pleased.

Occasionally I was reminded by a warmth in my belly of the hidden presence of the Ring Babette had given me, on the long-ago day I had left Galway City. Deep in my navel, at my precise centre of gravity, it seemed to gain energy from my walk.

Once, I woke in the night and saw a white light shining from within my navel, illuminating the branches above me into bright leaves and hard shadows. As I blinked, and tried to focus, the light faded to a dim pale green and dimmed again to a deep blue, and went out.

Steadily, I progressed towards London.

For three full days, I forgot the spark of individual humanity contained in each vehicle, and saw only one eternal river of life; a fluid, continuous flow of animate metal.

But late on the third day, a gust of warm air wafted up from the depths of my plastic bags, bearing the smell of bread perhaps from some warmed crumbs in the depths of an old bag, and I cried, "Mother!" An odd choice of word.

With a shock like a thump to the heart, One became Many, and what drove past were cars and trucks and vans made in Birmingham and Stuttgart and Japan. I felt tired.

I decided I would make camp early that night.

I made my way to an island, the largest yet, and the fairest. The curve of its shore was so gentle that it scarcely curved at all, and at its centre was a vast dark wildwood. Around it a snowy field ran in a great white circle.

The grass beneath the snow felt lush and thick beneath my feet, and the soil well drained. There was no human sign upon the land. No eight-ox team had ever broken this carucate of ploughland. This fair island had no antecessor. No loanland, this, nor held by any man in bookland tenure. My heart exulted. Neither inland nor warland, I would grant myself my own fief.

"I claim you," I said aloud to the island. "You are mine."

And so I walked my fief, a free man in England. Commended to no lord. A truly free man, neither king's thegn nor median thegn nor ceorl, I had absolute soke of my manor.

I had never been seised of land before: it was a voluptuous sensation.

On the northern edge of my demesne the ground softened, and I discovered a broad turbary which would yield, in a dry summer, eighty summa of turves.

When I had fully circled my island, I entered the wildwood.

In its heart I found a pleasant assart. Here, I would build my caput, hold my court: here would be my castle, in the heart of my honour.

The trees were chiefly ash, birch, beech and oak. In autumn they would provide acorns and beechnuts in abundance: fine pannage for pigs.

I set a fire, and began to tan a dicker of skins. Here I could be assessed for neither hearth tax, nor fumagium… I left the wood and walked to the foreshore, where they were spreading salt by the mitta, by the summa: such a wealth of salt, thrown to the road. I took the mere amber of salt I needed and returned to my fire.

I lay down to sleep, the small white pyramid of the hoccus a dancing yellow triangle in the fire's soft light before me. It continued to dance in the privacy of my mind for a minute after I closed my eyes, the triangle dancing, inverting, superimposing itself on its fellow to form a dancing yellow star.

As I relaxed, the yellow star flaked apart again into dancing triangles, which grew pink in the fire's flickering light, filtered through my eyelids' blood.

And so the pink triangles and yellow stars danced until I fell asleep, a free man in England, smelling a smoke no man could tax.

In the morning, the tiny hoccus was dry. At a touch it dropped, with a smooth flow, into a flatter, wider pile.

I stood, and walked out of the wildwood, and looked about my laund: defended by an eternal river, there could be no purpresture upon my demesne.

Alone in the cold morning air, a free man in England. I savoured my freedom. The snow began to fall upon my island.

"All this is mine," I said.

My words emerged in a warm breath that condensed into a white cloud above the white island. And my words moved off across the land, towards the dark wood.

Who heard them?

Only the creatures of the wildwood.

The little cloud of words, coded in my cooling breath, approached the trees.

When I died, my body, too, would return to the wildwood that I now claimed to own.

I watched my words cool further, from liquid to crystal, and fall as snow across the land they claimed.

No, I would not hold this land.

I would not be held.

I packed my camp and left the fair island.

I rejoined the great river of life. Made my way to the central path. Ahead lay my true love, my parentage, and destiny. The island disappeared behind.

Occasional buildings now appeared, off to either side.

I walked the snowy path. A free man in England.

The snow thickened in the sky and deepened on the ground, as I walked on toward London. No wind blew now, and the flakes fell straight down. Occasional buildings had become rows of buildings, far to either side. Soon I could see only their vaguest silhouette. Then the silhouettes themselves faded and were gone. The cars slowed now, thinned in number. Their vague bulks murmured by me at a fast trot, then a slow trot, then walking pace, so that they laboured to overtake me.

Now minutes went by without a car or lorry at all. When there was one, it was barely moving forward along the empty road, through snowfall so thick they must hardly see a yard, or the car had pulled in and stopped, and I was overtaking it, so that the natural order seemed thrown into reverse.

Then came a curious thing. The endless path ended. I stepped off the hidden grass and down, through the deepening snow, onto the hidden tarmac and strode straight on, toward the continuation of the interrupted path… or perhaps an island… and on I strode… and on… and there was nothing. I continued, guided by wheeltracks in the snow to the left and right of me, their edges softening and ruts filling under the relentless snow. Once, I thought I heard swans flying low and slow above me. But it must have been the slow, low beat of some other thing, inside me or outside, for I looked up into the falling whiteness and could see no whiteness move with purpose across the general pattern.

The twin rivers had ceased now entirely to flow. I waded on.

With no rabbits moving and no cars to kill them and no grass on which to track them and no burrows in which to find them, I decided not to eat.

With no islands on which to stop, and no materials to burn, and no trees for shelter, I decided not to sleep.

The snow being so heavy, the light so dim, I took off my goggles and put them in the inside pocket of my rabbit-skin jacket, beside Angela's lipstick. Against my heart.

I strode on. I ignored the occasional faint tracks, at right angles to my path, with their hints of other roads, other goals. I was intent on London, and my love. I did not stop: day died, night fell with the white flakes. The orange light of street lamps flickered and caught, and the flakes changed colour in mid-air.

Dawn came, pale, pink: the orange light died.

The flakes were white.

The cycle repeated.

The endlessness of the fallingness of the flakes in my vision led me at length to the curious illusion that I was rotating, backwards, endlessly, feet over head, and that the flakes were fixed points in the still air. The illusion was pleasant, and I indulged it. Hours passed. Days?

I grew sensitive to the weight of the invisible buildings, bulking to the left and right of me. I navigated by their mass. Perhaps I detected them by their soft effect on the infinite flake-fall.

And now the delicate crunch of the snow beneath my feet echoed softly from either side, as the buildings grew closer together and the road narrowed.

The sensation of a gateway. The tingle in my fillings as I passed under an invisible iron arch. The sensation of the path ending, buildings vanishing, a taste of distant trees, the smell of the memory of last summer's leaves. All was pleasant to my lulled and mesmerised senses.

I rotated endlessly backwards along the surface of an earth rotating around its axis as we both circled a sun, rotating as it circled a swirling galaxy whose intricate mechanism performed a collaborative parabola influenced by and influencing all the rotating, circling atoms scattered through a universe disguised as matter but, in silence under all, a single mighty mote of energy in flux and motion changing form and place through space and time.

Dizzy, I fell over.

As I slept, I dreamt that Angela's hand reached out to me, and I was happy: but her hand kept going, through my skin, into me: I was sad: her cool hand closed around my heart, and pulled it out.

Love's a puzzler.

I woke up.

Goats and Monkeys

That would be a glorious life, to addict oneself to perfection; to follow the curve of the sentence wherever it might lead, into deserts, under drifts of sand, regardless of lures, of seductions; to be poor always and unkempt; to be ridiculous in Piccadilly.
~ Virginia Woolf, *The Waves* (1931)

Sometimes while I'm writing I feel I'm the designer of a video game, and at the same time, a player. I made up the program, and now I'm in the middle of it; the left hand doesn't know what the right hand is doing. It's a kind of detachment. A feeling of a split.
~ Haruki Murakami, interview, *The Paris Review* (2004)

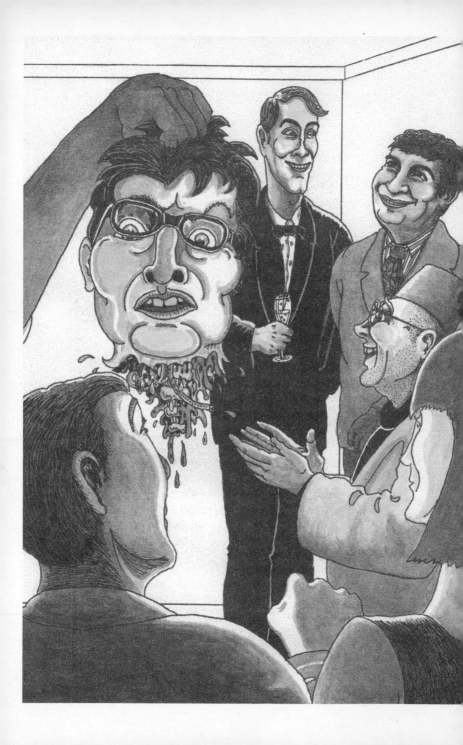

37

The lightest of snow had covered me, like a down duvet. My warm breath had kept open a breathing passage. I stood, stiffly, pushing up into the milky light, and broke the crust of snow, small sounds in the great silence. Swaying, I looked straight up: the snow had stopped: the sky was a deep, dark blue.

Back down, toward the horizon, it became a paler blue.

I looked around me.

I was standing on a bare, snow-drifted hillside. All was dazzling, and bleached of detail by the morning sun. About me were tall groves of venerable trees. This sylvan scene filled me with distress. I closed my eyes on it.

How had I missed London? I felt certain I had held to the true path and never once deviated.

Could I have walked through it unknowing, and out the other side? For how long had I walked?

There was another, more immediate enigma: something had woken me. I opened my eyes.

I stood in my suit of rabbitskin on the white hillside. With my hand, I shaded my eyes from the winter sun.

I looked all around me again, in a good, long, slow, full circle, to see not a sign of humanity.

This time the dazzle cleaned my eyes of sight and I stood snowblind.

I put on my goggles before reopening my eyes.

The amber plastic turned the snowy hills to dunes of amber sand.

The only trace of life upon the snow was of my own footprints, leading up the hill to where I stood.

I studied the crisp footprints with melancholy interest. How had they not been filled in by the night's snow, which had buried me so deep? And then I noticed, parallel to the deep, crisp footprints I had taken for my own, the faintest dimpled traces of my large footprints, and my heart rotated. I had had a visitor.

I looked back at the crisp prints. Small. Barefoot. And continuing past me up the hill.

I put my hand to my racing heart. It beat strong and clear, through skin, plastic and fur, to the flat of my hand. A moment of comfort: then, horror.

The lipstick was gone.

38

I dug, searching the snow where I had slept. Nothing. And the trail of footprints leading silently to me, and away. Dear God, had I been robbed in my sleep of all that I loved?

As I followed the footprints, up along the curve of the amber dune, I tried to get my voice back to work, after its long holiday.

"Pleased…" Too loud.

"I am…" Now too soft.

"My Name…" It cracked.

"You are…"

And it cut out altogether. I licked my mumbling lips with my clumsy tongue. My bowels felt loose. I stopped to make stool in the snow, buried it hurriedly and moved on.

The small, barefoot traveller had left an erratic, almost eccentric trail. Lost? Snow-blind? In some other kind of distress? And was it a child? Or the slight yet hardy native of a colder clime? Though small, it was not a feminine foot.

I waded uphill through the snow, and shivered to think how deep the drifts must be elsewhere in the sheltered places, against walls and houses, and in the soft folds of the woods.

The tiny footprints danced around in a circle, and off again.

My anxiety mounted the hill ahead of me. My nerves seemed extended from the skin. My eyes darted from blankness to blankness, across the featureless snowfield, in the useless hope of finding the lipstick discarded. Perhaps it had been opened and spurned as worthless, hurled far into deep snow?

As I crested the hilltop, a sinister figure came into view. The stranger, his back to me, gave a throaty laugh. The backs of his hands were as hairy as the back of his head, and he wore a blue woollen polo-neck jumper and denim dungarees. A shock of white hair emerged from under a black woollen hat. He resembled a small, elderly Frenchman.

I stepped as silently as possible to within a few yards of him. In his right hand he held Angela's lipstick, and with an almost drunken glee and much chortling he brought it, capped, to his nose: inhaled deeply: and then appeared to draw the sculpted plastic top across his lips, in ecstatic imitation of a woman. He howled with laughter.

I knew him!

I pounced: the Monkey, taken by surprise, gasped quite like a human and, inhaling the lipstick, began to choke upon my memento of Angela: my clue to my origins, worn always against my heart.

The choking monkey swooned backward into the deep snow.

I looked at my rival for Angela's affections. He had shrunk a little, and his hair had whitened considerably, but it was him. He had beaten me to London. Had he beaten me to Angela, again? Compassion and rage did battle as I pondered whether or not to save his life.

I fell upon him. Flipping him onto his front, I put my arms about him, beneath the ribs, and lifted him. He was lucky I knew what to do, for the Orphanage hurlers had all been taught Dr. Heimlich's Manoeuvre, after losing most of our midfield to a series of unfortunate incidents outside fish and chip shops, in the aftermath of Harty Cup victories.

Settling his buttocks into my groin, I pulled my doubled, joined fists up and into his diaphragm, to compress his lungs and blast the lipstick free.

I repeated this action several times, vigorously, with no result other than a loud whistling noise. The lipstick appeared to be caught sideways in the monkey's throat. With breath able to flow around it, the pressure of air could not build to blast it free. Abandoning my first plan, I bent the gasping monkey over my knee and slapped him hard with the flat of my hand on his buttocks, hoping that his involuntary cry of protest might cause such a spasm of the throat as to dislodge the tube, and that gravity would then assist it to the snowy ground.

The lipstick shifted, and became lodged at a less advantageous angle.

The monkey began choking in earnest.

I became aware of a distant noise to my rear, growing closer, but my mission was now urgent. I slapped again, with no useful result. Hooves thundered to a halt behind me, as the tips of the monkey's ears turned blue. I was being too gentle: I steeled myself to slap harder.

Then, a voice.

"Please, cease spanking my monkey. It is, I believe, illegal on the Heath."

The voice was too late to slow my hand and I dealt the poor creature a blow of some ferocity.

The wind whistled out of his lungs as he howled: the lipstick came free, propelled by air and outrage to land at the feet of a young man as he dismounted a fine snorting chestnut mare of some eighteen hands. A second, unsaddled horse, a prancing, nervous black gelding with a small white blaze on the forehead, was loosely tied by long leading reins to the pommel of the mare's saddle.

The projectile, and the sobbing breaths of the monkey, clarified the situation better than any verbal explanation.

"Egad, sir, I must apologise. You have saved my Monkey," said the young man, leaning down to pick up my lipstick. He put out his other hand. "Alex Fromblur. Minor popstar, aesthete and dandy, at your service."

"Jude, from Ireland," I said. The first word too soft. The second, in compensation, too loud. But I was grand by the time I got to Ireland. I held out my hand.

We shook.

Alex's horse shifted nervously, alarmed by the monkey's strong smell, or perhaps mine.

"Your face looks funny… Of course, I am on Mescaline, so everything looks funny, but your face looks particularly funny. Your darling dimple is darling, darling," said Alex Fromblur. He handed the lipstick back to me.

"Where did you get this monkey?" I said.

"No idea. Woke up with him one morning."

"No recollection at all?" I prompted. "Was he, perhaps, with a woman?"

Alex Fromblur shook his head, and winced. "Don't think so. Of course, I was *extraordinarily* drunk that week."

So: no clue to her whereabouts. I sighed. Still, though… if Angela had forsaken the monkey…

… it might mean she still loved me.

"Where am I?" I asked.

"Hard night, eh," said Alex Fromblur. He slapped me on the back. "We're on Parliament Hill. Hampstead Heath." He took my elbow, guided me a few yards uphill, and turned me ninety degrees.

Floating above the trees of the Hill, emerging from a sea of snow, close and sharp enough to touch, yet far away and far below, A City. It stretched out endless to the far, faint horizon. A city the size of County Tipperary, a city that filled the visible world, a city to swallow a man. A city to swallow a girl.

A city a lifetime could not fully explore.

Oh, London.

"Excuse me. I am temporarily overwhelmed by information," I said, and sat down in the snow. The monkey gently stroked my hand.

Somewhere in that city was my first, my final love.

"I can offer you a lift into town," said Alex. "I'm exercising a racehorse for a pal, but he doesn't mind chaps riding it. Good for it in fact. Can you ride bareback?"

"Of course," I said. It was customary on a Saturday night for the older Orphans to joyride Riggs-Miller's horses, to impress the Convent Girls.

Using the mane of the black gelding for leverage, I vaulted astride him from a standing position.

Alex put his right foot in the right stirrup and swung aboard the chestnut. He unlooped the black gelding's leading reins from the pommel of his saddle, and threw them to me. I shortened the reins, and dug my knees in firmly.

We began to trot the horses through the heavy snow. A moment later we were set upon by two tall men, who emerged from the shadow of a broad oak in our path and advanced on us crying "Mah'k W'llan Jer! Mah'k W'llan Jer!" The deep black of their face and hands made a striking contrast with the white of the snow. One waved a long black spear on the tip of which was impaled a limbless, woolly creature. The other raised a heavy metal object to his shoulder and pointed it at my head.

I heard a click resound across the still snowfield.

39

"Egad! Brigands!" cried Alex Fromblur, his horse rearing.

The lead brigand kept his Engine pointing at my head.

The second brigand, running close behind, swung his stick lower, toward me. As it came close to my face, I studied the woolly Thing atop it with concern.

"Oh," said Alex. "It is a Boom Mike."

I looked around me. "What is a Boom?" I said. Should I correct his erroneous impression – no doubt attributable to the Mescaline – that my name was Mike? Looking back to the first Brigand, I found myself staring down the barrel of his shoulder-mounted Device. The barrel was stoppered by a clear glass lens, through which I could see, opening and closing restlessly, a kind of mechanical sphincter.

"Why, I do not believe they are Brigands at all," said Alex.

"Then why," I said, careful not to make any sudden movements, "is he pointing that Weapon at my head?"

"It's a Camera," said Alex.

The man with the Camera swung to point it at Alex, then me, then Alex.

"You are not Mark Wallinger," he said to Alex, and frowned.

"No, I am not," said Alex. "I am merely exercising his horse. My God!" said Alex. He opened his palm to the two men, in that gesture of understanding and surprised recognition which I believe may not have its own name, though it is common. "I know you chaps. You're Mark Wallinger's Ethiopian Documentary Crew! You were shortlisted for the Turner Prize last year!"

The taller winced. "We had that misfortune, yes."

"Man, I thought you guys were great. You were robbed, robbed. I guess they just didn't want to give it to him twice."

"Yes, life would have been very different had we won." The tall man's eyes grew dreamy. "No doubt we would have been bought by Tate Modern… perhaps put on permanent exhibition… or at least had the shelter of a storeroom with constant temperature and humidity. At least that."

Alex put his hand on the man's shoulder. "Mark's at the Groucho. We're heading there now. Do you and your Sound Man ride?"

"Not really. Only mules," said the man. "In our youths."

"Well, the snow's soft if you fall off," said Alex. "Hop up."

The man spoke to the other in a tongue unknown to me. They put away their equipment in black nylon bags, then mounted – the Camera Man behind me and the other behind Alex. The monkey, chattering, climbed onto Alex's shoulders.

We passed the leafless oak under which the two had sheltered. A large black bird glided down from its branches to alight, fluttering, on the Sound Man's shoulder. The bird made the sound of bacon frying.

"That is a nice bird you have," I said across to the Sound Man.

"Pah!" he said. "She has been utterly corrupted by the West."

"How so?" I said.

He sighed. "When I bought her in the bird-market of Mogadishu, she spoke perfect classical Arabic, and recited verses of the Koran in the innocent voice of a child. Now, she recites A Vindication of the Rights of Women in a Hounslow accent." He fell silent.

"Zach is not a fan of Modernity," said my Horsemate.

Zach said, "Had the world not grown Modern, we would not have known what we missed. We would have accepted, unquestioning, the iron frame of poverty to which we were strapped. But the Modern World broadcasts its existence on all frequencies, into every dark jungle, every arid valley. And so we came to know that life could be better than subsisting, half-starving, labouring till dark every day, and then dying. And so we came to suffer, suffer, suffer, from the worst of the afflictions unleashed by Pandora when she opened her Box: the bitterest curse, kept till last: Hope. Hope. Hope. A life lived in contented ignorance is, abstractly, sad. A life lived in hope forever unfulfilled, is tragic."

He fell silent again.

We trotted down Parliament Hill.

"So," I said, turning to my new companion. "You are an Ethiopian Documentary Film maker."

"No," he said.

"Ah," I said. There was a pause.

"I am neither Ethiopian nor a documentary film maker. I am from Somaliland, in the former Somalia," he said. "Oh, it is a long story." He fell silent.

"Tell me the story," I said, for I liked stories, and found comfort in the novelty of a human voice after so long alone.

"Very well…" His frown became a smile. "If you are really sure?"

I gestured to the snow, the sky, the silence. "What better way to spend the golden coin of time?"

"Indeed… Ibrahim Bihi," he said, extending his right hand. "Dr. Ibrahim Bihi, of Somaliland."

"Jude," I said, extending my hand. "An orphan of Ireland." We shook.

He cleared his throat, and began.

"Once upon a time, I eked a meagre living, arbitraging a fundamental structural discrepancy in the price of Goats." He looked me intently in the eye.

"You've lost me," I said.

"I must apologise," he said. "My degree is in economics, and it has had an unfortunate effect on my conversational English. Allow me to begin again…" He composed himself. "My story is a sorry tale, of the Dismal Science, in the heart of the Dark Continent…"

"Lost me," I said again.

"A Story. Of Economics. In Africa."

"Ah, grand. I have you now," I said, entirely gratified by this excellent clarification. "Now we're sucking diesel! On you go."

He settled himself more securely on the gelding and, after a pause, continued.

"After the final collapse of the Somali state, the confiscation of my property, the destruction of my possessions and my repeated relocation due to the to-ing and fro-ing of multiple overlapping civil wars, I eventually found myself in Hargeisa, owning only a goat."

"What was she called?"

"Who?"

"The Goat."

"She was a goat. She didn't have a name."

"I find it hard to follow a story without a name," I said. "It is a weakness in me."

"Call her anything you like."

"Can I call her Ethel?" I said, for I had a fondness for the name, it having been the name of the Orphanage Cook. Ethel gave the orphans a small bag of Emerald Sweets to share between them every Christmas. Thus, every third year I got a sweet and, by rationing my consumption of it to a single lick at bedtime, could usually make it last till the taking down of the decorations on January 6th, or even a little later. Indeed, the sweet wrapper, stored under my pillow, often maintained a trace of coconutty, chocolatey fragrance till mid March.

"Feel free to think of the goat as Ethel."

"Thank you." I closed my eyes. Ethel the Goat shimmered and came into hard focus, chewed meditatively, and tilted her head to one side, fixing me with an unblinking stare.

Opening my eyes again, I urged Dr. Bihi to continue.

He continued. "I was caught on the horns of an acute economic dilemma. The forced sale of a goat in wartime is unlikely to realise the full value of the goat."

I mentally substituted the word "Ethel" for the terms "a goat" and "the goat", and the meaning became entirely clear. I closed my eyes and smiled fondly at Ethel, as he talked on.

"Yet the slaughter and personal consumption of the goat, while keeping one alive in the short term, would lead in the medium term to having no goat. In the long term, with neither assets nor capital nor cashflow, death would inevitably follow. Luckily, my PhD had been devoted to the exploitation of price discrepancies in imperfect markets. I thus resolved to apply my knowledge of temporary market inefficiencies to my Goat."

He thus resolved to apply his knowledge of temporary market inefficiencies to Ethel, I said under my breath.

"This last, or ultimate, goat, on which all my hopes rested, had only three legs, due to shrapnel from a mine stepped on some weeks previously by my second-last, or penultimate, goat, on the trek to Hargeisa."

I hastily named the penultimate goat Charles, and exploded it immediately, before I could Bond with it. Then I removed Ethel's rear left leg.

"Thus the surviving goat's movements were slow, and my search for economic opportunities was limited to the immediate vicinity of Hargeisa airport, where I was sleeping at the side of the runway, for the UN presence at the airport made it a safer place for the homeless, friendless wanderer than in the lawless town proper."

I was stymied by the runway till I remembered seeing a postcard of Knock Airport, sent to Brother Madrigal by Monsignor James Horan to congratulate the Orphanage on winning the Harty Cup. I imagined Knock Airport, removed the drizzle, clouds and fog, drained the bog, covered it in sand, and increased the temperature by twenty degrees. As an afterthought, I mentally relocated, just over the horizon, all the stories I had heard the older orphans tell of Limerick City, including the one about the lad getting stabbed in the head with a screwdriver, the one about the ten-year-old in the Bus Station toilets, and how Aengus McMahon smuggled the bar-stool out of Driscoll's after the Microdisney gig.

"I thought long," he continued. "I thought hard. To aid my deliberations I ate the final remnants of my penultimate goat, which I had cured in salt and carried on the tottering back of my ultimate goat to Hargeisa. I came up with a plan. The next day, as I refined my plan, I ate the mutilated fourth leg of my ultimate goat. I wiped my mouth as I finished, and drew a deep breath. It was now, or never. I had neither friend, nor relative, nor roof, nor occupation. I had, in all this world, one solitary three-legged goat. This poor goat, which I had come to love – its hazel eyes; its trim beard; its dry dugs – this poor beast comprised all the Surplus Value I possessed. It was the Rock of Capital on which I stood, raised above the perilous sea in which so many of my countrymen around me desperately swam or, ceasing their struggles, drowned."

In life, in front of me, Dr. Ibrahim Bihi closed his eyes and drew a deep breath. His voice began again, filled with a strengthening passion.

"That poor goat was my stepping-stone to a safer world, a better world, some greater island raised higher above the perilous waves of Life. My first stepping-stone to the Capitals of Capital: to London, Tokyo, New York, all thrusting so far above the sea of subsistence that the people there think the world dry land; they fly from great Island to great Island far above the sea of suffering, never looking down. Some glance perhaps out the windows of their planes: but if they see us they must think we are waving, not drowning, for they do not come to save us. They do not come."

I was rather keen for him to get back to the story of Ethel. I cleared my throat meaningfully, but he was off on one now.

"Not from England, who once owned our country; who took over the Gulf slave trade from the Arab slavers, and built Bristol and Liverpool from the profits. Not from America, who built her wealth upon the surplus labour of twenty million African slaves. I believe some troops arrived in Mogadishu. Eighteen died:

they went home. A million of us not worth eighteen of them. A million, not worth eighteen. There was no Marshall Plan for Africa. There was no Marshall Plan for Africa."

"What happened to Ethel the goat?" I said, somewhat appalled that he appeared to have forgotten her plight. In my mind's eye, she teetered bravely on her three legs, yet still stood proudly erect, the hint of a tear in her hazel eye.

"Eh? Oh." Dr. Bihi opened his eyes. "I waited until the daily UN food plane was committed to its final approach: as its wheels touched down at the far end of the runway and I saw the puffs of dust, I drove my goat out of the long grass and into the middle of the runway and, leaving her standing bewildered and blindfolded where the tyre-tracks were thickest, I ran back into the long grass. The plane was laden, the suspension heavy, the engines slung low: the propeller took her head off and the headless corpse went under the wheels."

"Oh no," I said, wishing now that I had not visualised Ethel quite so intensely.

"Oh yes," he said. "I went straight to the control tower and demanded to see the airport manager. In Somalia, it is the custom to pay a man double the market price if you accidentally kill his beast. I had the price of two goats in my hand before the plane had finished taxiing back to the terminal."

"What luck!" I cried. "What did you do with the money?"

"I went to the market, of course, and bought two goats."

"They could be friends to each other," I said, pleased.

"The next day I drove the two goats into the path of a turbo-prop from Riyadh. Leaving their corpses on the runway, I went straight to the control tower, demanded to see…"

"I get you!" I said. "Because, in Somalia, it is the custom to pay a man double the…"

"I see you appreciate the genius of my notion," said Dr. Ibrahim Bihi. "I had the price of four goats in my hand before the plane had finished taxiing back to the terminal."

"Yes…" First upon my fingers and then in the quiet caverns of my mind I extrapolated from one to two: from two to four: from four to eight: and so on for some time. "And thus," I said after a while, "you quickly became infinitely wealthy."

"Sadly, no," he sighed. "It is the tragedy of arbitrage opportunities: they are killed by those who love them. The Market abhors a price discrepancy… But oh, it is beautiful to watch the market corrected by the invisible hand! The success of my scheme was noted by others: by the third day, rivals were driving goats onto the runway ahead of me."

"Hold on there a minute," I said. "There's an invisible hand?"

"Yes," said Ibrahim Bihi.

"There's an invisible hand, driving goats onto the runway?"

"Yes."

I was not happy with this turn of events. "So now we're in some kind of ghost story?" I said.

"No," said Ibrahim Bihi. "It's not a real invisible hand."

"How can you tell?" I said.

Dr. Bihi began to breathe a little heavily. Asthma, perhaps. "The invisible hand of Adam Smith!" he said. "The great Scottish economist? Born in 1723?"

"Adam Smith had an invisible hand?" I said.

"No," said Dr. Ibrahim Bihi, "he invented the invisible hand."

"Ah, I have you now," I said. "He lost his hand in an accident, and made another one. Out of some transparent material, no doubt?"

"No!" said Dr. Bihi. I looked at him with some concern: he appeared to be having considerable difficulty breathing. Perhaps he had lost his Inhaler. "I occasionally worry about the future of a society in which nobody understands the true basis of that society's wealth," said Dr. Bihi. "You are familiar with the words 'Love thy neighbour as thyself'?"

"I am," I said, with great satisfaction. That was an easy one.

"Well," said Dr. Bihi, "the invisible hand is as fundamental to the economic health of your society as those noble words are to its spiritual health."

"So the Invisible Hand," I said, "is like the Holy Ghost?"

"Look," said Dr. Ibrahim Bihi. "The invisible hand is a metaphor. It is not real. The invisible hand is a poetic term for the power of market forces to swiftly and efficiently deliver capital and goods to where they are most needed. With nobody in command. Nobody ordering it so."

He gave me a Look. I gave him a Look back. This conversation was giving me a ferocious crick in my neck. I began to wish we could be seated facing each other rather than front-to-back on a horse.

He sighed, and said, "In a free market, increased demand drives up prices, and profits. New suppliers move into the market to take that profit, until oversupply drives prices back down, whereupon some suppliers leave, to use their capital more profitably elsewhere. The invisible hand regulates both supply and demand far more efficiently than the clumsy iron fist of state control. Capital is always in movement to where it is most needed."

"I have you," I said. "So the invisible hand drove the goats onto the runway."

"Yes," said Dr. Bihi. "For there, the profits were highest."

There was a thoughtful pause. The horses made steady progress through the snow.

"Do you know," I said, "I think I see where this might be going."

Dr. Bihi nodded. "Yes. Our competition in the market that afternoon drove up the price of goats. Thus, the market price of two goats, paid to us that morning at the airport for each one of our slaughtered goats, was by that afternoon unable to buy us two goats in the market. Goat hyperinflation had set in, for at the airport the next morning we demanded double the new market price for the goats we drove into the path of an old Aeroflot Tu-144. The airport manager agreed to this new rate of compensation. Thus, the compensation now being indexed to the market price of the goat, where the price of the goat is n and the compensation is 2n, capital was in effect free: no matter how high the goat price soared, the fresh capital for the next round of goat finance soared along with it. The tap was held artificially open, and a speculative bubble made inevitable."

"Fascinating!" I said. "…What does the 'n' stand for?"

"What 'n'?"

I quoted from memory: "'Where the price of the goat is n and the compensation is 2n.'"

"It stands for any number."

"'Any number'," I pointed out, "begins with an 'A'."

"No," said Dr. Bihi, "in mathematics, n stands for any number. It is a mathematical formula. Whatever the price of the goat, which we shall call n, the compensation for the goat would be twice that: 2n. It remains true no matter what the number is."

"Oh, you were speaking Mathematics!" That explained it. "Can I translate it into English?"

"Be my guest."

I muttered, "Where the price of the goat is a fiver, the compensation is a tenner… Where the price of the goat is a million, the compensation is two million… Ah yeah. Got it," I said, louder. "Carry on."

Ibrahim Bihi also muttered to himself for a minute, before carrying on. "However, soon the doubled and redoubled prices paid out by the airport manager had reached such giddy heights that the merchant class grew greedy and joined in. No other asset could offer so high a rate of return as the goat, so capital was now diverted into goats and out of every other asset class, and all but the goat traders were starved of investment. Men sold their very houses to raise the price of a single goat.

"Word had spread, and men drove goats in any condition to Hargeisa from all over Somaliland, and even the other statelets of the fragmented Somalia: from Puntland, from Middle Shabelle and Lower Jubba in the chaotic southern rump state, even from Ethiopia. The market was soon flooded with goats, many of them sick or lame. However this did not matter, for the demand for goats had become infinite. The runway, being entirely unprotected around its perimeter on either side, was the Platonic ideal of a free market: there were no barriers to entry.

"However, planes were by now reluctant to land in Hargeisa."

Wishing to pull my weight in the conversation, I ventured, "Too many goats on the runway?"

Ibrahim Bihi shook his head. "The goats were not the problem. Certain economic firebrands, frozen out of the goat market, had attempted to introduce the cow as an element of trade at the airport's morning meetings."

"Ah," I said.

"The goat cartel fought this fiercely, as it endangered their near monopoly, and threatened an uncontrolled, overnight devaluation of the goat which could badly shake confidence in the market. Also, the pilots were very unhappy. More importantly, the UN, as issuers of fresh capital and guarantors of the liquidity of the market, opposed the introduction of the cow. Any decent-sized aircraft could plough through almost unlimited numbers of the lightweight native Somali goat without risking much more than a puncture from a shattered pelvis or horn, but a couple of cows could take the undercarriage off a passenger plane. The replacement cost of an aircraft dwarfed even the inflated cost of the goats, and the UN made an informal deal that if we kept the cows off the runway, they would continue to pay out for the goats."

"That was good?" I ventured.

Dr. Ibrahim Bihi nodded. "Of course, some fiscal conservatives within the UN wished to unilaterally halt the goat payments entirely. It was, however, too late to do this. An enormous re-allocation of capital had already occurred, and the personal wealth of the entire Hargeisa middle class was by now tied up in goats, as indeed was that of many enterprising UN employees, and most of the pilots and crews flying the route. To abolish the payments would have lead to a collapse in market confidence, the panicked sale of goats, a flooded goat market, and subsequent price collapses that would have ruined most.

"As you can see, we had entered a classic momentum market, where the price of the goat had decoupled from the fundamental value of the goat: the cost of a goat now vastly exceeded the capital returns which were possible over the lifetime of the goat from sale of milk, cheese, and, ultimately, meat and skin. However, vast fortunes can still be made in strong momentum markets, regardless of fundamental values, as long as you are not the one left holding the goat when the reversion to fundamental value occurs. In the poetic words of Chuck Prince of Citigroup, 'As long as the music is playing, you've got to get up and dance.' And so I stayed in the market, fully invested in goats.

"By this time the goat craze had become a mania. A severe shortage of goats, and infinite demand, led to excesses. The price of goats became ludicrous, and many animals were led to the town market that were loudly proclaimed to be goats but which, on closer inspection, proved to be mutilated dogs. They were purchased anyway, the frightful creatures, at grotesque prices.

"The sheer length of the boom was now leading to increased confidence. There was a loosening of credit. It seemed madness not to lend to a man who could pay you back handsomely the next day. And as a creditor, once you'd borrowed and repaid with interest a couple of times, the banks began to persuade you to borrow more. Indeed, as the banks began to package and resell the goat loans, it soon became in the banks' interest to expand the market. New products were developed; soon buyers were flying in from as far away as Switzerland, New York, and Basildon."

"But what would some Millionaire from New York City know about goats?" I said. "They have no background in goats, them fellows. Did they really know what they were doing?"

"It is true," said Dr. Ibrahim Bihi, "that buying individual goats can be a tricky business, requiring an expert eye. But that problem was soon solved by Securitization." He caught my Look, and sighed. "Overseas buyers no longer purchased their goats directly," he said. "Instead, they purchased a bundle of goat-backed securities. Rather than owning a goat, they owned a share of the future revenue stream from a number of goats. This spread the risk. Each goat-backed package was rated by the ratings agencies. And thus their quality was assured. Some critics – pessimists, doom-mongers – argued that an agency who refused to give high ratings would soon lose business to an agency with looser standards. Such downward pressure, they argued, meant that even a herd of sub-prime goats would soon be rated Triple-A. A few, in their madness, even abandoned the mathematical models and began to examine the actual goats. But these voices, which threatened the stability of the market, were soon shouted down. Even if their wild claims were true, all the mathematical models said that this should not matter. The price of goats had *never* fallen nationally, year on year, in Somaliland, since records began."

I nodded. It seemed impeccably Scientific. "When did records begin?" I said, to show I hadn't fallen asleep.

"Well, let me see…" Ibrahim Bihi thought back. "It would have been earlier that month," he said, "when we set up the ratings system. Many borrowed to get into the market, and soon the total value of goat-related loans outstanding was greater than national GDP – a tribute to the flexibility of our young and dynamic banking sector. Somaliland, lacking a government of any kind, was not hampered by over-regulation. Thus, we could experiment with absolutely free markets. The leading bankers of many smaller nations, such as Iceland, Ireland, and England, soon came to Somaliland to learn from our success."

"But surely there were natural limits to the boom?" I said. "I mean, what did you do when you ran out of goats?"

"True," said Dr. Ibrahim Bihi, "the physical shortage of actual goats briefly threatened to slow the market's rate of growth to something dangerously close to its natural level. But the market was evolving all the time. There was such money to be made in goat-related financial services that the sector attracted the country's, indeed the world's, brightest minds. They came up with a magnificent range of goat futures, and goat options, and developed some highly innovative goat derivative products…"

"Such as those inexpensive drinks in red cans, that spell Coca-Cola with a K, in the hope of fooling the less literate?"

"No," said Ibrahim Bihi. "A derivative product is one whose value *derives* from something else that is not part of it. In this case, a goat derivative derives its value from the price of physical goats, but does not itself consist of a goat. Thus, derivatives can be created in unlimited quantities, though the thing they derive their price from may be in very limited quantities."

I regarded the muscles of the horse moving smoothly beneath me, and had a think about this. "So they derive their value from the price of goats, in the same way a betting slip derives its value from the speed of a horse in the Grand National?"

"Yes. An excellent metaphor," said Dr. Bihi. His asthma seemed to suddenly improve. "You could extend it: the bookies are the rating agency, who analyse the data for you, and then issue the odds. The odds are the rating that says, this is your chance of getting your money back."

"So you don't need to own the actual horse," I said, "or know anything about the horse, in order to bet an unlimited amount on the performance of the horse?" It seemed quite brilliant.

"Or, in this case, goat," said Dr. Bihi. "Yes. But derivatives have one immense advantage over betting slips: the banks will not loan you thirty times your assets to bet on horses."

"But they will loan you thirty times your assets to bet on goat-backed securities?" Now here might be a way of making a Million to win Angela's heart.

"Yes," he said, "because the goat-backed securities are rated triple A, after a careful and judicious analysis of all the data since records began. And thus there is no risk."

"I see," I said. "They're a dead cert."

"Yes, a dead cert," said Dr. Bihi, and sighed. "So crucial to the economy were goats now, and so fatal to our people any collapse in the goat market, that the UN appointed an Official with

Special Responsibility For Goats. Around him swiftly sprung up a bureaucracy. A well-meaning man, his attempts to stabilise the goat market were well-intentioned. However, this intervention by the authorities was, as ever, late and ineffectual. Indeed, it was counterproductive. Reassured that the UN wouldn't let the market collapse, prices soared higher. It had become a one-way bet.

"The Airport Manager had by now begun to fly in goats, to sell at market for more than he was paying out, thus financing further imports. This meant both more goats and more planes arriving to run them over. Now that everybody was benefiting there seemed no need for the boom ever to end. True, the UN budget for Somalia was paying out increasingly large compensation fees to the owners of dead goats, but one of the first moves by the UN High Commissioner with Special Responsibility For Goats was to make the goat compensation fund self-funding by means of a hedge."

I nodded. "To feed the goats."

"What?" said Ibrahim Bihi.

"The goats," I explained, "could eat the hedge."

"It was not that kind of hedge," said Dr. Bihi. "A hedge is a protection against risk. In this case, they hedged it in goat futures."

"Oh. Goat futures," I said. "Right… You mean, like, death? And being made into a handbag?"

"No," said Dr. Bihi, when the spasm had passed. "A futures contract is, in this case, a contract to buy a goat at a future date, but at a price set today. If the price of goats soars higher than the set price by that date, you make a profit, because you can now buy the goat at the old, lower, fixed price. And then sell it at the new one."

"Ah!" I said.

Dr. Bihi smiled. "Indeed… Now, every time the UN pushed up the price of goats by paying out double the market price, it regained the money fourfold, as its goat futures contracts soared in value.

"The only drawback was that the slaughter on the runways each day was by now so great that it was becoming a hazard to land, and it frequently took till nightfall to execute all the goats, with planes forced to slaughter animals all the way down the runway, then often all the way back again, to hit the ones they'd missed and to finish off the wounded, and then again all along the taxi-route back to the terminal. Takeoffs were being delayed while the bodies were removed from the runways, which lowered the number of flights and thus the potential revenues generated for all."

"And so that finally brought the boom to a natural and a peaceful end," I said, satisfied.

"You underestimate the ingenuity of economists," said Ibrahim Bihi. "The problem was solved by bringing in an electronic Goat Accident and Compensatory System, or GACS, to replace the cumbersome physical system. Now, instead of herding your one, then two, then four, then eight, then sixteen goats onto the runway each afternoon, each of which then needed to go through the laborious process of being physically hit by a landing aircraft's undercarriage, wingtip or propeller, you simply input your goat numbers into the GACS. The airport manager then allocated each flight its goats, and the compensation due each trader came up on the Big Screen.

"The numbers we dealt in were by now so vast that the few remaining physical goats were a financial irrelevance of purely historical interest and, indeed, a source of slight embarrassment to the newly wealthy traders of goat derivatives. The vast new electronic Goat Exchange replaced the old, dung-stinking Central Goat Market, from which the last surviving obsolete goats were released to wander where they would.

Some of us missed the blood-soaked runway of the old system, the shouts of the traders, the roar of the engines and the shriek of the goats, but all acknowledged the increased efficiency of the new system. Often two full trade cycles could be executed in a day, doubling turnover. By the end of the year, Hargeisa contained fourteen thousand millionaires and the UN were running a paper profit of over a trillion dollars." He sighed.

"Then what happened?" I said.

A curious sorrow seemed to fill him. "Now that we were trading virtual goats, a peculiar lassitude began to sweep through the trading classes. Oh, certainly, paupers were becoming millionaires, and millionaires were soon billionaires by merely getting out of bed and showing their faces at the beautiful new Goat Exchange, but the heady joy of the early days had gone. The Millionaires envied the Billionaires, while the Trillionaires feared the Millionaires. Trade became vicious yet meaningless. Everyone was growing richer, yet somehow more anxious. Without a solid goat to give value to the figure, one's wealth only had meaning in relation to another's wealth, and was thus never enough. Someone, somewhere, always had another zero. On the day I became a billionaire, I felt poorer than when I had owned but a single goat."

"I know the feeling," I said. "My pocket money, back in the Orphanage, was ten pence a week. I remember the traumatic shock when I discovered Waxy Tracy was getting a quid."

"Precisely," said Dr. Ibrahim Bihi. "But what could you do but trade more, trade harder? The social anxiety and sense of failure felt by the millionaires and billionaires in a city of trillionaires caused despair, self-harm, even suicide.

"Trade went on all night now: men hardly slept, or saw their wives and families. They spoke of nothing but goats, yet had soon forgotten what the word goat had once referred to: many younger traders had never seen a goat.

"Yet the new wealth was meritocratic: old money, in property or cocoa or oil, was easily overtaken by that of young, brash goat traders who better understood these new rules.

"Confused by all I had wrought, and by now so rich that there was no word in common use that could describe my wealth, I returned one day to the old Hargeisa airport runway, the site of the birth of my glorious notion. It was disused now, of course, for our wealthy nation had outgrown the source of its wealth. The transport of goats was no longer necessary, and we no longer needed aid. Our luxury goods arrived through the new, modern airport and electronic Goat Exchange on the far side of Hargeisa.

"The long grass had spread from both edges to reclaim the old runway. And there I found, munching quietly, disregarded in the long grass of the abandoned airfield, two goats."

Nell and Mick, I thought to myself, and saw them clear as day before me. Though grumpy, they were in love: Mick nuzzled Nell. Nell kicked him.

"And what happened then?" I asked, as Mick mounted Nell in my mind.

Dr. Ibrahim Bihi sighed. "While I stared at the two goats, I received a frantic call from my office: the arse had fallen out of the market, and we had all lost everything. Now tell me: who could have predicted that?"

"Who, indeed?" I said.

"The dream had ended, and everything went away as fast as it had arrived. The luxuries, the money, the gleaming towers of steel and glass. The people lost faith in the system, as good companies followed bad into ruin, for it turned out that those not trading goats had yet been corrupted by them. Envious of our billions, they had fiddled the figures and diddled the books. Now all that had seemed sane behavior in the long dream of the bubble looked criminal madness in the cold light of day. Heroes of the goat market were fired, divorced, jailed for the very ambition and creativity that had made them heroes. All fell apart. The delicate fabric of society unravelled. Somaliland lay again in ruins. I again had nothing. It was as though it had never been… I cut a stout stick from the bushes, and slept at the edge of the runway to escape my hostile creditors, investigators, prosecutors."

"What did you do then?" I asked. "Poor, alone, and friendless, again, in poor Somaliland?"

"I had learned my lesson. I had heard that the US were conducting tank exercises across the border in Djibouti. In

Djibouti," said Dr. Ibrahim Bihi, "it is the custom to pay a man triple the market price if you accidentally kill his beast. I raised my stout stick, and drove my two goats North, before me, through the minefields. But that is another story."

Without our noticing, it had begun to snow.

"Please," I said. "Tell me the story. I like stories."

In my mind, Mick got off Nell. Yes, in Spring, there would be a baby goat. A Kid.

"Very well," said Dr. Ibrahim Bihi, and cleared his throat.

I closed my eyes as the first flakes fell. Yes. I would call her Ethel.

Tales were told. Snow fell. Our black horse continued to follow the chestnut mare, into the heart of London.

40

At last Dr. Ibrahim Bihi's story reached the present moment, on a horse, in London. I thanked him.

We did not speak, for a while.

Alex Fromblur's monkey, having groomed the mare's mane, leaped aboard our horse, and combed its mane too, for burrs. Politely, but firmly, I ignored my rival in Love.

As we made our muffled clop through the streets, past the great houses, the first signs of human life assailed us. Children emerged shyly into gardens, then less shyly, then shouting. Fathers supervised the building of snowmen. At times, a nod greeted us. One child threw a snowball, which fell far short of our horse, for the child was small and fat and, encumbered by many layers, could barely swing back his arm. Nonetheless, it was a brave try, which I acknowledged with a wave, the monkey with a hoot, Ibrahim with a smile – and the child waved, hooted and smiled back at us.

Then a curious thing began to happen. I found myself fondly recognising things I had never seen, and bitterly remembering things I had not myself done. Certain buildings, glimpsed for the first time, were familiar to me. I shivered, and the plastic bags grumbled and crumpled beneath my fur. We turned a corner: more long-smouldering memories of experiences which were not my own ignited.

I shook my head, and closed my eyes against the vision, and saw behind my eyes a paler version of the vision, colourless, shrunken: a city in snow.

Which visions were Visions? Which Real?

But I now noticed the quality of my Visions was poor: detail was lacking, they wavered, whizzed up off the top of my vision occasionally, then reappeared at the bottom of it. My Visions also came only in black and white. Nor did it ever stop snowing in my Visions, although in Reality the sky was now as blue as the eggshell of a Mistle Thrush.

The houses became grander; stranger; taller. The children vanished. I began to relax. But no: certain buildings, certain views, continued to summon in me ghostly memories of things I could not have seen. In all these Visions, it was snowing.

Indeed, my Visions were beginning to remind me of something…

They were Televisual Images! I had seen London before, on the Television! Dear God, are all new arrivals to the modern city Tormented Visionaries? Are all convulsed thus by sudden revelations?

Overwhelmed, my mind sought relief in the past: I flashed back in time to my first memory of Television: that unforgettable day.

Every four years Brother Madrigal used to borrow a Television set, to try it out, from Paddy Thackery of Thackery Electrical. This television was Tried Out for the three weeks of the World Cup Finals, then switched off and returned with a note regretting that the Orphanage had decided, on mature reflection, that it could not, after all, justify the expense.

Any Orphan who wished to see the Television had to go to Brother Madrigal's room. However, the only excuse for an Orphan to go to Brother Madrigal's room was for a beating of such seriousness that it could not, for reasons of insurance, be carried out by an ordinary Brother. Competition for a Senior Beating was soon intense.

I myself first won the privilege by claiming responsibility for setting fire to Waxy Tracy's hair. The deed had, in fact, been done by Null-Set Kenny, taking advantage of a diversionary Fit thrown in the back row by Mona Minihan. But before Kenny could confess, and request his prize, he was tripped and sat upon by

Knacker Nagle. While the other Lads were busy extinguishing Waxy's blazing ringlets with their fists and boots, I seized the golden moment, released Brother Scully from the cupboard, and took all credit for the conflagration.

How well I now remembered the mingled trepidation and anticipation with which I knocked on Brother Madrigal's door for my first Senior Beating. Even through the door I could hear the low, unceasing whisper of the Television.

"Come!"

I entered, and immediately sensed a flickering, shifting, clouded presence in the corner of the room, in the corner of my eye. My eyes snapped shut in terror.

"A Senior Beating, Sir," I said. "Please."

"For what crime, boy?"

"Arson Of The Person, Sir."

"Sss. Dth, dth, dth! Boy or Master?"

"Boy, Sir."

"Successfully extinguished?"

"Yes, Sir."

"Oh, no harm done. Still, rules are rules, are rules... are rules. Bend!"

Cracking open one eyelid to squint at the floor, I trembled my way towards the noise of the Television, found a low chair, and bent over the back of it.

As the beating commenced, I considered the sound of the Set from the darkness of my self's interior.

The hissing, from which emerged thin, human voices – this I was prepared for – this was Radio, familiar.

Likewise the huge emotions carried by these tiny voices. Every word was charged till it trembled, even "the" and "and". The voices moved from anger to terror to sorrow, and back, rapidly, endlessly, so that my heart sped up in sympathy.

Reassured and at the same time exhilarated I took the leap.

I opened my eyes: it was a box: the front was open, yet glassed over: it was flat, yet deep: in it was a snowstorm through which tiny figures struggled. I could not focus, or the television would not focus, I could not be sure. I moved my head from side to side, I covered one eye: the snowstorm was in a kitchen: I saw a tiny woman lift a kettle, her back to a tiny man who sat in a snowy chair at the far side of a snowy table. "Where's my tea?" he said in his tiny voice. I relaxed: it was a picturebox: it was as they had said: there was nothing to fear.

Then the couple and the kitchen vanished with horrendous abruptness: my mind reeled as I was confronted with an enormous Kettle, too large for the box, yet jammed somehow into it. Steam, pouring from the kettle, vanished upward, yet did not enter into our room, it could not leave the box. A hand, dear God, a monstrous hand was gripping the handle of the kettle! The hand was pouring torrents of boiling water downward, toward the floor of the box, where the tiny people still must be! A savage, disembodied voice came from the torrent: "Here's your bloody tea." The tiny couple had nowhere to run to, nowhere to hide: the appalling torrent obscured their fate in a wreath of steam and a storm of snow.

I could not bear it any longer, and closed my eyes.

After the beating, I rejoined my classmates. Brother Scully, overwhelmed by the administration of so many Junior and Intermediate Beatings, had sustained a minor internal catastrophe and had left the class. My fellows surrounded me.

"What did you see?"

"A horror film," I said, and told them the tale of the supernatural kettle and the severed hand.

That was the beginning of my great Love Affair with the Medium.

Soon, I was slipping with ease from stories of Frogs in Borneo to stories of People in Manchester. Indeed, I probably saw more television during that World Cup than anyone at the Orphanage – bar Brother Madrigal himself, of course. Most of the Lads were interested only in the Ireland matches proper, which were so popular that mass Senior Beatings had to be arranged, at which the younger Brothers acted as stewards, and Brother Madrigal's door was removed from its hinges to ease the congestion.

Memories of that World Cup summer lingered long after. Tele-Visual images would flash back into my mind, as I tried to kick Riggs-Miller's old mare into a trot on snowy Tipperary evenings. In that great hallucinatory light, the fields growing dark under darkening skies and the world turning from colour to black and white, those images seemed more real than the fields. Would I ever see such sights in my true life?

For a moment, in the Real World, I was riding a horse bareback while looking at London buildings, which reminded me of looking at London buildings on a Television, which reminded me of looking at Television in Ireland, which reminded me of riding a horse bareback in Ireland while remembering looking at London buildings on Television while wondering would I ever look upon such buildings in the real world.

Riggs-Miller's old mare halted abruptly, deep in my layered reminisce, and hundreds of miles away, many years later, I fell off a perfectly blameless gelding.

"You hurled yourself from your horse," said Alex Fromblur.

"I did," I replied. There was a pause, as I regained my feet.

"I do not mean to pry, but why…?" said Dr. Ibrahim Bihi.

"It is nothing, thank you," I said. "Just a sudden attack of Memories."

Ibrahim helped me back aboard the placid beast. "I, too," he said, "suffer terribly from my Memories." We moved off again.

"Oh," I said, "the Memories from which I suffer are, luckily, not my own. Chiefly police dramas, and the odd News Report."

We had entered narrower streets. On our left, the snow drifted to six feet so that bright shop signs sat at the crest of blank drifts. The horses trotted tight to the right-hand walls now, where the snow merely reached their bellies.

At the crossing of two streets, Alex swung right.

I looked up and read the signs, high on the brick walls. We had ridden down Old Compton Street. Now we joined Dean.

"It's open. Splendid," said Alex, dismounting into deep snow. "Tie the horses to the bicycle racks, if you can find them..." He dug down the face of the wall to find a metal loop beneath the snow, bolted to the brickwork, and looped the reins loosely through it. Dismounting, I did the same.

Straightening up, I read the small brass sign by the glass door. "What manner of place is this?" I asked.

"You've never been to the Groucho? Gosh! Well, it is a private members' club for anti-establishment mavericks and rebels, the kind of people who sneer at the whole idea of clubs and just want to get away from the whole wretched English Class System for a while."

I nodded. Splendidly true to the Marxist spirit.

We stepped over the frozen corpse of a beggar and entered the building.

41

In the small Foyer, a Lovely Girl greeted us from behind a great sweep of Desk. Were I not already exhausted from excessive Love, I would have fallen, again, deep in deepest love. Indeed, the doors of my heart shuddered and bent in, but my heart was already full: she could not push through. I was relieved and sorry. She was blonde and happy.

"Hullo Alex," she said. "Food's off, I'm afraid, no deliveries because of the snow. A lot of us slept here last night, couldn't get home. What larks! Mark said to say he's in the pool room."

"Thanks, Sweetie... I'll just sign you lot in as my Guests," said Alex, and scribbled in an open book on the counter-top.

"Would you like me to hang your... er...?" said Sweetie the Lovely Girl, indicating the Jacket of my rabbit-skin suit, which was an increasingly ambiguous garment, all right. I had recently extended its hem with the skins of several particularly fine rabbits. I considered the question. Not having removed it for a number of days, indeed since its last extension, I had grown comfortable in it. "On balance, no," I said. "Thank you. But..." – a wonderful thought struck me – "If I could leave my bag..."

"Sure. We've made an emergency cloakroom through there... bit stuffed, I'm afraid, with so many people crashing here..." She opened a door beside the reception desk.

I walked down a short corridor, and found a small room filled almost to the ceiling with bags, knapsacks and suitcases.

I removed the strap of my black bag from my shoulder. Blood hesitantly returned to the deep groove in my shoulder's flesh. My left arm began to rise of its own accord as long-numbed nerves began to fire in blood-starved muscle. It was an exquisite relief.

For a silent moment I simply stood there, enjoying the sensation of lightness and freedom.

Then I picked up the bag, by handle and strap, and attempted to loft it onto the stack of bags and cases.

However, my arm failed me halfway through the arc, and spasmed my bag hard into the middle of the stack. I stepped closer, to halt the sway outward of the top baggage, and stepped heavily on a protruding ski. This levered the entire pyramid away from the wall. It fell on top of me.

Buried in bags, and winded, I tried to haul myself out of the pile. The first strap I tugged ripped open a knapsack which spilled folded white silk all over me.

So did the second.

At last I managed to swim to the surface through a sea of what appeared to be two vast wedding dresses. It took some time to rebuild the stack of bags. It was nearly impossible to return the unfolded seas of silk to their packs. The design was atrocious. With one tug, they would spill again. I stitched both packages tightly shut with a few quick loops of rabbit sinew, and returned to the foyer.

42

"Ah, there you are," said Alex. "Dr. Bihi and Zach have gone to look for Mark…" He opened a glass-panelled door and ushered me into a pleasant, noisy Saloon.

A tall man in a grey suit stood in the centre of the swirling crowd, staring up at the ceiling. By his left side stood a short man in a black suit. The men were linked by a short tube, emerging from the trouser pocket of the Black suit, to vanish under the coat-tails of the Grey.

Alex led me up to the short man in Black and placed a hand on his shoulder. "This is Lord Cümerbund, the greatest Buyer of the Age," he said. "He has bought more British art, by weight, than any man alive, and is single-handedly responsible for putting the British Art scene on a sound industrial footing."

"No, no…" murmured Lord Cümerbund.

"Yes, yes!" said Alex. "Already he has been granted the Queen's Award for Industry, and been elevated to the peerage."

"Come, come," spoke Lord Cümerbund softly. "I do not like to hear such trifles mentioned in the same breath as… Art!"

A beautiful woman walked past. Lord Cümerbund stepped to one side to let her by. There was a loud pop. At once, the tall, Grey-suited figure beside him slumped to the floor.

"Fuck, I've unplugged Lord Grey. Hang on a minute…" Lord Cümerbund reached down to grab the free end of the transparent tube, from which now pulsed a thin spurt of red liquid. He put his thumb over the end of the tube. Lifting Lord Grey's jacket tails with his other hand, he plugged the tube back into an unseen socket.

Lord Grey lurched erect. "Tube come unstuck?"

"'Fraid so."

"Damn... Excuse me, but I must intercept the bubble before it arrives at my brain, slaying me." Lord Grey slid his forefinger into the inside corner of his right eye and flipped the eyeball out. It dangled halfway down his cheek, on the short tether of the optic nerve, staring floorward. "Shoes need a shine," he murmured. His other eye looked at me. "Got a little valve in here... the timing's crucial... don't want to leak too much blood..." His index finger hovered inside the vacant socket, then poked. A little jet of gore shot out of the socket, followed by a whistle of air, followed by a very brief second spurt of gore, before Lord Grey shut the valve. "There! Done. Those little air embolisms can be the very devil."

"Lord Grey and I suffer from related rare disorders of the blood," said Lord Cümerbund. "Each needs the other in order to survive. Thus we share a single circulatory system. I have a supplementary pump in my pocket."

"It is a marvel of modern science," said Lord Grey. "A supremely contemporary arrangement, vastly superior to the discredited old system of individuated circulation of the blood. And have you seen these Eyes? Just look at these crazy Eyes. Far better than the old kind." He held out to me the dangling orb of his right eye, then tugged at the back of the orb. The optic nerve came free, and was revealed to be an electronic cable, ending in a tiny plug. "Fibre optic cable... astonishing resolution... *vast* bandwidth..."

I took the eyeball in my hand. The front was hard and cold, the back warm and wet.

"I don't believe we've... met," said Lord Grey, staring at me. Or perhaps not. It is hard not to seem to stare, when you've only the one eye, and an empty socket.

"I'm Jude," I said, transferring the loose eye to my other hand so that we could shake.

"Jude, this is Lord Grey," said Alex. "Head of the Tate, czar of the modern arts in Britain. He is the Medici, the Borgia, the Peter the Great of the age, and even now is making the final preparations for the Turner of Turners. London speaks of little else... But there's Mark!" said Alex, pointing to the top of the stairs.

"Oh," said Lord Grey, "would you drag him down to join us here? I've some questions regarding the Award Ceremony."

"Righty ho," said Alex. He bounded away and up the stairs.

"And what," I asked, "...for I am newly arrived from Ireland... Is the Turner of Turners?"

"A contest," said Lord Cümerbund, "In which thirty years of Turner Prize winning artists, and some old, dead artists that should have won it, and some artists we own a lot of stuff by, are pitted against each other in a Winner Takes All Blaze Of Immortal Glory!"

Lord Grey clapped his hands and bounced up and down. "Plus, all the truly great Turner Prize guest hosts, duking it out! Brian Eno and Madonna! Together at last!" A moist patch appeared at the groin of his grey suit.

"Lord Grey, you have again come Unplugged," I said, in warning, pointing at the spreading patch.

"Eh? No, no, aesthetic bliss, dear boy! Aesthetic Bliss!"

I thanked them for explaining to me the Turner of Turners. "But what," I asked, "is the Turner Prize?"

"The Turner Prize is the greatest Prize in Contemporary Art," explained Lord Cümerbund.

"It gets ten times more coverage than all the other Arts' Prizes in Britain put together," explained Lord Grey.

"It is the most Modern," explained Lord Cümerbund. "It is..." he inhaled deeply, "Hip."

"Is Hip still Hip?" said Lord Grey, frowning and touching his crotch.

"Hip is retro, but hetero," said Lord Cümerbund.

"Retro but hetero..." murmured Lord Grey, writing it with his finger on the screen of a handheld electronic device of exquisite miniaturity. "Is that H-E-T-E-R-O, or H-E-T-R-O?"

"H-E-T-E-R-O, but pronounced hetro... Take great care, though. Retro but hetero is on the way out," said Lord Cümerbund. "It will be gone by Christmas."

Lord Grey sighed, his finger held high. "What is the new retro-but-hetero?"

"Oof... the future is for the young... ask young Toby Bostique there. It is one of his Special Areas... Toby!"

"Lord Cümerbund?" said a young man, approaching in spats, loons and fez.

Lord Cümerbund leaned toward me and whispered, "A brilliant Creative mind. He works at my... it debases and degrades me to say it... Advertising Agency." Straightening up, he said "What is the new Retro-but-hetero?"

Toby answered immediately. "Fantastic in plastic. Though that is mutating into Groovy Vinyl."

"So hip is still, ah, groovy vinyl?" said Lord Grey, fingering his tiny device.

"I'd stick with fantastic in plastic till retro but hetero is gone," said Toby. "It's not a good thing to be two terms ahead of the Herd. They resent it."

"I wish they would bring back Old Skool," said Lord Grey, with a sigh.

"It's due to be revived next autumn, but it will require ironising quotes," said Toby Bostique.

"Really?" Lord Grey's eye widened. "Would I be on the, ah, suffering edge, if I used it in late summer?"

"Very late summer," said Toby, with a wag of his finger.

"I don't know what I'd do without you, Toby," said Lord Cümerbund, pushing him away.

I returned Lord Grey's right eye to him and, slowly and carefully (for I felt the question was somehow at the crux of it), asked, "And what – for we have none in Tipperary, though obviously I have heard of it – is Art?"

Lord Grey plugged his eye back in, and stared at me in stereo.

Lord Cümerbund and he simultaneously opened their mouths.

At that very instant, though, Alex arrived with Mark Wallinger.

"Have you met the Somali gentlemen who were looking for you?" I asked him.

"Pardon?" said Mark Wallinger.

"Oh yes," said Alex. "I forgot to mention. The ones in that conceptual piece you put together last year, 'Ethiopian Documentary Crew...'"

"Oh yes, I nearly bought that one," said Lord Cümerbund.

"Oh, *nearly*," muttered Mark.

"Well," said Alex, "They're here, looking for you."

"Ah," said Mark Wallinger. He gulped. "Ah."

"I don't understand," said Lord Cümerbund, frowning, "weren't they actual, real Ethiopians?"

"Well, we meant to get Ethiopians," said Mark Wallinger, "but they turned out to be surprisingly expensive."

"*Really?*" said Lord Grey. "I thought there were warehouses full of them in Calais."

"Well, maybe back in the 1980s, yes, but they're quite impossible to get hold of these days," said Mark Wallinger.

"Well I never," said Lord Grey.

"I suppose they were the height of chic around Live Aid," said Lord Cümerbund.

"... But a bit naff now," said Lord Grey.

"Oh yes. Bit *too* eighties," said Lord Cümerbund.

"Which of course was the *point*," said Mark Wallinger, "a bit naff, eighties, retro..."

"... but hetero," said Lord Grey, laughing.

"Ha ha yes, a bit groovy vinyl," said Lord Cümerbund, also laughing.

"Plastic *fantastic*," said Lord Grey, snorting wildly.

"Yes," said Mark Wallinger. "So Ethiopians were out, I mean, my dealer wanted ten grand *a piece*. Outrageous! I mean *they* were paying *him* twenty a piece just to get them here, it was pure gravy for him."

"Shocking," said Lord Grey.

"So I thought, well, I can still *call* the piece 'Ethiopian Documentary Crew' even if they're not–"

"You're the Artist," said Lord Cümerbund.

"Absolutely," said Lord Grey.

"– Ethiopian. And of course Somalis look exactly like Ethiopians – lots of Somalis in Ethiopia – it's a bit of a joke border, one of ours I think – let's draw a line from here to that mountain, stick a Union Jack on it... *Anyway*, my chap sourced them from Germany, brought them over through Bruges, sixteen grand the lot."

"Lovely... was that for three?"

"Two, but he threw in some *qat*," said Mark Wallinger.

"Oh *really*?"

"They like it, you know. A sort of bush, that they suck," said Mark Wallinger.

"So what were they like? I never actually saw them..." said Lord Grey.

"Well, funnily enough," said Mark Wallinger, "neither did I."

"Richard," said Lord Cümerbund, nodding.

"Richard," said Lord Grey, nodding.

"I love Richard," said Lord Cümerbund.

"Richard, my fabricator, assembled them in the workshop in Staines, dressed them up, showed them how to use the camera, the boom mike, we went with a lovely old-fashioned analogue tape machine with that *look*..."

"Perfect," said Lord Grey, removing and fondling an eyeball.

"Exactly, perfect... So Richard dressed them and I meant to meet them, brief them myself, but I had to meet someone about the Biennial, and the concept was simple, so I let Richard brief them, their English was very good, I believe one of them had studied economics, and of course Somalia used to be British, well the North... So I never met them... And then the piece never quite *clicked*..."

"Such a disappointment," said Lord Cümerbund.

"And after such a good start in the *Sun*..." said Lord Grey.

"Oh yes, ha ha! 'Has The World Gone Mad?', *great* editorial, and the Littlejohn column, and that cartoon!" said Lord Cümerbund.

"Yes, but *The Times* wouldn't bite," said Mark Wallinger, "*lukewarm approval,* you know, crushing – and not a single letter of outrage or complaint…"

"*No*, really?" said Lord Cümerbund.

"Appalling," said Lord Grey.

"I know, they didn't print one, they wouldn't touch it. And I wrote them *five.*"

"Afraid of the piece," said Lord Cümerbund.

Lord Grey replaced his eyeball and sucked his teeth. "It was too powerful for them."

"And it was an expensive piece to run, you know, I installed it in a suite in the Kensington Hilton, you know, nice reference, the Hilton/journalism/imperialism/Vietnam… American Imperialism, but *black.*"

"Brilliant!"

"Brilliant *touch.*"

"Yes, but expensive. So I wound the piece up." Mark Wallinger sighed. "I wonder what happened to them?"

I felt that I could at last make a useful contribution to the conversation. "I believe," I said, for Dr. Ibrahim Bihi had filled me in on this, "that they were thrown out of the Hotel when you ceased to pay the bills, and found themselves illegal aliens in England. They then tried to claim asylum, as they risk persecution in their increasingly violent and savage failed state of Somalia, exploited, destroyed and then abandoned by British and Italian colonial regimes. They were then put in a Camp, fed alien food which their stomachs' enzymes could not break down and which made them sick. They were forbidden to work. When they protested, they were rehoused on an estate in Scotland, attacked nightly by racists, campaigned against as spongers by the local newspapers, given Social Welfare vouchers instead of cash, for which the local shops were not legally obliged to provide change, and forbidden to move, and forbidden to work. When they fled to London illegally, and worked illegally, they were paid half the minimum wage, housed in portable cabins, then arrested for working illegally, and had their asylum claim turned down for breaking the law. They are now on the run, facing deportation home," I concluded, "where they will be tortured or killed."

Mark Wallinger frowned, and sucked in a sharp breath. "Yes, life is hard, very hard, for a failed piece of conceptual art, one that has almost, but not quite, clicked... Almost... ah, that terrible word, almost." He shook his head. "Poor devils... Perhaps, perhaps if I had pickled them... But no, no regrets, regrets are useless. In any case, pickling was past its vogue... And yet... The sheer cheek, the instant-retro flash, the sly nod to Hirst, could that have swung it? Or put them in a case, yes, and filled the case with flies, yes...! Oh, bitter, bitter my tears of regret..." He started. "Ah! Now there's a thought. Perhaps if I bottled my tears of regret? Yes, in cobalt-blue bottles... Yes, marked 'poison'... Fantastic! Someone poke me in the eye, quick!"

He chucked his brown drink over his shoulder and with oaths asked a passing waiter to poke him in the eye with a forefinger. He caught the tears in his tumbler.

"I'd love to know what those two are doing now..." he said.

"They're over there," I said, pointing.

Mark Wallinger looked toward the stairs, down which came Ibrahim and Zach, looking annoyed after their fruitless search of the Pool Room.

"Bloody scroungers," said Lord Grey.

"I can't stand these Bogus Asylum Seekers," said Lord Cümerbund. "Did you see that piece in the *Mail?* Apparently, they can give you cancer. And the Vaginas of their Women contain Teeth."

Mark Wallinger, setting down his tumbler, sank slowly to the carpet. Quietly and swiftly, he crawled past me on all fours and disappeared into the dark gap between a large brown leather sofa and the wall.

43

Mark Wallinger held them off for some time, using the sofa as a defensive parapet, and swinging the tall, steel column of a standard lamp very effectively at head height. Soon all were focused on the drama.

"Help!" cried Mark Wallinger.

"Ooh, it must be the new Mark Wallinger... *Do* look Robert," said the lady beside me to the man beside her. Zach landed a savage blow just above Mark Wallinger's right ear, with a tripod.

"It's a Matter of Life And Death!" cried Mark Wallinger.

"Excellent title!" cried a short man in short trousers from halfway up the stairs.

"Referencing Powell and Pressburger's *A Matter of Life and Death*," murmured a nearby young man to another nearby young man.

"I knew that," snapped the second young man. "Oooh!" – Dr. Ibrahim Bihi had broken Mark Wallinger's nose – "*Brilliant*."

"Lots of *Zulu* references..."

"Battle of Rorke's Drift... heroic English last stand... lovely..."

The siege ended, as the attackers finally clambered over the back of the sofa, and slew Mark Wallinger.

He weltered briefly in his own gore, and expired.

A lengthy round of generous applause slowly shook the quivering cocktail glasses on the piano an inch to the left.

There was a pause after the applause.

"Weren't they *Welsh*, rather than English, the soldiers at Rorke's Drift?" said the short man in shorts.

"Well, that's exactly his point... The power struggles of Empire were more complex than we give them credit for…" said a tall woman in camouflage gear.

"Astonishing realism… I swear, I saw real emotion, real tears, real blood…"

"A lovely, wry comment on…"

"The post-colonial dilemma of…"

"A minor work, but touching…"

"Just a little naughty, very post-Obama."

"An amusing deconstruction of the Savage Negro Myth."

"A *very* amusing deconstruction of Mark Wallinger."

"Yes, the severed head and bulging eyes…"

"Wonderful."

"And the way he's inserted the, um…"

"Yes, right up his, ah…"

"Cheeky chap…"

Toby Bostique bent over and peered sideways. "All the way up, look, it's almost disappeared."

Lord Grey poked at a nondescript piece of Mark Wallinger with his shoe. "Oh dear," he said. "This is most unfortunate."

"Most," said Lord Cümerbund. "He's not a named artist on the death-exempt list. If the silly ass had given you notice, but…"

"The rules are quite clear," said Lord Grey. "Mark has disqualified himself from the Turner of Turners with that piece, I'm afraid."

"What a pity," said Lord Cümerbund. "I was thinking of buying it… *A Matter of Life and Death*… Still," said Lord Cümerbund, "all is not lost. We have an opportunity to nominate an unknown artist to fill his place. Imagine the drama! A last-minute entrant! A game outsider, naïve, overwhelmed, yet poised to beat the odds! It will put half a million on the viewing figures." He smiled, and closed his eyes.

"But who?" said Lord Grey. "Teddy Tucker-Harvey? Tara Frith-Rees? She has cancer, nice angle… Young Tom Churchill? Little Jemima Freud-Waugh?"

"No. We need a prole. An oik. A skanger, minger, chav or blot. A true outsider. A People's Champion. Someone utterly unconnected with the establishment, someone who's there purely on merit, through sheer hard graft. Someone who wouldn't be seen dead in a place like this."

"How about Jude here?" said Alex.

Lords Cümerbund and Grey studied my home-made clothes, my wind-chapped, sun-burnt visage. They inhaled my strong odour appreciatively.

"Great," they said.

"He has the look," said Lord Cümerbund. "But can he Talk the Talk?"

I cleared my throat and spoke urgently. "I fear I will disappoint you, for I am still searching for an answer to the question, what is art?"

"Perfect!" shouted the Lords. "You're in!"

"Congratulations on being nominated for the Turner of Turners," said Alex, shaking my hand energetically. "I told you I'd get you a job."

44

"What are my chances of winning the prize?" I asked.

They laughed heartily and slapped me on the back.

"He will need a Theory," said Lord Grey.

"Toby!" shouted Lord Cümerbund. Toby Bostique appeared. "This young man has been nominated for the Turner of Turners."

"Oh, congratulations…" said Toby.

Lord Cümerbund kicked him. "Idle chit-chat on your own time, Toby… He needs a Theory. Some basic dichotomies, a paradox, the usual drill. He's naïve, stress that, an outsider, stress that, authentic, *stinks* of authenticity… Press release goes out in an hour. Off you go."

Toby rubbed his shin. He circled me. He tilted my chin up, then down. He pondered.

"Nested Paradoxes," said Toby Bostique. "A hint of the Spiritual. And I've three fresh oppositions."

"Go on," said Lord Cümerbund.

"Well, start off with a couple of golden oldies, don't want to frighten the punters, his work is 'rooted, yet floating', 'firm, yet yielding', 'bleak, yet strangely uplifting'. Then a bit of Marx, bit of po-mo, maybe a reference to Thatcher for the nostalgia market…"

"No," said Lord Cümerbund.

"*Blue Peter*? Sticky-back plastic?" said Toby.

"Yes," said Lord Cümerbund.

"Then we're into 'reinforced, yet invertebrate'…"

"Oh jolly good," said Lord Grey, clapping his tiny hands.

"'Thuggish, yet dainty'…"

"Mmm," said Lord Cümerbund.

"And 'anguished, yet serene'."

"OK, that'll do," said Lord Cümerbund, and kicked Toby Bostique in the left shin. "Back to work!" Toby hopped away.

I tried to visualise my Art from Toby's description of it. I swayed and my head began to hurt. A disturbing flaw in their grand plan occurred to me.

"But I'm not, actually, really, an artist."

They all smiled.

"The true artist always denies his artistry," said Lord Grey, clapping his tiny hands together.

Another flaw occurred to me. "But I don't have any Art!"

They all laughed. "Oh, you'll think of something. The ceremony isn't till tomorrow," said Lord Cümerbund.

"I'll tell security to let you in early," said Lord Grey. "Bring along anything that will help you illustrate your Theory, and chuck it on the floor somewhere. It's a big room."

"But…"

"Ah yes, expenses," said Lord Grey. He reached out a hand to Lord Cümerbund. Lord Cümerbund tapped at his pockets, and shouted "Toby!"

Toby Bostique hopped back. Lord Cümerbund clicked his fingers. Toby handed over his wallet, Lord Cümerbund removed a handful of banknotes and handed them to Lord Grey, who stuffed them in the top pocket of my rabbitskin suit, over my heart.

Before I could think of another flaw, a man with passionate yet authoritative hair arrived, and introduced himself. His upper face was masked in a hard, black plastic. Preoccupied with my new life as an Artist, and distracted by the mask, I missed his name. As the conversation became general, he addressed me.

"What to London brings you? Are there certain things you hope to purchase cheaply, in the winter sales?… Incidentally, Alex, go see Terrence Malick's latest. It's his greatest, or so says the Prince of Wales…"

I told the masked fellow of my life to date, of my Quest for True Love, and for the secrets of my Parentage. At the mention of Pat Sheeran he awoke with a start.

"The morphine... makes me woozy. Half a gram: a doozy. Still, you can't be choosy and it's helping with the pain... Your name isn't Jude? I don't mean to be rude, but Jesus Christ you're screwed. Pat told me on the plane. The Secret of your Birth – and the mystery of your Name..."

A Beeper beeped beneath his fleece.

"Bollocks, got to run, police... Jude, catch you again."

He hugged Alex manfully, and headed out into the foyer. I tried to follow him, but Lord Grey's grip on my elbow was too strong. By the time I had peeled his fingers loose, it was too late.

"Who was that masked man?" I asked Alex.

"That was the Poet Laureate," said Alex. "He is on his way to join the Princes, Harry and William. The Special Protection Unit just paged him the location of the rendezvous."

"But what does a Poet Laureate do?" I said, confused as to why a Poet should require Special Protection.

"It is the Laureate's job to modernise the role of Official Poetry, to capture the State of the Nation under her Majesty Queen Elizabeth the Second, to celebrate the achievements of both Royalty and the People, and to mourn their disasters."

"That does not sound particularly dangerous," I said.

"Pah! He is lucky to be alive. Now, the Queen is safe enough – though he did get athlete's foot off her, after he loaned her his boots to cross a puddle... And Charles is OK... But the Princes..." Alex sighed. "Well, put it this way, his sonnet sequence 'Licking Coke Off Naked Debs With William' left him in rehab. His 'Ode To A Royal Drink-Driver' left him with broken ribs and facial scarring. And the charming *ottava rima* squib, 'A Bungee Jump From A Windsor Castle Tower' came at the cost of fractures to both cheekbones and a depressive fracture of the nose which he was lucky did not pierce the brain."

"How that man suffers for his art," said Lord Grey.

"Where's he off to now?" I said. I could yet find him, and the secret of my birth...

"Oh, it's all top, top secret, for Security reasons. Adventure sport of some kind, I think. Poor bastard."

"An excellent Poet Laureate," said Lord Cümerbund. "Delightfully anti-American."

"Oh, I rather like the Americans," said Lord Grey.

"The Americans are just a bunch of cunts," said Toby Bostique beneath his breath.

This seemed to me an inaccurate generalisation. I had met a number of Americans over the years, in Ireland, not least the excellent fellows of the Brotherhood of Brothers of Mohammed in the Hood, fine Americans all. And of course the splendidly vigorous capitalist, Barney O'Reilly Fitzpatrick McGee. Although, being more Irish than the Irish themselves, he perhaps did not count. But his daughter... yes, Babette was American, I supposed.

I thought about Babette. About our time together, back in Ireland. Helping her to build the Workers' Paradise, in the abandoned Yuppie Estate at the edge of Galway City. Making love each night. And morning.

And after lunch.

And before dinner.

And the way she might look at me. And I at her.

It was almost as though...

Yes, I liked her... a lot... A curious image arose in my head, of Babette and of Angela, though I had never seen them together. I remembered my last sight of her, on the station platform. The Ring she had for some reason given me. I felt my heart speed up. I decided I would tell them about Babette.

"I knew a nice American girl once..." I said. But they did not hear me, for Lord Cümerbund was now loudly attacking the Americans, Lord Grey defending. Toby, emboldened, spoke up in support of his boss.

"I knew a nice American girl..." I said, louder. And broke off again. No good, they were too caught up in their argument. I stepped forward, deep into their gesticulating group, and tried one more time. "I knew..."

"The Americans are just a bunch of cunts."
"Well, that's a rather sweeping thing to say."
"I knew a nice American girl once…"

"I married one: the woman was a dunce."
"Because she was born in the USA?"
"The Americans are just a bunch of cunts."

"They do tend to have these enormous *fronts*."
"Which is rather nice, in its own way."
"I knew a nice American girl once…"

"I don't think much of their intelligence."
"Do you mean… IQ? The CIA?"
"The Americans are just a bunch of cunts."

"Their cinema's an art of bangs and grunts."
"Well, ours is unambitious, cheap, and grey."
"I knew a nice American girl once…"

"We're jealous of their wealth and confidence."
"We love them, fear them, envy their display."
"Although the yanks are just a bunch of cunts."
"I knew a nice American girl, once."

I said it to myself, too softly, I thought, to be heard.

Deep within, I felt the most extraordinary Feeling. Almost as though… the woman I loved… was Babette O'Reilly Fitzpatrick McGee. Absurd.

There was a sudden shriek in my ear as the shrunken Monkey leaped on my back and ruffled my hair. He was still looking for lice. Alex had returned.

"A nice American girl, eh?" he said. "Your One True Love?"
"No," I said.
"Oh," he said.

I shook from my mind these visions of Babette. "My One True Love…" I said, "Is…" And so, softly, I told Alex the tale of my One True Love, the quest she had set me, and my pursuit of her through shipwreck and blizzard.

A silence followed its finish.

"You loved her surface," he eventually said.

"To be sure I loved her surface, but what else may I know?" I asked.

"Her surface is a mere accident of birth," said Alex. "It has nothing to do with her, with who she is."

I had pondered this question often, during the more philosophical moments of my long and arduous Quest for True Love, and so was ready with a reply. "Her surface is an accident, yes," I said, "but so is her talent, her intelligence, her wit, her depression, elation, triumph, despair. We are toyed with by chemistry, genes, and the weather. The woman I love is the woman I see. There can be no purer love."

"Nor stupider."

I acknowledged that he might have a point.

"Describe her surface," he continued.

I described the surface of Angela, from her crimson toenails to the birthmark in the shape of Zanzibar at her hairline.

"My God!" said Alex. "I bought the monkey off her! Oh, she's in London alright…"

My throat dried on the instant and I swallowed and swallowed.

"I do believe I've fucked her," he said. "Lovely girl. Two streets over, green door, up some stairs."

I trembled, and turned, and pushed through the crowd.

She was here, just two streets away…

I strode out the door of the Groucho, into a breeze that was unseasonably warm. The great banks of snow were stirring, slumping, vanishing, the length of Dean Street.

I walked the warming, melting streets in search of my True Love.

As I grew near the building in which Angela dwelt, a trembling took my frame and shook it. My bones shivered in me, and I, in turn, shivered in my rabbitskins, causing the plastic bags beneath the skins to rattle at the creases. Perspiration emerged in a sudden surge from every pore, and made me slick inside my plastic. With every step, small puffs of steam were driven from my neck-hole and out the ends of my jacket-arms and trouser-legs.

I saw the green door.

It was open.

I looked inside.

On the wall was a notice, written by hand:

1st Floor,
New Model,
Caprice,
French

And another beside it in a shaky hand:

Second Floor
New Model
Angela

So, she had become a painter's model. Muse to a thousand artists. Her beauty made immortal, again and again. It seemed right and proper… Above me, the dimly lit stairwell turned and turned again, retreating out of sight.

No, I could not enter; the very air seemed solid. She should not see me so tattered, with no riches, no Million to lay at her feet. I could not bear to feel her gaze upon my face. I recoiled and fled.

I fled I knew not where, round one street's corner, then another, till I stood gasping and steaming beneath a great Canopy. Thrusting out from the wall, it creaked beneath its burden of heaped and melting snow.

THE MODERN THEATRE, said the sign. From it hung two huge masks, so true to life I mistook them at first for the faces of giants. One smiled, one frowned. I surmised it was a warning, that this theatre sometimes put on Good plays, but sometimes Bad.

I threw my head back, to face the sky above the city. A yelp of anguish escaped my throat. Far above me, a cliff of snow overhanging the roof-edge of the Theatre trembled at my yelp, and shuffled further down the slates. Again I yelped; my tiny noise travelled up and out, expiring in the manner of expirations, moving more and more of the world less and less as it went; till it reached the overhanging cliff of snow as the faintest undulation of the air.

The snow cliff shifted; began to slide; accelerated; toppled over the roof's edge; fell.

The canopy above me broke the snow cliff's fall; and the snow cliff's fall, in turn, broke the canopy. Both crashed down all about me in exploding tubes of glass and sheets of plastic.

The Masks lay in the snow before me; I picked one up in my right hand. It was heavy. I picked up the other in my left. It was light. I examined them. The heavy mask looked old and stained and battered, and was of a metal painted to resemble bronze. Stamped inside its chin were the words 'Made in the USA'. The light mask was new and of a plastic made to resemble bronze, and bore the words 'Made in China'.

I pressed the cold metal of the mask in my right hand to my face: My nose shrank back at its touch: My breath issued a jet of steam through its frowning mouth. Crushing it to my face, my features moulded to its cold surface, my perspiration formed a seal. It stuck firm to my numb face.

I slipped the other mask into my bag; turned; and retraced my steps to Angela's building, my identity concealed.

My breath steamed out through the cold metal mouth of the mask. The rims of the mask's eye-holes cut off the edges of my vision, and reminded me that my own eyes were but traps for light to fall in. My hearing, too, seemed somewhat changed by the weight of the mask. How strange are these holes in the face, into which the universe pours water and matter and light and air, and the vibrations of the air, unceasingly, year after year.

Alice in Ordnung

We are born with a destiny. The destiny is bliss,
absolute, sensuous, blissful, carnal knowledge of the
universe, fleshy union with all things.
- Nina FitzPatrick, *Fables of the Irish Intelligentsia*

I have always imagined that paradise will be a kind of
library.
- Jorge Luis Borges

47

I hesitated once more in the doorway.

Well, I was an Artist now; and she was a Model; it was almost as though it was meant to be.

This time I entered.

Made my way to the second floor.

Knocked loudly on the door.

She opened; changed and yet unchanged, familiar and yet unknown. She seemed smaller than I remembered. But it was hard to focus in such low light with my heart beating so fast.

"Angela," I said. She peered round the door at the notice taped to it.

New Model.

Angela

Blonde Beauty

No Rush

"Er, yeah," she said. Her accent, in so brief a time, had gone completely London. I had seen the phenomenon before: some of the Lads, after a weekend in Limerick, would return to the Orphanage with accents so foreign they made the younger Orphans cry.

"You are wearing a mask," she said.

"I am."

"Why are you wearing a mask?" she said.

"I was disfigured in an accident," I said. It was not a lie.

"You remind me of someone I know," she said.

"You remind me of someone I once knew," I said.

We stood looking into each other's eyes. "You have lovely eyes," we said simultaneously.

She laughed. "Come in," she said.

I followed her inside the door, and looked about me, at a tiny room with a sofa and a small television set, switched off.

She put out her hand behind her. I put my big hand in her little hand. She led me across the tiny room and through another door, into a large bedroom. A lamp on a bedside table filtered its dim light through a purple shade.

On the far wall, between the shuttered windows, hung a number of schoolgirls' uniforms and young girls' dresses, as well as a whip, a cane, a pair of handcuffs and a nice straw hat. Angela caught my glance. "A lot of my clients are teachers," she said.

I nodded. It is very natural, this urge to paint what one knows.

"Would you like me to dress up?" she said. "It's extra."

"Understandably," I said. "No, please, don't dress up."

How beautiful her form. She wore a brassiere of swirling black lace, cupping her magnificent Bosom. A translucent triangle of black material framed her mons veneris. Words were newly tattooed just above it, but I could not read them in the dim purple light.

She turned toward the bed, and I watched the swing of her long golden hair across her slender back.

The black strap above.

The black string below.

Who could bear such sorrow? She did not know me; I had failed utterly in my quest to earn a Million Pounds. My face, my present to her, the face I had had crafted to her design, was not enough. I would not declare myself. I would not plead for a love I did not deserve.

Yet I could not bring myself to leave.

"So, what would you like?" she said, and removed her brassiere.

She pulled at the dark silken triangle, and rolled its little strings down her legs, and off.

Her beauty hurt my heart. There could be no finer Model in London. No finer Woman in the World. The curves of her breasts so complex, so subtle, so simple, so perfect. The way her waist dipped in above the hips.

The flare of her hips, the giddy fall of thigh through bend of knee to calf, to the foot's perfection, ending in a display of toes each perfect in its difference.

Perhaps I looked too hard, too much, too intently. Something broke in my brain, and she fell apart, yet without changing. Nothing was different and all was transformed.

I had never before seen a woman in this way, as angles and light, as curve and surface, as no longer one thing indivisible but as a series of tones, curves, colours; intricate, separate, related.

Yet, yes, this was her. Shadow below her breasts, Shade between her thighs. The pale skin and the darker hair, in half-moons and triangles. And I realised that if I could catch, in oil paint on canvas, in pencil on paper, in Photons on Film, these shifting signals, symbols, signs; shade, and shadow; angles and light; I would have saved something of her essence from the wreck of time.

"I would like to Do You in Oils," I said.

"That'll be another thirty," she said. "And another twenty again if you want Positions."

"I will only require the one Position," I said.

She sighed. "Ah, I'll throw in Positions for nothing," she said. "I get cramp with just the one."

"But chiefly just the one," I said, for I did not want her moving once I'd nearly got it right.

"Fine," she shrugged.

"Can you hold it for an hour?"

"You've got ten minutes," she said, plucking Toby Bostique's banknotes from my top pocket. Yes. The Expenses, for my Art. "I've customers waiting."

I had neither brush nor canvas, easel nor paints. Yet as I stood there, I was a Painter; I was an Artist, in the artistic heart of the most artistic city. I painted her curves into memory. I captured her shades.

I saved her shifting signals, symbols, signs.

I moved my mind back and forth, between her Signal and my Image of it, perfecting the outlines of perfection.

And there she stood before me: the image of my image of her. Oh, Angela.

And now, I thought, for the details: and I began to scan her at a different level of intensity.

She moved away.

"You want to take off your clothes? Why don't you lie on the bed? I'll get ready," she said, and left the room.

I was somewhat confused. I had always been under the impression that, traditionally, the Painter remained clothed and upright, and the Model lay unclothed upon the bed. Had I missed something? Or was this a sophisticated modern form of Painting, in which Model and Painter were equally nude? Perhaps it was to set the Model at her ease? Or a form of the Equality of the Sexes I had heard existed in England? Could it perhaps be Oppressive of the male to stand back, fully clothed, and paint…

The more I thought about it, the more fair this new approach to painting seemed to me.

I looked at the double bed. Long days of walking, and nights spent sleeping in my clothes in snow-holes, made the bed almost shimmer with attractiveness. Its sheer *bedness* was so exciting I began to tremble. I put down my bag, and removed and unpeeled my rabbit-skin suit, my plastic-bag suit… Piling them neatly beside the bed, I inhaled my odour appreciatively. Seldom, if ever, had I smelled more overwhelmingly manly.

I lay down on the bed with an involuntary whimper of pleasure. As soft as a mother's embrace, no doubt. I lay on my right side, and reviewed my memory of Angela's curves and shadows. Yes: every inch of her was secure in memory. She would not be lost to time. I buried my masked face in the pillow and closed my eyes. No, I thought, shaking my head emphatically, she will not be lost to time.

When I awoke, Angela was sitting naked in the chair beside the bed, watching me. She glistened as though wet, in the light of the little lamp.

"You looked so peaceful, I let you sleep," she said.

"Oh I'm sorry," I said. "Have I cost you business? Your other customers…?"

"Oh them." She shrugged. "The snow's killed business. I've been stuck here for three days and you're the first one I've seen. Even the maid went home yesterday as soon as a snowplough came through."

"I would imagine you normally have a lot of customers," I said, and felt a pang of envy for all the men who must have painted her before me.

She shrugged again, and stood. Her golden hair glowed softly in the half-dark.

The mask felt heavy and burdensome, and I small and alone behind it.

"You are very beautiful," I said.

"Thanks," she said, and sighed.

She grabbed my Cock and began to Jiggle it.

"Ah, you've lost me now," I said, mystified.

"There, it is hard," she said and unrolled a rubber Sheath down the length of my cock with her other hand. She lay on her back beside me and spread her legs wide. "Put it in me."

"Ah!" I said, realization slowly dawning. And I marvelled at her generosity of spirit, and at the swiftness of her perception. She had seen my great love well up in me and, without recognising me, had recognised that love, responded to that love instantly and generously. I did as she commanded.

As we made love in position after position, I examined closer still the curved, oiled surface of my love. Though the light was dim and it was hard to see her face clearly behind the great curtain of her blonde hair, through the eyeholes of the frozen mask, yet I thought Angela greatly changed. She seemed older, and smaller, and more worn by care than I had remembered her. Sweet sorrow filled me, that I had been unable to save her from worry and harm, from shipwreck, rough travel, uncongenial work.

But sorrow made way rhythmically for joy. Joy rose from the physical deeps, summonsed by the friction of our surfaces. Joy descended from the conscious heights, with the knowledge that I was finally consummating my true love; that the one I loved had set aside the terms of my Quest and welcomed me, accepted me, loved me as I was. Joy vanquished sorrow, vanquished the universe, and I spent myself within her.

As I cried out in an Ecstasy of Ecstasy, and joy transformed my features, my cold and frowning Mask was dislodged and flew off, bouncing from Angela's shoulder to the thin carpet. Angela turned to look upon my face.

As she did so, I made my final shuddering thrust; my hands upon her shoulders; my knees between her parted knees, resting upon her long and golden hair. The suddenness of her turning, and the weight of my kneeling on it gave her hair a mighty tug; it came clear of her head in a mass and fell to the bed, then slithered to the floor. Lying limp beside my icy mask: a wig.

And Angela looked upon my face and I upon hers and my shout played low harmony to her scream.

"Leonardo DiCaprio!" she screamed.

"You are not my Angela!" I shouted.

We disengaged hurriedly.

She put her wig back on, and adjusted it.

"Angela?" she said.

"Yes, I seek the true Angela, of Ireland."

The woman frowned from the shadows of her hair.

"There's a new girl," she said, "an Angela, started working this street recently, Irish alright. She's using the name Caprice..."

"But your sign says Angela," I said, as I looked around for my clothes.

"Today my sign says Angela." She shrugged. "It will say something else tomorrow. Let us say my name is..." She glanced at the young girls' dresses on the far wall. "... Alice. A lot of clients like to call me Alice. You can call me Alice..."

"So she's on the first floor? Caprice?" Unsure what to do with the frowning mask, I put it in my bag alongside its smiling companion.

"The Irish girl? Yeah, she was. But she's moved a few doors down the street. The Caprice below is now a girl from Nigeria."

I found myself shivering with post-coital and emotional shock. If she was not my True Love, what did that mean? I wrestled with the philosophical implications. I could know nothing of the world but through my senses; and my senses had been utterly convinced, at the time, that I was consummating my union with Angela, my True Love. Indeed, had I died at the Moment of Consummation, my final experience and memory would have been of the ecstatic certainty of our glorious Union. This new information could not go back in time and erase that glorious Certainty, though it could certainly play merry hell with it from the present moment on; therefore, that glorious Certainty in its magnificent Moment still existed, though I may be moving away from it now into the uncertain future; all moments, all memories, all truths, were potentially subject to such revision.

Yes, I had indeed consummated my Union with my True Love. Greatly relieved, I thanked Alice fervently for her generous contribution to the emotional and spiritual highlight of my young life.

"You're welcome," said Alice, helping me remove the rubber sheath.

"I certainly am," I agreed.

She began to stroke my cock and balls. "Listen Leo, if you'd like to…"

"No, thank you," I said. I began to dress hastily. I wondered if I should relieve her of her misconception that I was the famous American film star Leonardo DiCaprio. But it seemed too complicated, and I was eager to find the true Angela.

She got up, and left the room. "Well, that was on me," she said, coming back into the room with her clothes.

"It was," I agreed, "though there was that interlude where you were on me. And also the sideways stuff."

"No, it was on me in the sense that I won't charge you for it," said Alice, handing me back Toby Bostique's banknotes. "I couldn't charge the hero of my favourite film for sex." She added coyly, "You know I'm in the movies too."

"You were charging for Sex?" I said, astounded.

Alice slipped into new white knickers, and then an old-fashioned dress that made her look like a Victorian schoolgirl. Her head popped out the hole. She reached over to me and affectionately stroked my furrowed forehead with an oiled finger. "What did you think I was doing?"

I told her that I had thought her an Artist's model.

When she had got over her surprise, Alice explained the nature of her business, the meaning of the term Model in such a context, and the economics of the sex industry in London, with particular reference to the negative effect on pricing power of the new Eastern European sex workers and their putting out of business of the native English sex worker.

"They'll do anything," explained Alice. "For peanuts."

"Like elephants," I said, nodding absently.

Alice frowned. "Well, I've seen one suck off an Alsatian for eighty, but I think they draw the line at elephants. But if that's what you're into, I've got a friend who works in catering at London Zoo… Do you know what time it is? I've got to make a phone call."

I had no idea.

She rummaged in a bedside drawer and found a source of time. "Oh, shit. Great talking to you, but I've got to run. I've a Regular to do, before the Film." She pulled on transparent high-heeled shoes. "Just pull the door closed on your way out."

She ran.

I finished dressing in my rabbit-skin suit, and lay back on the bed, my thoughts drifting in post-coital bliss. The downstairs door slammed.

I shot erect. She had not told me where I could find my True Love. The Real Angela. I knew only that she was somewhere on this street…

I'd forgotten to put on my under-suit of plastic bags. I hesitated over the pile on the floor. Some, biodegradable, had begun to disintegrate. I sniffed them. No…

I left the degraded remains in a pile in the corner, and ran off after Alice.

Oh, how blind had I been? It was there all the time, written in felt-tipped pen on fluorescent pink card, that she was a Model. Not Real. Not Real…

A snow plough had cleared the road, and lorries now moved slowly past, but the pavement was still caked with melting snow and ice. Alice seemed remarkably confident in her see-through high heels. She hopped over heaps of slush, all the time muttering, "I'm late! I'm late!"

She stopped just a little way down the street at a locked wooden door, and pounded on it with her little fists.

The door did not open.

"I shall be too late!" she cried. She looked all about her, and ran to a much smaller metal trapdoor a few yards away, set flat into the pavement. It was open.

A couple of delivery men stood by their lorry, with their backs to us, lighting cigarettes.

She hopped through the trapdoor and vanished down a steel chute or tunnel.

Not pausing to think, I stepped into the trap.

The tunnel went straight on for some way, and then dipped suddenly down, so suddenly that I had not a moment to think about stopping myself before I found myself falling down a very deep well.

I fell very slowly, for the steel chute down which I slid was barely my width, and my rabbits' fur was compressed tight to my body by the tight tunnel.

At length I came to land upon a burlap sack of sand.

Where was she?

There she was.

Alice's little white dress bobbed away into the darkness. Vanished.

I stood, and looked about me.

How would I get out of here? The chute was unclimbable, and I could see no door.

Hard to see properly, in the odd, silvery light.

What were those?

Columns, of…?

I stretched my hands out, to left and right. My fingertips touched cool curves of metal on both sides of a narrow aisle… curve after curve, like silvery pillars packed together to make high walls. A framework of slim, steel beams supported the pillars, like scaffolding.

From the far darkness, sudden wild, animal cries. They shivered the silvery pillars beneath my finger tips, died away to a gasp. A moan. Silence.

I walked, cautiously, ahead. What was that?

A human voice. Not hers. Around a corner.

No doubt the owners of the voices would be kindly. Yet I shivered in my rabbit suit, and felt a strange anxiety.

I took a deep breath, and stepped around the corner.

In the dim silver light, a small man talked softly to himself in the hum.

"Hello," I said. He leapt a foot, which made me leap a foot.

"Could you tell me where I am?" I said.

The man turned to face me and I saw, by some misalignment of our faces, that he could not see me. "Why, you are in the Great Library," he said softly.

"And you are…?" I asked.

"I would prefer not to be categorised or filed. But if I must be described in a single word, that word might be 'Librarian'."

"A blind librarian," I said.

"The finest kind. All great librarians go blind. Do you like the new system?"

I looked around. There was no sign of Alice. Hmmm… It was a funny-looking library. "Where are the books?" I said.

"Here," he said, his blind hands stroking a smooth silver curve beside him. "Oh, the Book is constantly changing,"

It looked suspiciously familiar. Smooth, curved steel – or was it aluminium – and that symbol, embossed on the metal… not the harp of the government of the Irish Republic, but its mirror image… a far older symbol, long preceding the Republic…

"It doesn't look like a book," I pointed out.

"No," he agreed. "But the Form does not matter. Only the Content."

The cylinders of curved silver, stacked in immense pillars rising to the ceiling, were aluminium kegs of Guinness. The National Drink of Ireland. The Black Holy Water in which all our great writers were Christened.

The Librarian slapped a keg, and it rang. "The Glory that was Rome! Plautus!" He slapped the one beside it. "Horace!" Another, higher. "Virgil! Under the old system, there was little demand in recent times for these great products of the human mind. But repackaged thus, with New Technology, delivered down Pipes, demand is insatiable!" At the far end of the aisle, a red light flashed, and a beeper sounded. "Dear God, they have exhausted Sappho of Lesbos! Again! Already!" With difficulty, from a high shelf, he hauled down a keg, breaking its fall with a fat burlap sack. The impact drove a few fragments of cork out through a small rip in the bag.

"Are you not, perhaps, misinterpreting Reality through a faulty Metaphor?" I asked.

The blind Librarian shrugged. "Is there any other way of being human?" It was a fair point. He began rolling the keg of Guinness down the aisle, gasping.

"Here, let me help you," I said, and we rolled the keg towards the beeping light.

At the end of the aisle were a large number of kegs, attached to pipes leading up through the ceiling.

The assembly attached to one keg flashed and beeped. Together we unscrewed the old and screwed in the new.

As we finished, a second keg gurgled, and its meters began to beep and flash. He touched his way to the beeping keg.

"Beowulf! Their thirst for great literature is insatiable!"

I felt a discomfort in the middle of my forehead, where Alice had gently touched me. I hoped I was not getting a Spot...

"How do I get out of here?" I said.

"Why would you ever want to leave the comfort of the Library?"

"Hmmm," I said. "What happens if you don't change the keg?"

"Eh?"

"If you didn't do it, wouldn't someone else have to come down here?"

"Perhaps... perhaps..."

"Don't change that keg."

"What? But they thirst for…"

"Let them thirst," I said.

I studied my Face, by the flashing red light, in the distorted curve of a barrel of Guinness. Yes, there was something in my face I didn't like the look of. It revealed something repressed, deep within.

I looked closer.

Oh, I would have to do something about that.

I looked around me for a Biro.

Yes. László Bíró's disposable plastic ballpoint pen had never been improved upon, for the task I had in mind.

There, in the very centre of my forehead. A blocked pore, and behind it a tremendous buildup of I didn't know what. And getting worse all the time.

A Biro's inner, ink-filled plastic tube is your only man for removing a blackhead. The soft plastic – firm yet flexible – of the tube's open end spreads the pressure evenly in a ring around the offending pore, and eases the obstruction free, up into the tube, without breaking the delicate capillaries of the face.

Above us, a trapdoor slammed open in the ceiling and a cage began to descend. Excellent. I put my arm around the Librarian, and led him away. He was as light and bony as a cat, or bird. Beyond the Librarian, the descending cage came to a halt; a man emerged blinking, half blind in the dark. There was something wrong with his right hand. He began changing barrels, left-handed, oblivious to us, as the blind Librarian talked on. "Of course after the Great Depression, the Novel had a nervous breakdown…"

The middle of my forehead began to itch. I scratched, but the itch grew worse.

"Why do you despair?" said the blind Librarian.

"I need a Biro. Urgently."

"I have Inspired you! Perhaps you are the One who will fill the final gap." He pointed blindly to a narrow space at the base of the pillars. "The Novel that describes a free and independent Ireland, as she truly is in the new Millennium, remains to be written."

I crouched lower. True, there was a gap or hole.

I leaned closer, and saw that the slim steel frames, supporting the pillars of kegs, were neatly labelled, as though they were indeed former Library shelves. Glued to them, every few feet, were yellowing cards on which were neatly typed, by an ancient manual typewriter, the words and numbers of a filing system. Embossed on each card, too, were patterns of dots. He ran his fingertip delicately across a card and smiled, and I realised that he was reading the bumps with his skin. Beside the card for 21st-Century Irish Literature, no keg. Just an awkward, asymmetric space, trapped in a triangle between England, America, and Europe. Hmmm. And there were so many full kegs in the many towering, half-toppled pillars marked 20th-Century Irish Literature that they'd crowded into the new millennium's space, leaned over it, shadowed it. I peered closer.

"It would have to be an odd shape," I suggested.

"It would," he replied. "Form mirroring Content."

"A bit funny-looking," I said.

"The insightful words of a True Novelist!" he said. "Yes, it would have to be disguised as a comedy. So, are you the Special One, sent to fill Irish Literature's Hole?"

"I am not," I said firmly. True, a good number of Government Inspectors had travelled to the Orphanage on several occasions and made energetic attempts to label me Special, but I had evaded them all each time, and hid out in Ballylusky Bog till they were gone.

"Then why do you so urgently look for a pen?" said the blind Librarian.

Would he think the less of me, if he knew of my disfiguring Spot? As I hesitated, Alice ran silently from the darkness beyond the blind Librarian, past the labouring man, into the cage.

Feck.

"I must go," I said, and took a step, but the blind Librarian halted me, gripping my elbow with fingers like twigs.

"What is your buried childhood Trauma," said the blind Librarian, "that drives you on?"

A memory lurched up, almost as though I had a buried childhood trauma. Luckily, I knew I did not have a buried childhood trauma, so I quickly knocked the memory back down again without bothering to look at it.

Ooh, I felt a little queasy.

"I have no buried childhood Trauma," I said firmly. Then for some odd reason I smelt in memory the perfume of Ethel the Orphanage Cook, and was afflicted briefly by a vision of… I gave myself a slap across the jaw. Ah, that did the trick.

The cage began to rise.

The labouring man turned in the distance, shouted, and ran towards the cage. But it had risen high above him toward the light, and now Alice leapt up with great grace and a flash of her knickers, and out through the trapdoor.

The floor of the cage sealed the gap, and cut off the light and noise.

The labouring man cursed in darkness.

My forehead bulged, throbbing, hot.

"You do not understand the depth of the crisis," said the Librarian.

I gently corrected his misapprehension. "I do not give a shite about the crisis," I said. But he must not have believed me, for he did not let go my elbow.

"Ours is the first generation in three hundred years," said the Librarian, "in which the Novel has made no progress. Indeed, it has retreated. And a novel which is not novel is not a novel."

"This crisis has nothing to do with me," I said.

"A crisis that does not recognise it is a crisis, is in crisis," said the Blind Librarian.

The man in the distance summonsed the cage; the trapdoor poured down light and sound. I had to get out of here.

I took another step towards the way out, almost toppling the Librarian. He gasped, "Here, then, take this on your Quest: the world's finest pen. Solid gold."

It was a lovely pen, but, lacking an open-ended plastic refill tube, not of the slightest use in removing a blackhead.

"No, thank you," I said. "A simple Biro is all I require."

"You have passed the final test!" he cried. "And so…. here."

He pushed something else, something hard and cold, into my hand.

I brought it up to my face.

Stared into its face.

A large gold watch.

"There you are. And now you must run," said the blind Librarian. He released his grip. "For you are late."

"Late?"

Its ticking ran up through my little bones and agitated my heart.

"The door has been revealed to you."

And he was gone.

The ticking of the watch was very loud and my heart sped up to meet its speed: a tick and a tock each second, one hundred and twenty per minute, so few minutes in a day, how soon life would be gone. I had never had a watch. I had never felt like this. My teeth clattered together as though I were cold in my rabbitskin suit.

"I'm late," I said. "I'm late." And I ran.

The cage was rising as I reached it, the man within looking up at the light.

I jumped high, caught the edge of the rising platform, and was borne aloft, dangling.

I swung my feet up, into a loop of cables beneath the platform. My weight on the cables unplugged something, and sparks flew about my ankles. There was a smell of hot metal and overheating plastic. I swore as quietly as a man can swear, slipped my feet free again, and hung full length.

The man standing invisible above me seemed not to have noticed.

I prepared to swing myself aboard the platform. Too early, and he would have time to hurl me to my doom. Too late, and my fingers would be crushed…

But in the event, the platform juddered to a halt a few feet short of the top. The man swore as loudly as a man can swear, and climbed out. His accent was oddly familiar.

Once he'd gone, I swung a leg up, and over, and clambered aboard the platform.

I lay there, squinting up at the brightness, till I had recovered my sight.

My breath.

My courage.

I stood, and hauled myself up through the trapdoor and into a warm, luminous space. My fur gleamed, clean and bright. All around me was a great noise, AUM... AUM... A profound and sacred noise, strangely familiar.

Voices, rising and falling, in the great collective wisdom of a thousand-throated conversation.

It calmed me.

Looking around, I saw walls covered with inscribed mirrors advertising whiskeys.

A few highly polished kegs of Guinness, purely ornamental by the look of them.

Some half-familiar signs so authentically Celtic in their ornate antique calligraphy and obsolete accenture that it was impossible to read them.

It did not help that my view was half-obscured by a dangling bicycle.

I had emerged behind the bar of a pub of almost excessive Irishness.

I sniffed. The warm, mellow, sweet smell of wood soaked for decades in porter.

There. The man, his back to me. He worked in frantic haste behind the bar. Cleaning, stacking, pulling, spilling, wiping with his twisted right hand. As he worked, he muttered something that sounded like "Alice in Ordnung" again and again. I stepped up behind him, and waited to catch his attention. I did not wish to startle him, for he seemed in a state of high tension.

He stood on his toes, to apply black boot polish to the tyres of the dangling bicycle.

We were both standing at the very end of an immensely long wooden bar counter that curved gently away into the distance. A small sign hung on the Guinness tap, saying... I turned it round, and tried to disentangle the imitation Book of Kells lettering... If that angel's open mouth was an O... those cow's udders a U, the wooden table in profile a T... that dog's arsehole was another O, and the man leaning over attempting to suck his own... Ah!

OUT OF ORDER.

That explained why this end was so quiet, and the bar stools at the other side of the counter empty.

My view down the full length of the bar was blocked by something large and white. Several feet high and several feet wide, featureless and flat-sided, it sat the width of the counter.

From beyond it, further down the bar, came a roar of conversation, and the clatter and chink of glassware and coins, of customers and other barmen, but we seemed insulated from it all down our quiet dark end.

The pub's warmth, after the cool of the cellar, made the Spot on my forehead hot and itchy. Reaching up to scratch it, I tickled my nose with the fur of my sleeve.

I sneezed into the Barman's ear.

"Sorry," I said, when he had climbed back down from the counter top.

"*Mein Gott*," said the Barman, "a talking rabbit."

He cleared his throat.

"And sure what will you be having, yourself, there, at all at all?" he said in an entirely different voice, his rheumy red eyes blearing down at me from beneath two thick black bushes of eyebrows encrusted with the petrified froth of old Guinness, like two blackthorn bushes on a hillside, their hard blackness softened with the fleece of passing sheep.

"Stop it," says I. "You're scaring me."

"And how is that, now?"

"With an excessive Irishness which is overwhelming in nature."

"Bedad, and I'm sorry," he said, relenting the relentlessness of his Gaelicism. "But we pride ourselves here on the excessiveness of our Irishness; our training in Rotterdam, Rostock and Oslo is lengthy and rigorous; we are exposed, day and night, to works, in both English and Irish, by Brian Ó Nualláin, Myles na gCopaleen, Flann O'Brien, An Broc, George Knowall, and Brother Barnabas, the whole of it tuning us to a high lyrical pitch of Gaelicism, before we are let near a pint." He reached up to polish the iron pump of the antique bicycle. "I myself am originally from Schleswig-Holstein, but a miasma of Irishness has permeated me, till I am scarcely distinguishable from an inhabitant of the Dingle Peninsula. Accept my apologies, for I had not realised you were one of our own. Great is my shame in the not-recognition of it. What'll you be having? It is on the House."

"I need a Biro," I said.

"We only have Guinness. And we don't even have that."

The pipe to the Guinness tap gurgled. The Barman gave the lever a squeeze. After a pause, Guinness poured into the splash tray.

"Tell a lie, we do." The Barman cut off the tap, and removed the sign. The blind Librarian had evidently attached the new barrel.

I assembled the courage to make a shameful confession. "Though Tipperary-born and, quite possibly, bred," I said, "I have – through an unfortunate series of mishaps and catastrophes – never drunk Guinness."

The Barman stared at me. He began to pull a pint, without his gaze leaving mine.

"It is a weakness in me, I know," I added.

"Never?" he said at last. "You astound and faintly disgust me. Are you an Irishman at all?"

I assured him that I was. But my Irishness seemed to me now a weak thing compared to the magnificence of his.

"Get around to the other side of that counter," he said.

Shamed, I did not even lift the hinged flap at the end of the bar, but ducked under it, and made my way around to an empty barstool, near the large white obstruction on the counter.

I leaned closer and examined it, to hide my blushing cheeks. Stacks and stacks of sheets of paper. Some scribbled on. Some blank. From deep within the stacks came the noise of a man slowly sawing wet timber.

"Why the pen?" said the Barman.

I put my palm to my forehead, and sighed. "Something has built up inside me," I said, "and must be released."

"What?" said the Barman, picking up a pint glass. He leaned forward over the bar, and looked me in the right eye.

"I won't know till I see it," I said. The Spot throbbed. "It lies deep within."

"Spoken like a true Writer," said the Barman. He polished the glass.

Ah for feck's sake, I thought. Is there one who understands me? The sound of a man sawing wood increased in volume.

"Oh, if you want to be a Great Irish Writer, then you need a Pint," said the Barman, topping up the one he'd left to settle.

"I need," I said firmly, "a Biro."

"You... need... a... Pint."

He slid my fresh pint towards me along the wooden bar counter. It stopped by my strong right hand, its cream head rocking, too thick to spill.

I took the cool, bedewed glass in my right hand, and sipped the cream foam and, bursting through it, the black. I tasted its tar and malt on my tongue, and swallowed.

The Barman got up on tiptoes to knock dust off the cracked leather saddle of the suspended bicycle, and there was, for a moment, the faintest smell of nun.

I swallowed again.

"Fascinating," I said, pushing the pint of Guinness away from me, and with it the threat of becoming a Great Irish Writer. "I am thirsty, but not for that. Could you bring me, instead, a pint of milk? Full cream, unpasteurised, warm from the udder?"

The Barman sighed, and headed off to a storeroom, in the dark at the counter's end. As he walked away, I noticed that his trousers were tight on the right buttock, yet baggy over the left. An odd sight. He gave a tug sideways on the loose cloth as he disappeared into the store.

54

I leaned around the great pile of paper, in search of the source of the sawing sound, and perhaps a Biro.

A man, on a barstool, snoring.

Fresh white sheets of paper fanned out in front of him, in a great arc along the curving counter. He lay slumped across them.

I leaned over him.

Something was moving on the counter beyond him. It scuttled back and forth, back and forth, across the great spray of white pages.

His right hand, bearing a Biro, writing, writing, all the while.

I gave him a poke in the armpit with my finger, and he jerked erect.

His eyes snapped open, and the snoring ceased.

"May I borrow your Biro?" I said.

"Can't you see I'm WRITING?" roared the man.

He closed his eyes, and fell asleep again, while the pen in his bold right hand raced back and forth across the page.

"When you're finished, so," I said, and gave my forehead a cautious rub. The Spot was growing, and bulged uncomfortably. No point being led to Angela in a disfigured condition. This would have to be dealt with first.

The Barman returned with a pint of white milk in his crippled right hand.

I sipped the cream foam and bursting through it, the white.

"Would you have a Biro?" I said.

"No." The Barman nodded at the sleeper. "He is the Writer in our family."

The drone-note of the great AUM suddenly doubled in volume, and I jumped.

"It's only my brother, snoring."

I turned back to the unconscious writer.

"Isn't he a lovely sight?" said the Barman.

I couldn't honestly say that he was.

"He's dreaming now," said the Barman. "And what do you think he's dreaming about?"

"Nobody can guess that," I said.

"Why, about you!" exclaimed the Barman, clapping his hands. "And if he left off dreaming about you, where do you suppose you'd be?"

"Where I am now, of course," I said.

"Not you!" the Barman retorted. "You'd be nowhere. Why you're only a sort of thing in his dream."

I stared at the slumped figure, asleep, and writing all the while.

"How do you know what he's dreaming?" I said.

"We are Siamese twins," said the Barman. I looked at him. "Former Siamese twins," he amended. I looked at his brother, and back at him. They scarcely looked the same species.

The Barman put on the kettle behind the bar. "Until recently, I was translating my brother's mighty work into German," he said.

"A hard task."

"Harder than you know," he said. I stared at the Barman's crippled right hand. "German words are long," he said, "and my brother writes fast. Now I am merely a Barman. But I am proud of his success."

Then the huge white object on the bar was a Book being born. I had never seen a live one, in the wild.

"So people do still write them," I said. I wondered what would become of it, in this Modern Age.

"Yes, he is a Great Irish Novelist now. But we both started out as Translators." The Barman nodded at his brother. "He translated *Finnegans Wake* into English."

The brother groaned in his sleep.

I acknowledged the immensity of the feat with a nod. Several of the Lads in the Orphanage had lost a year of their lives in attempting to read that same book, after hearing it contained filth. Kevin McGee had never been the same after.

The kettle clicked off. The Barman scooped some coffee into a cone of filter paper that sat in the mouth of a glass jug. He poured boiling water onto the coffee. Some splashed his sleeping brother's resting left hand. "Sorry," said the Barman, and did it again.

The Novelist awoke. He blinked and rubbed his eyes with the back of his left hand.

"Seriously, though," I said. "May I borrow your Biro?"

The novelist gave his eyes a last rub, and grabbed the soft pale fur at my throat.

It was not the reaction I had hoped for. My left eyelid began to twitch in time with the dripping of the coffee into the jug.

"Look at my Nose," he said. "The little hairs emerging from my nostrils, for lack of a woman's love."

I stared up the writer's nose.

He grabbed tighter on the fur at my throat, and pulled me closer.

"Look," he said, "at the gaping pores, opened by the steam from the countless cups of coffee slowly going cold beneath it, on this counter, while I write here, right here, all the while…"

The softness of my fur seemed suddenly to register in his consciousness.

"My God, I love your suit," he said, loosening his grip in order to caress the lapels. "Issey Miyake?"

Was he my yakky? "No," I said. "He is my rabbity."

"Pah!" said the novelist. He grabbed my throat once more. "I used to be a hep-cat, in the jazz scene in Congleton." As he spoke his bold right hand wrote on. "Played everywhere, Wilmslow, Runcorn, even Macclesfield. Oh I was known the length and breadth of Cheshire."

"You were born in Cheshire? Raised?"

"Yes. Yes."

"But you seem Irish. Your brother said…"

"I am Irish."

"But…" I frowned. "Your brother is German."

The Novelist shrugged.

"And was born in Schleswig-Holstein," I pressed. This conversation was giving me the most fearful throb in my Spot. Without thinking, I gave it a vigorous rub, and a bolt of pain went through my forehead and out the back of my skull.

"There is probably a Gene for it," said the novelist.

"But you were Siamese twins!" I said, blinking the tears from my eyes.

"Non-identical Siamese twins," said the novelist. "Born in different countries. Speaking different languages…"

I looked from one to other.

"Extremely non-identical," said the Barman, frothing at the hatch. The warm milk rose in the steel jug, and he began the assembly of an intricate milky coffee.

The novelist nodded. "It is extremely rare." He sighed a long sigh. "But we were talking of Jazz. The *Cheshire Jazz Gazette* said I played the trumpet like Thelonious Monk."

I frowned, distracted from my own problems. "Thelonious Monk played the piano," I said.

"Sadly, yes. Now I am a novelist," said the Novelist. "Attempting to write the Ultimate Novel."

"As is every other novelist," murmured the Barman, and pushed the frothy coffee under the Novelist's nose.

"Isn't there already an Ultimate Novel?" I said.

"It's a century out of date," said the Novelist. "Each age needs its own."

"What is it?" I said.

"*Ulysses*, by James Joyce. You are familiar with it?"

"Oh, indeed I am. Sure, didn't they name the largest car ferry in the world after it. It sank beneath me, in the Irish Sea."

"But have you read the actual book?"

"Ah…" I said. "No." I glanced down into the darkness of my bag, hoping the Salmon of Knowledge would give me a dig out. The Salmon cleared its throat.

"Never did I read such tosh," it said. "As for the first two chapters we will let them pass, but the 3rd 4th 5th 6th – merely the scratching of pimples on the body of the bootboy at Claridge's."

Virginia Woolf on *Ulysses*, in a letter to Lytton Strachey, 24 April, 1922

Hmm. That hadn't really helped. I scratched my Spot without thinking.

"What is it about?" I asked, when the pain had abated.

"Ah…" said the Novelist. He scratched his right buttock. "Well… The book describes the twenty-four hours of a day with such thoroughness that it, itself, fully occupies those twenty-four hours. It is a book designed not to depict life, but to *replace* life. You could live entirely in the Dublin of June 16th 1904, if you wished, merely by rereading *Ulysses* every day. While insomniacs may use *Finnegans Wake* as a replacement for their lost dreams… There has been, since, no need for another book."

"Yet you are writing a book," I said. I eyed his Biro as it wrote.

The Novelist leaned closer and whispered, "I have surpassed it… Joyce caught a full human day, at one second per second. But it took him seven years of writing and rewriting and at the end of it what had he but a single day. I," he paused, but his right hand wrote on, "have trained myself, by methods Western and Eastern, to write a Novel that fictionalises life, at a rate of one second per second, day and night, unceasing. As I sleep, my loyal hand writes on, in the language of dreams. As I wake, my prose returns to the conscious and prosaic world… Nothing is lost to time."

"Mighty," I said. "What is it about?"

The Novelist scratched his left buttock for some considerable time.

I noted a certain bagginess to the pant-cloth.

"Like any novel worth a shite," he said, eventually, "it is an attempt to replace this universe with another, better universe."

He lifted his cup of coffee from the saucer left-handed, and the bubbles fizzed and burst in the milky froth as the pressure waves passed through them. "As a novelist, I want to replace this cup of coffee with another, better cup of coffee."

The Barman, unseen, frowned at his brother from behind the bar.

"No, really, though," I said. "What's it *about?*"

"Here, have a look." The former jazz-playing hep-cat from Congleton passed me a pile of pages as heavy as a man's head.

I prepared myself mentally for the ordeal of reading a Modern Novel.

He grinned, showing his strong white teeth.

And as I read the words, the curves of the dark marks hooked me and hauled me in to the world of the word.

I grew less and less aware of the black marks; soon the black marks were converted, instantly, on arrival, into vivid images in my head. My conscious mind, busy with these images, now paid no more conscious attention to the flow of black marks than it did to the flow of air as I breathed.

And out beyond the world of the page, the previously solid world, in its turn, began to grow flat; and lose its colour; and fade away.

First the pub fittings at the edge of my vision gradually vanished; then the wooden counter of the bar; then the Congleton jazz man began to disappear.

First his arm vanished; and then his body; and then his hair, his chin, his ears, his nose… Soon nothing remained of the Cheshire Cat but his grin, floating in the air in front of me.

After a while, even that faded and was gone.

55

When I reemerged from the Book, some time had passed.

"So, what do you think?" said the Novelist.

"There seem an awful lot of allusions to the works of James Joyce and Samuel Beckett," I said. "Also to *Alice in Wonderland*, and some German fellow. Would you not be better off writing an Original Story?" For I had heard that Originality was a virtue in Fiction.

"The very idea!" sniffed the Novelist. "As if such a thing were desirable, or possible! What is this pub made from?"

I looked about me. "The gutted interiors of previous pubs."

He nodded. "Any novel is, likewise, made from the gutted interiors of previous novels."

"But... but... how do we get new stories, so?"

"Because the novel is a Linear Accelerator!" said the Novelist. "Yes, it merely smashes together the existing Elements of Fiction, to release their hidden energies. But in doing so, it inevitably creates new Elements, never seen before."

Ah, turning Lead into Gold... Or Gold into... An exquisite Thought occurred to me. "A Literary Novel can be sold for money, can it not?"

His right hand hesitated for a second, and wrote on. "Technically," said the Novelist.

Oh yes, I thought. There was after all more than one way to wield a Biro. "Good," I said. "I need to make a million, to win my True Love."

When he had stopped laughing, I said, "I could not, then, expect a million?"

"No," he said. "The average advance for an English Literary Novel is about five grand."

"Five pounds?" It did not seem grand to me.

"Five *grand*. Five thousand pounds."

"Oh," I said, relieved. So I would only have to write... two hundred literary novels to make a million pounds and win Angela's heart. I pondered this. "And how long do they take to write?"

"About two years, on average. Though an ambitious one will often take twice as long. And a very ambitious one longer again."

I re-pondered. It did not look good.

"To summarise," said the Barman helpfully, "it would take you a minimum of four centuries' constant work to earn a million pounds as a literary novelist. And it could easily take you a thousand years."

"And you would earn between ten and thirty times as much working as a barman," said the Novelist.

Well, that was out, then. Indeed, this fellow seemed to have chosen the most extraordinarily unrewarding and difficult route through life. "Is a Cheshire childhood not a drawback for an Irish Novelist?" I said.

He shrugged. "The Ultimate Irish Novel will turn out to be the Ultimate English Novel. England is Ireland in a mirror."

"Or, contrariwise," said the Barman, "Ireland is England through the looking-glass."

"Each defines itself as the reverse of the other," said the Novelist, "both blind to half their single history."

"They are in fact," said the Barman, heading over to the coffee machine, "identical twins, standing back to back."

My Spot was killing me. I wondered would I have to fight them both, to win the Biro. Perhaps the Barman would be going off duty soon... Meanwhile, keep them talking.

"You are entirely sure you were Siamese twins?" I said.

"Yes," said the Novelist. "Conjoined, if you prefer."

I studied the Novelist. "Where were you joined?"

"The buttocks," said the Novelist. "Oh, we didn't know whether we were coming or going. Yet it had its compensations."

"How happy we were as children," sighed the Barman, returning from the coffee machine, "dancing cheek to cheek!" He placed a fresh coffee in front of his brother. "But we wished to be Individuals; and so we had to part."

"We had our first argument over the division of the buttocks," said the Novelist. "I got custody of the Right buttock."

"Of course," said the Barman, "pointing contrariwise, I also got custody of the Right buttock."

"And so we both entered the world of the Individual," said the Novelist, "both of us with a Right buttock, neither with a left buttock; still fundamentally identical."

"Ah," said the Barman with a sigh. "To the man with one buttock, every Stool is a hard Stool."

The novelist nodded. "Many times we have repeated to ourselves the words of the old lady in Voltaire's novel, *Candide*: 'I have grown old in misery and disgrace, living with only one buttock, and having in perpetual remembrance that I am a Pope's daughter.'"

"Of course," said the Barman, "neither of us was a Pope's daughter."

"Indeed," said the Novelist, "it was the total lack of so much as a single full sentence in all of world literature with which I could identify that drove me to become a writer. I would write the book I wished to read."

"I once read a book containing a character with whom I could identify," I said. "It was a voluptuous feeling, all right."

"What drove you to identify with the character?" said the Novelist keenly. "The genius of the prose? The subtlety of the psychological observation? The sensation that you were being vouchsafed cosmic truths?"

"Er, it was more that we had the same name," I said. "Jude."

"Ah! *Jude the Obscure*!" the Barman cried. "Thomas Hardy!"

"No. Jude the Entropic Man," I said. "Marvel Comics."

The Lads in the Orphanage had been mad about the ancient, yellowing comics they had found under Brother Quirke's bed after his death, and delighted to discover a fellow with my name, turning men to dust with a touch. It had brought me great status and prestige, and, for months after, the younger Orphans ran away from me screaming.

"Jude battles The Thing," I explained.*

The Novelist stared at me. The Barman sighed.

At the far end of the bar, dazzling lights came on. There was a distant sense of urgency, movement, a hush. Something was about to Happen.

"They're Shooting my Book," said the Novelist, in explanation.

I shivered in my furs. They shoot books in England?

The Barman noted my confusion. "Filming his novel," he explained. "As fast as he can write it. They await only the final scenes."

And indeed, as he spoke, a young fellow ran up to us out of the darkness, grabbed a stack of pages, and ran off again towards the bright lights.

"It will be the Ultimate Film," said the Novelist, grabbing my arm with his left hand. "Even better than the film of my last book... you may have seen it, Tim Burton directed... Have you read Kafka?"

I shook my head.

"Well, I translated Franz Kafka's most extraordinary book into English," said the Novelist. "Kafka had neglected to name the central character, who is powerless... acted upon. I felt that this was an essentially feminist novel about a woman in a world of arbitrary laws, designed to oppress her. I gave her a simple, English name, and called the book, *Alice in Wonderland*."

I wriggled. He let go my arm. Far away, the lights turned blue, and somebody screamed.

The Barman nodded, and gripped my arm weakly with his ruined right hand. "I translated Lewis Carroll's extraordinary masterpiece into German," he said. "The central character is a

---

* In issues #42 and #43 of Marvel Two-In-One! – *Smilin' Stan Lee.*

cipher, an everyman figure, oppressed by terrible arbitrary laws designed to destroy the innocent; and is ultimately judged and condemned to execution without ever understanding the crime the poor creature has been accused of. I called the novel *Der Process*, or *The Trial*."

The Novelist turned to the Barman.

"You will recall that extraordinary line from Franz Kafka, 'I know you are a friend... you won't hurt me, though I am an insect.'"

"Ah yes, yes," They began to weep.

"Very sad," I ventured.

"No, no, no," they said. "It is a joke."

"You shouldn't make jokes if it makes you so unhappy," I said.

I felt my heart hammering, ticktockticktockticktockticktock, a second vanishing every second.

The Novelist talked about Samuel Beckett for a minute. Then he talked about James Joyce for an hour. I couldn't understand a word of it. Eventually I could endure no more.

"Stop, stop," I said. He ground to a halt.

This was worse than my Spot.

I had to deal with it.

56

I applied my mind to translating the Novelist's speech into English.

"James Joyce," I said. "Did he ever work as a journalist?"

The Novelist frowned. "Well, he did the odd bit of journalism, early on, yes. Incisive analysis of Ireland's paralysis, from the traditional thousand miles away…"

Excellent. I'd thought as much.

A journalist.

Wore glasses.

Lived in exile, from a lost and distant world to which he could never return.

Yet of a sunny disposition.

And, deep inside – hidden from everyone – all-powerful.

Super-vision, with a thousand-mile range.

Able to stop the turning planet with his strong right hand, so that a single chosen day would last forever.

I translated James Joyce into Superman.

In my imagination, the modest and bespectacled figure carefully removed his glasses, stepped out of a Parisian telephone box, and leaped a building in a single bound.

So, James Joyce created a world in a book…

I imagined Superman labouring night and day to carve, from a planet, a book. Letters like cliffs girdled and regirdled it in a spiral, and God read it as it rotated into the sunlight, and vanished back into the night-dark.

OK. Now Samuel… The Novelist started off again.

"Stall the ball there a minute," I said. "I'm translating Samuel Beckett into English."

The Novelist looked at me with a new respect.

OK. Samuel Beckett…

Younger than Superman.

More tortured.

Bit of family money, so he never had to work.

Looked on humanity with a certain despair.

Batman. Obviously.

This Literature lark wasn't as hard as it looked at first sight.

"And who," I said keenly, "is Spiderman?"

A certain amount of confusion ensued before I worked out he was Flann O'Brien.

"Did the rest of the globe not supply a few of these superheroes," I said, "or is Literary Modernism a strictly Irish sport, like Hurling?"

"Well," said the Novelist, "later on, William Faulkner attempted to do for his own part of the United States what Joyce had done for Dublin…"

So, this William Faulkner was a patriotic, but inferior, rip-off of Superman… Oh this was easy. Captain America.

"And were there any English modernists?" I said.

"Oh yes. All shit," said the Barman. "Except for Virginia Woolf."

"Ah!" I said. "Wonder Woman!"

"Precisely," said the Novelist.

"And what did these superheroes do?"

"They fought," said the Novelist.

"And what did they fight for?"

"Truth."

"And what did they fight against?"

"Bought words," said the Novelist. "Comforting lies. Mass-produced thoughts. They fought against the romantic novel, the formulaic thriller, and the Walt Disney Corporation."

"And so they lost," I said.

The Novelist shrugged, grimaced, and tipped the last of the sugarbowl into his coffee. "It is too early to say." He sipped.

The Barman vanished into the stock room, for more sugar.

My Spot throbbed. I eyed the Biro. OK. I was going to go for it. I would distract him with a last question that had been troubling me.

"So, if no normal person reads them... and the job pays twenty times less than a barman's... why do you write Literary Novels?"

"Well..." The Novelist looked around him, and lowered his voice. "There is always the microscopic chance of winning one of the Great Literary Prizes. And you know what that means!"

"Millions, is it?" I said.

He nearly dropped his coffee. "Good God, no. The Great Literary Prizes usually give you about enough to lease a parking space in one of the less fashionable boroughs of London. No, you get to have a lot of sex with those impressed by such things. Chiefly..." – he winked – "Librarians."

"That is good... is it?" I said cautiously.

"Oh God, yes. Best. Sex. Ever. Librarians lead repressed lives, in environments where loud cries are not encouraged. The tension builds; and must be released." He licked the froth off the lip of his cup. "Lord, you haven't lived till you've spread a Librarian."

Well, that was the mystery of literature solved. I was satisfied.

Up close, now, I watched intently as the crab of his hand scuttled, back and forth, across the white page. The hand's grip on the Biro seemed secure. The muscles of the arm bulged from the manly exertions of the writing life.

This would not be easy.

I reached across the counter towards the scuttling pen...

57

I caught him unawares and, in his surprise, the Biro fell from his hand.

I had not consciously noticed the constant, urgent, low scratch of pen against paper; but now it stopped, and the silence was terrible.

It drew the Barman back out of the Stockroom. Damn.

The Novelist stared at the white page.

"My Book!" the Novelist shrieked. "And I was nearly finished, too!"

The Barman snorted. "He's been saying that for ten years."

The Novelist went for me.

We commenced the battle proper.

The Barman let us get on with it.

The black Biro itself soon lay disregarded on the counter, as the Novelist and I rolled around the floor among the legs of the barstools, knocking seven types of ambiguity out of each other.

A crowd, attracted from further down the bar, soon gathered, and cheered us both impartially.

I got astride him.

"Put this in your book!" I said, and slammed his face off the floorboards.

He dislodged me with a flailing elbow that caught me on the bridge of the nose.

It took me a moment to recover from the white blast of pain. I attempted to staunch the blood.

The Barman sighed. "I'll go get ice." He vanished back into the store room.

The Novelist stood, and plucked from the dangling bicycle the long, black, iron bicycle pump.

He advanced on me slowly, the heavy iron bicycle pump in his bold right hand. He slammed it into his left palm, to judge the heft of it. Then he stopped, reached over the wooden counter with his free left hand, rooted around behind it, and came up with the short, sharp knife his brother had used to slice lemons.

My body attempted to haul my dangling testicles up to safely inside my abdomen. The attempt failed. They would have to take their chances.

The Novelist feinted at my head with the iron bicycle pump.

I raised my hands without thinking, to protect my bloodied face.

He lunged with the knife at my unprotected heart and I smelt lemons.

The knife crunched and snapped into my chest. The hammering stopped.

Everything stopped.

But I was still alive.

58

There was a sound like coins hitting the ground.

I looked down, to see the Novelist withdraw the knife from my chest.

No.

Just the handle.

The shattered pieces of its broken blade still hopping silver across the wooden floor, in among the shoes of the crowd.

It had sliced through my rabbitskin jacket. There was a glint of... blood? No.

Gold. A glint of gold.

I reached into the wounded jacket, and took out the gold watch given to me by the blind Librarian. Its soft yellow metal, scored deep by the steel blade. Its glass face shattered. Its cogs stilled. The relentless reminder of time's onrush had stopped.

My heart slowed to its natural rhythm.

I felt a great calm.

The Novelist came at me with the iron bicycle pump.

I backed away, along the counter. Past the piles of manuscript, the coffee cups...

I had no weapon.

In the moment of my greatest need, the Salmon spoke.

"Parried again. He fears the lancet of my art as I fear that of his. The cold steelpen *[sic]*."

James Joyce, *Ulysses*. From the Telemachus episode, in which Stephen Dedalus, a character

212 • JULIAN GOUGH

representing the young writer James Joyce, does battle with Buck Mulligan, a character representing the young writer Oliver St. John Gogarty

Sick, indeed. But quick thinking, as ever, from Superman.

I seized the disregarded pen from among the debris on the counter. The lancet of my art.

59

It takes a long time to kill a man with a Biro, but it can be done.

My final blow drove the pen so far into the Novelist's chest cavity, in search of his heart, that only the last inch, bearing the cap, protruded.

I stepped back, to find that a mighty crowd of people – Great Irish Writers by the look of them, for each held a Pen, a Pint, and a Whiskey Chaser – had gathered around us. A cry went up that shook the dangling bicycle.

"You have killed him surely, the last post-modernist of the Literary World!"

"The Death of the Author is on your conscience!"

It was. "Sorry," I said.

I mourned the Death of the Author. And yet...

And yet, by God, it was curiously liberating. He'd annoyed the living hole off me with his booktalk. There were more shouts from the crowd.

"Who will replace him?"

"Who will finish the Story of Ireland?"

And one by one they rushed up, and attempted to remove the Biro from deep in the Novelist's chest.

All failed.

They milled about, in their strangely familiar dark clothing, weeping.

Oh, my Spot was murdering me.

"I need a BIRO!" I roared. "Or what is deep within me will go septic!"

The crowd trembled, and refused to look upon my bloodied visage with its swollen forehead. Heads bowed, they offered me the finest pens available to humanity. Pens named after Swiss Mountains. Pens used by Kings of Sweden. Pens hand-cast by Japanese masters in ceramics.

Fountain pens.

Propelling pencils.

Swan-feather quills.

I spurned them all as unequal to my task. They murmured to each other.

"Look, he spurns them all as unequal to his task!"

"He wishes only for the humblest Biro…"

"Ah, the true Author craves not a Golden Pen…"

"Only one who is Innocent and True… − indeed, perhaps a bit of a Gom −…will be able to pull forth the Pen from its resting place…"

I stuck a foot on the Novelist's chest. Leaned down. Grasped that which I most desired. Warm blood still fell from my elbowed nose, splashing my hands, the Biro…

The crowd's murmurs stilled.

I had laid it to rest there, in its deep bed of bone and muscle. I knew its angles and its stresses, the arc of its release. Also, the other lot, all their muscles atrophied by the literary life − bar those of whichever arm they used for writing and drinking − hadn't given it nearly enough welly.

Effortlessly, I drew forth the Biro.

Ooh, I felt a little weak myself, from loss of blood.

The Barman reappeared behind the bar, with a bucket of icecubes. He rolled them up in a tea-towel, crushed them with a small hammer, and handed me the package. I pressed it to my nose, which began to shrink, constricting the outflow of my heartsblood.

"Poor eejit," said the Barman, looking down at the corpse of his twin. "Probably a good career move, though, at this stage."

I readied myself for combat.

A distant clock chimed the hour. The Barman put on his coat. "Well, that's my shift over," he said in a thick German accent.

"*Auf wiedersehen.*" He left.

I was relieved to discover that it was true the Germanic peoples were not demonstrative in their grief. I put the ice on the counter. My nose had shrunk to a nubbin, and the bleeding had ceased. I stared at the Biro. The crowd gathered round, to congratulate me on my triumph.

"How Innocent you are!"

"How Spontaneous!"

"How Authentic!"

"God, you're the spit of Leonardo DiCaprio!"

OK, I had the Biro. Now all I needed to do was release what was in me.

I staggered and fell to my knees, exhausted.

A man pressed through the throng. He held out his strong right hand.

I stood, slid the Biro behind my ear, and wiped the blood off my fingers. We shook till I swayed, and had to grab left-handed at the barstool beside me for support.

"Professor Raglan Kibosh," he said. "I hold the Chair of Anglo-Irish Literature and Drama at University College, Dublin."

"Jude," I said, "I hold this bar stool."

The crowd murmured.

Yes, they had the noble and dilapidated look of writers all right. But there was something about their clothing…

"Diagnose the ills of the Nation," said a short story writer.

"Soothe us with honeyed words," said a tall story writer.

"Renew the National Project," said a squat novelist.

"What are you on about?" I said.

"Why, you drew forth the Biro of Destiny," said Professor Raglan Kibosh. "You must finish the Ultimate Irish Novel." He looked at me expectantly. "Don't worry; simply replace *Ulysses.* Off you go."

The Salmon snorted.

"An illiterate, underbred book it seems to me; the book of a self-taught working man, and we all know how distressing they are, how egotistic, insistent, raw, striking, & ultimately nauseating"

Virginia Woolf, on James Joyce and *Ulysses*. From her diary, 16 August, 1922.

I sighed, to hear Wonder Woman speak so disparagingly of Superman behind his back. They did not love each other, then.

"What's stopping you?" said Professor Kibosh.

I pointed to the tiny, dark pore at the centre of the vast bulging Spot on my forehead. "Blocked," I said.

"Ah yes," said Professor Kibosh, "the terror of a book-ridden culture is most present to him who would be the pioneer of a national poetic and not just an innovator..."

Terror?

"Don't worry," said Professor Kibosh. "I'm here to help."

"Look," I said, "I just need a mirror."

"A fine start," said Raglan Kibosh. "Yes, Art holds a mirror up to nature... for the world regarded through a Looking Glass is curiously transformed..."

Ah yes; the walls were lined with mirrors advertising Irish whiskeys. I turned and walked towards them.

60

The mirrors glittered in the gloom. I moved my face close to the first. It sported a map of Ireland, with "Paddy" written on it. I searched for my Spot.

Good God. My blemishes seemed enormous.

"You don't want that one," said Professor Kibosh hastily. "It is the cracked looking-glass of a servant."

I moved on to the next one.

"Jameson," it read. But it distorted my features till they were unrecognisable. I sighed. Being Catholic, and Bastard, I was no doubt not eligible to be a true son of the Protestant King James, who had ordered the Bible translated into English. Fair play to him.

I moved on to the next.

Power's.

At last, a Mirror fit for Superheroes! Though poorly punctuated. I stared into it, and sure enough I could see my Powers clearly.

"But I cannot see my faults and blemishes," I said.

"Exactly," said Professor Kibosh. "It was the most popular mirror in Ireland, from 1922 till late October of 2008."

"This mirror will not do," I said.

"Those are your only choices," said Professor Kibosh.

"Is there not a Tipperary spirit, holding its own mirror up to nature?" I said.

"Well, yes, Ireland, of course, once had as many distilleries as Scotland," said Professor Kibosh. "Each distilled the spirit of its place, each different from the other. But after Independence, from the 1920s onwards, Éamon de Valera dealt firmly with this pantheistic anarchy, and forced the industry to consolidate. By 1971, with Éamon de Valera still president, there were only three

Irish whiskeys – with a single owner – and all three came out of the same factory in Middleton."

"How can Three come out of One?"

"The Trinity is a Mystery," said Professor Raglan Kibosh. "Nonetheless, you may only choose from the mirrors of Paddy, Jameson, or Power's."

"You should rejoice," said the short story writer, "for Éamon de Valera finally converted a nation, whose many and conflicting Spirits were far too complicated, into a simple brand, easy to understand, which could be sold around the world."

"Eventually we learned to like the taste of it ourselves," said the tall story writer.

But I mourned the lost spirits of Ireland, for in de Valera's mirrors I could not see my face.

The Biro trembled in my hand.

The crowd held their breath.

From the dark interior of my bag, the Salmon of Knowledge gave a gentle cough.

I hauled the Salmon back out of the pool of darkness, but there were no words on its smooth screen.

And now even the screen's light faded and was gone. All that I saw on its dark and glossy surface was my own face reflected back to me.

Was this Knowledge?

It was.

I had found a mirror with nothing written on it by history. It reflected only my own face, undistorted, with my own faults and blemishes perfectly clear.

Most of the crowd were still holding their breath. I began to fear for their brain function.

I stared into my face, and saw the blemish.

Professor Kibosh passed me a fresh sheet of blank paper.

I nodded, and put down the piece of paper on the bar.

"I will Pick carefully," I said.

I held the Biro delicately between finger and thumb.

The crowd gasped down a quick gulp of air, and held their breath again.

I pinched the head of the Biro, and slid my fingernail into the crack where the ball-pointed cone joined the outer plastic tube. I popped out the inner plastic straw. It was almost empty of ink.

I placed the open end of the plastic tube carefully in the precise centre of my forehead, so that the small circle of plastic surrounded the blocked pore, and pushed down gently.

The blackhead emerged from its shelter and slid up the tube, followed by all that had been hidden and repressed. Mingling with the remaining ink, it soon filled the tube.

Oh, sweet relief. My smooth forehead no longer throbbed. I had dealt with my buried trauma, and now I could move on. I carefully reassembled the Biro, and turned to face the crowd.

"That's it," I said. "I'm done."

The crowd looked from my face, to my Biro, to the unmarked page.

Those at the back sought whispered clarification from those at the front.

"Has he refused the task?"

Their murmur became a roar.

"He has refused the task!"

They surged forward, some spilling their fresh pints.

Oh dear.

"You'd better write the book they want to read," gasped Professor Kibosh, holding them back from me with some difficulty.

I wished to oblige this kindly old man. But at his words, I became aware of a resistance in me... connected to a buried trauma...

"There is a resistance in me," I said.

"Please, for my sake," said Professor Kibosh, "overcome your resistance. Or they are likely, in their Enthusiasm, to kill the two of us..."

It was such a small thing to ask. And – an important point – it would save us both from death and mutilation.

Yes. Swiftly finish the Ultimate Irish Novel, and move on.

I paused.

My pen, above the blank page placed in front of me by Professor Kibosh.

The crowd of Great Irish Writers pushed closer, and stared at me intently.

"Why," I said, "are you all dressed as priests?"

They blushed and shuffled.

"Well, you can pick up the outfits surprisingly cheap these days," said the short story writer. "And the thick serge provides wonderful protection from Electricity."

"It also helps ensure you are not mistaken for a crime writer, chick literatus, or stand-up comedian," said the squat novelist. "I myself was able to pick up the Bishop of Cloyne's entire wardrobe for a song, after his shock resignation."

"Ah, I love the smell of incense in the morning," said the poet, adjusting his soutane. "It gets you in the right mood for Marian Finucane."

"I find the stole and chasuble peculiarly comfortable," said the tall story writer, "when writing the Bishop of Limerick's former spiritual advice column for the *Limerick Leader*. And they don't show the dirt."

"You don't find the cincture chafes," said the squat novelist, "when addressing school assemblies?"

They began to swap tips on the right tone to take when writing about Ireland's spiritual crisis. Agonised, or merely sorrowful? Merely sorrowful for the *Irish Times*, but agonised for the *New York Times*, seemed to be the general consensus. The conversation petered out, and they stared at me again.

Concentrate.

Yes.

Just finish off the Ultimate Modern Irish Literary Novel.

The pause grew intolerably long.

It wasn't as easy as it looked.

Where to begin… Perhaps there were role models. "I am aware," I said carefully, "of the Superheroes of the Modern Novel, who bestrode the early 20th century like Colossi, selling hundreds of copies of their world-moulding books. But are there modern Irish writers?" For the Orphanage Library had ceased to buy Irish fiction rather abruptly in 1879.

"Oh, there are many fine Irish writers," said Professor Kibosh, pointing at the crowd.

"You can tell that we are Good Irish Writers," said the short story writer, "because the English give us prizes."

I nodded, and turned back to Professor Kibosh. "And what do they write about?"

"Well…" said Professor Kibosh. "From John McCool to Shawn Bawn… From Colm Tóbleróne to Anne Onnymuss… they are infinitely diverse! But generally… as a rule… men, at dusk, looking backwards; and women, at Funerals, in the rain. The best combine both, and have men looking backwards at women at funerals at dusk: or women at men's funerals looking backwards in the rain."

I felt a quiver in the pit of my stomach at his words. "And the Pleasure," I said, "lies in…"

"Pleasure?" said Professor Kibosh. He frowned. The crowd muttered among themselves. "Oh, I suppose… the pleasure lies… in being Harrowed! It is all wonderfully… harrowing!"

Ah. I had often seen the Harrow at work in Riggs-Miller's small field: and once I had seen a myxomatosised rabbit, its eyes gummed shut with an orange fungus, wander in its bewilderment into the path of the harrow and all its iron blades, and come out the other end of it changed utterly.

Harrowed.

"I am not sure if I want to be Harrowed," I said firmly. "Or to Harrow."

The gathering crowd murmured like the sea, in the dark.

"Hand me another key," I said, "to writing the Ultimate Irish Literary Novel."

"There is always a family secret," said Professor Kibosh, "far in the past, which explains everything."

Well, that was no use to me. Being an Orphan, I had no family secrets. Why were my knees trembling?

"Usually a memory from childhood," said Professor Kibosh, "which comes rushing back, a couple of hundred pages into the book."

"A memory of what?" I said, as my hands began to shake.

"Oh, generally a traumatic event, befalling a child…"

The memory came rushing back.

61

I was but a child, and in the private quarters of Ethel, the Orphanage Cook.

I was there to put up a new bookshelf.

Ethel was a woman of boundless intellectual ambition, and had read the first chapters of innumerable Irish Classics from the Golden Age. But she was not prejudiced, and also condescended to read books for pleasure. Thus, she required a new shelf annually, at the beginning of the Reading Season. Putting up a new bookshelf for Ethel was one of the most sought-after jobs in the Orphanage, for she would give you an entire Sweet, to yourself.

I had consigned a number of smaller Orphans to the Infirmary in my eagerness to win the task.

Ethel leaned over.

Her perfume filled my senses.

"Put it up good and level, now," she said. "Young Mong Mangan's last shelf was pure useless. My Sophie Kinsellas slid themselves out the window and into the yard, from all the vibration of the senior team practising Off-The-Ball Incidents up against the end-wall, and I never did get back *The Secret Dreamworld of a Shopaholic*." She gave me an Emerald Sweet, all to my Self. "And you know the Golden Rule: don't touch the books on my Special Shelf."

And then she headed off to have tea with her unmarried sister.

Leaving me. Alone.

For the entire afternoon.

I sighed. I had been hoping for a bit of... Ah well.

As soon as she was gone, I went through the cupboards.

There. The cardboard box, containing a lifetime's supply of Emerald Sweets for the entire Orphanage. I dragged the claw of my little hammer the length of the taped seams. They split with a silky hiss.

I tore open the first bag of Emerald Sweets.

Stood on a chair.

Reached up.

And took the first book from the highest, most inaccessible shelf.

Ethel's special, reinforced shelf. It had taken a team of Orphans three days and three nights to erect it.

The shelf bearing all of Ireland's Great Literary Prize Winning Books.

I sneezed the dust from the first book, cracked its unbroken spine, popped a couple of sweets in my mouth and I was off...

Every burning second of that fateful afternoon returned to me now.

The unsmiling faces of Superhero after Superhero, grimly staring up at me in black and white from their book jackets, as I slowly inched my way along the Shelf.

Battling Evil had clearly taken its toll.

John McCool.

Colm Tóbleróne.

Anne Onnymuss.

Shawn Bawn.

Oh God, memory after memory.

Sentence after sentence.

Book after book.

In excellent, realistic and lyrical prose.

    A funeral.

        Another funeral.

          The famine.

            A funeral.

          Another.

Oh, she's Emigrating. Maybe something will happen... No, she's back for a funeral.

Funeral.

Funeral.

The American Civil War... Battlefields. Funerals. Mice. Rain.

World War One... Trenches. Funerals. Rats. A great deal of rain.

The Easter Rising... Tenements. Funerals. Small horses. Hailstones.

A funeral.

Wifebeating.

A funeral. Funeral.

Funeral.

A children's book... great, a break from... no, wait, those aren't pyjamas... Ah feck, it's set in some kind of concentration camp.

Funerals.

Funeral.

Funeral.

Is this... yes, an excellent, realistic and lyrical funeral.

Funeral.

Funeral.

Oh, this one didn't have a funeral. No, hang on, that fellow's about to kill himself... there he goes...

A funeral.

Funeral.

Funeral.

Merciful... Jesus...

I had read my way to the end of the shelf, while eating ninety-six bags of Emerald Sweets.

I tried to banish again from memory the catastrophe of revulsion, regret, and remorse that followed. But I could not.

Dear God, the entire shelf!

The...

Entire...

Fecking...

Shelf...

"You have the wrong man," I said. "I can't do it."

"Why not?" said Professor Kibosh.

"Modern Irish Literature makes me puke my ring," I said.

The crowd sucked in an immense collective breath that made my ears pop.

Professor Kibosh winced. "Perhaps you would like to clarify... even qualify... your critical response," he said, "to contemporary Irish literary fiction..."

Another repressed memory returned.

"It gives me the yellow squirts," I said helpfully, to clarify. "And a scaldy hole."

The crowd gave a roar, and lunged at me.

"If you could phrase your reason for refusing in a more Literary way," gasped Professor Kibosh over his shoulder, holding back the crowd with difficulty, "it wouldn't annoy them as much."

The Salmon of Knowledge coughed discreetly, and came up with another nugget from your man Borges. I read it, and nodded.

"I am dissuaded from this by two considerations," I said. "My awareness that the task is interminable, and my awareness that it is useless."

"Ah, that should do it," said Professor Kibosh.

Sure enough, the huge crowd of Great Irish Writers calmed, apart from one at the back who'd just arrived in, and who continued to mutter. The top of his head looked awfully familiar.

"Well, we could use our sub to finish it, I suppose," said Professor Kibosh. "But he's in Ireland, at a funeral... Look, could you not just give it a lash?"

The crowd seconded Professor Kibosh's suggestion with a growl.

I eyed them. They looked as though they could grow rather emotional if thwarted. And it would be nice to Renew the National Project, and not be torn limb from limb.

"I'll try," I said, and closed my eyes, the better to concentrate on the task.

62

First, I had to translate these literary giants into something I understood...

McCool.

Tóbleróne.

Onnymuss.

Bawn.

Superheroes of the Silver Era, with their lesser but still considerable powers...

Four of them...

One woman, three men...

Ushering in a new era of naturalism...

Well, it couldn't be simpler. The Fantastic Four! A dysfunctional but loving family.

But who was who?

I studied them, in memory.

John McCool... Which ones were his again? *The Dark, The Pornographer, Amongst Women...* Ah yes. Clearly he was Mr. Fantastic, the older, more sophisticated leader of the Four.

Colm Tóbleróne... author of *The Heather Blazing... The Blackwater Lightship...* Hmmm, obviously The Human Torch.

Anne Onnymuss... slightly startled in her photograph, and looking as though she wished she could disappear... The Invisible Woman, so.

And loveable, crusty Shawn Bawn had to be everybody's favourite... The Thing!

As I mused, a thickset figure pushed his way through the throng.

The man who had muttered loudest at my refusal of the Task.

His cassock was caked in a thick clay that had cracked as it dried.

"I was at a funeral," he explained to those he moved past. "Fell in. It was raining."

He lurched free of the crowd, towards me. Oh, he was more than familiar...

"Feck," I said.

It was The Thing!

"Your notion that shouting the word 'feck'," said The Thing, "and being grossly scatological will make you seem echt Irish only harms your argument."

Echt Irish? I puzzled over this. Perhaps the "F" was silent. Well, it was not every day you got advice on how to be Irish from The Thing, author of *Mefisto*, *Kepler*, and *Athena*. "I shall ponder your Wisdom," I said. I pondered it.

Should I not shout "feck"?

Was I grossly scatological?

I contemplated the words I used. Could some of them be considered crude by listeners not of Tipperary, or in other ways linguistically impoverished? Hmmm.

It was possible.

Perhaps I was failing to fluently translate Tipperary into English.

I called to mind the Great Names of Modern Literature – several of whom I had read – and their use of the vernacular. Yes, I would study these Great Writers, and thereby improve my speech.

The Thing drew forth his ivory Mont Blanc fountain pen. Its silver nib glittered in the bar's low light.

He assumed the battle stance.

"We who were born and continue to live in Ireland," said The Thing, "are always distressed by the stage-Irish antics so often to be encountered among the sons and daughters of the diaspora."

The crowd roared their approval. Several threw their mitres in the air.

Wait, was he talking about me?

Though admittedly a Bastard, with no doubt disreputable origins, I was surely Tipperary from Braincase to Bollocks.

The Thing took a swing at me with his ivory Mount Blanc.

I ducked, and grabbed my recently reassembled Biro.

Battle it was, so.

I fended off his Mont Blanc with my soiled and bloodied pen.

Oh feck this. Killing The Thing with a Biro, through that thick crust of dried mud and a full set of vestments, would take forever, and I was already knackered.

I picked up a polished, ornamental keg of Guinness, and hit The Thing in the head with it, so hard that both were bent out of shape.

When the Thing stood up again, I saw the mark of the Guinness Harp embossed upon his forehead.

Reversed, to form the harp of the Republic.

He felt the mark with his muscular writer's fingers

"Dear God, the mark of the Irish is on me! I can no longer pass as European!" he gasped. "Nabokov will not speak to me in Heaven!"

He picked up his copy of the Oxford Treasury of Polite Synonyms – edited, I saw, by The Riddler, T.S. Eliot – and caught me an absolutely ferocious buffet, just behind the left ear.

My eyes came back into focus on T. S. Eliot's book, and read instead the anagram, Toilets. What? Had I suffered another Mental Catastrophe?

I groped about in my mental interior for an explanation. There: yes.

I had been pondering Great Writers; I had been pondering Tipperary Speech.

The blow appeared to have jangled the two word-hoards, so that the content of each had spilt into the other.

I reached for a Tipperary oath, and found sweet foucault.

Had he made shere hite of me, thus losing me Angela's hand?

The battle-frenzy of Cúchulainn bulged my muscles till they filled to the full the fur of my suit, and made the animal-skin of it as tight about me as the skin of a bodhrán played in sunlight, and caused the hairs of my body beneath the suit to stand so hard they pierced the rabbit skin, and caused the grey hairs of the rabbit skin itself to stand in sympathy, as steelstiff as needles, and pulled my tendons tight as the cables that hold a long bridge in a high wind, so that they made tents of my neck-flesh, and the drum of my heart beat the blood of battle to my every extremity, giving me a slight headache.

I slew The Thing, in combat fair and courteous.

It took some considerable time.

When I was done, I threw the crushed, misshapen keg of Guinness over the bar counter. It bounced once, and vanished down the open trap.

There was a dull *thunk* from deep beneath us.

A dragging sound.

A clank.

A satisfying click.

A cry of joy from the blind Librarian, ecstatic in his eternal darkness far below.

63

I stood over the body of The Thing.

Professor Kibosh joined me.

"Shite," said Professor Kibosh. "He was our sub."

On the floor, The Thing's left hand twitched... scuttled deep into a pocket of the muddied cassock... emerged from the darkness clutching an ebony Mont Blanc pen... and wrote!

I gasped.

Then sighed.

Of course.

Surely I, Jude the Entropic Man, had read enough comics to know that I could not kill The Thing forever?

The Thing staggered erect, bloodied and marked with a hundred harps.

The ebony pen in his sinister hand scored its letters deep and dark across beermats, cigarette packets and old serviettes.

"What are you writing?" I said, to make conversation before the violence began again, and my inevitable defeat.

"I'm not writing anything," said the Thing.

"Ah, you are though, Thing," I said.

"Father Ted has a lot to answer for," said The Thing.

"No, look," I said. "Seriously. You are."

The Thing glanced at his sinister hand, and gasped from the right side of his mouth, "My Dark Side! It writes again!"

The crowd moaned in horror, and a ghastly silence fell.

By my side, Professor Kibosh whispered, "You are familiar with the strange case of Dr. Jekyll, and Mr. Hyde?"

I indicated that I was.

"Well, Ireland's greatest writer," Professor Kibosh nodded at

The Thing, "writes Literature for the Elite, with his right hand, under the name Shawn Bawn. And Thrillers for the Unwashed, with his left, under the name Ben Black…"

Ah, of course. The Thing's original name – before he gained his Superpowers – was Ben… "What's the difference?" I said.

The Thing's clean right hand picked up the ivory pen, seized a clean white sheet of paper from the bar, and began a work of Literature narrated by a Greek God.

"Show-off," growled The Thing from the left side of his mouth. The Thing's filthy left hand wrote all the faster, with his ebony pen, on the brown cardboard flap of a Cheese and Onion Flavoured Tayto Crisps carton.

I leaned in and read a little. A detective thriller, narrated by a drunk.

"Slut!" piped The Thing. He spat at his left hand, from the right side of his mouth.

"It will not have escaped your attention," whispered Professor Kibosh, "that *Bán* is the Irish for White. Black and White are locked in eternal conflict – no resolution to his torment is possible."

I felt tremendous pity for this tortured Superhero. I'd always had a soft spot for The Thing, ever since he had been hideously transformed by cosmic rays. He was grumpy, but lovable.

"If the Noblest of the Noble are so divided," I said, "how can the House of Literature stand?"

"Feck off," said The Thing from both sides of his mouth.

And he came for me with both pens.

I had already given this battle my all: the best of which I was capable could not stop a Superhero with such extraordinary powers.

Jude the Entropic Man could not defeat The Thing.

No.

Only The Thing could defeat The Thing.

"But what if you had only the one pen?" I said.

I seized the little hammer used for crushing icecubes, and swung with all my strength.

The blow was easily parried by The Thing's strong right hand.

But the little hammer had crushed the Ivory pen.

The Thing dropped the white wreckage, and plucked the hammer from my hand.

I took a step backward, and scooped up the iron bicycle pump.

I feinted at his right hand, he parried. I struck instead at his left, with all my remaining strength.

The blow bounced off the iron-hard clay that caked his fist.

But the pump had crushed the Ebony pen.

The Thing dropped the black wreckage, took the iron bicycle pump from me with ease, and advanced.

Hammer in his right hand. Iron pump in his left.

I picked up my deconstructed, reconstructed Biro with its mingled inkstuff, black and white. My first and final weapon. "Excelsior!" I murmured. The Thing was almost upon me.

His strength was colossal, his powers without limit.

Yes, only The Thing could defeat The Thing.

I threw my Biro to the floor, at his feet.

"Choose," I said.

The Thing stared down at the Biro.

The hammer fell from his right hand.

From his left, the iron pump.

The Thing bent forward.

Reached for the Biro, from either side. With either hand.

The hands met above the Biro. Touched.

Seized each other!

The mighty writing muscles of both arms bulged, as The Thing began to arm-wrestle himself for possession of the Biro of destiny.

There was a straining sound.

A ripping noise.

The dried clay crumbled from his flesh.

The cassock gave at the seams.

The skin beneath ripped.

The muscle…

He tore himself in two.

The new shift's bar staff swiftly cleared away the remains, leaving only the Biro on the floor.

And he was gone, as though he were only a sort of Thing, in my dream.

I picked up the Biro.

64

Professor Kibosh lowered his head into the bowl of his hands.

"Shawn Bawn and Ben Black – both gone!" he said. "A double catastrophe. The Great Irish Novel will now never be written, and I'll also have nothing to read on the beach."

The crowd surged and roared. Yes, a more unruly element seemed to have arrived during my battle with The Thing. Readers, rather than writers, by the language out of them, and the absence of clerical collars.

A hand slid along the fur of my thigh, and in through the unbuttoned fly of my rabbitskin trousers. "Ah, there you are," said a voice. My pen shuddered, as I felt a small, cool hand cup my balzac. I looked down.

Angela!

No. Ah well. "Alice?" I said.

She looked up. "Got to get you ready, Leo. For your big scene."

She hauled out my john kennedy toole, and pinched me just behind my slightly saul bellow.

"What…?" I enquired.

But at that moment there was a shuffle in the crowd. The Great Writers of Ireland moved through the ranks of their Readers, to the front, and they formed a shape.

And each of them began to sing their own tremendous and imperfect words.

I looked closer at their faces, their dress. Several of them looked suspiciously like crime writers, writers of commercial women's fiction, and even, by their shifty look, stand-up comedians. They must have sneaked in through the toilet windows, while no one was looking.

They sang, the shabby women and men. The Crime Writers, in their black leather jackets. The Writers of Fiction Specifically for Women, in their little black dresses and peculiar shoes. The Literary Writers, in the cast-off habits of dead nuns, and the vestments of priests who had loved boys and women and God with a great, confused, imperfect human love.

They sang in their wild, unequal voices, oh hallelujah, sang the Irish choir.

And they sang Ireland into being.

And I wept.

But they hadn't finished yet.

Each Writer now sang their favourite word, and held it on their favourite note, to make a single chord between the lot of them, and the words made a story in the air.

And I realised that none of us had written the Story of Ireland.

Because it took all of us to write it.

And I cleared my throat and sang my one inadequate word, on its imperfect note. I tried to sing it as clean and clear as the perfect note in my head, but what came out was far too sharp, and when I went for the major it turned out minor, and went flat, and my wavering note was soon lost anyway in the great chord.

But it was part of the great chord.

The pen moved in my hand.

And the Story wrote itself, from our weak, imperfect Notes.

Page after page…

I stared at the pages.

It was finished, but it wasn't complete.

We held our Notes, and waited.

There was a shuffle in the crowd.

The Readers formed a shape.

And the Readers sang their wild, imperfect harmony in response.

The air hammered the walls till the mirrors shivered, then shattered, as we stood in the centre of the story we sang. The vibrations of the air moved off, down the trapdoor, through the cellar, up out the beer chute, across London, England, Wales, the Irish Sea, to West Britain, and the song moved across the bright and sunlit central plain of Ireland, the grassy hills, across the Tipperary bogs rich with knee-capped Bronze Age informers, suicidal farmers, unofficial babies, lovers who'd made a hames of love and, farther westward, the song danced across the sparkling Shannon waves. It consoled and tormented the four million orphans living in Ireland, and kept on going, across Atlantic and Pacific, tormenting and consoling forty million embarrassing stage-Irish orphans, sons of famine and daughters of war, billionaires and labourers, scattered round the world, the fecked Irish. And when they heard our song, they sang their rich and poor reply. The sound went round the world, and mingled with the songs of other choirs.

And they sang the universe into being.

The great song finally came back around the curve of the world improved by seven billion other voices, and reentered the Pub of Excessive Irishness through the open toilet windows.

We stopped singing, exhausted, and listened to a Song that was far better than the one we'd sung.

It ended.

The silence made my ears ring.

"Thank you," I said into the silence, to the Writers I had insulted, the Readers I had disappointed, to the Choir.

I looked around me at the corpses, at the broken-hearted. At the successful writers, weltering in their own gore. At the failed, drowned in sour Guinness. At the Readers, with their demands, and their refusals. At the entire tormented beauty of the Choir…

The Biro fell from my hand.

I felt even more light-headed than usual. I looked down.

Alice removed her jane smiley from my philip k dick. She had given me an updike with the durability and tensile strength of mahogany.

"OK, you're ready," she said. She hit my frederik pohl a thoughtful slap. It vibrated like a diving board. "If the shooting goes well you'll be finished by tonight. Easiest million you'll ever earn. Bring your Book."

"It's not my book…"

"Don't be modest. I saw you write it."

I picked up the pages. "But I was merely taking down…" Million?

"Come and meet the Director." She pinched hard just behind the head of my longfellow, and led me by my madison smartt bell toward the light.

65

We entered the blazing circle.

It was hot under the scaffolding which held up the lights. Alice stripped off her dress. I noticed again her pink tattoo, just above her white knickers. The words were easier to make out in this bright white light. I bent, to read them.

"**Eat Me**" they said, in letters about a quarter of an inch high. I crouched lower, to admire the delicate lettering. Pink ink, with a darker outline that was almost black.

Alice reached down, hooked her thumb through the thin central strip of her knickers, and pulled the blank white cotton to one side. "Feel free," she said. "It'll help you get bigger."

My lips were now level with her donna tartt. Pink, with an outline that was almost black. My nose began to swell.

"Thank you," I said. I stood, swaying slightly. "But I don't think I can get any bigger." I felt a little dizzy.

In front of us, the Director was sitting high up on some sort of stepladder, busy directing two actors. "Impenetrability!" he shouted.

I recognised them. The younger actor standing there naked was Gerry... no, Gerald... something. And the elderly naked man on all fours was one of England's many theatrical knights. I had seen his Photograph in the Newspapers in Tipperary. Their names were on the tip of my... Sir... no, it wouldn't come.

"Fluffer!" cried the younger actor. "Fluffer!"

Alice said, "Excuse me."

She walked over to the young man, knelt, and took his louis l'amour in her mouth.

Alice swiftly worked it up to a good nick hornby, before moving over to the pale theatrical knight. "Great Scott!" he said, as Alice grabbed him by the fitzgerald.

When it was of the desired consistency, she released it, and returned to my side.

"Alice," I said, "you said you knew the whereabouts of Angela…"

She looked blank.

"My True Love…"

Blanker.

"… the new girl walking this street, from Ireland."

"Oh yeah."

"Is she far?"

"Far?" She pointed at the ceiling. "She's working out of this building."

"Could you take me to her?"

"Sure, after your scenes."

I was about to insist, when she pointed into the circle of light. I looked.

Well, it would be polite to wait till I'd talked to the Director.

And I'd never seen a Film made before.

Of course, a million for a day's work in Film would considerably speed up my wooing of Angela…

Oh the fatal seductions of Cinema!

As Alice watched the scene before her, she absentmindedly gave a few tugs on my own shakespeare, for maintenance purposes.

The Director cried, "Lights!" and the lights grew even brighter than before. The theatrical Knight's buttocks glowed a brilliant white.

I heard a noise above.

Then a voice.

"Shit."

I looked up.

A fellow, high in the scaffolding, fumbled with translucent sheets of plastic in shades of green and red. His abundant hair was tied back like a pony's tail. The Director cried, "Cameras!"

People did things with cameras.

Above me, the man with the pony's tail slid a coloured plastic square in front of a glaring bright white lamp, as the Director cried, "Action!"

The plastic dyed the light an unpleasant green.

The young actor, very tentatively, brought his bright green seamus heaney closer to the older actor's parted, hairy, paul muldoons.

The Director shouted, "Cut! Cut! Terrible, terrible!" He gazed up. "A pink gel, you fucker, not green!" He turned back to the actor. "And you, for fuck's sake, this is supposed to be a passionate, frenzied love scene!"

"Well," said the young actor, "When I saw Keith had used the wrong gel..." The actor began to tremble. "I thought we wouldn't be using this take. Better to save my energy..."

The Director cut him off. "Wrong response! You never sleepwalk through a scene. If you think Keith has screwed up, then channel that anger. Attack the scene! Look at him." He pointed to the older actor. "Consummate professional. A living saint." The Director's voice softened so that I had to strain to hear him. "Look, I'm stuck with a colour-blind lighting technician. Can't fire him. Equal Opportunities bullshit. OK, I'm going to end up using takes that aren't perfect. But..." His voice hardened again. "Your job is to give a perfect performance every time, until I say cut. So, for the last time. If that asshole Keith dyes the lights the wrong colour. What will you do?"

The young actor mumbled.

The Director rolled his eyes and roared:

"Do not go gentle into that good Knight!
Rage, rage against the dyeing of the light!"

66

The Director issued orders to the Crew.

The pale Knight sat and dozed.

The young actor stood, picked up *The Communist Manifesto*, and began to read.

Alice whispered, "His family were more upset when he told them he was a Communist than when he told them he was gay. Oh, the blacks can be very conservative."

"He doesn't look particularly Black to me," I said. "My skin is darker than his."

"That's just the lousy lighting," said Alice.

We argued about the Red Queen's Race until we were exhausted, but did not seem to get anywhere.

"OK, nearly ready guys," said the Director. "Script! Bring me the last scenes. This one will be wrapped in five…"

An assistant climbed the ladder, and whispered in the Director's ear.

"Stabbed the writer?" said the Director. "Jesus, couldn't they wait till we'd finished principal photography? Fucking writers. And on our fucking last day. Fuck. Who are they getting in to finish it? Tell me it's Tom Stoppard. It better be Tom Stoppard."

The assistant pointed at me.

I waved weakly.

"You. Are. Shitting me," said the Director. "We're fucked… OK, again, properly this time. Assume your positions!"

The young actor put down *The Communist Manifesto*, and stood.

"What a shame it's not Stoppard," murmured the older actor, opening his eyes. "*Shakespeare in Love*, what a wonderful script.

Stoppard really captured what theatre was like in 16th-century London…"

"If you could get down on your knees, Sir," the young actor whispered.

"… He must be the quintessential Englishman… Quite astonishing to think he is Hungarian… Hmm?" said the pale knight, distracted by Alice's last-minute fluffing. "What the dickens…"

"Neil, gaiman!" roared the Director.

The knight knelt.

"Lights… cameras… action!" said the Director.

The Red Queen whispered, "Czech, mate," and took the White Knight.

"Cut! Print… Great." The Director threw the stack of pages high up into the lights, in the general direction of Keith. "OK, script, script, last scenes, come on," said the Director.

Alice nudged me, and I stepped forward, holding the Book.

The Director leaned down from his ladder, and grabbed it out of my hand.

"Leo took over from the other guy," said Alice. "Finished it."

"Well, actually," I said, "I just…"

"He's very modest," said Alice.

The Director snorted. "Books are bullshit, Leo. Stick to acting. You work in the only art-form that people give a shit about. What kind of a guy writes a novel, in the third millennium?" He leaned down off his ladder to look me straight in the eye. "A jerk-off… Well, you've got to be an improvement on the last guy, that fucking Novelist. All Novelists are just frustrated film-makers. *We're* the guys who tell stories in 3-D. Full colour. With surround sound. Totally immersive, and totally overwhelming. Totally invented, and totally real. Totally fantastic, and totally naturalistic. Totally…"

"Totalitarian," I suggested, hoping to help. It was a word I was fond of, though I did not know what it meant.

"We are Gods," he said. "We replace this universe with another, better universe." He lifted his cup of coffee from the saucer. "As a director, I want to replace this cup of coffee with another, better cup of coffee." A minion scurried up the ladder, and replaced his cup of coffee with another, better cup of coffee, leaving the old cup abandoned on the top step.

"Well, this is the Ultimate Novel," I said, "containing everything." I felt, having murdered the author, the least I could do was help promote his book. But I had one eye on the cup. God, I could murder a coffee.

"Ninety-eight percent bullshit," said the Director. "Had to dump thousands of pages. All the thoughts. Ideas. Most of the talking."

"And what's left?" I said.

"The good bits. Sex. And violence."

"But," I said.

"I know what you're going to say. You'd be amazed," said the Director. "They're always in there. My film of Kant's *Critique of Pure Reason* got an R-17 rating in America. Strong men fainted. Was the Novelist feeding you that bullshit about the sacred importance of the Novel? No, writers say it's a Vocation, an Art, a Mystery. Lying… little… shits."

Under the bright lights I could see myself reflected in his green eyes. He reached down and poked me in the chest with his finger.

"They write to beat up the boys who beat them up in school, and to fuck the girls who wouldn't fuck them. All art is sex 'n' violence… I read his account of your encounter; a thousand pages of bullshit. Just talk, about Ideas and Philosophy and Literature, which, I guarantee, his readers skip. At the end of which you murder him, in order to have sex with a woman you hardly know."

"He wrote about that?" I said. "In his Book?… He knew?"

"Yeah… That's your motivation, behind all those useless words."

I stared up the step ladder. I eyed the Book, in his hands. He had begun to thumb through it.

"He died rather abruptly," I said. "A lot of people helped finish it. So the plot may not cohere."

"Plot? 'The plot may not cohere'?" I thought he would fall

off the ladder. "Nobody," he said, "in the history of cinema, has ever come out of a movie and said, 'What a wonderfully coherent plot.' They say, what a great scene. What a great moment. What a great kiss. What a great car crash. She was hot. He was hot. I loved the bit where the plane hit the helicopter, where they fuck in the elevator, where she shot him through the door. Plot? Like life has a *plot?* Life is just pussy and revenge," said the Director.

I opened my mouth to object and he poured his old coffee into it.

I swallowed some. It was excellent.

"The 'plot' that writers worship," he said, "is just a bunch of dumb ways to delay the orgasm of the hero, and the murder of his rival. So it doesn't end after a minute. So you can charge twenty bucks."

I swallowed the rest of the coffee, in my shock. "You think Writers only write in order to win the heart of a woman?" I said. Oh, Angela, how I yearned to…

"No, you've got me all wrong. I'm saying you only write in order to fuck a woman." He snorted again. "Write? *Write?* We only live, breathe, eat, drink, think, exist in order to impress, trick, or trap women so we can fuck them." He leaned down closer to my face, perhaps in order to make his point more clearly, for fear I would misunderstand its subtleties. "All thinking is fucking." He straightened up again. "Thinking which leads to anything other than a fuck is an evolutionary dead end. Soon be gone."

"But…" I said.

"Wrong," he said. He put his hand on my shoulder and ruffled my fur. I was hot under the lights. "Leo, Leo, Leo. I understand. Right now, in this civilization at this time, genuinely believing it's not all about fucking, it works. Women like it. So a lot of guys genuinely believe it's not about fucking. Doesn't make it true. If a war broke out, and they were five minutes from getting their balls blown off…" He shrugged. "Your bodies would pull rank on your big, caring, sensitive, overdeveloped minds, and you'd be raping away like Cossacks. Happens in every war, in every culture."

He paused to breathe.

I went for the gap. "I…"

He slapped my pages back and forth across my face until he had finished his breath, and snorted "Art?"

"I never mentioned…"

"… All art is just sex temporarily deferred. People know this. Only artists don't know this. Walter Pater – total jerkoff – said 'all art aspires to the condition of music'… Bullshit. In the real world, all art aspires to the condition of pornography. Artists paint abstracts, but people buy nudes." He gave me a last slap with the Book, and sighed. "Stick to films, Leo. Films are more honest. Films don't do sublimation." He pointed to the pouting lips of Alice, and wrote a circle in the air around the pink words, Eat Me. "There is your philosophy of life. And it's a good one. You shouldn't feel ashamed of it, and you shouldn't dress it up."

He had run out of wind.

A thought occurred to me. "Why do women write, so?" I said.

"I have no idea," said the Director. "Writers, Jesus. Whine, whine, whine… Now shut the fuck up and let me read your fucking bullshit book." After a while, he looked up. "Too much talking. And thinking. And singing. But I can sex it up. It'll do." He read on.

A few pages later, the Director was frowning. "Ah, wait a minute." He looked up from the page. "How the fuck are we supposed to shoot this scene? I mean, I can show the ecstasy, rather than telling, but… too many characters, multiple climaxes, it would take an actor who had two…"

I cleared my throat and rubbed my nose vigorously.

The Director looked at me. "Makeup!" he shouted. "Fluffer!" He looked at me again. "Fluffers!"

67

The Crew prepared the Set.

The Director converted the Book into Script with a red pen, at surprising speed.

I was puzzled. Surely the final scenes of the novel were discussions of literature, and the ecstatic chorus of the Choir? But none of the many actresses, busy with their preparations, seemed to be doing vocal exercises. And they didn't remotely resemble the pale and feeble authors of the original scenes.

"OK, places, places, people," shouted an assistant. "We're shooting in sixty seconds…"

A tall, blonde actress with absolutely djuna barnes covered my jeffrey archer in a thick, dark fluid.

I began to think that the Director, in pursuit of his Vision of Cinematic Perfection, may have taken some liberties with the Ultimate Irish Novel.

The fluid stung in a way that was not entirely unpleasureable.

"What's that?" I said.

She held up a bottle, containing some kind of brown sauce.

Its label bore a picture of the Houses of Parliament, an image considered offensive in Tipperary on account of the eight hundred years of English Oppression. Ah, yes.

"For historical reasons," I said, "I don't eat HP Sauce."

"It's just for continuity," she said, "coming out of an anal scene. You don't have to eat it."

"Oh, fair enough, so," I said.

"Lights!" roared the Director. "Cameras! … Action!"

She turned around, leaned over, and wiggled everything in a friendly and inviting manner.

I launched my h p lovecraft up her aimee bender.

The sensations were so voluptuous that I entirely lost track of the script, and, in my rapture and confusion, stuck my h beam piper up her edgar allan poe.

"Cut!" said the Director. "Jesus H. Christ. Concentrate, Leo, for fuck's sake."

"Sorry," I said, somewhat dazed and confused.

"And get stuck in quicker, damn it," said the Director. "Less admiring the scenery."

We started again. This time, I concentrated harder, she bent over till she was at a more madeleine l'engle, and I managed to shove it into her wrinkle in time.

"And cut! Great! Makeup! Fluffers! Prepare the next scene…"

And so, Literary Ore was converted into Cinematic Gold in what, I gathered, was the traditional manner.

We arrived at the last scene. More actresses arrived.

I shook hands with them. We wished each other luck.

"OK," said the Director. "Almost out of time… We have one chance to get this right. Fuck up, you're fired and I'll sue you. No pressure."

68

Now, sex with a large number of women is confusing at the best of times. Many's the Lad had bitten his own most sensitive parts in error, at the height of his passion, while celebrating a Harty Cup victory with some Market Cross girls around the back of Frankie's Arcade. But the problem is considerably more than doubled for the man who has two penises. Mathematically speaking, the possibilities multiply as the square of the root.

I would need all my powers of concentration to get this scene right.

They set up the lights.

They perfected the set.

Checked the mechanics of the cameras.

The Director whispered "Action…"

We were off.

I gave the first woman a frank herbert up her carson mccullers.

The second, a more samuel langhorne clemens in her kathy acker.

The third woman then slowly lowered her edith sitwell onto my face.

My gene wolfe was exhausted, so I stuck my tongue up her leigh brackett, and tasted her slightly flannery oconnor. The script now called for penetration, but I realised I had currently no resources available for the task.

I marilyn frenched her fannie hurst, to buy me a little time. Then, all my other available parts being fully occupied or resting, I shoved my armistead maupin up to the elbow.

The sensation, as I had hoped, stimulated her greatly, and the sight and sounds of her pleasure gave me an absolutely norman mailer, with which I was able to perform my obligations, as specified in the script, with the fourth, fifth, and sixth woman.

Only one to go.

I turned to the seventh woman, sought out her heidi julavits, and licked her pearl buck till she moaned.

Then I pushed my roddy doyle down her patricia cornwell till I was deep inside her rather kurt vonnegut.

I felt her contracting in waves, and gasping with what I hoped was pleasure.

I too began gasping, as did the rest of the actresses, still busy with both me and each other.

Here comes everybody.

I felt a certain sense of modest satisfaction. We had successfully reached the end of the script, and the climax of the film.

The Climax went on for some considerable time.

"And... cut!"

I stood there, in my rabbit suit, swaying, with my kingsley amis tall, ruddy, at a drunken angle, and my martin amis small and wrinkled and smoking.

The exhausted women busied themselves with essential maintenance. The air was rich with the mingled smells of oil, lubricant and hot wax.

Some exercised their essential muscles.

Two lay on their backs, and played ping pong, without bats.

I stared out upon the vision. I did not understand my own feelings.

And I remembered Angela. She stood vivid and alive before the eyes of memory. I glanced back at the Actresses. These real scenes before me now seemed muffled and distant, as though seen through glass.

I shivered, despite the heat under the lights.

My fur rippled like a cornfield sensing an approaching stormfront.

We all made our way to the Bar, to celebrate the successful completion of the ultimate film.

I felt hollow, and sat at the very end of the bar counter, where I had first come in. My nose throbbed. I brought the soaking teatowel full of crushed and melting ice up, to shrink my nose, to maintain the illusion that I was Leonardo DiCaprio, the illusion that I was…

No. I dropped the teatowel. Ice clattered across the floor. They looked at me.

"I have a confession to make," I said. The words lurched out of me. "I am not the real Leonardo DiCaprio. I merely had my face rebuilt in his image, after an accident, with grafts from my genital region, to win the heart of a woman. Thus my erectile nose."

The Director snorted. "I suspected from the start you weren't really Leo."

"Really?"

"Yeah. You had way greater emotional range."

"So, I'm no longer a Movie Star." The thought brought me a strange kind of peace.

"Oh cunt rare!" said the Director.

"Excuse me?"

"Pardon my French… in that sensual tongue, it means 'on the contrary'… No, it's not being a star that lets you make movies. It is being in movies that makes you a star. You're in this movie: you're a star!" said the Director. "And, man, now that you're a writer too…" He whistled low. "You can script your own stories. Do whatever you want, to whoever you want. Make them do you, any way you want them to…"

He pointed to the long line of women sat the length of the bar. "All of this can be yours."

As his finger swung along the line, each woman pouted at me with both sets of lips.

I shook my head. "Film is of the surface. I need to explore the depths."

"Depths? DEPTHS? What is it with actors and depths? You're an actor, for fuck's sake! It's surface all the way down!"

"No," I said. "I need to go find my muse. My true love."

"Get real, kid," said the Director. "True love's just another fantasy of power and perfection."

"Nevertheless, though a folly, it is mine, and has meaning for me. This means nothing to me."

"Oh, Vienna!" said the Director, rolling his eyes. "Excuse my Austrian... OK, I suppose I can get the real Leo for the sequel. Though it won't be the same..." He scribbled on the back of a page of the Book. "Stars, Jesus... The fucking cunts treat us like pricks... excuse my English... OK, you're in breach of contract, so you forfeit the million, and I'll take the film rights to your life and your book and all that shit in lieu of punitive damages. Sign here."

I reached for... I had no Biro.

Alice handed me a stick of gold. I examined it. It wasn't a stick. It was a pen of solid gold. The blind Librarian must have given her one, just before I arrived.

I signed. The pen wrote *"Jude"* and I stared at my own name.

I looked up, and along the line of beautiful women. All I had to do was write it and it would come true...

No, the Life should come first, and create the writing. The writing should not create the Life. I was headed in the wrong direction.

"I need to get back to the source..."

"I'll take you to her," said Alice.

71

Alice led me from the Pub of Excessive Irishness, through doors, up and downstairs, the length of long passages, until we stood in a dim room containing only a table, a chair, and a mirror.

I looked closer at the large mirror on the wall. It was not a mirror. Though it reflected me and the dim room, dimly.

I could see through my own reflection, into another, more brightly lit room, at the far side of the glass.

In that brighter room was a large bed. On that bed lay Angela. The True Angela. The authentic Angela. I touched my throbbing nose to the cool glass.

"Careful," said Alice. "If you get too close, she might see you."

I pulled back. "Why... ?" I indicated the half-silvered glass. Alice shrugged.

"Some cannot Do It themselves," she said, "but they have a powerful desire to watch others Do It... You sure you don't want one on the house?"

"One what?"

She sighed. "A fuck. Sex. With me, Leo. On the house."

"No thank you." I said. In this weather? It would be freezing up there. "But I shall never forget our..."

She sighed again. "Yeah, whatever, Leo. It's been real. I gotta make a phone call." She rooted through her bag, and found a tiny phone. "Bye..."

And she was gone.

I stared through the glass at Angela. My Muse. My Love. She rolled over a little on the large bed and seemed to sigh in her sleep. Her thighs slowly parted. I looked into her... into her...

I slammed my head off the glass, but it did not break. She stirred in her sleep.

All my jangled words fell back into their respective boxes. Order was restored.

I saw her through a glass, darkly. But I wished to see her clear.

I reached into my bag, felt cold metal, pulled it out. Stared through the holes where its eyes should have been. Frowned. Hesitated.

I put the heavy frowning mask upon the table.

I grinned.

My white teeth reflected off the half-mirror in front of me. My sun-darkened face did not.

I took from my bag instead the light and smiling mask, and crushed my face into it.

The warm plastic stuck to my perspiration.

It was a better fit.

Turning, I lifted the chair in my two hands. I carried it around to the far side of the table, swung it over my head, and drove the four metal legs of it through the semi-silvered glass.

The shattered central slivers showered the carpet of her room, the remainder fell a moment later from the frame.

I stepped through the looking glass.

In this real room. In this real world.

Angela lay sleeping on the bed. How tired she must be, to have slept through breaking glass.

I kissed her dreaming lips through the warm smile of the mask.

"Leo," she murmured. "You've come for me."

"No," I said. "It is I, Jude, an orphan of Ireland; we met long ago, in Supermacs of Eyre Square, and you set me a Quest."

She opened her eyes and smiled and frowned up at my mask.

I stood back at the force of her look.

I had no million: I would not reveal my face: I would see if my true Angela would love me as I was, as the false Angela had done. As I had believed she had done… If not, if not, if not… then I would begin again, and earn the million, and reveal my face to Angela when I had fulfilled all the terms of the quest.

Angela glanced into the darkness behind the broken mirror, and paid it no more heed. She gave the impression of one who had seen worse things, regularly.

I did not know what I wanted to say to her. I opened my mouth anyway.

"Oh. Angela. You… are my true… l."

"Don't say it," said Angela.

"… luh…" I said

"Don't."

"What?" I said.

"Say the L word," she said.

"L…?"

"Quit it!"

"But I luh… love you," I said.

"You can shove your love up your arse," said Angela, sitting up on the bed.

This was not going as well as I had hoped.

"Love songs, love poems, love love love…" she said. "I have been muse to every gobshite in Galway with a tip on his pencil. There is little pleasure and no profit in it."

She lay back on the bed and wriggled out of her knickers while listing off the prices of entry to her various orifices.

"I had not in mind a commercial transaction," I said, standing at the foot of the bed. A small electrical fan heater on the floor, at the foot of the bed, blew warm air through my hair. She shrugged, caressed her clitoris and, by clenching and unclenching assorted small muscles, pouted at me simultaneously from three orifices.

"No," I said, though the temptation caused my nose and penis to lurch forward, so that my mask popped free of my face and hung suspended, my nose jammed, swollen, into the mask's hollow nose-space. I smelt hot plastic and felt the beat of my heart in the tight pulse of my injured and constricted nose. To have pursued my true love for so long, over land and sea, only to briefly rent a hole, seemed somehow insufficient and unsatisfactory. "I was thinking more of marrying you and having children, making a little house into a home, and, most of all, growing old together."

"Aren't we growing fecking old together now, isn't that good enough for you?"

I bowed my head, and saw my mask reflected in fragments of mirror on the floor. A **b**, reflected, its curves reversed, becomes a **d**, I thought. An opening bracket becomes a closing bracket. Yet a smile, reflected, its curves reversed, does not become a frown. I thought on the axes and symmetries and reversals of mirrors until I was lost.

I looked at her beautiful body, naked upon the bed. Pale as the moon. I thought.

I felt Time pass, it matters not how much. Our tiny life is nothing to the everlasting trillion-galaxied universe but that does not mean we have not lived.

The fan heater's blades rotated and the warm air blew.

I felt us very slowly growing old together.

Peace filled me.

I closed my eyes, and felt my nasal pulse pace out precious second after precious second of perfection till I could no longer count them. Abundance. The eternal, I realised, is not a Quantity of time. It is a Quality of time.

And so I stood, in the eternal moment.

A second, or a thousand years.

The fan heater's blades rotated and the warm air blew.

I opened my eyes.

"Yes," I said. "It is good enough for me." I bowed to her. Her right hand being still engaged in the desultory manipulation of her labia and clitoris, she extended her left, perhaps to draw me to her. Oh, her white hand, floating before me: its slender fingers, its pale back, the veins with their red blood so curiously blue beneath the skin: I lowered my plastic face to it. My lips, emerging past the smiling mask, caressed the warm skin of her perfumed hand: a static discharge from the nylon carpet crackled as we made a circuit and my lips burned blue, electric for a second on her fair skin.

"Oh," she said, "oh," and withdrew her charged hand from my discharged lips. I stepped back and bowed again. My skin had dried its perspiration in the dry heat of the electric heater: my nose had shrunk as passion had been replaced by something quieter: I smiled my joy. My smile exceeded the smile of the mask; my joy exceeded my previous joy; the mask leaped free and fell upon her knickers, on the carpet, so that the arched black cotton gusset protruded from the open mouth like a tongue. As my true love looked upon my face, her expression changed. I fled through the doors and threw myself down the stairs in great leaps, reckless of injury.

As I descended, a figure appeared in the doorway, on the lower landing, taking out a cigarette. It was the false Angela. Alice. She should not be here. But why not, why not. I slowed my descent. She seemed tired. She searched her pockets slowly.

I halted a moment, to say hello and goodbye. She seemed far away, and the holes in the centres of her eyes were very small. Not a lot of the world's abundant light could get in through there.

"Are you OK?" I asked, and handed her back her lighter. She lit her cigarette, and murmured, "Alice in Ordnung, sweetheart. Alice in Ordnung."

"Is that your full, true name?"

"It's German, sweetheart. Everything's fine. All is in order. Alles in Ordnung…"

I nodded. All is in order.

I passed on.

Gents Anal Cruise

In the autumn of 1967 a cloud in the shape of human buttocks appeared over Cracow.
- Nina Fitzpatrick, *The Loves of Faustyna.*

The winner of Ireland's top literary prize has been stripped of her title in a situation as bizarre as any novel.

The judges of the Irish Times/Aer Lingus literary award announced last month that the first winner of the annual prize was a previously unknown writer called Nina Fitzpatrick whose first book, Fables of the Irish Intelligentsia, had been greeted with wide critical acclaim.

Photographs of the author, a dark-haired beauty, appeared in all the Irish papers. Over the next few weeks, however, it emerged that the author's name was not Nina Fitzpatrick and that the photograph of her was also false.

- *Chicago Sun-Times,* 27 October 1991, "'Irish' author loses prize – Check shows she's Polish."

74

I ran downstairs and out into a blast of light so strong and disorienting I thought my forehead must have struck the lintel.

"Leo! Leo! This way!" said a voice. I turned towards it, into the most tremendous series of further flashes. I fell to the pavement, clutching my eyes.

"Piece of shit," muttered the voice. "Should have used my good flash."

Dazzled, the world dancing negative and positive, ghost and truth, every time I blinked, I cautiously stood. A dim human figure seemed to loom before me.

"Who are you?" I said.

"The Sun," he replied. He stuck a camera-barrel in my face and pulled the trigger. I smelt a faint singeing of the hairs in my nostrils, and went blind.

"Shit," said the voice of the Sun.

When I finally regained my sight, he was plugging a thick cable into the back of his camera.

"You're a photographer?" I said, blinking.

He shrugged. "Some call me the greatest Paparazzo of the age."

I felt rather than saw the next waves of light which blasted me.

"What… was that?" I said, when they had stopped.

"My good flash," he said, as my sight very slowly returned. "Top bit of kit… Old days, we had the flash guns, six volt, but then guys started to carry the big batteries, running twelve volt with a capacitor could blow your arm off, and then blokes started patching in 240 volt mains from a generator, solid wall of light, and now you're nothing if your flash ain't three-phase heavy cable electromagnetic crystal pulse flash, takes an ex-Russian military pocket-nuke battlefield generator to run them, bloke in Hounslow knows a chap in Kiev, obviously you got to run the generator as far away as possible, lead shield, bloody heavy, I pull mine on a trolley, but just the flash unit can stop pacemakers and give you a tan in ten seconds, we have to slather ourselves in zinc and engine oil to keep out the ultraviolet, and wear a bloody Faraday Cage or it fucks up our tickers. Here, listen."

He grabbed my head in his hand and squeezed me tight to his chest. I clearly heard a little metal valve tap open and closed, open and closed, on the beat and off the beat of his vast heart. "Ceramic and titanium," he said. "BUPA. Can't even get them on the National Health." He shook his head. "We should never have gone nuclear. Anyway, pleased to meet you, Leo. Been trying to bag you for months."

"What an extraordinary coincidence," I said, "that you should be passing as I leave this building."

"Eh?" he said. "Nah. Your tart tipped me off."

"Angela?" I said. "Or... Angela?"

"Yeah, Angela," he said.

The last of the snow had decayed in the tropical breeze. The melt-waters rushed along the gutters, and swirled down the capacious storm drains of the city. People of both sexes had emerged from the buildings in a great range of ages and skin-tones, and the vehicles had returned cautiously to the streets. A small crowd had gathered to watch the paparazzo shoot me.

"So," said the Paparazzo, "done."

"Good, good," I said absently, and turned away.

At least Love was sorted, after a fashion. For had I not made love to my True Love? Though, admittedly, she had turned out to be someone else. And had I not, subsequently, grown old with my True Love? Though, admittedly, that subjective eternity had, objectively, lasted less than a minute...

Well, it would have to hold me.

The time had come to solve the Secret of my Origins. I pulled in a deep breath. The air was very mild, and clean.

I took the lipstick from my pocket, slid off the lid, and carefully took out the triangle of burnt paper I had rescued from the blazing Orphanage on my eighteenth birthday.

"What's that?" said the Paparazzo, taking a quick photograph over my shoulder. The flash half-melted the remaining stub of lipstick, and crispened the already brittle scrap of paper. I slipped the triangle back into the tube, almost swooning from the thick, rich perfume of the molten lipstick.

"Go on, give me a look Leo," he said.

Reluctantly, I drew the scrap back out, and gave him a look.

... gents
... anal
cruise...

"I believe that contains the key to my happiness, and the secret of my origins," I said.

He studied it. "Oh, yeah, easy," he said.

I swallowed hard. "You have solved the mystery of Gents Anal Cruise?"

"Yeah, missing letters, innit? Simple stuff... Me and the boys used to do a lot of crosswords, while we'd be waiting for the Princes to come out of nightclubs. Now it's all soap stars and Sudoku. The secret of your origins is..."

I gasped.

So did a young man, nearby. He tilted back his shaved and balding head to face the lowering sky. His lips parted in a soundless cry: he pointed straight up into the bowl of heaven. All followed his gesture, as he spoke.

"Look, it is our noble Poet Laureate! Dear God, his parachute has failed to open! A rictus of horror suffuses his features! Look!"

The Paparazzo looked up briefly at the hurtling approach of the screaming Laureate, shrugged, and looked away again. "Nah, nice colour shot, Royal angle, but... still a fucking poet, innit? Can't risk it, mate. Your true Creator is tabloid death."

"Why is that, do you think?" I asked, and felt a slight annoyance at being distracted from my destiny. Still, there was plenty of time to get the secret of my origins.

The Paparazzo pondered. "Well, celebrities can be moulded by the inchoate desires of the Collective Unconscious to replace the lost Gods, can't they? Stands to reason. But your novelist, or poet, is a Creator: Already a God, see? And you can't mould a Creator, because he'll mould you right back. It fucks up the natural order. When a novelist is in the News Section, it's all gone wrong for everyone."

He briefly stopped speaking to watch, as the Poet Laureate plummeted. The screaming Laureate's shadow fell upon us.

I had a bad feeling about this.

The Paparazzo did not raise his camera, but merely closed his eyes.

"Anyway," I said, "that Secret…"

The Poet's hurtling form struck the Paparazzo at terminal velocity.

Both men changed shape and consistency.

I looked at the entwined and bloodied corpses lying broken in each other's arms, and sighed.

75

One of the bodies stirred.

A memory came back to me, from my brief time in the Groucho Club's emergency cloakroom. Yes, I recognised the small, unopened bag strapped to the Poet Laureate's back, and the smaller closed bag strapped to his front.

It had been an error, I realised, to sew both bags shut with strong rabbit tendon.

And I remembered something else. This Poet, too, had said he knew the Secret of my Origins...

The dying Poet pulled his broken body free of the dead Paparazzo. Bone-ends grinding, he dragged himself to the pavement's edge, and was stopped by the running water.

He cleared his throat. In a surprisingly loud voice, he declaimed,

"ON THE DEATH BY INTERNAL HAEMORRHAGE OF HER MAJESTY'S LOYAL SERVANT AND KNIGHT OF THE REALM, THE POET LAUREATE."

Pedestrians the length of the street stopped, as he continued.

"And so I watch my poet's blood enrouge
The dirty snow of Soho, W1
As sweet Diana shed her mortal juice
In that Parisian underpass: the fun
Is over now, the Laureate's race is run
Enjambed against the pavement, limbs askew
Fluid filling fast the limpid lung.

Bladder crushed in that sweet silken fall
I've spilled my guts again, for all to see
My loyalty to royalty was all:
I issue now, at last, the Royal wee."

He coughed, and the filthy snow beneath his hips turned slowly yellow.

The crowd had by now tripled in size. All applauded.

"Bravo!"

"Encore!"

"More!"

The Laureate waved, weakly.

I took a step forward, to get the Secret of my Origins off him before he expired, but the Crowd of English Poetry Lovers stepped between us.

"No, seriously, *more*," said the Crowd.

A woman nodded and removed a cigarette, then a lump of gum, from her mouth. "You're the fucking People's Poet. We're the People. Cough up." She replaced gum and cigarette, and added a sweet. The crowd roared their approval.

A shaven-headed man kicked the dying Laureate. "Oi! You heard the lady! Give us another quatrain, mate. We clapped, didn't we?"

"Yeah," said a little girl. "You deaf or what?"

The poet sighed, and a bubble of blood expanded on his lips. "OK." It popped in a spray of droplets on the kicker's white running shoes.

"As through this gaping wound I vent my spleen:
I'm still a little bit miffed with the Queen
She didn't read my stuff, so what's the point?
… Look, could you get my tablets, and some oint…"

He expired, to slightly smaller applause.

"Oh for fuck's sake," I said. There went the Secret of my Origins, again.

The crowd eyed me, but my nose and cheeks had by now warmed in the wintery sun, and achieved normal size, so that I no longer resembled an American Film Star. "Huh," said the crowd, and dispersed. I was left alone with the corpse of the Poet Laureate, and the corpse of the Paparazzo. I leaned over, and took back the paper scrap from the Paparazzo's dead fingers. I looked down in sorrow on the Laureate.

Wait…

Was that a breath, or the settling of his broken chest? I put my ear to the shattered barrel.

No sound. I put my palms to it, and pressed, and pressed again. A beat! Another beat. A…

Silence.

I stood, and looked around me. There! I took the bulky Flash from the Paparazzo's other hand. I unplugged the heavy cable from its back, pulled open the Poet's shirt, and pressed the cable's copper terminals to his chest.

Retracing the cables, I found the generator, then, beneath the Paparazzo, the camera itself. I pulled out the camera, stood well back, and pushed the button.

There was a blue flash, and the smell of bacon burning. The Poet Laureate's eyes snapped open, as his legs kicked. His great heart began to beat so strongly I could hear it three yards away.

I *am* I *am* I *am* I *am* I *am*…

"If you could…" I said.

He seized the scrap of paper from my hand without looking up at me, and began to sign it.

"Er, no," I said, "that's actually the clue to the secret of my origins…"

"Oh, sorry, force of habit. They thrust a paper? Grab it… A Laureate's life is hellish, all autographs and groupies demanding you embellish their kids' bellies with a couplet improvised, with relish and a smile, on each sextuplet. They trample on my *praxis*, if I don't rhyme they start swearing, and say "I pay my taxes!" Let me tell you, it grows wearing…"

"Please, there's no need to rhyme on my account," I said. "I'm Irish. Paying no hearthtax or fumagium, commended to no lord, neither Queen's thegn nor median thegn nor ceorl, subject indeed to no monarch, and beyond the reach of my own Republic, I am a free man in England."

"Well… if you're absolutely certain?"

I nodded. "Please, not so much as an accidental half-rhyme."

"Fuck me, that's a relief," said the Poet Laureate, and glanced down at my scrap of paper. "From a letter?"

"Yes."

"Top right corner?"

"Yes."

"Most likely the sender's address… Therefore a place… In an English-speaking land… torn and burnt at the start of gents and anal, the end of cruise… Why, it is not half a mile from here."

I gasped.

"I used to do a lot of crosswords," he said, "while waiting for the servants to dress and bathe the young Princes each morning, and prepare their hangover cures… Yes, the sender of this letter lives in Re*gent's* Park… on the Grand Union *Canal*… in a river *cruise*r!"

Astounded, I broke into involuntary applause.

"No doubt it was the careless omission of the apostrophe which threw you," he murmured. "Although it is frequently omitted in place names, even for London Regents College… within Regent's Park… itself…" His great heart now merely murmured I'm… *uh*… I'm… *uh*… I'm… *uh*… I'm… *uh*… I'm… *uh*… "The apostrophe… is a bugger."

I nodded.

His eyes widened, and I feared he had reached his Expiry Date. I'd better get the Secret, before…

"Wait!" he said. "I know who lives at that address… it's…"

I held my breath.

He stared into my face.

His eyes widened still further.

"Blessed union! Jude, isn't it? Oh, I know the Secret of your Origins... it's..."

I continued to hold my breath. It would be a tight race between Revelation and Death.

"Well, there are so many Secrets..." he murmured. "You yourself, of course, are... Wait! More importantly your Mother is... But wait! Far more importantly than that, your Father is..."

The strain of digging up so many long-buried Secrets in the one Go proved too much.

He expired for the last time, and my attempts to revive him merely barbecued his ribs. Drawn by the succulent smell, the Queen's Loyal Subjects returned, and began to feast.

The Secret of my Origins had eluded me once more. But the Poet Laureate had done his best. "Thank you, Sir," I murmured.

I left him, then, and walked in the direction he had indicated.

76

I soon entered The Regent's Park. How beautiful the flowers. I stopped in the shelter of a vast, calm oak, to admire an astounding stand of bluebells. They swayed gently in the breeze. So did I. Our swaying synchronised briefly, and I gained the illusion that the bluebells and I were fixed and immobile, while the world swayed gently in my peripheral vision. "You are beautiful," I murmured, before urinating on them. I resumed my walk, along a path overhung by trees.

The harsh edges of the world grew soft beneath a silken skin of dew. Before me now, the low sun caught the intricate mechanism of a spider's broad web, spun between the bushes to either side of the curving path and a branch overhanging it. The dew had jewelled every taut line with a thousand tiny diamonds. In each diamond was held an image of me, and of the world: and of every other diamond, and its image of the world: and every other diamond... This net of jewels held every living thing. Me.

My mother.

My father.

I paused to admire the beauty of the web swaying suspended before my face, and vomited through it.

The elegant web embraced the loose burst of spew, and gave it Unity, stretching with it as it flew. The stretching, reaching web gathered in its broad spread of threads the scattered splatters which haloed and pursued the comet-head of vomit. The long-stretched web's fibres shed their tiny dewdrops in a fresh mist, as the silken lines snapped free of leaves and branches. The webbed spew flew into a distant bush.

I closed my eyes, and opened them again.

Before me, where had been the web, a shred of orange stomach lining spun, suspended from a single silver thread. As I watched it sway, a blackbird flew close by my head, snapping up the spinning scrap of brightly coloured gut.

I walked on. The trees and bushes ended, and the path moved out across a great open space. The path began to swing uphill. Thinking it unlikely that I would find a boat or an open stretch of water at the top of a hill, I left the path and continued across the cropped grass of the park, sloping gently down. If the handwriting was male... If a man had written the letter... Then that man could, conceivably, be...

My bowels convulsed. I looked about me: not a human frame in all the great circle of my horizon. Cricket pitch after football field after bowling green, on they stretched, unpeopled, to the distant oaks and sycamores and plane trees that screened the City from the Park. I looked down, to see a hole surrounded by a piled ring of soil. A mole, I surmised, had made it. As Ireland has no moles, I had never seen a molehill, but this seemed the sort of hill and hole that would be best explainèd by a mole.

Undoing the bone-buttoned flap at the back of my rabbit-skin pants, I squatted above the mole hole, bent, and looked down between my legs. How strange are these holes below, from which the universe pours water and matter and darkness and air, and the vibrations of the air, unceasingly, year after year.

Cock and balls had shrunk to nothing in the cold. My eyes, being upside down, inverted my arse so that it now resembled rolling hills split by a large canyon. A cool breeze stirred the sparse hairs clinging to the high slopes of the valley of my buttocks, and puckered the sphincter. I loosened it, and to my inverted gaze gravity seemed defied as a small dome, then thicker cone, then yet thicker trunk of warm dung rose in a mighty column from the dark valley and into the sun. The sunlight sparkled on the dark sides of the pillar. Around the warm pillar an almost invisibly delicate sheath of steam formed, as the moisture evaporating from its surface met the cool air and condensed into the finest, air-suspended liquid drops, too fine to fall.

The column grew taller, broader: then it maintained its width, and emerged smoothly from the relaxed ring of the sphincter. Up it thrust, to my inverted gaze. It began to narrow: narrowed faster at the base, the sphincter beginning to close, and with great suddenness the dark column of excrement accelerated up and away, sparkling in the sun, before vanishing into the darkness of the mole-hole.

I plucked a dockleaf from the greensward and dabbed gently at my puckered sphincter; but so exquisitely compact had been the packet of faeces, so smoothly extruded and so satisfactorily sheathed in the mucal coating necessary to assist its passage, that the leaf returned to my eye unmarked.

Would that we could rid ourselves so efficiently of sorrow.

Anxiety.

Regret.

I rose, rebuttoned the flap, and walked on.

Soon, I reached the edge of the canal.

77

A boat sat on the flat water, a good fifty yards out, where the canal broadened. It was as immobile as a photograph or painting. Fifty yards. Must I swim? I quivered. To arrive unannounced, naked and wet, at the feet of one's father, seemed both excessively right and excessively wrong but in any case excessive. An unaccustomed shyness shook me. "Oh father," I whispered.

A hatch upon the unmoving boat crashed open, and a great wild head emerged, as though summoned.

"Father?" I whispered.

A body followed.

The wild head turned and saw me. Yes, a familiar head.

"Dear God, it's you!" cried Pat Sheeran. "Or is it..." He ran his fingers through the unruly hair. It snapped and crackled fiercely erect at the passage of his hand. "I build up an astonishing charge on the Water."

The boat sat as solid as the Rock of Cashel beneath him. "Come here to me, and let me see you, whoever you are," he said, and stretched his arms, inviting, wide. The low sun behind his head set all his bush of hair seeming aflame, and the crackle of it came fierce to me across the water.

"Come!" came the voice from the burning, crackling bush, and I in reflex at that great command stepped forward onto the surface of the waters: and the waters held me up: and I took another step upon the waters and I walked toward the light, my eyes open yet dazzled and blinded by the light, for I had attempted to look upon His face.

"Father!" I said, and the word echoed and re-echoed from the far bank, the near bank; the still boat: the still water.

"Eh? Jesus, no," said Pat Sheeran, "Whoever you are, son, I'm not your father. Christ, heaven forbid." My steps faltered, I slowed, slipped, fell, and nearly broke my arse-bone on the ice which covered the pond a foot thick beneath a half-inch layer of melted snow water.

"Whoops, careful…" said Pat Sheeran. "Will you come in for a nice cup of tea?"

78

"Is it Dublin I know you from?" said Pat Sheeran, staring on my face as I climbed aboard. "Angela's friend, isn't it? No wait, it was England... or perhaps Wales..."

"Yes," I said. "All those. But..." I hesitated. No, best to risk all, and find out. "But I am also the one you brought from Tipperary to Galway: the self-same-fellow, if you count the thing by continuity of consciousness. I have been transformed since then, my face rebuilt." I hesitated. "And... I am also that Jude to whom you delivered a Letter at the Orphanage." [†]

"Ah! Ah! I had my suspicions," said Pat Sheeran, putting on the kettle. "So you *are* Jude... Why on earth would you think I..."

"I am sorry I destroyed your meeting with the Minister," I said hurriedly.

"Oh, all is forgiven. You more than made up for it, setting me up with Westcom."

"It was the least I could do." Thank God, Barney had passed on my message. "And... how is the Wisdom Business, since your delivery of Wisdom destroyed the world's banks?" I was filled with a strange reluctance to pursue the subject of my parentage; to admit I knew nothing of the content of the letter; to find... to uncover... "Are you still in the gate-opening business?"

"Well, we've been trying to get out of gates. It turns out there's not a lot of money in gates. But the recent global economic difficulties, funnily enough..." He frowned, and looked in a high cupboard for Mugs. "... caused us some problems. Our Business Plan predicted that, in such a crisis, demand for Wisdom would

---

† See the thrilling events of issue #1, Jude in Ireland! – *Jumpin' Jules G.*

rise, not fall: for Wisdom is even more valuable in a crisis than when all is going well."

I nodded, in contradiction of my own feelings.

"But…" He shook his crackling head, and bowed it low. An empty transparent plastic glass rolled toward him and leapt up from the table, into the tangle. He looked up. "We had failed to realise that those most in need of Wisdom are too stupid to realise they need it."

"It has not, then, entirely transformed your fortunes?" I said.

"Not in the manner anticipated. But, thanks to your introduction, back when we first met, we have finally found the ideal customer for our product: the customer with the most Money and the least Wisdom."

"Barney?" I was surprised.

"Barney brought us the customer: The American Military. The future lies in Intelligent Bombs: Wise Weapons. Change is the cry across America! And few things deliver more change, more rapidly, than a good, big bomb. Having partnered with Westcom, we have lobbied hard, and donated freely to both the Democratic and Republican wings of the ruling party. Our arguments have convinced them: and we have sold the Pentagon our Software. It will soon be Installed in their Systems." He placed on the table a carton of milk and a bowl of sugar, and sat. "The current generation of missiles guide themselves Intelligently to their designated targets, in order to deliver Change: but with our technology, the next generation will Wisely choose the perfect target themselves: will launch themselves at threats and dangers before they are even Threatening or Dangerous. Soon, the world will be Perfect: it will mean an end to War. Within a couple of years the system will be in place, complete: and America will be able to declare Peace, and unleash the missiles."

"A magnificent achievement."

"And lucrative. In the brief transition period to Total Peace, tens or even hundreds of thousands of missiles a year may in their Wisdom decide to self-launch, in order to prevent Danger or Threat."

I opened my mouth to ask about my Parentage, but found myself saying, "I like your boat."

Pat Sheeran shrugged. "This river cruiser is all right, but I wish to build a boat of Wood. I have it all Planned. On that boat I will be Happy, although I like a good view… indeed, ideally, I would live in a wooden boat on a hilltop…"

"Would that not negate much of the point of living in a boat?"

"Some would say so, yes. But in my case, it is Boats I like, not Water. I cannot swim, and dislike the damp. No, to live on a boat far from water is my dream."

I tried to tell him that I had not read his letter; that I did not know that which he assumed I knew; that I yearned for, and feared, knowledge of my origins. However I found it hard to say these things. "But this," I said, "… is a very big boat."

I sighed and thought that if all possibilities were true in an infinite super-universe of all possible universes, then in many I had the courage to speak; in many I had read the letter; in more I was not an orphan at all; there were so many universes in which… in which I was…

"A fine big river cruiser, yes," said Pat Sheeran. "Plenty of room. I lived, briefly, on a narrowboat in my earlier years. When I qualified as a psychiatrist, I found that I could not produce my Art in a boat that was only five feet two inches in its internal width."

"I would like to know…" I began. But then I asked, "Why is that?"

"Because a crucial part of the psychiatrist's art lies in sitting quietly, off to one side of the couch. Placement is vital. It is important to be reassuringly far from the centre of the patient's vision; yet not totally out of sight. The standard psychiatric couch is six feet eight inches in length, though I gather sports psychiatrists in the United States of America who specialise in the treatment of troubled basket-ball players use custom-built couches of up to eight feet."

"It is a marvellous land, America," I said. "I hear of nothing but wonders from that place."

The kettle grew louder and louder. The lid rattled and a first wisp of steam came from the spout.

"Indeed…" said Pat Sheeran. "Your mother… as you must know…" He made as though to say more, and stopped.

My mother my mother my mother my mother, I thought, and I had a sudden vision of myself flipping open the hinged lid and plunging my hand in among the kettle-water's roiling molecules.

I did not like the vision, and my muscles spasmed involuntarily and my hand leapt from my lap and fell back and I blinked rapidly and imagined deliberately a soothing black square filling my vision. "Tell me more about the couch," I said.

Pat scratched his head vigorously with both hands, and items of plastic cutlery flew up out of an open drawer, across the room, and embedded themselves in his hair. The lampshade swayed. "A couch of six feet eight inches must run lengthways in a narrowboat. However, this presented me with a dilemma. At first I sat further along the narrowboat, down past the head of the couch, but this made the patients nervous. They had no way of looking, to see was I laughing at them, and I had a tendency to breathe heavily on the tops of their heads. Yet when I sat at the foot of the couch, I was so far away they could no longer hear my breathing. They were continually sitting up to check had I passed out, fallen asleep, or crept ashore; they could not relax. I decided I would have to sit alongside the couch, tight squeeze though it would be, and I ordered a custom-built bench, or shelf."

The kettle's roar quietened, as it reached the boil, where the water soaks heat in silence, in preparation for the great transformation.

"But crushed up alongside the patients was worse. Many patients reverted horribly. On one particularly bad Wednesday, I had to Section a claustrophobe: a former Nottinghamshire miner had a breakdown: and a woman reliving her birth-canal trauma got stuck halfway. I was forced to reschedule the next patient. It was then I decided the couch had to go in sideways: I took a foot and a half off it myself with a handsaw: and so began my career as a child psychiatrist." He sighed. "I did try to continue with my adult practice, but I found that dealing only with the psychological problems of people under five feet in height was depressing. The same stuff again and again. Especially the men. And a lot of compensatory aggression, of course. How I yearned for an apologetically tall basketball player, with a straightforward mother fixation perhaps."

My mother my mother my mother, I thought. My mother my mother my mother. "My mother my mother my mother," I said. The kettle switch clicked off. "Could you did you said you knew her."

"Yes. As I said in my letter…"

"The letter was destroyed before I could read it. All that survived was some of your address."

"So you don't know…"

"I know nothing."

"Oh! I am mortified. I am dreadfully sorry." He put a hand to his heart. "You must be dying to know."

I nodded.

"Well, your mother… she stayed with me on the narrowboat briefly, when she was pregnant and on the run…"

"On the run? From who? Or what?"

"She didn't say…"

"And my father?"

"She didn't say." He hesitated. "She hinted that your father was alive but… ah… in… ah… prison."

"Prison?"

"I may be wrong. But that was the impression I received."

"Where?"

He hesitated. "Somewhere in the United States of America."

"Do you know anything of…" I hesitated. "My Father?"

He hesitated. "No." He rehesitated. "She would say nothing of him."

I nodded, and my eyesight blurred and dimmed.

"I believe…" he hesitated. "They loved each other."

I heard a sound in the distance, like a motorbike.

"She left me a letter, as you know, to deliver to you on your 18th birthday."

"What did it contain?" I said rather loudly to be heard over the roaring sound, louder now.

"I do not know," he said. "It was small, in a small sealed envelope. I delivered it to you in my larger envelope with a note from myself, explaining how it came to be delivered 18 years later."

"Destroyed," I said. "Destroyed."

The roar deafened me now, and I realised it was coming from my own head, the bellow of blood in my ears. The room swayed and I fell back upon the couch.

"I know no more," said Pat Sheeran. "But one man may know... As you are probably aware, I am permitted to live in the Regent's Park by permission of the Royal Family. This is due to some work I did in my narrowboat days, as a child psychologist, on the two Princes."

"And did you fix them?" I said, relaxing, my cheek to the cool leather. "The motherless boys?" I curled into foetal position, to fit the short couch.

The kettle ticked as it cooled.

"It was before they were motherless," said Pat. "And I was not required to fix them, but break them. It is disastrous to grow up Normal and Natural, if the life you then have to lead as an adult is as Abnormal and Unnatural as that of a member of the Royal Family. In the old days, the Royals fucked up their children haphazardly, by mere trial and error, hoping thereby to help them survive. Nowadays the Breaking of Princes has been put on a firm scientific footing. A program of precise and helpful psychological damage is laid out for them from birth, so that when they reach their maturity they are exactly as abnormal and unnatural as the job requires... Of course, a similar system was traditionally used, on a more industrial scale, to prepare the children of the poor for factory and office work. The breaking of the spirit, the rigid hours, the enforced obedience to a system that is not run in your interest, invisibly chained to a desk until you internalise the chains and cannot imagine a life without the desk…"

"One man," I reminded him from the comfort of the couch, "May know."

"Oh yes. A friend of mine at the time came to know your mother well; he is the only man alive who could perhaps help you find her."

"And he is," I said. "He is… ?"

"He is the Poet Laureate."

The silence was long.

"I slew him," I said. "In error… in error…"

The silence was longer. I began to tremble.

"You seem upset," said Pat Sheeran. "Perhaps you would like to be Shrunk…

"Why, thank you," I said, and closed my eyes.

"What is the Trauma, from which you are running away?"

"I have no idea," I said. There was a lengthy pause.

"Well, go on, *look* for it," said Pat Sheeran eventually.

"Pardon?" I said.

"*Look* for it."

"Where?"

"Inside."

"Inside what?"

"Inside yourself."

"Pardon?"

"It is filed away, somewhere in your Interior World."

"I have an Interior World?" I said.

"We all do."

I nodded at this. I had always suspected I had one, but we were never taught to explore it, for it was thought it would render us Unfit for Factory Work. Indeed, the Abattoir famously let go an Orphan one summer who was caught exploring his Interior World on Company Time.

"Well, off you go and have a look round," said Pat Sheeran.

I turned, mentally, and looked around inside myself, and gasped. It was bleeding huge.

"Hang on a minute," I said. "This could take a while." I searched, internally.

I searched the Attic of my Self, but there was nothing there of interest bar the dusty files of Memory. I moved down the ladder and through the dreamy Bedrooms of my Self, but found nothing. The toilet of my Self, immaculate and functional, contained nothing of note. Through the Living Quarters: nothing. The Utility Room of my Self hummed gently with the quiet activities of the White Goods of Self, pumping, draining, cleansing, cooling, heating. A soothing sound, but not what I sought. Down, then, into the very Cellar of my Self. Against the Foundations of my Self lay a little box from which came a small, incessant noise: Here I am Here I am Here I am.

I went further, into the cool dark at the back of the Cellar of my Self and found there at the far wall under the creaking joists where the ceiling lowered so that I had to stoop, then crawl, a deep depression in the very Bedrock of my Self: a depression in the shape of a woman: the absence of my Mother. I crawled into the depression, and curled up till my knees were hard against the walls of it and my fists were up tight against my chin, and I shivered there, cold in the hole where my mother was not and had never been.

"No," I said. "Everything seems grand."

"Interesting," said Pat Sheeran. "Very interesting. Have a quick look through your memories."

I made my way back up through the house, and located the files of memory in the attic, and flipped through them, from beginning to end. Nothing. Then back again, to the start. Nothing. All was normal. All was as it ever had been. Except for one curious blip, or beep, or surge, or flash, or flare, or flush, or spurt, or blink, wink, nod or tremble of something different, once, in the idyll, in Galway... I flipped back to the idyll, slower, yes... shortly before I... yes, there's the...

Babette, whom I liked and indeed respected so much, had turned to me after lovemaking and put her little hands in mine and, looking me in the eye, my left eye, yes, looking into my left eye from very close with both of hers (and with both of my eyes flicking back and forth left to right to left to right, but never, oddly, away) she said to me, "Jude." And I said, "Yes." And she said. Yes. She said. "You are not alone." And at that moment I felt that curious blip. Or beep. Or tremble. But otherwise everything had been perfectly normal and pleasant both before and after that disturbing instant.

"Hmm," said Pat Sheeran. "The buried trauma from which you are running away appears to be a brief glimpse of Happiness."

"That... that was Happiness?" I pondered this. "And some live in such a state permanently?"

"They do."

"I take off my hat to them. They must have nerves of Steel. But what triggered this Happiness?"

"The knowledge that you were warm, safe, loved, and understood. No doubt you had also had a good meal."

I pondered this. "So I merely need to avoid the first four factors, or go hungry?"

"Yes."

I exhaled my relief. I had feared it could strike again.

"Well this is most satisfactory," I said, rising. "You have explained me to myself, located my Trauma, removed my essential Mystery, and narrowed the search for my parentage to a single Nation. I cannot thank you enough."

As I turned to go, I had a thought. A dream had puzzled me recently, in which three women surrounded my bed and reached down to me and I could not move. And I could not choose which hand to take. And I could not take a breath. One woman resembled the Lady Doctor in Galway Hospital. One resembled Angela. And one resembled Babette.

I gave Pat Sheeran the gist of my dream.

"That's easy," said Pat Sheeran. "Freud knew that one very well. It is the choice of Paris, the young Greek lad who had to award an apple to the most beautiful of three goddesses. It is the choice between the caskets of gold, silver and lead in *The Merchant of Venice*."

"You're not helping me," I said. "What does it mean?"

"Oh, the three women are always your Mother, your Wife, and Death."

"Thank you," I said, and turned away, and the blood roared in my ears.

I left the boat, walked firm-limbed and confident across the treacherous ice, leapt up onto the bank and walked briskly across the greensward in the direction of... the direction of... I fell to my knees. "Mother..." I sobbed, stood up and strode on.

Shortly afterward I fell to my knees again. "Father," I sobbed, stood, and strode on.

Then, almost at the trees edging the park, I fell sideways in a weakness, and a series of vibrant images from my childhood replaced my vision briefly. Rising, I strode on, before, in the shade of the first tree, falling forward in a swoon with the word "biscuits" on my lips.

I awoke to discover I had retraced my morning path. The mingled smell of bluebells and my own urine evoked an incident in the Nurse's quarters in my earliest years, an incident not recalled till now. Arising, I strode on.

The flicker of light through the bare branches induced a curious trancelike state in me in which unbidden came to mind my curious first encounter with a banana. Then that with a ripe pear. Figs.

The tragedy of the missing jigsaw piece.

Numberless accidental viewings of rutting beasts, a couple of deaths I had forgotten, and three innovative beatings.

There was also a most curious image of a big pile of shit coming toward me and hitting me in the face while my mother screamed. My mother?

I did not realise I had passed out until I regained consciousness. There had been no dreams. It was nearly dark.

Dear Lord, the Turner of Turners! I was on the Shortlist! The prize-giving was about to take place!

… I'd not even begun to make my Art!

I hurried across London to Tate Modern.

What a day! And I had never got my cup of tea.

King of the Artists

As a child I remember parents and teachers expressing a curious emotion of guilt at their aesthetic excitement over the beauty of the flames and the searchlights of the Blitz. The luridly lit, hallucinatory landscape of burning London went in the novels with themes of uncertain identity, treachery, unfaithfulness and some essential instability of the Self.
~ A.S. Byatt, "Fathers", from *On Histories and Stories* (2000)

It's like, if you've got the Mona Lisa on your wall, all you'd get is people coming in your house and going, 'Fuck off! Is it fuck!' Know what I mean? Nothing against the artist. It's been kicked up its own arse, the Mona Lisa. It's destroyed. It's been destroyed as an image.
~ Damien Hirst to Gordon Burn, from *On The Way To Work, Damien Hirst and Gordon Burn* (2001)

81

The Salmon whispered as I ran.

"What is to replace the missing object?"

Wassily Kandinsky, Russian artist, 1913, on the dilemma of abstract modern art, and its "terrible abyss"

I whispered the words as I crossed a great bridge, high above grey-green water. "Missing... Abstract... Modern... Abyss..." and the surging water far below flickered in and out of view between the strips of stone and steel that held me in the air, above the deep water.

The Salmon whispered back.

"And when you look long into an abyss, the abyss also looks into you."

Friedrich Wilhelm Nietzsche, German philosopher and writer, *Beyond Good and Evil*, 1885-1886.

I closed my eyes against the words and the flickering water.

It was late evening when I arrived. I approached a red brick cathedral, TATE MODERN written in a high band across it, the tower of its chimney capped.

Around the corner. Down a slope.

I stood before a vast glass door. It had been slid open the width of a broad man.

He stepped from shadow and stood in the opening. His face remained shadowed, beneath the peak of his uniform cap.

"Security," said the red band.

"Jude," I said, extending my right hand.

"Anton Ndele," he said, extending his. "I have been expecting you."

We shook.

We stood there for a while.

"So are you going to let me in?"

"Not at the moment."

We stood.

"Later?" I said.

"It is possible. But now is not the time."

I peered around Anton Ndele.

"If you are tempted," said Anton Ndele, "do try and enter despite my prohibition. But please observe: I am powerful."

I considered my options. Ah!

Toby Bostique's banknotes, which I had given to Alice, and which she had returned to me.

I reached into my pocket and hauled out the crumpled notes.

"May I purchase entry with money?"

He took the notes from me. "I am only taking this so you won't think that you failed to try everything." He did not step aside.

I felt very tired and weak and sat down. Behind him, through the glass, and the crack of the opening, I saw a distant light far inside the dark building flicker on.

It flickered off.

Eventually I beckoned him.

He leaned over. "You are insatiable," he said.

"The Turner of Turners is an immense event, I am told," I said. "How is it that I have seen nobody else seek admittance?"

"No one else can gain admittance here because this door was assigned only to you. I am going to close it now." He slid the vast door shut.

My eyes prickled.

"Also, you are very early," he said, leaning down, seizing my right hand and hauling me to my feet. "So, you're a Martin Scorsese fan? *After Hours!* What a film! So underrated." He shook my hand energetically.

"I do not know what you are talking about," I said politely. He laughed with great energy.

"You Wag! You Wag, you! But seriously," he said and ceased to smile. "Films are great, aren't they? So much better than Life, for instance. Or Art. Or Books." He rolled his eyes up, and back down. "Films are just *funnier* than books. That security guy, 'Now is not the time.' That is one of the truly great security guy scenes in cinema. You don't get great lines like that in books."

"I'm sure you are correct," I said, and wished that overenthusiastic Orphans had not burnt down the town Cinema some years before my birth, during a showing of the film *Bugsy Malone*. Had I seen Films, perhaps one would have contained a truly great security guy scene, which I could have shared, or even enacted, with Anton Ndele. "I am a book man myself," I said. "I did see several scenes of a film once, but I had to leave before it finished."

"You Wag! You Wag! Saw a film once! You devil! You madman! You card! This door is only for you! I am going to open it now! Go gettum, Tiger!" He slid open the great door.

82

I entered Tate Modern. The floor sloped away and down, beneath a high walkway, and out into one enormous Room. I walked for a long time, until I was in the centre of the Room, and looked around. I was obviously very early, for the Art had not arrived yet. Certainly there was more than enough blank space on the walls for it. It was a room into which you could have fitted Galway City's great Car Park of the Roaches itself. I had never seen the like. Its scale was inhuman. Yet the Tate Family evidently still lived here, and spent all their time in this room, for their possessions lay all about me. At the far end of the room, and proof I was in the right place, a stage stood before a backdrop of vast, dead television screens. Great lights, unlit as yet, hung above the stage from steel beams.

No doubt the Prize-Giving will take place upon that stage. Oh, I hope they will not be too disappointed that I have neglected to create any Art…

Perhaps I could make up for my failure by helping to get the place ready, before the other artists' Art arrived. I looked all about me.

There was very little furniture in the room, and that in bad order. The bed in the far left corner was in most need of attention, the sheets crumpled and filthy. The last party had obviously congregated here, for on the bed, the rug, and the surrounding floor, were empty cigarette packets, stubbed butts, vodka bottles and general debris.

It was an easy matter to collect the rubbish, turn the mattress, shake out the sheets, plump the pillows, and remake the bed. This ritual, familiar to me from the Orphanage, soothed. I sang softly as I worked. Too soft a sound to rebound in echo from the bare walls.

The fish tank proved trickier than the bed. Enormous though the tank was, the fish was far too big for it. I estimated the poor creature at thirty-five feet. Presumably, in the way of family pets, it had simply outgrown its accommodation. The older Tate children, who loved it, had themselves, I supposed, reached adolescence, and become too busy to care for it: and the aging parents slowly forgot it, in its forty-foot tank in the far right corner. Certainly, it appeared to have been dead for some time. Bubbles of decomposition rocked it occasionally in the thickening water, as they emerged from the decaying grey flesh. The top of the tank was sealed, which cannot have been healthy for the fish while it lived. Certainly, it made my task of emptying and cleaning the tank more difficult than it needed to be.

When I was finally done with the fish tank, I examined the room in more detail. The place was in a shocking state. The closer I looked, the more shocked I was. The very basics of child-rearing seemed to have been neglected by the Tate parents. Neither the young Tate children nor their many pets seemed to have been adequately toilet trained. There were lumps of elephant dung everywhere. Some had even stuck to the paintings, and dried there. It was a hell of a job to get it all off.

The children themselves seemed to go anywhere. I even found a bottle of urine with a crucifix in it. Sighing, I retrieved our Lord Jesus on his cross, and hung him back up on a clean wall.

I began to clean the handprints and splashes of dried mud off the end wall.

As I worked, others quietly entered the enormous room. Some introduced themselves to me, and shook my hand.

"Judges," they murmured.

"Brian Eno,"

"Brian Sewell,"

"Brian Balfour-Oatts."

"Fascinating piece."

"Please, ignore us."

"Carry on, carry on."

They crept into the shadows, murmuring.

"And while dressed as a rabbit! Brilliant!"

"I thought Mark Wallinger's *Sleeper* couldn't be improved on, but by golly…"

"I beg to differ…"

I finished cleaning the wall, and looked around. Still a great deal of work to do, to get the place ready… Unbelievable that a family as rich as the Tates lived in such squalor. Nothing seemed to work. I decided to fix the fluorescent light, which had been flickering erratically since I'd arrived. I tracked the fault to a hidden timer that someone had mistakenly set to turn the light on and off again every minute or so. It was a simple matter to route the circuit around it.

Even their big, new, colour television seemed broken. I couldn't get any sound out of it. It was showing a rather dull film, about a woman trying to clean a shower. The pictures had gone very slow for some reason, and were in black and white. The whole thing seemed banjaxed. I switched it off.

Then I picked up some old firebricks, which had been left lying where someone might trip. Gasps came from the shadows. Brian Sewell clapped.

I put the firebricks in an old, water-damaged shed. Its overlapping boards and weathered paint reminded me of the lakeboats of Lough Derg. A pleasing warm feeling rose in me.

Now to deal with the graffiti.

The older Tate children seemed to have thrown several parties recently, without the benefit of parental supervision. Many of their friends had scrawled their names, and worse, across all kinds of objects and surfaces. I set to scrubbing. An illiterate fellow called Chris, from County Offaly, seemed to be one of the worst offenders. I was sad to see a fellow Irishman letting the side down. *"Ofili"* indeed.

Tired, and in need of a break after removing the graffiti, I looked for the toilet facilities. A urinal was mounted in the centre of the room. It was mounted at a curious height, and on its back: but no doubt that was the modern way. Oh, more fecking graffiti... On its rim someone had scribbled their name, and the date or time of the party. R. Mutt. 1917? 19.17? 7.17pm? I carefully scraped it off, before urinating. My yellow stream tumbled into the urinal, pooled briefly, then overflowed out the hole through which, I now realised, the fresh water pipe should have been plumbed. Had the artists ripped out the pipes in their Bacchic frenzy? Urine trickled down the white plinth, to pool about its base.

Brian Eno walked across the room to look over my shoulder, and nodded. "Expressive and powerful, though not, of course, original. I myself urinated in Duchamp's *Fountain*, in the Museum of Modern Art, in New York, in 1990? '91? During 'High and Low', anyway, their big Modern Art and Popular Culture exhibition... Of course, I had to use a piece of clear plastic tubing reinforced by galvanised wire to reach through the gaps in the security glass. The young have it so easy these days. But yes, this youthful firebrand is winning me over."

Brian Balfour-Oatts nodded. "The ready-made urinal, decreed to be Art by the imperious Duchamp, is accepted as Art but then decreed to be a urinal by the imperious Jude. Bold. Very bold."

"I beg to differ," said Brian Sewell.

Others had now gathered in a wide circle around me, whispering and pointing. It was a curious sensation, to have a small crowd stare at me as I went about my business. I began to imagine myself through their eyes, as they saw me; then I began, in a shocking instant, to think about my actions as I did them: to analyse them: and then, in a slippage, to think about my actions in advance, analyse them in advance, and either terminate or exaggerate the planned action. My gestures grew broad, stilted.

By now I was attempting to clean out a large container of spoiled meat, near the endwall of the room. It was a see-through box, of plastic or glass, the size of a garden shed. An internal wall of similar transparent material divided it in half. In the right half, fat-bodied black flies flew about, and crawled in and out

of a box resembling a beehive for flies. In the left half, someone
had dumped a rotting cow's head beneath an electronic fly-killer.
Holes cut in the internal wall allowed flies to make their way
from the half containing the flyhive to the half containing the
cow's head. A small pile of burnt, shrivel-winged corpses lay on
the floor beneath the crackling electric fly-killer. I stared, back
and forth, at the flyhive, the cow's head, the killer, the corpses.
My eyes followed flies in dizzy flight, trapped in one half of the
box, then, rarely, a moment of sudden transition through the
transparent hole in the transparent wall, and they flew out into a
new trap of identical dimension. Some flew down to the flesh to
eat, some to the killer to die. The actions of the flies seemed the
more arbitrary the more I looked; but the little world in which
they lived and died seemed less and less arbitrary; more and more
willed. Yet I could not understand the point of this little world;
if it were designed to kill flies, the internal wall was a flaw in the
design, slowing the killing, protecting the flies. If it were designed
to protect the flies, the holes in the internal wall were a flaw: the
placement of the meat on the other side was a flaw: the fly killer
was a flaw. This world Sustained, and Killed: sustained, and killed,
in a meaningless cycle. I found that my breathing had grown fast,
as I watched and pondered.

I tried to slow my breathing. It sped up.

I picked out a single fly to watch, to distract me from my
gasping. Oh, little fly, I thought, please, little fly… it swerved
and dived. Rose abruptly in a spiral, almost to the transparent
roof. Held still in the air an instant, wings vanished with speed,
body still and black, high above the crowd that flew and crawled
around the flyhive.

Oh please, little fly.

It dived, forward, and down, straight at the transparent internal
wall and I realised as it reached the wall that I wasn't breathing.
My eyes stuttered at the invisible transition, half expecting a
stunned rebound, but my little fly had found by luck or judgment
one of the small holes and entered the left half of the space with

undiminished speed. I breathed out a great sigh of relief, as he continued across the new space and accelerated into the crackling bars of the electric fly killer.

His scorched corpse rebounded as though spat, and landed in the wet and cloudy eye of the severed head.

Wings burnt back to tiny, muscular stumps, his body lay on its side in the centre of the wrinkled eyeball. Half collapsed back into its gummy socket, the wet and rubbery eye was fringed and half-covered with tiny, pale, identical eggs. The moist caverns of the nostrils, too, I now noticed, were crammed deep with pale eggs. And inside its lips. The tongue thick with stacked eggs, back into the dark mouth. I looked back at the black body on the eye.

My body began to turn away, but my face would not.

The stumps twitched, and flickered into life. My gaze drifted away from the flickering stumps across the field of eggs, to the edge.

My mind filled with familiar images of home. Oh, Tipperary.

"Oh, Tipperary," I said.

The cow's long, curved, dark eyelashes, rising in a ring all around the open eye, were very beautiful.

I closed my eyes and walked away.

83

I closed my eyes and walked away. The salmon spoke as I tripped.

"Is it me or is it it?"

Brian Eno, English producer, composer, artist, on modern art. 20 October, 1995, diary entry.

"I say," said Brian Eno.

"How post-post-modern," said Brian Balfour-Oatts.

"I beg to differ," murmured Brian Sewell.

"It's Brancusi's fish," said Brian Eno. "He must have taken it from upstairs. Unscrewed it from the steel base."

I looked up at them, the Salmon spilled from my bag beside me. I looked back at what had tripped me. A small dead man.

"Who's that?" I said.

"Ron Mueck's dead dad," said Brian Eno. The tiny dead man was still. So tiny, and so still. I felt myself swell with unaccustomed feelings and I leaned over and touched the cold cheek of the small dead man. I was breathing in great gulps now and it was uncomfortable.

I needed to lie down, and made my way to the bed. I took off my suit of rabbitskin and climbed in, to murmurs of "Magnificent," "He has made the piece his own," "I beg to differ..." but I could not sleep. I thrashed onto my left, onto my right; onto my back. By now men and women were filling the hall. My bed was surrounded by cameras and microphones even larger than those of Ibrahim and Zach. Excruciatingly bright lights ignited above me.

I rolled onto my front. I covered my head with a pillow.

I could not sleep.

I heard myself murmuring amongst all their murmurings, "And, in a century, a dog will choke on the bones of your beautiful face, and I won't be there to care. " I did not know what I said. I won't be there to care. I did not know to whom I said it. Some half-remembered love song.

My eyes burned and itched beneath my eyelids, in the dark. I crushed my face into the mattress till the pressure on my eyeballs hurt, and purple and yellow nets and checks and herring-bone tweeds of light juddered and flashed across my sight, and I backed off.

"Dear God. The bones of your beautiful face."

And I could not sleep. Whose face? A tooth hurt me in a sudden stab and a blast of white light erased the fading nets. I thrust hard at the tooth with my tongue and it did it again.

I threw the pillow from me, and twisted in the bed and a shard of unnoticed glass, caught in the sheet beneath me, cut my side between two ribs. A trickle of warm blood on my cooler skin.

Something smooth against my face. I opened my eyes. Pale blue. Silk, or polyester. A woman's knickers. A trace of blood in the shape of lips on the white cotton gusset. I crushed it to my face, inhaled; but all its human fragrance had long gone. I pushed it away, and it silently fell over the edge of the bed.

A cold shape against my foot, down in the bed. I hoked it up with my foot, and grabbed it. A vodka bottle. How could I have missed that? I had not even made up the bed properly. I uncapped it and drank, but it was almost empty and I could taste no alcohol in the thin sup of liquid. What what what did I want? I leaned out, searched under the bed, found a book of matches. Found a full, shop-bought cigarette, intact.

I carefully put the end bearing the little painting of a cork into my mouth, as I had seen the Lads do: and I lit the other. It burned with a swift, fierce, dry crackle. I inhaled slowly: it burnt back to the cork stump in a long single breath. A little, thin smoke trickled into my mouth and tickled my throat. I dropped the stub into the vodka bottle, where it sizzled out in the wet corner. I dropped the bottle to the rug.

Everyone applauded. The room was full. "By God, he may have swung it," said a Brian.

Two figures approached the head of the bed.

"Hi. Me, I'm the Artist formerly known as Tracey Emin," said a slight lady with somewhat bruised-looking features.

"And I used to be Eminem," said a tall, shaven-headed man with somewhat bruised-looking features.

"Love what you've done with my piece. It reminds me of me," said the lady. I stood and shook their hands, wrapping the filthy sheet about my nakedness in the manner of the Romans. The man threw his arm around the lady. She looked up at him. Each seemed to glow with pride. I exhaled a long breath. How lucky their children.

"You make a lovely couple," I said.

She nodded.

"I do believe we were Born to be Together, sir," said the man. He gazed upon the face of his wife and smiled, before returning his gaze to mine. "We have founded a movement, to fight for the rights of women. It is modelled on the Be-ism of John Ono Lennon and Yoko Ono Lennon. Except they used pacifism, and we use violence."

"Fair play to you both," I said.

"We call it Feminemineminemism," he said.

"It rolls off the tongue," I said. "Eventually."

Tracey Emin-Eminem tugged upon her husband's sleeve. He rubbed the bandaged knuckles of his right hand against his thigh, and sighed. She pointed to a stranger at the far side of the room.

"He called me a slut nine years ago, in Brighton," she said.

"Excuse me, Sir," said Eminem Emin-Eminem. "*Acrissime navigate, torpedinum obliviscens*," and he left to punch the stranger.

"Use the replica gun!" shouted his wife. "Pistol whip him! The face! The face!"

Eminem Emin-Eminem halted and turned. "Jeez, Tracey, you don't have to tell everybody it's a replica. The whole point is it looks like a *gun*, a real *gun*, or I might as well walk up with a little bitty *stick* in my hand. Jeez. No, don't cry. You know I love you honey… Jeez, please, bitch, just shut the fuck up, people are looking, honey."

Tactfully I left them to it, for I had seen a familiar bulky figure limping across the crowded floor towards me. My heart beat the faster. An unfamiliar figure followed in his wake. I looked to either side of them, but I could not see Babette. As I walked towards them, I bent to pick up my bag, and the Salmon. I felt a sharp pain, and fresh blood from the gash between my ribs stuck the thin sheet to me.

Barney O'Reilly Fitzpatrick McGee greeted me. "Revolutionary! Destroyer of my Property! Leader of my Workers! Misleader of my Daughter!"

I noticed a small pistol with a long silencer in his right hand. No doubt, as a wealthy American in a room full of impoverished Artists, he needed it to protect himself.

"That's me," I said, "Jude's the name," and put out my hand.

"Wrestle my gun from me, would you," said Barney O'Reilly Fitzpatrick McGee.

"Righty-oh," I said and took a step forward, but before I could oblige he had taken a step back, trodden on the instep of his following friend, and, attempting to recover his balance, tripped backwards over Ron Mueck's dead dad.

As his friend and I bent to help Barney's unconscious form, the lights changed; the crowd surged forward, carrying me with them; and Lords Grey and Cümerbund stepped together into a single circle of Light upon the stage before me.

"The moment we have all been waiting for," said Lord Cümerbund, with a smile. His magnified voice filled the vast space.

"The announcement... of the winner... of the Turner... of Turners," said Lord Grey.

"Jude! Jude! Jude!" cried the crowd, and attempts were made, by thin arms, to lift me onto thin shoulders.

"Please..." All looked to Lord Grey, who held aloft his pale right hand. The chant died away, and I was dropped. Lord Grey lowered his hand. "Let there be no hasty rush to Aesthetic Judgement. We must not be carried away by our mere Emotions: by our fallible, biased, fatally compromised, subjective, disgusting, personal taste. More sober, objective, scientific, impartial criteria for judgement must be found."

He reached into his right-hand trouser pocket with his right hand; Rummaged; his hand emerged empty. "I would appear..." He twisted to rummage in his left pocket with his right hand. "To have left the house without..." He twisted yet more, to rummage in his back pockets, tugging, in his anxiety, on the life-line joining him to Lord Cümerbund.

Lord Cümerbund reached into his own pocket, and drew forth an object. It appeared to be both Wallet, and Pump. Clad in pale leather, it pulsed at something just below the natural rhythm of a Human Heart. A tattoo upon the wallet-skin read Mother. Mother, transfixed by an arrow, encircled in a Heart.

Lord Grey's fragile tube led into the pulsing wallet, through the 'o' in Mother, and came out its shadowed back, to vanish into the deep pocket of Lord Cümerbund.

Lord Cümerbund cracked open the pale, pulsing wallet and slid into the leather slit two fingers: There was an impression of delicate digital manoeuvring.

The fingers emerged with a golden coin. It shone.

Lord Grey took the coin delicately from Lord Cümerbund, and turned to face the hushed crowd.

He spoke.

"Heads, he is the Genius of the Age: tails, he is a provincial, buffoonish charlatan."

The great Hall held its breath.

84

Lord Grey put forward his right hand, as though to shake hands. He gently curled his forefinger about the tip of his immaculate right thumbnail. Then he rested the coin flat upon the middle knuckle of the forefinger, so that the coin's near edge overhung the trapped thumbnail. He tensed the Thumb – it strained – its knuckle whitened... The Queen's head, calm above the shadowed, straining thumb, was perfectly visible to me. As the cameras pushed in closer, rose higher, she appeared now upon the cliff of television screens behind the tensing Lord; in the countless million homes and bars of Britain; bigger, brighter, dramatically filling the pulsing screens.

The reality of the coin, unmediated, seemed stale and small in comparison. The great bright screens drew my gaze repeatedly; and yet, the quiet thrill of the real drew me back; and so I would glance up, or left, or right, at these enormous electronic reconstructions; then back to reality, and away, and back.

Finally, by increased pressure from the straining thumb, or by decreased pressure from the restraining finger, or by a combination, the long and graceful Thumb escaped, or was released, or both, and transferred its pent-up energy to the golden coin, hurling it high into the glaring air beneath the television lights, up above the lights into cooler air, glinting as it spun...

I looked away from the coin on which my fate depended, to find the woman on whom my fate depended. There! Babette, looking straight at me from the stage.

An astounding thought occurred to me.

I indicated to her, using universal human gestures, that it was her that I loved after all. Or at least in addition. She, in gesture, indicated that she was pleased to hear it.

The coin began to descend.

She spoke briefly, in gesture, of the crisis of faith afflicting Socialism, the crisis of faith afflicting Capitalism, and the possibility of harnessing the virtues of the second to the virtues of the first, and vice versa, without killing too many people.

I stepped toward the stage edge, and her.

She stepped between Lords Grey and Cümerbund, toward the stage edge, and me. The tube connecting the two Lords pulled tight around her hips; strained; then snapped free, and shot into the audience.

The coin, observed by millions, landed on her Head.

Lord Grey, unplugged, collapsed.

Lord Cümerbund, his wallet wrenched from his hand, dropped on all fours to retrieve it.

Babette, a writhing Lord at either foot, stood magnificent in the spotlight. Reaching up with her right hand, she slowly and delicately lifted the gold coin, and brought it carefully down without rotating it. All the cameras thrust their lengthening snouts toward its surface, ablaze in the light.

"Heads," said Babette, as the Queen's head filled the screens.

"He is the Genius of the Age!" roared the crowd, thousand-voiced, and their cheers echoed and re-echoed throughout the vast Hall.

Babette frowned, running her delicate fingertips beneath the golden coin. She turned it slowly over, to reveal the identical head of the self-same Queen.

"It is heads both sides," she said.

"Hurrah! Hurrah! He is Twice as Brilliant as even we thought! Hurrah!" replied the crowd.

"I think you are missing the point," said Babette.

"Eh?" said the crowd.

She explained, to gasps, the significance and implications of the double-headed coin, and went on to critique the very system of the Coin; explain the role of the Coin; discuss its symbolism, etc. I must confess I did not follow all of it myself.

The crowd slowly quieted, the better to digest this rich feed of information and its interpretive sauce. Babette ceased to speak: I admired her, a very Goddess in the spotlight.

And I do believe, had there been no spotlight, I would have admired her nonetheless; and that she would have been, without benefit of illumination, nonetheless a Goddess.

At length the swiftest thinker in the crowd, having thought his way at full-pelt through her speech, came to his fearful Conclusion: "Dear God!" the thinker cried. "He is, in truth, a provincial, buffoonish charlatan!"

The crowd in the instant became a Mob: silence, bedlam. They lunged, to rend me limb from socket.

And then she reached down her hand to me, and I reached up mine; and our fingers touched and I swayed and had to hold myself from fainting; and she pulled me up onto the stage and into the light and began another speech, in favour of my actions, not as Art, but as Artistic Critique. I was not worthy of Establishment Acclaim… the crowd bayed… No, I was worth far more than *that*: for mine were Radical Subversive Gestures. The crowd gasped, then cheered. Indeed, she read a great deal more into my actions than I had consciously put there. And I marvelled at the cleverness of my subconscious, which seemed to me well worthy of a Prize.

The silence was most exquisite in its perfection as she reached the end of her ringing oration. The crowd looked at her: looked at me: dropped their eyes.

"For Shame! For Shame!" they wept. "He has done so much for us, for us! For our sins! For our sins! And we so nearly destroyed this good, good man!" And they began to rend their garments, weeping.

"Artist of Artists!" one cried, "King of the Artists!"

And all joined the cry.

"Hail, Hail, King of the Artists!"

Weeping, a young woman threw herself at the stage, grasped my feet, she wept upon my feet and dried them with her hair.

"Speech! Speech! Oh King of the Artists, Speech!" came the new cry. I wished merely to stand hand in hand with my Babette, a little to the side of the brightest light; but I was pushed into the hot core of the overlapping beams by the sweating workers of the Television companies. I resisted, pulled back; but my elbows were grabbed by the Art Critics of the major Newspapers, their plastic identification tags swinging wildly from cords about their necks; and I found myself caught between *Mirror* and *Observer* – thrust into the light by *Sun* and *Star* – and held in its glare by *The Times*. Crowd and critics howled, "Speech! Speech!" in a frenzy to hear me speak. But I had no words.

Then, oh my anxiety became immense and my sight grew dim and I swayed under the unending torrent of light.

A Television Worker pinned a tiny model of a Microphone to my bloody loincloth and whispered loudly in my ear, "If you could just make a short speech, of five to six minutes, that will bring us up nicely to the break."

A speech? A speech, to these thousands? These millions? Sweat sprang up, along the length of my spine, across my shoulders, my brow. My white sheet clung flat to the cold sweat.

Luckily, Lord Grey now chose this moment to attempt the removal of his eye, in order to intercept the bubble on its way to his brain. The crowd, seeing this, gasped.

A thin, male Artist cried, "Dear God, he is clawing at his own eye! His mighty Eye, which once did so much for British Art Exports, in the face of a strong sterling and a philistine Press!"

A thin, female artist wept, "Dear God! Detain his reckless hand, for he knows not what he does!"

The slender Artists bounded up onto the stage, followed by others. They were frail but many.

In vain, Lord Grey protested. They sat on his right hand and on his left hand. They sat upon his feet.

The bubble reached his brain, and he shuddered, and expired.

"Great television," murmured the Television Worker at my side. "So, four minutes to the break, *go*." And he was gone. And all the lights came on above me. And every camera swung to face me.

My sweat dried. Every eye, except for Lord Grey's, followed the lighting's glare and the cameras' stare. I opened my dry mouth and wished for Wisdom.

And the Salmon leaped in my bag.

I drew it surreptitiously forth, but the lights above overwhelmed its little screen, the crowd its little voice. I held it up, above my head and slightly in front of me, blocking out the brightest lights to read the Wisdom from the Screen.

The crowd gasped. "He has made a Fish appear!"

"Brancusi's Fish…" said one, then another.

"What can this portend?"

"That the Fish shall be our symbol!"

"Henceforth we shall eat Fish on Wednesday, in Memory of Jude!"

One, in error, said "In Memory of Brancusi!" and was pummelled to the ground.

"Jude has Appropriated it! Refreshed it! Made it New!" they cried as they pummelled. "How dare you ascribe this fish, which is Jude's, to Brancusi, who is dead and does not live, who is the past…" But others argued that Brancusi came first to prepare the way for me, and was thus worthy of veneration. Taking advantage of this argument, the pummellee crawled between their legs, and away.

"Shhhhh!" said the others to the arguers. "Speech! Speech!"

And I spoke. I had used the brief brawl to check the start of the Quote, and its source. Gerhard Richter, German Artist, from his diary or notes, 8 December 1992. And, indeed, it started well.

"Artist: more of a title than a job description…"

The crowd roared, "Artist! Artist! King of the Artists!"

When they had stopped, I continued. *"It's a word that still earns you considerable respect."*

They laughed, believing I had praised their baying. It was

extraordinary the perfect fit of the Quotation; and I read on with perfect confidence.

"People associate it with splendour and misery, with the attainment of freedom and with unexampled independence. Artists' lives seem exceptional and exotic: they are ahead of their time: their works are among the loftiest works of the human race; their undaunted courage defies the incomprehension of the philistines and the persecution of the dictatorships!"

My breast filled with pride, that I was an Artist. The exclamation mark was my own – for the original text had neglected to include any – and it added immeasurably to the effect. The crowd improvised Hats from items in their pockets, and from the nearby objects, and threw them in the air. I felt a swelling Joy, to be so loved. I looked out upon their loving, swollen, reddened, wild-eyed faces, and smiled, and continued.

"Artists are the truly creative ones, the geniuses; their fame and the fame of their works derives from their God-given talents and from their passionate devotion to their work, which they perform with intuition and intelligence on behalf of the community. They are always progressively minded and critical of society, always on the side of the oppressed; and, rich or poor, they are always privileged."

Lengthy roars of approval were interrupting me every few words. The Quotation, though short, seemed, thanks to the interruptions, likely to provide me with a speech of roughly the right length. The thought that this would soon be over, the relief that I had been saved by Wisdom, the adrenaline coursing through me as a result of the ordeal, all lent passion to my voice as I continued to read out Mr. Gerhard Richter's excellent and life-affirming words. It was perhaps the translation from the German which gave it its great confidence and power, imbuing the English version with a certain lumpiness which added much to its authority. I bellowed the last:

"Understandably, everyone would rather be an artist than endure the shame of some ordinary occupation. But the artist's image is going to be adjusted, sooner or later, when society realizes how easy it is to

be an artist, and to set down (on or off the canvas) something that no one can understand and consequently no one can attack; how easy it is to inflate one's own importance and put on an act that will fool everyone else and even oneself. By then, if not before, the title of artist will induce nausea."

When I had finished, there was a silence as they processed my full speech. They had ceased to smile. I did not like this silence. I felt I would prefer anything to this silence.

However, I was wrong.

"*Artists…*" they said at length. They took a step toward the stage, knocking to the floor, crushing against the stage-edge, or throttling with the cords of their own name-tags those few artists who had not been pistol-whipped earlier by Eminem Emin-Eminem. The frail, artistic bodies vanished under the savage assaults of the crowd. Only occasional bloodied scraps of clothing, hurled aloft by the Mob, indicated what was happening at the core of these tornadoes of fist and boot.

A particularly tall and wild-eyed gentleman, bow-tie askew, white shirt-front spotted with crimson, looked up from the dismemberment of Martin Creed and, over the heads of the crowd, pointed straight at my beating Heart.

"The King of the Artists!"

"Kill! Kill! Kill him!" came the chant of the crowd. "Kill the King of the Artists!"

"It is best if we flee," said Babette.

We fled.

Behind the backdrop of screens, we entered an almost silent chaos of smaller screens and large machinery, controlling sound and vision for Great Britain's televisions. Figures in black moved like monks among the machines, murmuring to themselves. Hand in hand, Babette and I ducked under thin cables and jumped over thick, until a man moving among the monks confronted us.

It was Barney O'Reilly Fitzpatrick McGee.

"Father," said Babette.

"Shut," said Barney O'Reilly Fitzpatrick McGee, grasping Babette's left hand and pulling her behind him, "up."

He took a deep breath.

"You," he said to me, "you have taken my sweet daughter, the apple of my eye, the comfort of my decrepitude, and you have parted her pale thighs, her innocent thighs, you have caressed the tender flesh of her belly and breast, you have taken her breasts into your mouth and sucked her nipples hard against your soft palate, spread wide the warm lips of her slim labia with your thick tongue, you have moved her warm hair out of your eyes as you have plunged your engorged manhood into her liquid depths: you."

"Yes," I said, nodding. "That was me all right."

He swung wide his arm to welcome me to the bosom of his family. Unfortunately, in doing so, he struck me surprisingly hard on the left temple with the silencer of his pistol.

When I woke up, it was Thursday.

A clock said so, on the far wall of…

The room was strange, and white, and bright.

Yes. Five to Nine. Thursday.

Lord Cümerbund's face eclipsed the clock.

"Creative," he said. "Unspeakably talented… yet brave enough to say the Unpopular Thing, in the teeth of danger, to the very face of the Mob. You, sir, are the man I need." He grabbed my limp right hand and hauled me to my feet. "I took the liberty of having you dressed while you slept."

I felt my head. My hair had been tied back in a manner which caused it to resemble the tail of a pony. I looked down. My loincloth had been replaced with a loose, floppy suit, and a shirt in a violent colour to which I could not immediately put a name.

Lord Cümerbund looked me up, and down. "Yes, I believe we have captured your Creative Spirit… Come, the meeting is in four minutes." He hauled anew.

I grabbed my bag from the bedside table and teetered after.

A silent man in a black suit, also sporting a pony's tail, seized my other elbow and half-carried me toward the door.

"Where?" I said.

"The Medical Unit of Cümerbund, Cümerbund & Cümerbund."

"Who?" I said.

"My brothers and I set up Cümerbund, Cümerbund & Cümerbund in the Seventies. But I like to think I drove its Vision."

I was, I noticed, being dragged along a long corridor. Sweet memories of the Orphanage afflicted me.

"Cümerbund, Cümerbund & Cümerbund brought the modern, hot-desking, multi-tasking, rank 'n' yank, lockershocker, root & shoot work environment to the staid world of UK advertising."

"Babette…" I said.

"Ah," said Lord Cümerbund. "Barney has sent her to the United States of America for… well, we shall speak of this after the meeting."

The United States of America…

We were approaching a long row of lockers, which ran down the middle of the corridor. A number of young men, half-dressed, looked up, and sprinted or, hobbled by their trousers, shuffled from sight, some taking shelter around the far side of the bank of lockers, some leaping into their locker and slamming the door.

"Other agencies," said Lord Cümerbund, "are divided rigidly into Suits and Creatives, each faction despising the other. But at Cümerbund, Cümerbund & Cümerbund, no one is merely a Suit, no, nor merely a Creative neither, though by your smiling you seem to say so."

"There was no such stuff in my thoughts," I said.

The last locker door slammed, concealing a man with his head trapped in a poloneck too small for it, and vast loons or flares, or twin skirts, about his ankles.

"Every Morning, every Partner arrives at work and must decide for himself or, theoretically, herself: Am I a Suit today? Or am I a Creative? This mental flexibility brings astonishing rewards." We stopped at the lockers. Lord Cümerbund fanned out a series of small rectangles of lined card, of several different colours, and, plucking one, read it. "Cuthbertson!" A head of curly blond hair appeared slowly around the far end of the row. "I'm rooting for you, Cuthbertson!" shouted Lord Cümerbund down the line of lockers.

"Very good Sir! Thank you, Sir!" shouted back Cuthbertson, and vanished.

"Sing!" cried Lord Cümerbund. There was silence. "Sing, damn you!" shouted Lord Cümerbund. Several quavering voices came from behind the lockers.

"And did those feet…"

"Dancing Queen…"

"Lager, lager, lager…"

"Shut up!" They ceased. Lord Cümerbund looked back at the card. "Edward Singh! New boy, a little nervous," said Lord Cümerbund to me in an aside. "Come out like a man, wherever you're hiding."

A locker door swung open beside us, and a tall man with a sheet wrapped around his head unfolded himself from his place of concealment. The silent fellow in the black suit released me. He put his hand on Singh's elbow. Singh fell to the ground, sobbing. The man in the black suit produced a small pistol and, placing it in the back of Singh's left knee, shot him once. Edward Singh cried out, then bit his hand and was silent.

"Very good," said Lord Cümerbund. "I'm afraid it's only an air pistol," he said, turning to me. "The pellets seldom lodge deep. But nonetheless, an excellent motivational tool, and it makes sure everybody starts the week on their toes. Except him, of course. They prefer it to detention, though. And you seldom have to shoot the same fellow twice. Now," he said, giving Edward Singh a hand up, "I hope to be Rooting for you next Monday, Singh."

"Thank you sir, I hope so too sir, I shall do better sir, it was my dying wife sir, you may remember my mentioning her, but she is dead since Tuesday sir, so you should see a marked improvement."

"Yes yes, I'm sure I shall." Lord Cümerbund slapped him on the back. Singh fell over.

We continued on.

Around the corner, and near the corridor's end, was a single isolated locker.

A delicately built fellow reached very slowly for the locker handle. He wore only white underpants, with the name Calvin Klein stitched neatly onto the waistband. A small yellow stain appeared low on the front of the underpants, as his hand closed the last few inches. There was a blue flash, a whip-crack of sound, and a strong smell, as of the seaside on a hot day, as a cataract of electrical energy poured through Calvin's frame, convulsing him. He fell to the floor, and lay there blinking rapidly, as the small yellow stain on the front of his underpants spread until the entire garment was pale yellow.

"Got the shocker locker, again? Second time this week, isn't it? Not very good that, is it? Frankly, I don't know how you keep making it through the rank'n'yank." Lord Cümerbund kicked him below the ribs and moved on. "The boy's not even trying," said Lord Cümerbund as we approached the big double doors. "I don't know, I may have to Discipline him, but I don't like doing it."

Loud footfalls behind us, as a half-dozen Suits and Creatives caught up with us, panting.

"My Lord,"

"My Lord,"

"My Lord,"

"My Lord,"

"My Lord,"

"My Lord."

Some were perspiring heavily. "Nervous?" said Lord Cümerbund. All nodded. One fainted. "Never fear. Oh, we've a tough customer lying in wait for us in there, but," said Lord Cümerbund to the sweating advertising executives, lifting my weak arm, "this is the fellow will turn this account around!"

All nodded.

I attempted a smile. Failed.

Another fainted.

I entered the room on Lord Cümerbund's arm, followed by the surviving Creatives and Suits, the former still clipping on their ponies' tails.

88

A half-familiar man sat at the far side of the table, beside a woman unknown to me. "Sit!" he said.

We sat. The morning light poured in the windows behind him. Creatives and Suits drew dark glasses from their pockets, and put them on. I squinted, and regretted the loss of my amber goggles. Unless…

I had a dig in my bag and found them beneath the Salmon. I put them on, the caress of the pale fur against my nose exquisite. The Creatives gasped and the Suits muttered. "Retro, but hetero." "Fantastic in plastic!" "Groovy vinyl…" "Couture." "Italian?"

I could see the man's face more clearly now. Where…? Yes, I knew him. Barney O'Reilly Fitzpatrick McGee's trailing companion yesterday, at the Turner of Turners.

"Right," he said. "What the heck is wrong with this country? I pay you guys for penetration and I'm not getting any. None! I need penetration here, guys. I sell more pants in Lithuania! And you guys give me a draft campaign where *you cannot see the clothes*. Where the brand is *not visible*. *My name* is… *not there*. What are you trying to do to me? I'm the second biggest name in US fashion! Black urban teens love me, because they think white preppies wear my stuff. White preppies love me, because they think black urban teens wear my stuff. Everybody wants to get into my pants. I am huge. I am enormous. I'm down the left leg of half the pants in America this season. And in the UK I cannot give them away! What is it?" His voice fell. "Is it because I'm Lutheran? It's because I'm Swedish-American, right? Is that it? It's an anti-Scandinavian thing, right? Tell me!"

The Suits looked at the Creatives. The Creatives looked at me. I looked at Lord Cümerbund.

Lord Cümerbund coughed. He steepled his fingers. "You have a very powerful brand," he said.

"Very, very powerful," said a trembling Creative.

"Almost," said Lord Cümerbund with a light laugh, "... too powerful."

The Swedish-American clothing magnate leaned half-way across the broad table. "That's just... just... bull chips! *Bull chips!* Tommy Hilfiger..." The woman beside him shuddered at the name. "... has a brand identity almost as strong as mine, but I see his stuff everywhere: Tommy! Hilfiger! Everywhere! Where am I, Lord Cümerbund? Where am *I*?"

"Mmm. Mmm. Yes. Every market is unique, though, presents its unique challenges, and your very strong, powerful brand..."

"Very very strong," whispered the trembling Creative.

"... is itself uniquely challenged in the British urban streetwear youth market. Penetration will be difficult. Perhaps painful... adjustments may have to be made."

"... so if my brand's too strong, what's your excuse for doing nothing with my ladies' line? New line, new name in honour of my lovely lady wife, new brand, limitless potential – limitless!"

She blushed, at her husband's side, and looked at his profile from under her eyelashes. In her lap a small child slept.

"And you guys can't even get it into the stores... Wait, *what* freaking adjustments?"

The Creatives looked at the Suits. The Suits looked at Lord Cümerbund.

Lord Cümerbund looked at me.

I coughed. Lord Cümerbund indicated that I should rise. I rose. Lord Cümerbund indicated I should make my way around the long table and approach the furious clothier. I did.

"I don't believe you have met," said Lord Cümerbund.

"Pleased to meet you," I said, extending my hand, "I am Jude."

"Creative… Artist… Genius…" glossed Lord Cümerbund from the far side of the table. Beside him, the trembling Creative fainted, and fell from his chair. Nobody else moved.

"Jude…" The clothing magnate extended his hand. "I am, of course, naturally, as you well know, Frigg Fingerwank." As I shook his hand I digested the nature and size of the problem. "And this is my wife, Fanny."

Releasing his hand, I took the hand of Fanny Fingerwank.

"And our son," she said. "Cnut."

I shook the tiny hand of the sleeping Cnut Fingerwank, while looking from Fanny to Frigg.

They looked back at me.

I cleared my throat.

89

After I had solved Frigg and Fanny Fingerwank's UK marketing problem, we all arose, to go to dinner.

"Fantastic," said Frigg, shaking my hand.

"Fabulous," murmured Fanny.

Cnut hiccupped.

Lord Cümerbund slapped me on the back.

We walked towards the double doors.

I glanced out the window. Far below, in the marina, a lone white yacht sat foreshortened on the calm water.

"You are admiring my yacht," said Frigg to me.

"Yes," I said.

"Frigg sailed here, you know," said Lord Cümerbund, "from the States. He sails everywhere."

"Flying is for faggots," said Frigg, nodding. "Many Americans are afraid of the sea, but I, being of Scandinavian stock, understand the sea; I understand its murderous, treacherous ways, its brutality, its stupidity, its ignorant philistinism. I understand what too few Americans understand, that we can never make peace with the Sea; it must be told who is master; it respects only strength; it must be tamed, drained, and settled with people of good Lutheran stock." Frigg Fingerwank threw an arm about my shoulder. "My yacht is ready for anything – it is armed, and armoured, and contains at all times enough stores to last a Year. You must sail with me some time, Jude."

"Thank you," I said.

We passed through the double doors. Those Creatives and Suits who had remained conscious throughout were now Whooping, and leaping high to slap each other's palms. They were also slapping me on the back, and offering to buy me alcohol.

In the corridor Lord Cümerbund said to Frigg and Fanny, "We would eat at my house, but I had to fire my cook."

"Why?" asked Fanny Fingerwank.

"He threw out something he should not have."

"Oh I heard about that," said Frigg. "I'm very sorry... Hey, I need a cook for my voyage. Is he a good cook?"

"Terrific," said Lord Cümerbund, frowning. "Just tell him not to throw anything out before checking with you."

"It was a Hirst, was it not," said Fanny, "which he disposed of in error?"

"Yes. A very personal piece that I had commissioned."

"Yes, I gathered from the *National Enquirer*, not that I read it," said Frigg, "that it was your brother, in a glass jar, pickled."

Lord Cümerbund sighed, and cleaned his shoes on an unconscious Suit. "I would prefer to say no more, for legal reasons... Excuse me a moment, gentlemen." He took me aside.

"Well, we're off to dinner with the Client, to celebrate the extension of the account," he said.

"Excellent," I said, "for I am rather hungry." It had been a good while since I had had my last rabbit.

"Ah," said Lord Cümerbund, and glanced across at Calvin, lying trembling in his urine by the shocker locker. "Tut. Tut. No improvement. I shall have to send MacNally to discipline him after all..." He tugged his earlobe, and looked at the ceiling. "I meant to mention it, but it slipped my mind... You won't be coming to dinner with us... you fellows go on ahead, the Ivy, I'll catch up..." He turned back to me as the Suits and Creatives led Frigg, Fanny and the sleeping Cnut down the corridor, weaving around their fallen comrades. "Yes... I'm afraid I had to cut a deal with Barney. He was very keen to... well, you know. You and his daughter, you know. Very old-fashioned fellow. Not to put too fine a point on it, he wanted to take you out."

I was delighted that Barney, celebrating my relationship with his daughter, wished to treat me to dinner. "I understand," I said. Indeed, everything seemed delightful to me, after a day's sleeping and fasting. And whatever Drugs they'd put into me in the Medical Unit.

"Nothing personal," said Lord Cümerbund, shaking my hand. The others had gone.

Barney O'Reilly Fitzpatrick McGee came round the corner, towards us, holding a somewhat larger gun than last time, with no silencer.

"Not here, Barney, for God's sake," said Lord Cümerbund, on seeing him.

I nodded. I had never heard a good word said for canteen food.

Lord Cümerbund walked rapidly away, pausing only to kick Edward Singh, who had just crawled around the corner after Barney, murmuring, "I'm late! I'm sorry! I'm late!" The kick doubled or tripled Singh's speed toward us. "Thank you! Sorry! Thank you!"

Lord Cümerbund was gone.

I took a step towards Barney and put out my hand.

He took a step backward, and tripped over Edward Singh.

As I walked toward Barney, and reached down to help him to his feet, he scrambled back, and stood up.

"Hah! Hah!" he said, "Hah!"

I was pleased he was amused rather than disgruntled at his mishap. I took another step, and went to shake his right hand, which contained the gun.

"Hah!" he said, "I shall not fall for that old trick twice!" and he took a further mighty stride backward, stepping over the quivering body of Calvin. "Hah!!" Unfortunately, the extreme length of his backward stride meant that the shiny leather sole of his bright new shoe landed hard and at an oblique angle in the yellow puddle surrounding Calvin, on the polished wooden floor. There was a muffled tearing noise, as he did the splits and landed hard, on his groin, on Calvin.

Calvin ceased to tremble and began breathing regularly.

Barney did the opposite.

"My groin..."

From around the corner came the man in the black suit with his little pellet gun.

I smiled reassuringly and reached out both hands across Calvin's sleeping head, to help Barney up.

"You will not disarm me!" said Barney. I thought it charming, that he found my smile disarming, and I leaned closer, over the puddle.

"No!" Barney, proud fellow, spurned my helping hands.

Before I could warn or stop him, he had grabbed hard and pulled on the projection above his head: the handle of Calvin's shocker locker.

The energy blew blue bolts through the wet soles of his shoes, snapped all his muscles tight, brought his legs together, whipped him upright, and, unfortunately, clamped his hand immovably closed on the electrified handle. The locker door swung open, masking Calvin's body from the view of the man in the black suit who now loomed behind Barney's convulsing body.

MacNally, I thought. Oh dear, he's going to discipline the wrong...

"Suit, huh? Too late, dancing boy," said the man in black, and shot Barney O'Reilly Fitzpatrick McGee in the back of the left knee.

90

After MacNally had left, I tried to assist my wounded future father-in-law.

When he had stopped spasming, he fired three trembling shots at me from his pistol, narrowly missing my groin and scorching the cloth of my new suit. I looked at him in astonishment. "You could have injured me," I said.

"That would have been a pity," he said, "for I am trying to kill you."

I took a step back. He took trembling aim at my heart.

It dawned on me that I had misunderstood the situation. Much became, in retrospect, clear.

I would have to find my own dinner.

I made my escape down an emergency staircase, and out an emergency exit, to the marina. Alarms ringing, I ran. Behind me, very slowly, limping and trembling, Barney emerged from Cümerbund, Cümerbund & Cümerbund, in slow pursuit.

I ran the length of what turned out, unfortunately, to be a Pier; and found myself at the end of it, surrounded by water. Frigg Fingerwank's yacht lay to my left, and a shed lay to my right, as Barney limped trembling on to the Pier's far end.

I looked at the yacht; voices came from it. Barney's friends, or the employees of Barney's friends. No.

I threw open the unlocked door of the shed, entered, and slammed it behind me.

A little light came through the high, barred window over the door. It was a storeroom of some kind: foodstuffs, in enormous industrial containers. Giant sacks of rice, of coffee-beans, of oats. Giant jars of pickles, of jam... Crates of tea, huge tin boxes of biscuits, bales of plastic straws, of serviettes, pallets of butter.

They almost filled the room. There was no space to hide. The butt of Barney's gun banged upon the door. I was doomed.

I deliberately disordered some of the supplies to my left. I then moved to my right and, climbing the crates of tea, slid and crawled across the supplies to the back, and a row of vast glass jars. With great difficulty in the confinèd space, I unscrewed the lid of one, to reveal Jam, almost to the brim: no use. But the next contained, by its smell, an Oil: yes, the lid was stamped in black letters "Extra Virgin Olive Oil: first cold pressing. Produce of Spain". There was a good gap between oil and lid. As the door began to splinter around the lock, I slid slowly inside the Jar, holding the Salmon aloft. A shame to ruin the new suit Lord Cümerbund had provided, but… The oil rose, reached the rim, spilled silently over and flowed down the sides. Would I leave the Salmon outside? I hesitated: no, the risk it would Leap, and alert him to my presence, was too great. I lowered it beneath the surface, and let it go: it drifted down through the muffling oil to rest at the bottom of the jar. I scooped more oil over the side, to create a breathing space, and I closed the lid.

I tilted my head back. I had just room, between oil and lid, to breathe: but I could not hear, with my ears under the oil: and so I reached up and I unscrewed the lid. It slid silently open on its oily threads. I raised my head till I could see out the crack between rim and lid, from my dark far corner. I tilted my head left and right, and the oil cleared my ears.

Barney O'Reilly Fitzpatrick McGee was in the room and roaring.

I could hear him, over in the corner which I had disordered as a decoy, kicking sacks. "Deflower my Daughter, would you! Come out, you little bastard!"

But I did not come out. It was now my firm belief that he did not have my Best Interests at heart.

He stopped kicking, and began to leap up and down. His face and staring eyes appeared and disappeared, appeared and disappeared, in the clear space between the stores and the roof. I did not flinch, or blink, as he stared in my direction. I was familiar with the optical parameters of the situation from my idle summer days, hunting rats for tenpence a tail in haybarns. Staring into darkness from light as he was, it was only my movement which could give me away. Even that would register on his vision more as a temporal asymmetry in the reflection of photons than as an image.

And so I stared from under my lid, unblinking, as the top of his head rose and fell above the rim of the piled tea-crates. He grew so carried away in his rage that he began to loose shots into the Darjeeling; at which point Frigg Fingerwank's crew, alerted by the sound, left the yacht, entered the storehouse, disarmed Barney O'Reilly Fitzpatrick McGee, beat him severely, dragged him outside and, by the unmistakable sound, dropped him into the harbour.

During this lengthy interval, I did not emerge from my oil. Any intervention of mine, I felt, could only complicate a situation which was resolving itself perfectly well under its own momentum. Also, I was growing increasingly comfortable, as my body adjusted to the temperature of the oil, and the oil slowly rose to my body temperature. I grew, indeed, a little drowsy, and almost slipped beneath the surface; but at length the beating was administered, the dragging and dropping done, the store's door shut and locked. The crew returned to their ship, and all was quiet.

Exhausted, perhaps from the sedation in the Medical Unit, I decided to stay where I was. To break noisily out of the locked storeroom now would be to invite a beating from the adrenalised crew. Here was as good as any place to rest; yes, the search for Babette would best be served by a rested mind and body.

I thus improvised a long breathing tube by ramming many wide-bore drinking straws hard into each other, in sequence. As straws of identical bore do not naturally fit inside each other, insertion was achieved by putting a slight crease, or V, in the tip of the straw to be inserted. With its bore narrowed, it slides inside the, now higher-calibre, outer straw for perhaps an inch. Of course, the crease being merely at the tip of the inserted straw, the inner and outer straws are soon again of the same bore, and the one gets stuck hard in the other. The slight elasticity of the plastic means that in practical terms a most satisfactory seal is made along a good length of the overlap.

Of course, some would argue that a short slit, rather than a crease, could be made at the tip of the inserted straw: the cut edges, overlapping, would shrink its bore and allow its insertion: but I feel it is an error to compromise the bodily integrity of the straw in this way. Such damage, done along the grain, can so easily travel further, should the join come under unanticipated pressure from within or without.

And a split of the *exterior* straw's tip, with a mind to *spreading* the cut to allow insertion of an uncreased, uncut interior straw is a plan so obviously and fundamentally flawed that I shall not spell out the catastrophic vulnerability of such a join to almost any stress whatsoever, in any direction.

And so I made my little breathing tube, popping a discreet hole for it in the thin metal lid of the jar.

I plugged each of my nostrils with a single large coffee bean. Most pleasantly, the beans released a rich coffee fragrance. Indeed, as the hard beans pressed into the soft moist flesh of my nasal membranes, I absorbed certain volatiles directly, across the membrane, and grew giddy and dizzy; but as the volatiles slowly exhausted themselves, this passed.

The dozens of cardboard boxes of wide-bore drinking straws were held together in their large bale by a thin, clingy transparent plastic sheet, shrunk to fit. Carefully, I unpeeled a long strip of it. I put a final straw in the corner of my mouth, pointing up, and wrapped the strip of plastic around my lower head, till my mouth was sealed.

I was suddenly struck by the unwelcome possibility of sneezing my beans loose.

A disagreeable prospect. I wound the remainder of the strip higher, and covered my nose.

I breathed easily and cleanly through the broad red straw. I mopped up my oily foot-prints, my hand-prints, my drips, as I retreated to my jar. I hurled the soiled tissues into the Disordered Corner, and lowered myself gently into the oil.

Then the tricky task of screwing on the lid, from below, and reassembling my breathing tube without filling it with oil. Carefully, I pushed the sections of tube up out of the hole in the lid as I went. But at length it was done, my tube assembled, I slotted it into the straw in my mouth, pushed it tight.

Still a little knackered from the previous day's exertions, I sank slowly beneath the oil, my long tube descending with me. The nature of the overlaps ensured no join caught the edge of the hole on the descent. Weightless, in utter silence, free of obligation to self or world, I closed my eyes.

I slept the sleep of the immortals, or the dead.

93

I woke to a burst of light, to see a Cook's face, under a Cook's hat, over a Cook's apron, staring in at me, distorted by oil and the curvature of glass. Reciprocally distorted, I stared back. And so we stared, for a while. I did not blink, or move. He did not move, but blinked excessively. Perhaps he had got dust in his eye, moving crates and boxes. For I now had a clear line of vision, past him and out the open door into sunlight. I read his lips through the distortion. "Not again," he seemed to say. "Not again." The repetitions made me think I had it right.

A tranquility had come to me in the night. Content in my weightless state, I could not bring myself to act in my own life's drama. And so I watched, unblinking, as men pulling steel trolleys entered, and removed the crates and sacks and jars and bales and boxes.

First they came for the flour.

Then they came for the coffee.

Then they came for the condensed milk.

Then they came for me.

The light was too bright outside, even when filtered through the beautiful pale green oil, and I closed my eyes. How pleasant, the heavy drift of my lids, as my lashes dragged through the oil, then halted. Eyes closed, and the end of resistance.

I forgot, somehow, to open them again. There was a jostling, or a pressure wave through the oil, as perhaps I was set down somewhere. But I was half asleep, then all asleep, and I dreamed I was asleep and dreaming.

The Journey in Oil

To have original, extraordinary, and perhaps even
immortal ideas, one has but to isolate oneself from
the world for a few moments so completely that the
most commonplace happenings appear to be new and
unfamiliar, and in this way reveal their true essence.
- Schopenhauer

There are now no more horizons. And with the
dissolution of horizons we have experienced and are
experiencing collisions, terrific collisions, not only of
peoples but also of their mythologies. It is as when
dividing panels are withdrawn from between chambers
of very hot and very cold airs: there is a rush of these
forces together... That is just what we are experiencing;
and we are riding it: riding it to a new age, a new birth,
a totally new condition of mankind – to which no one
anywhere alive today can say that he has the key, the
answer, the prophecy, to its dawn. Nor is there anyone
to condemn here... What is occurring is completely
natural, as are its pains, confusions, and mistakes.
- Joseph Campbell, *Myths to Live By*

Gardening. No hope for the future.
- Kafka. From his diary.

94

When I awoke, it was dark. I floated, blind, deaf, dumb. The hiss of air through my straw, I heard. But, hearing it constantly, I did not hear it at all.

When I woke again it was still dark, and I had the most terrifically pressing need to evacuate bowel and bladder. My penis was as large as I had ever seen it, and more rigid than I could ever recall. There was no give in it whatsoever. Could I, indeed, get out through the narrow neck of the Jar in this condition? I did not wish to soil my oil, but nor did I wish to leave the Jar.

I floated there, pondering, as unknown amounts of time passed, minutes perhaps, or hours. The situation, however, did not remain static while I pondered it. Fluids within me performed their various functions and, molecule by molecule, the liquids I had done with found their way to my bladder. My bowel, too, continued to fill. Then there came a period of precarious balance: once all the food I had eaten had made its way to the far end of my alimentary system, the Bowel situation began to improve – for the water, comprising perhaps half that waste, continued to be absorbed stealthily by the membrane of the bowels, thus lowering somewhat the pressure in my rectum and lower bowel. But that water, absorbed, soon made its way to the reservoir of my bladder, thus raising the pressure there. As a side effect, it stiffened my penis to the point of pain, for the enlarged bladder was constricting the outflow of blood from my penile root more than it was constricting the deeper blood vessels controlling inflow.

My urethral sphincter creaked.

The situation was growing intolerable. Soon my Body would make a command decision, whatever my Mind continued to think.

I pondered. Despite my discomfort, the pleasures of my situation were great; yet, by failing to make a difficult and unpleasant decision now, I ran the risk of destroying my future happiness.

I surfaced; deconstructed my breathing tube; unscrewed the loosely closed lid; and climbed with a certain difficulty out of the Jar in my saturated suit.

I tilted my head from side to side, and the oil cleared from the bends and traps of my ears. The drums again made contact with the general air.

How loud is silence! I was entranced by its richness. So different to the interior richness of deafness, to the bellow of blood through the body, the rumble through the bones. This silence was so crisp, so clean, so light, so much more highly wrought, and delicately textured.

Most notably, most originally, it creaked. But it also hummed, at both ends of the sonic spectrum. Oh, all silences hum: but these seemed modern, almost electrical. A vibration that seemed unrelated to either hum also enriched this silence. Much muffled, far distant, were human cries. Then the loudest creak yet, and immediately after, and many orders of magnitude louder, a Bang, grotesquely close. The silence had been so rich I had forgotten it was silence, and had thrown open my senses excessively. I also appeared to have been hit, hard, as though with a plank, the full length of the left side of my body.

Sight! I thought. The very moment for it. Sight is a magnificent way to lower the volume of the world. The mind, when processing the vast, unending stream of the Visual, assigns considerably less attention to the Aural.

I opened my eyes. What a sight! A magnificent darkness, too rich and complex to describe in detail. I shall not traduce it with a summary. Suffice to say I was on my side: and by ruthless logical interrogation of the Darkness and the Silence, I made clear my position. I was in a storeroom; in a boat; on the high seas; the semi-circular canals of my inner ear had, in the absence of vision, caused me to fall over.

How? Thus: The Ship had rolled heavily to its right; I had reflexively hurled myself left, rather late, to balance myself; whereupon the ship had also rolled left, so that instead of balancing myself upright, I had thrown myself hard at the floor.

I stood, cautiously, feet wide apart, and groped forward, as my eyes began to make better sense of the rich darkness. Then, shocking and wonderful, moonlight began to trickle, then pour, into the storeroom through a high small window as a cloud outpaced us, or was outpaced. Crates!

I urinated by moonlight into an open crate of Earl Grey tea. The liquid swiftly vanished, absorbed by the loose, dry leaves.

Solid waste was more difficult: thanks to the lengthy absorption of water, it had grown dense, and compacted. An enormous jar of pickled whole cucumbers seemed my best bet: I opened it and, perched upon a pallet of tinned tuna, relaxed my anal sphincter – I began to strain – but then I thought a moment, and re-puckered. I reached down below me and took out a whole pickled cucumber, and ate it with a great hunger I had not till then realised I owned.

Another.

And another.

With the pickles devoured, I returned to my task, and voided into the pickle jar. My waste floated, indistinguishable, to the casual glance, from the few remaining cucumbers. I replaced the lid. The suit trousers, as I pulled them back up my legs, felt cold, and constricting. No... I removed all my clothes, and hid them where they would never be found, in a crate of unsalted rice cakes. There.

Naked, I returned with relief to my own Jar.

Pipes behind it, in the corner, warmed my Jar, my Oil.

Back below the surface, deep in the warm oil, I closed my eyes, and dreamed a selection of dreams.

95

I woke and slept.

I dreamed, and I did not dream.

Occasionally, I left my jar to excrete and eat. But this I did less and less as time went by.

I soon discovered that I could drink the oil in which I dreamed. Unplugging my breathing tube at the first joint, I would pinch the disconnected tube closed, so as not to fill it with oil. Dreamily I drank as much oil as I liked through the straw in my mouth, and reconnected the breathing tube when I was done, sucking the last oil down the straw to clear it.

This became my habit.

As it both satisfied my hunger, and produced very little waste, I found I left the jar less often.

Eventually, I was producing only liquid waste. Nothing solid had emerged for several sleeps. And so I arranged a second tube, from my penis, up through the lid, and discretely down into a crate of Earl Grey at the back of the stack.

Back in the jar, urinating uphill was difficult: but once the urine first crested the jar lid, and began to flow downhill, gravity was again my friend. The siphon effect made subsequent urination effortless.

And so I could spend the timeless days submerged in my jar, deaf and blind and ecstatic, eating and breathing and excreting with no effort, weightless and safe.

Rarely, there was the sensation of strong light on my closed lids. The door had been opened: and no doubt the Cook or a sailor took tea, or tuna, or toothpaste from the stacks, and left. Stored

safe and high, at the far back, with other jars of oil in rows ahead
of me, all the way to the front, I knew no one would bother
me, and I did not stir or fret. The sensation of light soon ended.
In time I slept through their visits, unless it is that they began
visiting less often.

And once, there was a day, or two, of grinding and shouting:
and the smells of jungle and of industry: and I thought we had
Arrived. But it passed, and later I realised we must have travelled
the length of the Panama Canal, and were now in the Pacific...

Then I noticed that the surface of the oil was dropping in the jar:
for I was taking my sustenance from Inside the jar, yet excreting
my waste Outside the jar, thus lowering the reservoir.

There was nothing for it but to raid another jar of oil, for to give
up my Bliss was unthinkable. Already the top of my head was
occasionally exposed to the air, as I moved at the bottom of the
jar in my shrunken bliss.

And so I raided another jar for oil.

96

The lid put up stiff resistance, but the issue was never really in doubt: I had opposable thumbs and a burning desire for oil: it was only a lid. With a satisfying pop the air gushed in, the lid was off, and the oil was mine. Using pipes and containers, I carried the oil to my jar.

I filled my jar as high as I could and still fit in it. And by it I enjoyed great quietness; and the taste of it was as the taste of fresh oil.

And I drank my oil and waxed fat, and no torment touched me. And I was content, slumbering submerged in my jar.

But at length, this oil, too, ran low: and I was forced to seize upon another jar and suck it dry of oil. And all the time my wastes were filling the cases of tea, the sacks of rice, soaking the dried biscuits and the Ryvita Crisp-Bread, till it was crisp no more.

Until the day came when, having pissed and shat in everything, I finally ran out of oil.

I left my jar a last time, and laid my wastes in the final untouched boxes. I stood, oil dripping from me, and took the last tissues from the last enormous tissue box. I wiped clean my traces, as I stepped back, towards the safety of my jar.

I stuffed the tissues down the back of the jar. That gap was almost solid now with oily tissues. The pipes which heated my jar, heated, too, these oily rags. I thought I smelt a trace of combustion, a hint of charred paper under the stronger scent of hot oil.

I climbed into the corner to check, and, pushing, headfirst, down through the warm, soft, oily pile of paper, I uncovered the ventilation grill into the next room. My ear beside it, I heard a woman's "Oh!" and a familiar, oily, regular, slapping sound.

"Frigg!" said Fanny.

"Fanny!" said Frigg.

Both in the urgent accents of love.

The slow, rhythmic slap of lubricated scrotum on buttocks continued. Oh, I said, not aloud, but in my head, audible only to me, alone. Not audible at all. A mere imaginary sound. No instrument but my consciousness to record it. I had not, I think, felt alone in that storeroom till that moment.

I love you, said the thin voice of Frigg to me through the ventilator grille.

Oh Papa, I said, upside down, to the air.

I love you, honey, gasped Fanny through the wall.

Oh Mama I replied, warm in the hug of oil and tissue. Almost loud enough to hear myself.

I love you so much, said Frigg.

I love you too, Papa, I whispered.

I love you so, so much my darling, said Fanny.

I love you too, Mama.

They finished at last, and slapped to a halt, and spoke no more.

The conversation had filled me with an emotion. I could not be entirely sure if it were sorrow, or joy: and I returned carefully, brimful of it, to my jar, to lie low in the last of my oil. There I slept like a baby, waking every hour to suck and chuckle and cry.

There was the sensation of light on my closed eyelids. But this time it did not swiftly cease.

Groggy from my sleep, and tears, and laughter, I lifted my heavy head till it cleared the oil's low surface, and I tilted my head left and right till the oil cleared my ears: and I listened as the sailors found all spoilt, further and further back, toward me. And they swore, and they laughed, and they cried.

"We'll take in new stores at Paradise Rocks, USA," said the Cook. "We should be there by dawn. And all this can go then."

And I was content, for my love had been headed for the United States of America; my father was imprisoned in the United States of America; and now fate or chaos was leading me there: and so my destiny would play itself out, if I had a destiny. Or my life, if I had merely a life.

And I sank back into the oil to sleep, and to conserve my strength for the challenges of dawn.

At dawn they threw me overboard, in my jar.
The jar hit the water, and I hit the jar.

I woke to a sensation of panic, rising and falling, breathing and choking.

The jar, containing so much air, and oil, and my silent Salmon, and me, bobbed upon the Pacific waves, rising to a crest and plunging to a trough.

The battered tip of my breathing tube, outside the jar, was sometimes in water and sometimes in air; and so I breathed, and choked, and rose, and fell, with the expansion and contraction of the moon-torn Sea, as it reached up in yearning for the moon, and was spurned, endlessly. The clear jar, the green oil, the clear air, the green sea – All rocked, and pulsed, and thickened and thinned; darkened and lightened, in waves.

I was rocked, in my oil, in my jar, in my sea; and, breathing and choking, I found the new rhythm of it; and I breathed on the crests and did not in the troughs; and rocked by the waves, not knowing what else to do, having no better plan, being content in the moment, torn by no urgent needs, having over the past while lost the habit of desire, I slept.

I awoke early the next day.

And the day was very long.

At first, I tried to keep track of up and down: I could tell which way was up by the dark blue of the ocean, the light blue of the sky.

The miles of water under me, the miles of air above.

But then there came a point, in the dusk, where the light sky grew dark and the million stars of the Milky Way appeared; and the dark sea grew bright with a million phosphorescent lights; and the darkening blue of the sky met the lightening blue of the sea, and they were the same blue, above and below and around me.

And even though the oil was gone, the world was very beautiful.

I looked neither up nor down at the little lights, the near and far, the cold glow of the jellyfish and the fusion-driven stars, in their galaxies and clusters, rotating in the void all about me: Everything was one and all was infinite.

I was almost sorry to leave the sea for land,

When I rolled ashore

In my empty jar

Up the crunching sand.

HERE FOLLOW THE FIRST THREE PRIZE-WINNING CHAPTERS OF:

Jude in Ireland

(formerly known as *Jude: Level 1*)

in which are recounted Jude's adventures prior to his arrival in London.

If I had urinated immediately after breakfast, the Mob would never have burnt down the Orphanage. But, as I left the dining hall to relieve myself, the letterbox clattered. I turned in the long corridor. A single white envelope lay on the doormat.

I hesitated, and heard through the door the muffled roar of a motorcycle starting. With a crunching turn on the gravel drive and a splatter of pebbles against the door, it was gone.

Odd, I thought, for the postman has a bicycle. I walked to the large oak door, picked up the envelope, and gazed upon it.

Jude
The Orphanage
Tipperary
Ireland

For me! On this day, of all significant days! I sniffed both sides of the smooth white envelope, in the hope of detecting a woman's perfume, or a man's cologne. It smelt, faintly, of itself.

I pondered. I was unaccustomed to letters, never having received one before, and I did not wish to use this one up in the One Go. As I stood in silent thought, I could feel the Orphanage Coffee burning relentlessly through my small dark passages. Should I open the letter before, or after, urinating? It was a dilemma. I wished to open it immediately. But a full bladder distorts judgement when reading, and is a great obstacle to understanding.

Yet could I do justice to my very dilemma, with a full bladder?

As I pondered, both dilemma and letter were removed from my hands by the Master of Orphans, Brother Madrigal.

"You've no time for that now, boy," he said. "Run off and organise the Honour Guard, and get them out to the site. You may open your letter this evening, in my presence, after the Visit." He gazed at my letter with its handsome handwriting, and thrust it up the sleeve of his cassock.

I sighed, and went to find the young Orphans of the Honour Guard.

2

I found most of the young Orphans hiding under Brother Thomond in the darkness of the hay barn.

"Excuse me, Sir," I said, lifting his skirts and ushering out the protesting infants.

"He is Asleep," said a young Orphan, and indeed, as I looked closer, I saw Brother Thomond was at a slight tilt. Supported from behind by a pillar, he was maintained erect only by the stiffness of his ancient joints. Golden straws protruded from the neck and sleeves of his long black cassock, and emerged at all angles from his wild white hair.

"He said he wished to speak to you, Jude," said another Orphan. I hesitated. We were already late. I decided not to wake him, for Brother Thomond, once he had Stopped, took a great deal of time to warm up and get rightly going again.

"Where is Agamemnon?" I asked.

The smallest Orphan removed one thumb from his mouth and jerked it upward, towards the loft.

"Agamemnon!" I called softly.

Old Agamemnon, my dearest companion and the Orphanage Pet, emerged slowly from the shadows of the loft and stepped, with a tread remarkably dainty for a dog of such enormous size, down the wooden ladder to the ground. He shook his great ruff of yellow hair and yawned at me loudly.

"Walkies," I said, and he stepped up to my side. We exited the hay barn into the golden light of a perfect Tipperary summer's day.

I lined up the Honour Guard and counted them by the front door, in the shadow of the South Tower of the Orphanage. The butter-yellow bricks of its facade glowed in the diffuse morning light as a late fog burned off.

I checked I had my Travel Toothbrush tucked safely into my sock.

We set out.

3

From the gates of the Orphanage to the site of the speeches was several strong miles.

We passed through Town, and out the other side. The smaller Orphans began to wail, afraid they would see Black People, or be savaged by Beasts. Agamemnon stuck closely to my rear. We walked until we ran out of road. Then we followed a track, till we ran out of track.

We hopped over a fence, crossed a field, waded a dyke, cut through a ditch, traversed scrub land, forded a river and entered Nobber Nolan's bog. Spang plumb in the middle of Nobber Nolan's Bog, and therefore spang plumb in the middle of Tipperary, and thus Ireland, was the Nation's most famous Boghole, famed in song and story, in History book and Ballad sheet: the most desolate place in Ireland, and the last place God created.

I had never seen the famous boghole, for Nobber Nolan had, until his recent death and his bequest of the Bog to the State, guarded it fiercely from locals and tourists alike. Many's the American was winged with birdshot over the years, attempting to make pilgrimage here. I looked about me for the Hole, but it was hid from my view by an enormous Car-Park, a concrete Interpretive Centre of imposing dimensions, and a tall, broad, wooden stage, or platform, bearing Politicians. Beyond Car-Park and Interpretive Centre, an eight-lane motorway of almost excessive straightness stretched clean to the Horizon, in the direction of Dublin.

Facing the stage stood fifty thousand farmers.

We made our way through the farmers to the stage. They parted politely, many raising their hats, and seemed in high good humour. "'Tis better than the Radio Head concert at Punchestown," said a sophisticated farmer from Cloughjordan, pulling on a shop-bought cigarette.

Onstage, I counted the smaller Orphans. We had lost only the one, which was good going over such a quantity of rough ground. I reported our arrival to Teddy "Noddy" Nolan, the Fianna Fáil TD for Tipperary Central and a direct descendant of Neddy "Nobber" Nolan. Nodding vigorously, he waved us to our places, high at the back of the sloping stage. The Guard of Honour lined up in front of the enormous green cloth backdrop and stood to attention, flanked by groups of seated dignitaries. I myself sat where I could unobtrusively supervise, in a vacant seat at the end of a row.

When the last of the stragglers had arrived in the crowd below us, Teddy cleared his throat. The crowd fell silent, as though shot. He began his speech.

"It was in this place..." he said, with a generous gesture which incorporated much of Tipperary, "... that Eamonn DeValera..."

Everybody removed their hats.

"... hid heroically from the Entire British Army..."

Everybody scowled and put their hats back on.

"... during the War of Independence. It was in this very boghole that Eamonn DeValera..."

Everybody removed their hats again.

"...had his Vision: A Vision of Irish Maidens dancing barefoot at the crossroads, and of Irish Manhood dying heroically while refusing to the last breath to buy English shoes..."

At the word English the crowd put their hats back on, though some took them off again when it turned out only to be shoes. Others glared at them. They put the hats back on again.

"We in Tipperary have fought long and hard to get the Government to make Brussels pay for this fine Interpretive Centre and its fine Car-Park, and in Brünhilde DeValera we found the ideal Minister to fight our corner. It is therefore with great pleasure, with great *pride*, that I invite the great grand-daughter of Eamonn DeValera's cousin ... the Minister for Beef, Culture and the Islands ... Brünhilde DeValera ... to officially reopen ... Dev's Hole!"

The crowd roared and waved their hats in the air. Long experience had taught them to keep a firm grip on the peak, for as all the hats were of the same design and entirely indistinguishable, the One from the Other, it was common practice at a Fianna Fáil hat-flinging rally for the less scrupulous farmers to loft an Old Hat, yet pick up a New.

Brünhilde DeValera took the microphone, tapped it, and cleared her throat.

"Spit on me, Brünhilde!" cried an excitable farmer down the front. The crowd surged forward, toppling and trampling the feeble-legged and bock-kneed, in expectation of Fiery Rhetoric. She began.

"Although it is European Money which has paid for this fine Interpretive Centre... Although it is European Money which has paid for this fine new eight-lane Motorway from Dublin, this Coach Park, this Car Park, that has Tarmacadamed Toomevara in its Entirety... Although it is European Money which has paid for everything built West of Grafton Street in my Lifetime... And although we are grateful to Europe for its Largesse..."

She paused to draw a great Breath. The crowd were growing restless, not having a Bull's Notion where she was going with all this, and distressed by the use of a foreign word.

"It is not for this I brought my Hat," said the Dignitary next to me, and spat on the foot of the Dignitary beside him.

"Nonetheless," said Brünhilde DeValera, "Grateful as we are to the Europeans...

...we should never forget...

...that...

...they..."

Fifty thousand right hands began to drift, with a wonderful easy slowness, up towards the brims of fifty thousand Hats in anticipation of a Climax.

"...are a shower of Foreign Bastards who would Murder us in our Beds given Half a Chance!"

A great cheer went up and the air was filled with Hats till they hid the face of the sun and we cheered in an eerie half-light.

The minister paused for some minutes while everybody recovered their own Hat and returned it to their own Head.

"Those Foreign Bastards in Brussels think they can buy us with their money! They are Wrong! Wrong! Wrong! You cannot buy an Irishman's Heart, an Irishman's Soul, an Irishman's Loyalty! Remember '98!"

There was a hesitation in the crowd, as the younger farmers tried to recall if we had won the Eurovision Song Contest in 1998.

"1798!" Brünhilde clarified.

A great cheer went up as we recalled the gallant failed rebellion of 1798. "Was It For This That Wolfe Tone Died?" came a whisp of song from the back of the crowd.

"Remember 1803!"

We applauded Emmet's great failed rebellion of 1803. A quavering chorus came from the oldest farmers at the rear of the great crowd: "Bold Robert Emmet, the darling of Ireland... "

"Remember 1916!"

Grown men wept as they recalled the great failed rebellion of 1916, and so many contradictory songs were started that none got rightly going.

There was a pause.

All held their breath.

"...Remember 1988!"

Pride so great it felt like anguish filled our hearts as we recalled the year Ireland finally threw off her shackles and stood proud among the community of nations, with our heroic victory over England in the first match in Group Two of the Group Stage of the European Football Championship Finals. A brief chant went up from the Young Farmers in the Mosh Pit: "Who put the ball in the England net?"

Older farmers, further back, added bass to the reply of

"Houghton! Houghton!"

I shifted uncomfortably in my seat.

"My great grand-father's cousin did not Fight and Die in bed of old age so that foreign monkey-men could swing from our trees and rape our women! He did not walk out of the Dáil, start a Civil War and kill Michael Collins so a bunch of dirty Foreign Bastards could..."

Here I missed a number of Fiery Words, as excited farmers began to leap up and down roaring at the front, the younger and more nimble mounting each other's shoulders, then throwing themselves forward to surf toward the stage on a sea of hands, holding their Hats on as they went.

"Never forget," roared Brünhilde DeValera, "that a Vision of Ireland came out of Dev's Hole!"

"Dev's Hole! Dev's Hole! Dev's Hole!" roared the crowd.

By my side, Agamemnon began to howl, and tried to dig a hole in the stage with his long claws.

Neglecting to empty my bladder after breakfast had been an error the awful significance of which I only now began to grasp. A good Fianna Fáil Ministerial speech to a loyal audience in the heart of a Tipperary bog could go on for up to five hours.

I pondered my situation.

My only choice seemed to be as to precisely how I would disgrace myself in front of thousands. To rise and walk off the stage during a speech by a semi-descendant of DeValera would be tantamount to treason, and would earn me a series of beatings on my way to the portable toilets.

Yet the alternative was to relieve myself into my breeches where I sat.

My waist-band creaked.

With the gravest reluctance, I willed the loosening of my urethral sphincter.

(*The above extract is from the opening chapters of* Jude in Ireland)

ABOUT THE AUTHOR

Julian Gough was born in London, to immigrant Irish parents living in a bedsit. When he was seven, the family returned to Nenagh, Co. Tipperary, when he was educated in a Christian Brothers school so tough that one of his teachers ran away.

Julian gained a degree in English and Philosophy in Galway, where – lacking a private income, but desirous of becoming a writer – he signed on the dole for ten years. In that time, he learned how to write fiction, and crafted the lyrics for four albums by underground rock band 'Toasted Heretic'.

His first novel, *Juno & Juliet*, was published in 2001. He has spent the subsequent ten years writing the *Jude* trilogy. At the height of the Irish property bubble, in 2006, he was evicted, and spent a year living in friends' empty houses in Dublin and France. (He now lives in Berlin.)

The first volume of *Jude* was published in 2007 as *Jude: Level 1*. He has since won the BBC National Short Story Award (with *The Orphan and the Mob*), an American Pushcart Prize, and been shortlisted for the Bollinger Everyman Wodehouse Prize. He represented Ireland in Best European Fiction 2010. His popular BBC radio play, *The Great Hargeisa Goat Bubble*, has been adapted for the stage, and will be produced next year.